The Soulkind Master

Book 3

Steve Davala

For my family

You have supported me throughout all of these adventures.

Acknowledgements

This book would not be here today if not for some special people. Laurie, your constant editing, rewriting, and feedback were all invaluable, even though I might not have been the greatest sport about it all the time.

Tanner Thompson is an amazing artist, and I thank him for his beautiful work imagining the Soulkind lands.

Danny Susco narrated/produced the audiobook on Amazon, Audible, and iTunes. Amazing work!

Chapter 1

"Jace!"

Karanne dropped to the stone lip of the tower, reaching toward Jace's plummeting body so far out of reach. He disappeared from sight without even a struggle, almost as if he accepted it. The breath in her chest expelled from her like taking a punch to the gut. The canopy of trees masked Jace's fall and she reeled, grasping at the railing at the edge of the tower. Last time he fell off the Library roof, the Soulwash had saved him. This time, he fell off the wrong side, and her heart dropped with him.

Karanne lifted her eyes to where Cathlyn stood on top of the Library. Jace had been beside her only a moment ago. She vanished in a flash of light.

Why had she not saved him?

A lone hawk circled the Tower of Law overhead. "Valor?" Karanne's vision blurred and before she could tell if this was Jace's hawk, it disappeared. Tears dropped to the stone ledge.

This was Fay's fault.

Power grew inside her, a cauldron of fire. She was a Soulkind Master. She wiped the tears from her cheeks and squinted her eyes at the Library roof for her enemy.

No sign of Fay. Something was there, though. A broken body lay smashed up against the ledge near the rooftop, its arms bent at unnatural angles. And was that blood on his head? No, just red hair.

Jace couldn't be dead. He wasn't. When the first image of him lifeless at the base of the library crept into her mind she immediately squashed it down.

But he could be hurt down there. The stairs flew by quickly and she was halfway down before realizing it. She emerged from the Tower and sprinted across the courtyard to the Library with a single thought in her mind. Find Jace. The full light of dawn wasn't too far off now, yet the sky over Beldan glowed red from the campfires spotting the fields. The clamor of the Darrak swarm entering the city finally rose over the sounds of the town's cries and alarms. There wasn't much time until they overran the city. She couldn't face them and escape, not with their numbers. But none of that mattered. Jace was alive. And she would find him.

Her palm suddenly itched and the lines of her marks lit up. The Fireflash shot out, bright and strong. It buzzed and whipped around in front of her face.

"Move!" she shouted as it attempted to block her way to the glade behind the Library.

The Fireflash intensified in brightness and got right into her face. Karanne stepped back. Was it trying to tell her something? But this thing, this magic came from her. How could it be trying to tell her anything she didn't know?

"I've got to find my son." How could she be arguing with a ball of light? And yet she continued. "He might need me." She pushed forward and again the Fireflash stopped her. Fresh tears fell upon her cheeks. "What do you want from me?" She gazed up at the Library and the Fireflash darted into her sight. "You want me to go up there?"

The bolt of light pulsed and Karanne sighed. The sounds of the approaching army grew louder. She held her palm upwards and the ball of fire returned to her hand. "This better help me save him." Doubt slipped from her, though. She had ignored the magic before, almost to her undoing. With a deep breath, she skipped three steps at a time to race into the Library.

Jace had to be alive. He wouldn't be simply a spirit for her to collect. As if in response, memories of those she had collected thumped unbidden into the back of her head. They were fighting her again. Fighting to be released from her protection unto the families and friends that awaited news of their deaths.

Time slowed. She raced past shelves full of the books that taught Jace and his friends what she could not. The weight of possibly losing him nearly caused her to fall. Her hand pulsed again as she wondered if coming this way was the right thing to do. The stairs to the rooftop finally came to an end and opened onto the place Jace had been. She raced out and scanned the area. It didn't take long to find Jervis' body since he hadn't moved from where she saw him across the courtyard. In fact, it didn't look like he was able to move at all.

"Oh great," he whispered hoarsely as she approached him. "You're here." His arms hung at awkward angles at his sides.

"Serves you right for siding up with the enemy." She knelt beside him. "You never were very smart." He would tell her everything about Fay now. It wouldn't take much to end this, just a little fire. Her fingers glowed with magic.

The Fireflash shot out again and pushed her back a couple of inches with its blazing light.

"Why did you bring me here?" Karanne stood and clenched her fist.

Her eyes settled on the ice covering Jervis. This wasn't from his magic. Frozen shards stuck out like needles all across his body, drawing thick lines of blood. The Fireflash subsided gently.

"She... did this to you?"

Jervis nodded weakly and grimaced from even that slightest of movements. Karanne reached out and put her hand on his shoulder. The tightness in his body relaxed a little. "Can you stand?"

Jervis coughed and his body convulsed again. "You're dumber than you look." Each breath brought a pained wheeze from his chest.

"You're going to make it."

"Good one." Jervis furrowed his eyebrows. She looked around for anything to help him, maybe some water. He gripped her weakly and she paused.

Tears dripped onto her hands. How long had she been crying? This was Jace's worst childhood bully. A boy who had betrayed everyone to help Guire and Fay back into the world. He deserved to pay for what he did. She ought to kill him right now. Instead, she held his hand.

"Those Darrak are coming," he said. "You've got to get out of here." Jervis drew in one last jagged breath. "Tell him I'm sorry." And then his eyes went glassy and he said no more.

Karanne knelt there for a few moments until the screams and cries of fighting down below woke her. The Fireflash had already absorbed Jervis' broken body and planted his spirit into her memories with all the others. A wave of dizziness shook her and she wavered. Who would she share this one with? He had no family and certainly no friends she could think of. Was this why the Fireflash had guided her here?

She stood and ran. The Library, quiet and empty like a tomb, amplified her clamping footsteps as she raced through it. Once outside, the glade of trees and stones below where Jace had fallen seemed even quieter than inside.

He's dead. That fall killed him.

The thought popped into her head and she squelched it under her boot heel like a bug. Curse these Soulkind. They had been Jace's dream for so long. And now that they had finally awakened, they brought him nothing but suffering.

Pine trees whipped past her as she brushed through the glade. The Library wall looked so tall from down here. How had he survived the drop when he was a kid? And now, without water, he didn't stand a chance. Why hadn't Cathlyn saved him? She only saved herself. The same questions spun in her head and the rage burned deep in her chest again.

Several colorful stones on the mossy ground sparkled in the sun that shone through the branches. Jace would've added them to his collection for sure. Dread crept into her heart when she thought of finding him, seeing him as broken as Jervis had been. But where was he? This had to be the place he had fallen.

There was something. His pouch. A small scattered pile of stones lay around it, spread out from the impact of the fall. Fresh tears burned her eyes while she gathered his memories. Heaving a great breath, she went back to her search. It was something she had to do.

Only, she couldn't when she tried. She sat down upon a large stone and hung her head in her hands. From the corner of her vision, she saw something out of place beneath a bush. It was a boot. One of Jace's. She ran to it. The other lay a few feet away. Karanne spun about. He had to be near. Something in the trees caught her eyes. Was that… a cloak? And pants, and a shirt. All fluttering like flags hanging in the trees.

"Of course he's alive," Karanne uttered and reached for something to steady herself. "But where in the suffering is he?"

Chapter 2

Karanne scoured the area for any more signs of Jace. The only other thing she found was a familiar looking metal rod and so she pocketed it. Something about it felt important. The treetops swayed in the early morning breeze, bowing as if nothing had happened. As if Jace didn't matter at all.

As she stuffed Jace's boots into her pack her palm shook with a sharp jolt. Her Fireflash. What now? She slipped beside a tree trunk and scanned the area. Her blood froze. Something moved through the branches of the small grove. Not a squirrel or a bird, but something smooth and liquid. Motion she knew too well. For a second she forced herself to forget it, to think it wasn't possible for anything worse to happen to her than losing her son. But another blur through the trees made her curse. A group of Darrak wound their way to the Library like snakes through grass. How was she going to get out of here?

The Darrak had been right outside the city, she should've known they were coming. And now they stood between her and the way back around the building. And the way behind her? Was that safe? The crashing of the waters upon the rocks in the Crescent River told her otherwise.

In moments five Darrak reached the wall and began to scale it. They clambered up like spiders, their claws gripping easily onto the solid rock. They didn't even notice her? They might be easy to get past after all.

A sound, as thin as a whisper caught her ear and she turned. The tree behind her splintered and a massive spear tip blossomed through the flying pieces of wood. She stumbled forward and spun trying to spot who attacked her.

Her breath caught in her throat.

The Darrak before her stood several feet taller than the others, a thicker set of scales covered its body, and yellow fangs rested in long grooves outside its shorter snout. After it caught her in its gaze, she was unable to look away. With several sharp bellows, the Darrak called to the others climbing the Library. This was no soldier following blindly, but a leader.

The climbing Darrak all dropped to the ground. From that height, even these creatures had to feel the force of the fall, but if they did they didn't show it to her or the leader. Quickly, they surrounded her.

Karanne summoned her Fireflash into a brilliant blast, and the Darrak were caught staring right into the blazing light. The five creatures clawed desperately at their eyes, and one dropped to the ground. The leader, however, blinked slowly and took several steps toward her. Startled, Karanne walked back onto some wet leaves and slipped.

The Darrak snorted and the mist of its breath curled in the cold morning air. It grasped the metal spear still embedded in the tree and with one fluid motion yanked it out, shredding the trunk to pieces. The rest of the tree tumbled into the side of the Library with a deep crack.

Karanne stood and raised her hands. She grinned and reached for the magic she used to smite Guire's darkness in the Tower of Law. "You asked for it."

Nothing. Only emptiness and weakness stole into her body. Nearly tripping backwards again, she gestured with her hand and her Fireflash burst toward the Darrak's chest. It only bounced off the thick plating.

The Darrak raised the spear over its head and pointed it directly at her.

By this time the other Darrak regained their vision and began to close the gap around her.

Okay, so maybe the Crescent River actually didn't look so bad, did it?

The large Darrak threw the spear as Karanne lunged at the closest enemy. She spun the creature to where she had been standing and the massive weapon buried itself into the Darrak's chest.

With speed she didn't know she could muster, she dashed off between the trees toward the river with her heart pounding in her ears. Behind her, the Darrak leader howled and she ran even faster, somehow. She jumped down the embankment amidst large boulders and found herself both rolling and sliding down the muddy slope to the churning waters below. The river couldn't be as bad as all that up above, but as soon as she hit the freezing waters, she almost reconsidered.

This was a good idea?

That thought buzzed loudly in Karanne's head as the relentless icy water shoved her against a jagged river rock. Her breath squeezed out of her chest and her vision blurred. Up above on the hilltop the first of the Darrak appeared. Maybe they'd let her go. They didn't know who she was, right? How could they? Still, they saw her use magic, and that was probably enough to follow her.

She pushed off the rock with her quickly numbing fingers and reached out for the next one as the river fought to pull her under. The strong current slammed her against an outcropping of rock and an intense pain shot through her arm. Slowly she made her way from one rock to the next always thinking she'd be dragged under. When she reached NorBridge, she dragged herself ashore,

She stood for a moment letting the water run from her clothes. Her teeth chattered uncontrollably and blood soaked through her sleeve. Gingerly she touched her arm and winced. If it wasn't broken there would certainly be a huge bruise. She lifted a thick blanket from an abandoned booth and draped it over her head and shoulders.

And now to find Jace. She headed south of town with a nervous glance over her shoulder. None of those Darrak from the Library seemed to be following her but she quickened her pace nonetheless. Time to pay Turic a visit.

Getting through town was easier than she thought it would be. People scattering and screaming through the streets provided her with some cover. They carried their meager possessions, if any, and crowded the marketplaces. If fear of Guire and Fay hadn't sent them running, the Darrak filling the streets surely did. She frowned at their distraught faces. She would help them when she could.

In the distance a gang of Darrak swarmed into the street, waving their weapons in the air. Some people cowered from them and others ran, right into Karanne's path. "Get back inside!" she shouted, but no one even glanced at her. All the shouting over the clanging of the alarm bells only added to the chaos.

Someone small bumped into her from behind and then sprinted past. Maybe it was the way she threaded through the crowd practically untouched or perhaps the subtle embroidery on her hood, whatever it was, the kid was definitely a part of the Guild.

Karanne curled her tongue and pursed her lips to emit a high pitched whistle. On cue, the freckle-faced girl slowed her pace and turned around. "Hey, what are you doing out in the streets?" Karanne asked.

Warily the girl took a couple of steps back and eyed Karanne without a word.

The guild wasn't safe. Clearly, Caspan had been compromised. But what about the rest of the thieves? "Do you have a place to go?"

The girl shifted her gaze from Karanne to the streets. She tensed up like a spring trap ready to trip.

"She's ok, Evvy," an older voice called from behind Karanne. "She's one of us."

"Picks!" Karanne turned to the old lock master with a relieved smile on her face.

"What're you doing back here?" Picks put his arms around Karanne's and Evvy's shoulders and led them down the street. "Everything's turned sideways since those two came to town. And now these…"

"Darrak," Karanne said, following the two into a side alleyway. "We've got to get you out of here. They'll kill us as soon as look at us." Though at the moment, they didn't appear to be killing anyone, only herding people through the streets. "And hey, what are you doing out of the guild? You never leave."

"A lot has happened," Picks said. "Just follow us, we're heading to the Old Guild. The caves have been taken over, we got nowhere else to go. Speaking of that, you look like you need a place to hide, too."

"I do. But I've got to go outside the city walls, to find my friends."

"It's too late for that," Picks said, wheezing as he fought to keep up.

"I'll figure it out," Karanne said. "I need to get them first. But tell me, is Caspan with you?"

"They captured him," he said.

"I know, and now he's working for them. But he's not with you now, right?"

Picks shook his head. "They must've got something on him, something that made him switch sides."

"They got anything on anybody else I know?" Karanne stared at Picks.

"No, not me, but thanks for asking. They only wanted Caspan. Threw the rest they managed to capture into some prison camps. Unfortunately, they got some of the other guild bosses. The whole place is falling apart now. I got the kids out, brought them up to the Old Guild."

Karanne patted him on the shoulder. "Sorry, I had to ask. With what's going on I had to know."

Picks grinned at her. "It's all right, K. You always did know when to check things out first. Now, where was I? Yes. After I got the kids out, I heard Jace was taken to the Library. That's where Evvy and I came from."

"Yeah, I got him out of the prison there," Evvy said. "He's your son, right?"

Karanne stopped walking. "He... he fell off the roof."

"What?" Evvy said. "But he's okay, right?"

The confusion Karanne had at the base of the Library shook her again. "I saw him fall, but he wasn't there when I got there."

"I hope he wasn't captured," Picks said.

"Or injured," Karanne added.

They reached the outer wall near a grove of short, wide trees. Picks started to pull aside the loose stone that would lead them out of town. The massive boulder shifted smoothly and slid into place with enough room for them to fit through, another one of the thieves' ingenious devices.

"I'll meet you there," Karanne said after they passed through the wall. "I'm heading the other way first. And I'll be bringing those friends."

"Friends," Picks said. "Don't expect a warm welcome. Ever since Caspan left, the place ain't what it used to be."

"Thanks for the tip." Karanne smiled at him before pulling the rock back but waited a second to see Evvy and Picks disappear into the underbrush before she closed it fully and returned to within the city walls. In a hundred feet she would be through the archway leading out of town. She quickened her pace, not knowing when the Darrak would shut down this exit.

Only a few people, some with small children, made it to the path leading out of town. How did so few make it out?

A fierce cry and a black blur gave Karanne the answer she was dreading. The blur, a winged Darrak, swooped down from the city walls and she instinctively pulled her hood over her red hair. Did it see her? Was it one of those that attacked her at the Library? Well, if it was coming for her, she wouldn't let it kill her as she ran. The people around her screamed and scattered but she stood like a boulder in a

9

river, parting them about her with her hands upraised. The Darrak, however, veered off and dove to grab one of the children near the escaping adults. Karanne's blood boiled. She reached for her magic but she didn't use it. Too many people around her that might get hurt. The Darrak flew back to the city entrance with the little girl in tow and the family running after them screaming the child's name. The remaining families clutched their children close, but the three other Darrak on the road in front of them made them think better of trying to escape. They followed the others back.

Wake up, stupid!

Karanne started at the thought and let her magic go. She ran to a patch of thick trees at the edge of the road and she ducked under their cover. She held her breath as she scurried from tree to tree, with one eye on the Darrak and the other on her footing. She couldn't help these people, not now.

From there, it was only a short trip to Turic's cottage. It was dark, but Karanne knew the way with her eyes closed. She stopped frequently to listen for anyone following her but never heard anything besides her pounding heart. Without knocking, she stepped into the house and met Burgis and Tare standing guard on either side of the door. They lowered their weapons and quickly shut the door behind her. Tare gave her a hug. Karanne smiled and patted his back.

"Have you seen Jace?" Burgis asked.

Her smile faded and she walked in past them.

Turic entered the room with Allar, Brannon, Danelia, and Ranelle. "You made it!" Turic walked to her but stopped when he got a look at her face. "Something is wrong. Tell us."

"I saw Jace, but…" She finally gave in to her tears and slumped onto her knees. Allar helped her up and led her to a bench near the empty and cold fireplace.

When she was able to speak again she told them everything. From the encounter with Guire in the tower, to her discovery about her necklace, to Jace falling off the roof, and Cathlyn letting him fall.

"My sister? You saw her? Is she all right?"

"She disappeared before I could talk to her," Karanne said and unconsciously clenched her fist. "She almost trapped the magic again."

"That explains what I felt," Turic said. "It was as if I were being split in half, but then it stopped." Allar nodded quietly next to him, staring at Karanne.

She felt everyone's eyes on her and she shifted. "What's wrong with Danelia?" The blond-haired woman seemed abnormally pale and shaky.

"She's been like this ever since we got into town," Allar said. After a pause, he added, "She's sick, but Newell hasn't told me exactly what he senses inside of her. I know it isn't from Guire's handiwork, though."

The same dizziness from before passed into Karanne again, and she held her breath when the pain hit her. When the wave passed, she met Danelia's knowing eyes. "I think I've got the same thing she does."

Turic approached her but she held her hand up to him.

"It's not safe here," Karanne said. "The Darrak are everywhere. Have you seen the town?"

"We saw it," Turic said. "And it is only getting worse. Brannon thinks we need to find his father."

Brannon straightened his cloak. "Not everyone will bow to those two. If we find him, I'm certain he'll have others ready to fight back."

"There wasn't any sign of him in the tower," Karanne said. "It's a prison now, and you won't believe who they have in there. Come on, I know where we might be able to get some help."

Chapter 3

Karanne led the others several miles south of the city along twisting paths near the river and through the trees. She had to backtrack several times to find her way but eventually stumbled onto the Old Guild. It had been a long time since she had been here, but she'd never forgotten the place. Several thieves were posted along the path, some in trees, others in stone shelters. Turning her body so she could fit between a narrow path between two massive boulders, Karanne glanced up to see silhouetted forms up above. She flashed the signals necessary to pass through alive while the others behind her remained oblivious.

"Oh, I should mention to you that if you ever tell anyone about this path or anything of what we see today you'll probably be dead before you know it."

Finally, they reached the entrance, a gaping hole in the side of the stone wall. A cool breeze blew out from the inside. No one stood guard besides those they passed and the eyes Karanne could feel yet not see. Karanne ushered her friends inside and plunged into darkness.

"Best not to use our magic here," Karanne whispered, resisting the urge to summon her Fireflash. "Well, maybe to light a torch. But not around anyone. Never know how they're going to feel about it."

Yeah, they're a touchy bunch.

Tare led the way, his fiery brand casting flickering shadows on the damp walls. Several minutes in, loud voices clashed with each other in the distance. Soon they drew nearer to the arguing and to a bigger room with its own light.

"I say we make a run for it!"

"Go to Myraton!"

"You know we wouldn't make it past them things."

"We'll be safe here until they leave."

"What if they don't leave?"

In a wide, round room, about fifty thieves stood or sat upon the gray stones, shouting back and forth. Others lined incoming passages on the other side of the room or hung in openings near the ceiling.

12

Karanne nearly lost her footing as she stepped into a sea of indecision and panic. She scanned the room for familiar faces. Finally, she saw Picks, hanging back to the side in a heated argument with two others she didn't recognize. As she approached him, he looked up and limped toward her through the chaos.

"Took you long enough," Picks said. "Those your friends?"

Karanne nodded. "What's going on here?"

"Well, with Caspan and the other leaders gone, nothing's getting decided. The different families are falling apart, now that the town is crumbling." Picks stumbled backward when a man and woman noisily shoving each other bumped into him.

Well, this isn't good.

Other fights broke out quickly and Karanne was pushed to the ground. Turic tried to step back into the tunnel but two others screaming and pointing at each other blocked him. When they saw him they both stopped their own fighting and turned their focus on him. Brannon stepped in front of Turic and raised his hands. They glowed a deep red.

"No, Brannon." Turic put his hand on Brannon's shoulder and the glow faded.

Tare helped Karanne back to her feet and pushed back a thief who got too close to her. Something in the air shifted and Karanne searched for the source. Someone in a hooded cloak, his face entirely covered, walked toward the center of the room. As he passed thieves, he laid his hands on their shoulders. Quiet swept across the room like a ripple spreading over a pond. When it reached her, a sudden cool wave washed over her, her arms and shoulders loosened and she was able to draw a deep breath. The entire room stared silently.

Who is that?

But her heart already knew.

"Jace!" she shouted through the absolute silence and pushed through to her son.

"Karanne!" Jace wrapped his arms around her tightly. Ash nudged past him into her side and she reached over to scratch his ears. When Jace saw her face it was lined with tears. "Are you all right?"

Turic and the others circled around Jace to greet him, pushing Karanne aside for a moment. Jace clasped Turic in an especially large hug. There was so much he needed to talk about, with everyone, but first, there was the issue of all the thieves staring at him.

"No shoes?" Karanne stared at his bare feet. She pulled out his boots from her pack. "You've got a lot of explaining to do."

As Jace strapped on the leather boots with a wry smile, Picks walked to his side and gestured to the gathering.

"Say something, kid. You've certainly got their attention now."

Jace stood up on a stone used for addressing the room and cleared his throat. "Some of you know who I am. I used to be one of you, as did Karanne here." Jace knew that she had recently been working with them, but he left that part out. He wasn't certain how he felt about her keeping that away from him. "Caspan Dral may be gone, but that doesn't mean you have to fall apart."

The thieves kept listening in silence.

"There is a great deal to discuss, and I believe Picks will help us to figure this out." Jace welcomed his old master to the front of the group, and a few appreciative cheers broke out. "I'm pretty sure all of you know you can trust Picks, we've all sat through his classes. And jokes." More than a few chuckled in response. Jace waved his hand in front of Picks, welcoming him to talk.

"First let's get our food and water in order," Picks said, addressing a woman next to him. After she left Picks' side, she sought out a few people and formed another smaller circle to continue the discussion.

Picks addressed everyone again, but by this time Karanne put her hand on Jace's shoulder, pulled him to the side of the room, and looked him square in the eyes. "I saw you fall… How did you survive that?"

"It has to do with the boots," Jace said, smiling.

Karanne cocked her head and raised an eyebrow. "Not going to tell me more?"

"Later."

"Well, soon, I'm not sure I can stand it. And here's some of your stuff that I found below the Library. Not much. I had to get out of there pretty quick." Karanne handed him a few knives and the metal rod.

"We've got a lot to talk about." Jace stowed his things away into a leather pack. "And thank you for helping me back at the Library, I knew that was you from the tower." He pointed to his temple where Fay's ice had blocked his magic.

"Yeah, I've learned a few new tricks, too." Karanne bent forward abruptly and she pressed her hands to her temples. Jace tried to put his arms around her but she held him back and shook her head. After staying in this position for several seconds, she gestured with a nod for him to follow her into a side passage. Picks pretty much had the room under control, and even Allar had joined a circle of thieves, though they eyed his worn Guardian cloak.

When they got to a side tunnel and out of hearing range, Jace hugged Karanne again. He pointed to her white stone necklace. "I know how you got that in Myraton."

Karanne raised her eyebrows. "What? How?"

"With my Soulkind. I saw everything, I saw… I saw *her.*"

"Your mother." Karanne reached out for him but pulled her hand back. "I couldn't save her…"

"I know. It wasn't your fault," Jace said. "I don't think I ever said thank you for bringing me to Beldan. I never knew what you really did to get me here."

Karanne rubbed Jace's mother's necklace.

"You dove out the window of a three-story building? Are you insane?"

Karanne gave him a hug and ruffled his hair. "I don't think you're one to talk about jumping off of buildings." After a laugh she continued. "Speaking of that, you owe me a good story for that last one."

Jace nodded. "It'll be better if I show you sometime."

Karanne stroked the white stone at the end of her necklace. "Jace, this— I don't know how— became a Soulkind."

Jace's eyes widened. "What? I *knew* there was something different about it. And you're the Master?"

Karanne shrugged. "Looks like it."

"That's amazing! What does it do? Can you show me? You have got to talk to Graebyrn."

"Slow down," Karanne said. "I'm sure I will, but we have other things to sort out first."

"Straeten." Jace frowned. "I've got to help him. Does anyone know where he is?"

"I saw him at our house, he had already turned. Caspan told me what he did to the others at the Guild. I can't believe Fay got to him."

"He saved me before we got to Beldan by using her magic." Jace shook his head. "He held off as long as he could until it was the only thing he could think of."

"Then she just took over?" Karanne asked.

Jace nodded. "I can't believe he's gone. Do you think we can get her out of him?"

Karanne rubbed her forehead. "Allar helped the Followers back in Varkran. He removed Guire and his sickness from them. Maybe he can help Straet?"

"I don't think that's how it works, unless Straeten has any of Guire's magic. I'm pretty sure only Fay is in there."

Karanne scrunched her eyebrows together. "Maybe Turic can help. Fay actually… planted … some ice in my head—"

"She what?" Jace said. "Are you okay?"

Karanne nodded. "Yeah, it was scary though. If it wasn't for Turic being around to melt it, I don't know what might have happened. I could've become like… well, like Straeten."

Jace placed his hand on Karanne's shoulder and gave it a squeeze. "That was close then. We've got to get the guild to help us find Straeten and then get Turic to him. As he learns more magic, Fay's grip on him will tighten. And if Guire teaches him, too, it'll get even worse. I wish Cathlyn were here."

Karanne grew silent after he spoke her name.

"Is everything all right?" Jace pulled back his hand when her neck muscles tensed.

"She didn't help you," Karanne said, through clenched teeth. "I know you're all right now, but she didn't help you up on the roof. What if you had died?"

"She did everything she could."

"You mean after she tried to kill everything up there?" Karanne said.

"That wasn't her fault." Jace rubbed his forearm. "She was confused, and drugged by Mathes."

Karanne shook her head. "That's a lot of confusion for someone who has the most power around here."

"That's why we'll help her," Jace said and slumped onto a stone bench. "I don't know where she went."

"Me neither," Karanne said. "She disappeared."

Jace sat in silence for several moments. "Did you see what happened to Jervis by any chance?"

Karanne traced the markings on her palm. "He was trying to help you and Cathlyn."

"You saw that?"

16

"I did. And talked to him. He seemed to know something about what Fay was going to do here, but I couldn't get it before… Fay ended up killing him."

"I can't believe he's dead," Jace said. "I mean, he tried to kill me, but still."

"He told me to tell you that he was sorry." Karanne closed her hand in a fist. "He died with a better heart, I think."

"I don't know about that," Jace said under his breath. "All right, let's go back and see if Picks will help track down Straeten."

"One thing first. We've got to talk about Blue."

Jace froze and let out a long sigh. "Karanne…"

Karanne held her hand up, and her palm glowed slightly. "Ever since you showed up here, I've had this feeling that I *need* to share her spirit with you. I know you didn't want to deal with it before, but I have to give it to you. I know she'd want that."

Jace nodded. She was right. He let Karanne sit next to him and place her hand on his forehead. "Do you think she blames me?"

Karanne smiled. "I know she doesn't."

Warmth flooded into him, images of Blue washed over his eyes, and the pit where her spirit once lay in his chest filled again. Shame for not accepting this before briefly flashed into him, but Blue shone over all of that. He was aware of his dark mark again, but with that awareness came deep understanding. With Blue here now, he would never use it.

Karanne's face lightened, as if a great weight had been lifted. "You all right?"

"I feel better. But different." Karanne stared at her hands.

"Thanks for holding onto her for me," Jace said. "Let's go check on the guild, all right?" He took a deep breath and smiled.

Jace led Karanne through the shifting tunnel back into the cave. Although it wasn't as calm as when they left it, everyone still seemed to be working together. Picks caught his eye as they walked back in and Jace gave him a small signal with his hands. The old thief stood on a stone bench and got everyone's attention by holding up his arms.

"I feel we're making headway. But there is someone that knows this place almost better than me. And with Dral missing, I want to put in a bid for my new commander. Karanne?"

Cheers from the thieves resounded within the room. Karanne stood shock still in the entrance at first, but then patted Jace on his shoulder. "You had something to do with this, didn't you?" she said under her breath.

"I couldn't think of anyone better for the job," Jace said.

Karanne walked to Picks and began talking to those around her, looking at papers and log books. It was true, with Karanne here, getting thieves to find Straet would be a lot easier. Before long, Karanne sent over a slightly familiar girl about Jace's age. She stood a little below his height and had short, black hair nearly covering her dark eyes.

"Karanne said you needed help with something," she said.

"You ready?" Jace asked. When she gestured with her hand to proceed, he continued. "I need to know who runs your routes, how open the city is for us, and where Guire and Fay are hiding."

She eyed him and crossed her arms over her chest. "Don't you want to ask me how I'm doing first?"

Jace furrowed his brows.

"You don't remember me, do you? That cuts, Jace." He couldn't tell if she was serious. "You and Jervis used to practically run the boy's gang a few years back."

She knows you, dummy. Come on, don't you remember her?

"And me and Tarolay led the girls. Don't pretend you don't know who I am."

Jace pulled his shirt collar from around his throat. It had grown uncomfortably tight. "Uh, I remember you…"

Shey, idiot!

"Shey, right?" Wow, where did that thought come from?

A small smile played on her lips. "Well, that's better. I was about to walk out of here and get your mom to find someone else." She sat down on a stone bench and patted it, motioning for him to sit. "You going to join me?"

Ash, who had been standing behind Jace trotted over to Shey's side and sat next to her leg. "See, at least your dog is showing some brains."

Jace took a deep breath and caught Karanne's eye in the center of the room. With a slight tilt of his head, he gestured to Shey. Karanne laughed. This couldn't be payback for promoting her to second in command, could it? The stone bench seemed to shrink when he sat next to her.

You tried to forget everything about this place, huh? Even the good things.

Were there ever any really good things about this place? Jace's hand hovered over his pouch of memory stones Karanne returned to him. He had very few memories from the Guild after he and Karanne had left years ago. Sure, he had more stones back then, but he left them behind. To start fresh.

"Now what do you want to talk about?"

Jace stammered. This was Straeten he was trying to save. He had no time for this. Someone tapped him on the shoulder and he turned to see three other girls standing there.

"Tarolay runs the routes, Ansa can tell you about the best way to get through the city, and Welly knows all about where those two creeps are holed up." Shey's three friends stood crossing their arms and tapping their toes behind Jace. He turned back to Shey to see her quickly motioning with her hand. She stopped and smiled. "And this is why the girls always beat the boys. Now, Picks has got us doing three other things, so if you're done sitting around I would appreciate getting down to business."

Jace finally laughed. "Same old Shey. All right, sorry to waste your time. I'm looking for an old friend."

Chapter 4

"You don't have to come with us," Jace said to Shey behind him. "Believe it or not, we know our way around the town."

Karanne slapped Jace on his arm. "Things have changed since we've been here last. Don't be rude."

"It's okay, Karanne. At least he hasn't changed much. Now look over there." Shey crowded next to Jace on top of the large statue of Atturan, one of Beldan's ancient founders and heroes. "They're here, just like I told you."

It was midnight and from their vantage point, they were able to look down upon the entire length of NorBridge. The Darrak had set up makeshift camps in the city and their fires glowed upon the houses and shops. The streets were quiet since the townsfolk had all gone inside.

"How many people are in the Hall?" Jace asked in a whisper. No one was walking across the bridge, or even anywhere near it. The lamps along the way were still lit, though.

"As many as they could fit." Shey crawled a little higher on the statue and peered toward the Hall. "Tarolay said that the rest are being held in some of the warehouses on the north side. She couldn't get a closer look to see what they were doing with them."

"And Straeten?"

"They tell me that some big guy with magic comes to check on them every couple of hours from the Hall," Shey said. "That sound like him?"

Jace nodded.

"Any idea where we could get him alone?" Karanne asked. "It wouldn't work if there were Darrak around."

"I was thinking about that," Jace said. "If we could get him anywhere near the alleys by the docks, we'd probably be okay."

Karanne laughed. "Remember where you learned how to fish?"

Jace nodded and smiled. "That would do. If only we knew where Straet was."

"Should be coming from the Hall any minute now," Shey said.

Overhead, Valor flew past, barely more than a whisper on the wind. Jace wasn't sure he would've been able to spot him if he hadn't sensed him. Wait, if he could sense Valor, Straeten could too.

"I think I need to leave." Jace started down when Karanne clasped onto his wrist.

"He's here," Karanne said.

Jace froze and watched as a cloaked person stepped on the bridge from the Hall. That was him. That was Straeten. He'd know his long loping stride anywhere. He resisted stretching out and contacting him. Two Darrak walked close behind.

"Now don't do anything stupid," Karanne said. "We're scouting things out here. Plus, they all think you're dead, right?"

Fay saw that drop off the roof, but did she see anything else?

Jace nodded. "As far as I know."

Straeten paused in the center of the bridge to look upstream. Jace called upon his Soulkind and his vision swept through a tunnel of light until he settled behind Valor's eyes. Circling above, he was far from Straeten's gaze, but close enough for the hawk's sight to clearly see his eyes.

A steady, piercing blue.

Not a hint of brown.

Straeten paused only for a moment, turned his head slightly and then continued walking toward Beldan.

"Is Tarolay out there now?" Jace pulled back to his own vision as Straeten reached the end of the bridge.

Shey nodded. "She'll be on the roof."

"You know which way he goes from here?"

Shey shrugged.

"We've got to follow him." Jace looked down but Karanne held him fast again.

"Just check things out," Karanne urged. "It's not safe in town for you to walk through. No matter what you think of yourself."

You going to listen to her?

Jace felt a bubble of anger arise with this stray thought but he quickly pushed it away. "I've got this," he said. "Remember the thing about my boots?"

Karanne tilted her head at him in confusion.

"I think I've figured out that problem." He jumped off the statue. Magic flowed through him, enveloping him in its warm folds. The wind blew past his face and he alighted upon the outstretched arm of the statue. He flapped his large wings for a moment while Karanne and Shey gaped at him.

With a sharp cry, he dove into the darkness. His heart raced and pumped wildly with the speed of the wind racing past him. Spinning in wide circles, he soared silently at a distance. Straeten was easy to follow at first, as the streets were wide and lit, but as the stone covered path led down to the river, buildings clustered closer together, blocking Jace's view. He and Valor abandoned the wide open for the tight alleys and dimly lit side streets. Several dark figures joined Straeten and the two trailing Darrak.

So much for getting him alone.

The black water of the Crescent River lapped against the shores where the docks met the streets. The warehouse ought to be close, according to Shey. Valor's gaze scanned further to the north and past the city walls, to where the Darrak army swarmed like insects upon the great fields.

This town couldn't be their final destination. Maybe they were going to set up a base here first, bleed Beldan dry of food and resources, then move on to bigger places. And what could stop them?

Straeten entered a building near the docks and disappeared. Now what? Valor swooped through the narrow alley but Jace didn't see any sign of Straet, the windows were all darkened and the Darrak stood waiting outside. Pumping his wings, Jace swept up to the slightly pitching roof. This had to be the place Shey was talking about. A scrawny girl with freckles and dirt peppering her face hunched over to peer into the roof's opening. Tarolay. About twenty feet from her, Jace called on his magic to drop out of Valor.

With slightly more grace than last time, his body ripped out of Valor's and rolled onto the roof. He came to a stop after sliding unceremoniously into a brick chimney and stood up, patting himself down.

"What...?" Tarolay hissed.

"Hey, at least I ended up with my clothes on this time." Good thing he'd finally mastered that skill. Jace crept to her side.

"What do you see?" Jace asked between deep breaths. He peered into the dim warehouse through the opening.

Tarolay took a step back. "How did you do that?" She didn't stop staring at him.

"That's my ride." Jace pointed to Valor now flying solo in the cloudy night sky. He smiled at her gaping expression. "Did *you* have problems getting here?"

Tarolay caught herself and shut her open mouth. "Just because you left the Guild doesn't mean we all forgot how to be thieves."

Jace nodded and watched a crowd of Darrak striding through the warehouse. "You seen Straeten, the 'big guy?'"

"Yeah, he walked in right before you showed up. Through there." Tarolay pointed to a door at the end of the warehouse. Above the door, he thought there might be a larger room, some sort of office or meeting place. Two Darrak stood guard, possibly the same that followed Straeten from the Hall. He couldn't be sure.

"What are they doing with the people?" Jace asked.

Tarolay shrugged. "Slaves, I think."

That had to be it. This massive army needed to be supported with food and labor. These people would easily fill that purpose. "And they'll ship them out from here. Like cattle." There went his idea to scout this area. He had to stop this. Now. Stop Guire and Fay and then get the army out of the city.

Easy, no problem.

He laughed.

Jace motioned to Tarolay that he was heading across the roof. Shouts and cries from the townsfolk came through the roof opening. Jace checked the door to the structure and found it locked but with a few quick twists of a pick, the door opened silently. He still had it. The steps creaked slightly as he went down them, but the sound from inside the warehouse was surely louder. The shouts were muffled, but a few voices made their way up clear enough for him to understand. One was Straeten's.

"And the second unit will take two hundred with them tomorrow," Straeten said in a flat voice. "Women only."

Jace froze on the steps, still out of sight. Two hundred? This was worse than he thought. How was he going to cripple this army and Guire and Fay as well? It was too big. Jace took a few more steps and peered into the room that sat above the rest of the warehouse. Straeten and a few other men stood in front of a large opening that overlooked the floor below. Jace could see the cages through the opening and the half dozen Darrak keeping guard down there, too.

"More Darrak are on the way from the mountains," a voice said. "What does Fay say about them?"

"She is meeting with the leaders tomorrow," Straeten said. "She hopes to station more in the city."

"The Hall probably holds some of this information, but I should bring her this ledger," the other man said. He continued in a low voice Jace couldn't hear over the rustling of papers.

"She assumes little will come from the north, even when Myraton hears about it," Straeten replied. "Spies have already made their way through. Show me the holding cells."

The shuffling in the office soon fell silent and the door leading down to the prisoners shut with a click. Jace didn't waste any time and stepped quietly down the stairs from the roof into the dim office area. He continued to the opening to look down below more closely. Flickering torchlight filled the large area. Screams and cries arose from the cages.

Straeten and the other man walked casually past barred doors, as if they were inspecting livestock. How could Straeten be so far gone? Fay had a strong grip, but he had to be in there somewhere. He would come back.

Darrak stood by and the human guards with Straeten eyed the scaled creatures uncomfortably. Jace waited until Straeten checked other cells further down the line before rifling through the papers on the large table in the middle of the room. A ledger sat atop the pile. Jace flipped through quickly seeing logs of the people now stored down below. Jace stashed the book in his pack, but then rethought the idea. If they noticed the book missing, they'd put the guards on high alert. The last thing they needed was more Darrak. He placed the book back on the table.

A crashing outside the door startled him. He rushed to the opening, keeping his head down, and listened. New shouts, this time the lizard screams of the Darrak, rose above the others. Two of them carried a kicking and struggling person past the cages toward the stairs. Tarolay. Jace darted for the staircase back to the roof but froze when he heard more shouts from that way. Darrak.

Great.

Not up to the roof, not down into the warehouse. What was left? Without thinking, he climbed through the opening from the office and out onto the rafters above the prisoners. The rough wood cut into his palms as he hung exposed to anyone looking up at him.

They're going to see you, idiot, hanging outside the room.

True, he needed more cover. He scrambled up the rafters into the shadows further away from the office. A quick check below assured him no one had seen him. None too soon, either. Straeten gripped Tarolay's arm and pulled her up the wooden stairs. She yanked against his hold yet the fear in her eyes froze Jace's heart. How could Straeten be doing this?

Tarolay's eyes darted back and forth across the warehouse, from Darrak to locked door. She wasn't looking for an escape.

She's going to rat you out.

Anger built in Jace's head again. She would tell Straeten not only about him running around in the warehouse but also about the thieves back in the hidden guild. The whole plan would be for nothing, and any chance Beldan had for freedom would be gone.

He rubbed his forehead and the sudden anger seeped away. What was wrong with him? It wouldn't be her fault if she did. She would have to spill everything or die. Jace had to do something first.

But what? Other than getting caught trying to free her by himself, he really couldn't think of anything. He edged back through the rafters to the opening above, only to see Tarolay tied to a chair. She cried out, whether from pain or something else, and earned a strike across her cheek from Straeten. Jace knew what she was doing, though.

"You're a thief, aren't you?" Straeten asked, his face close to hers. "Where are they all hiding? They fled like rats when Fay arrived."

He sounded like Straeten. It was his voice and all, but the way he spoke and the things he said... And those blue eyes.

"But, if they left, then why are you here?"

Tarolay wept openly and spoke through the sobs. "My mother is in here! Let her go! Why are you doing this?"

Jace smirked as he watched her hands behind her back.

"That's a good story." Straeten moved even closer and gripped her shoulders gently. In the next moment, Tarolay shrieked. "But you're a thief."

A dim blue glow emanated from her shoulders around Straeten's fingertips. Thin blue lines traced across her skin. Tarolay's head jerked forward and short spasms shook through her body.

"Do I have to ask you again?"

Thieves were good liars, but Tarolay wasn't trained for torture. This would all go horribly wrong soon. Jace needed to create a distraction.

As if in answer, Valor flapped his wings and settled onto the beam in the rafters. That would do. The power from the Soulkind filled Jace and pulled him through a light into Valor's body. Jace felt more in control this time. His wings beat quickly as he entered the room. With a shrill cry, he rounded past Straeten, startling the two Darrak. He weaved through the rafters and turned to face them. Straeten rushed forward and locked his bright blue eyes with Valor's.

Straeten kept staring and Jace smiled to himself. The distraction was working.

His smile fell abruptly, though. Something was pushing into his head, a feather in his thoughts, and it took him a few seconds before he realized that Straeten was using a spell. His spell.

Guire and Fay thought Jace to be dead, didn't they? If Straeten pushed any harder, he might sense Jace in there, and any chance of surprise would be lost. Jace called on the power of his Soulkind and the magic coursed through his mind and body. The tickle on the border of his thoughts brushed closer. He pulled back while at the same time pushing his own thoughts elsewhere.

The Darrak beside him barked a question but Straeten held up his hand and closed his eyes. Straeten gripped onto the wooden frame before him, but then his fingers relaxed. "It's nothing.".

Jace let out his breath. He'd get out of this yet.

The air around Jace suddenly turned frigid. Frost formed around the rafter and dusted his talons. Branching veins of ice grew through the beams, reaching for him. So much for getting out without a fight.

Valor flapped his wings to dive into the warehouse, screaming a shrill cry through the attack. Jace glanced back to the room where Straeten was standing but there was no sign of Tarolay. Straeten turned around as if reading his mind. He shouted something unintelligible to the Darrak, sending them running toward the roof.

An alarm bell started ringing, thin and tinny. Great wooden bars dropped into place before closed doors on all sides of the warehouse. Long beams dropped outside the shuttered windows. The wailing of the hundreds of slaves grew louder.

This is 'just checking things out?'

Jace stretched and pushed with Valor's wings toward one of the few windows still open and Valor's heart beat even faster in his chest. Then the cold erupted all over his body and his legs seized up.

26

His instinct took over and he let go of the magic tying him to the hawk. His own body ejected from Valor's, bursting the layer of ice off of both of them into tiny shards. He careened into the rafters, only just catching onto them as he fell. Valor flew through the open window and Jace scrambled up to it.

Before he could get to the opening, a thick covering of ice sealed him inside the warehouse. He slammed his fist into the frozen barrier and pulled out one of his knives to chip into it. Only a few bits flew from his hand with every chop yet he didn't slow down.

"Jace?" Straeten shouted.

Jace hacked harder at the ice.

"That *is* you. Come on down, you're only making a fool of yourself."

"I'm doing okay up here." Jace scanned back and forth, looking for the closest shut window, and wondered how quickly he needed to move to avoid another blast from Straeten.

"Fay told me you died," Straeten shouted. "Fell off that roof. Again."

Jace took one final swing at the ice. It was no use.

"That's a neat trick with Valor, huh? Maybe you could teach me that before I bring you back to Fay."

Jace stretched out his mind for the hawk, but couldn't sense him through the building. He tried to enter back into Valor's body again but something prevented him from reaching his magic. Probably that ice around the building.

"Are you going to make me send a couple of Darrak to bring you down? This could get really messy."

"That depends."

"On what?"

Jace glanced around again. "Yeah, never mind." He sheathed his knife and started to climb down a massive wooden beam supporting the rooftop. Several men with clubs and nets stood at the ready, waiting for him to reach the bottom. "It sounded good in my head."

"Bind him. Search him," Straeten said when Jace got to the floor. "And if he tries to use any magic, stop him. Any way you need to."

One man roughly searched his body, removing several knives hidden beneath his cloak and one in his boot.

"What's going on, Straet?" Jace asked. "Why are you doing this?"

"Quiet."

"I know you're in there," Jace said.

"Your friend is gone." Straeten's blue eyes, someone else's eyes, met his, freezing Jace to the core.

"No." Jace searched around for something in his head to force into Straeten's. A few memories of Straeten and him as kids flashed past his eyes and a rush of power from his Soulkind filled his chest. But it evaporated when one of the guards shoved him forward. He dropped to his knees. The man bound his hands together.

"For a thief, you're exceptionally good at getting caught," Straeten said with a laugh. "Fay will be happy with me. Probably teach me something new."

"That's why you're doing this? Since when do you need power? This isn't you."

For a second Straeten stared blankly. Then his blue eyes changed slightly, as a rock dropped into a clear pool might stir the sediment beneath it. But only for a moment.

Chapter 5

They entered the office where Tarolay had been held a few minutes before. Did Fay already know what was happening? Could she *see* through Straeten's eyes? Once in the room, Jace glanced at the staircase that led up to the roof. A single Darrak stood guarding it, his eyes glued to Jace. Straeten shoved Jace into the chair and turned Jace's dagger over in his hands, scanning the Darrak etchings.

"How can you remember things, and still do as she says?" Jace gently called on his magic, feeling the power creep into his body. There was a way into Straeten's thoughts, he knew it. He'd almost had it before. If he could peer into his mind and see something, anything, it might help him unravel whatever this was.

Straeten's eyes twitched, signaling to someone standing behind Jace, and then a crushing blow struck Jace on the side of his head. Pain shot through his body yet he resisted shouting out.

"I don't recommend using your magic again," Straeten said. "As for my thoughts, I know everything about 'Straeten.' But he is gone, I can assure you. Now, I will ask you what I asked your friend. Where are the thieves hiding?"

Jace scoffed. "What, you didn't finish your business with them?"

Straeten scowled and turned out Jace's pockets. He held up the metal rod. "I remember seeing you with this. Why do you still carry it with you? What good will it do you?"

Jace looked to the stairwell again. The Darrak hadn't moved. Straeten followed his glance and shoved the metal rod inside his cloak. "You're not leaving that way." Straeten pulled one of the men close so he could say something under his breath. The man promptly left the room.

Straeten then returned his attention to Jace. "They can't save you in here." Straeten stepped to the window's edge and peered down into the warehouse.

"Who said anything about saving me?" Jace said.

"You didn't have to," Straeten said, glancing back. "You do this sort of thing for each other. It's pathetic." After a minute, the man returned with a piece of paper and handed it to Straeten.

"We don't have enough here," he said while Straeten read.

"I can see that." Straeten handed back the paper. "They'll be coming for the slaves. Hold them off while I take the prisoner to Fay. Send a runner to the Hall requesting more support." The man left the room as soon as Straeten finished.

Straeten motioned to two Darrak and they strode quickly to his side. They pulled Jace roughly from his chair, draped a black cloth over his head, bound his hands together, and dragged him down the stairs.

Jace couldn't see where he was going, but this wasn't the first time he had been blindfolded. He measured out the number of steps he took, listened to the sounds of the people around him and of the river as he was brought outside. He dragged his heels as much as he could, but Straeten or someone else struck him on the back whenever he did.

But then, they struck him every fifteen seconds or so no matter how he walked. He lost track of where he was now, or how long he had been walking. He had to be somewhere on the streets back to the bridge, but where exactly, he didn't know.

The Darrak shouted something, although their words were lost on Jace. The cloth blurred the sounds, plus the pain from the constant beating didn't help. Even so, he could tell the Darrak were arguing with each other over something.

"Shut up, you two!" Straeten shouted from behind.

Jace heard the sound of a collision behind him. In the moment's pause after, he struggled against his bonds on his wrists. Whoever tied them hadn't spent too much time, and, having trained as a child to do this, Jace had his hands free in seconds. He whipped the cloth from his face, squinting to see what was happening.

One of the Darrak had tackled Straeten and was pounding him with his clawed fists. The other approached Jace quickly now, raising a foot-long cudgel over his head.

"Stop!" Jace shouted, holding up his hand. The Darrak faltered and then looked at his partner. Jace saw their eyes meet, and the one still pinning Straeten to the ground nodded as it reached inside Straeten's pack and pulled out the metal rod.

"I told you! It is him!"

In that pause, a blast of ice struck the Darrak in the chest. Icy veins crept over its arms and torso and savage screams filled the tiny alley. Straeten leapt up and released an icy bolt at the other Darrak.

"I know where I am," Jace said as he scrambled away. The stones on the street, the familiar buildings. Without a glance at the Darrak or Straeten, he turned to the alley on his left and sprinted as hard as he could toward it. He shook his head to clear out the lights that flashed in his eyes and tried to avoid the patches of ice that formed on the ground. Twisting his body, he barely fit through the narrow alley.

Jace stumbled and slipped on the slick stones. He glanced back and saw Straeten behind him, pushing and cursing his way through the alley. "You going to fit?"

Straeten gave a frustrated grunt and cast another spell. The bolt of ice careened off the narrow walls and crashed into the ground.

"Remember this place?" Jace shouted. Straeten didn't reply. "Can't speak? I always told Straeten to get in better shape. You ought to work on that for him. He'll thank you when he's back."

The sound of breaking glass crashed behind him. Jace turned around to see a part of a building crumbling from Straeten's attack. Bricks shattered and fragments of them pelted his face. He abandoned the constricted alleyway and entered into the fishing district next to the river. The cover from the building had ended, but hopefully his luck hadn't.

"Stop!" Straeten bellowed.

Jace froze. Not from a spell, but from the desperation in the words. He turned around and held his hands up. "You're not going to bring me to her."

Straeten smiled. Not his own smile, it came from whatever was controlling him. "No need to bring you anywhere. She is already coming."

Jace dropped his arms and scanned the area. Much shorter buildings here, stalls mainly for the selling of fish. The smell of it hung heavily in the air. He edged his way to the center of the marketplace keeping an eye on Straeten as he approached.

"You remember this place?" Jace asked again.

Straeten shook his head quickly. "No. Never." But Jace heard the strain in his words and saw the struggle in his eyes.

"Over there," Jace gestured. "You were trying to steal some fish with me that one time."

Straeten's brown eyes left Jace's for a moment to glance over at a red painted booth. "And…" He paused. "And I knocked over the whole stand."

Jace laughed. "I still don't know how we got away after that." He took one step closer to Straeten, calling upon his magic once again to see into Straeten's mind.

The blue glow in Straeten's eyes flickered. "That's far enough." He raised his hands.

A brilliant flash of light erupted in front of Straeten's face. He shouted and rubbed at his eyes.

"Now!" a voice called out. It was Karanne.

Shey rushed out between two stalls. She reached for Straeten's arms to pin them back and bind them, but he swung about wildly casting bolts of ice in every direction.

"Fay!" Straeten called.

Amidst the shower of ice cascading through the market, a Darrak crept and limped up behind Straeten. With one wide sweeping motion, he struck Straeten's neck with the rod and he crumbled to the ground. The Darrak fell in the next moment, clutching his chest.

Jace rushed to his side. The Darrak's arms were covered in a layer of ice and large shards protruded from his stomach. With raspy breathing, he handed Jace the rod.

"It is you," he uttered. "You can help us. Bring this to our camp."

"To who? Where?" Jace asked.

"Go!" the Darrak croaked. "She is coming." And then, releasing its grip on Jace's arm, it breathed out its last. Jace watched the insects completely return its remains to the earth and he gave silent thanks to the Darrak.

Karanne and Shey walked out onto the street.

"Nice work on the ambush, thanks." Jace put the metal artifact into his pouch and looked over at Straeten. "Give me a hand with him." Jace lifted Straeten's deadweight body and both he and Shey draped his arms around their shoulders.

"Tarolay found us," Karanne said. "She told me what happened in the warehouse. Luckily you went where I thought you would."

Jace nodded his agreement. "She did great in there. Where is she now?"

"I told her we would head to Turic's cottage after this," Karanne said. "Allar and Turic should be on their way."

"That Darrak told me Fay was coming," Jace said.

"You can understand those things?" Shey asked, struggling under Straeten's weight.

"It's one of my many talents," Jace said.

"Cute."

Jace smiled. "Karanne, grab his legs."

Karanne hoisted up Straeten's legs and wedged them under her arms. "He's definitely not lighter than he looks."

The three of them skirted through the side alleyways unseen like any respectable thieves would, though with the darkening night their skills weren't needed. They walked farther from the fire posts along the river district.

"There's someone up ahead," Jace whispered.

"How do you know?" Shey said between breaths.

Jace gestured with his chin to the rooftop beside them and the black silhouette of Valor bowed to Jace below. "This way."

Karanne and Shey followed his lead left through an archway toward the river.

Soon the path led to the city walls and a post guarded by two men. It seemed to be the only way outside. "Let's put him down for a minute." Jace placed Straeten onto the stones and rubbed his arms.

"He's not going to be out much longer," Shey said, stretching her back.

"And sounds like they're already on to us." Karanne pointed to the Hall across the water. A distant ringing sounded and more torches brightened along the bridge.

"Then let's get moving." Shey quietly unsheathed a curved knife from her belt and crept toward the guards.

"No knives," Jace said.

Shey didn't put it away. "We're going to get caught if we don't." She crept into the shadows and climbed onto an overhang.

"Shey!" Jace whispered loudly but the thief didn't stop climbing. He turned to Karanne. "Why did we bring her along?"

Karanne smiled. "You don't like anything unpredictable do you?"

"Not if it can get us killed."

Shey had already scrambled up onto the roof near the guards. One of the men stared off to the south and the other faced the town. A single rope leading to a bell hung between them.

Shey could easily off them both.

True, but he wasn't willing to kill anyone if he could help it. "I'll be right back," Jace said.

Power swirled through Jace's mind as he gripped his Soulkind, ignoring the metal prongs attached to it. All the magic he created washed over him. What would help? He knew what would finish the attack quickly, felt the lure of his dark mark call to him. The guards' minds were easily grasped. But the spirit of Blue neighed in his head and made his mind up for him. He knew what to do. He reached out with the power flooding through him toward Valor. "Karanne, get her attention for me."

Karanne's wrist twitched and a pulse of light darted out and flitted up toward Shey, now creeping along the roof. For a brief moment, her face glowed in the flash of light and she reluctantly nodded.

Jace signaled for her to hold off as Valor leapt from the roof and swept silently toward the guards. He fluttered through the window, flapped once around the room, and then gripped the lantern. The two guards waved their swords up at him.

Valor wrenched the lantern from its hook on the wall, and with a mad flurry of feathers, dragged it through the window, leading a guard away from Jace. After flying a few feet, Valor lost his grip on the lantern, and oil spilled as it fell, igniting a small stand nearby. The guard knelt beside the flames and pulled boards and boxes away from them.

Jace sprinted toward the other guard just as Shey jumped through the flames and onto him, knocking him off balance and into a stack of crates. She stood up and brandished her blade.

"Call for help!" the guard shouted and held up his arm to block her.

Valor swept in front of Shey, stopping her from striking with her knife. Instead, she kicked the startled guard between his legs. He dropped like a rock. She kicked him again in the face with the heel of her boot. The other guard standing in the room's entrance gaped at the scene. He turned quickly into the darkened room.

Great, you blew it, idiot.

Jace started after him but the guard stopped and backed out slowly. A low growl emanated from within the room. Jace smiled. A gray snarling dog stepped forward. The guard raised his sword.

"Stop!" Jace shouted.

He turned to Jace. Another figure emerged from the dark and struck the guard against the side of his head, felling him like a tree.

"Tare!" Jace patted his friend on the shoulder. He felt Ash nuzzling alongside him and kneeled to scratch his ears.

The silent boy saluted Jace and then hustled off toward Karanne. He easily lifted Straeten up and the two of them carried him, Jace holding his legs. Jace entered the room, squinting his eyes for a moment before pointing to the alarm bell.

Shey walked up quietly behind him. "You've got to trust me." She disarmed the bell with a quick slice of her knife.

Jace walked past her still carrying Straeten.

"Are the others close by?" Jace asked. Tare nodded. "Turic, too?" Again, a sharp nod.

"That will only have slowed them down a little bit," Karanne said, breathing hard.

Jace huffed and readjusted Straeten's legs. "You let me know if I'm going to walk into a hole or something." Tare smiled.

Ash ran off ahead of them. Jace closed his eyes.

"Can you get Ash to bring the others?" Karanne asked.

"Trying."

The smooth paved stones of the city turned to dirt and then to rounded river rocks. Just when Jace thought his arms would give out entirely, he sensed something up ahead and then heard someone talking.

"There they are!" Allar shouted.

Jace placed Straeten on the ground. His hands shook. This was it, their chance to free Straeten. The river roared past them, bubbling up onto the shore. "Come on!"

Allar limped into the clearing alongside Burgis and Ranelle. Ranelle. She smiled and saluted him when he met her eyes.

"Glad you could make it," Jace said. He clapped Burgis on his shoulder and waved to Allar who was still focused on Straeten stretched out on the ground.

"Bind him," Allar said. Shey quickly removed some rope from her belt and tied Straeten's feet together, then moved on to his hands.

"Where's Turic?" Jace asked.

"He's upriver a bit," Burgis said. "I'll go get him."

"Hurry."

Burgis ran into the shadows along the riverbank. Allar stood over Straeten and held out his hands to expose Newell's shield-like Soulkind on his forearm. "He has the taint of Guire upon him."

"Can you get it out?" Karanne asked.

A bright light grew from inside Allar's shield and then flew into the clearing above Straeten. It hovered over him but flickered about uneasily. "I can't get a grip on it, something's wrong," Allar said. "His sister helped me last time."

"Your sister, you mean," Jace said and tried to catch Allar's eyes, but he kept his focus on Straeten. "If they're looking for us, this is going to be a big sign to them." Jace pointed up to the trees.

The light settled upon Straeten.

Allar stood over him, gripping his shoulder with his shield arm. Something happened, something Jace couldn't see but felt in his chest, like sensing a ripple in a still pond. Allar's face strained. A vein bulged in his neck. "Something's holding me back. I… can't do it."

"You have to," Jace said, standing beside him.

"He's holding on too tightly."

"Straeten, or Guire?" Jace asked. If it was Straeten, he could do something about it. Jace knelt and pulled out his Soulkind. The power flooded over him as he channeled his magic first to calm any turmoil inside his friend, then into his eye-shaped mark.

He closed his eyes and floated, drifted, closer to Straeten's mind. A storm of thoughts swarmed him and pushed him back. But this was Straeten. Nothing could stop him. Not this storm in his head. Not anything.

It was almost as if he turned the magic sideways then. Instead of fighting the stream, he just cut right through it. Straeten stood before him in a strange void, his eyes closed as if sleeping. Jace knew it was Straeten, but a swirling light coursing over his body made him think he wasn't alone. Fay's orb had grown inside him, covering Straeten's chest with its icy tendrils. Others would remove that, he wasn't about to get drawn into her magic again. His job was to help his friend focus. He centered on his calming magic, felt its waves pass over him, and remained untouchable. Straeten's other magic hovered around him like giant lightning bugs tethered to the glowing symbols upon his body— red fire from Turic, Karanne's white Fireflash, and a green glow from Jace's magic.

And still another presence pulsed its sickness into Straeten. Charred and moldy growths reached into Straeten's back, coursing with Guire's evil. The growths pulsated like a beating heart pumping dark fluid across his back under his shirt. An outside force yanked at them, but their plant-like tips pulled back, trying to remain rooted. Straeten convulsed as the darkness resisted and folded in on his body.

36

"Straeten!" Jace called out but Straeten's eyes remained closed, only twitching slightly. "Wake up!"

Jace's Soulkind beckoned. His own magic swelled within him, flowing through Straeten into the familiar orb, one he had formed through countless connections with his companions.

The beam of light to Straeten brightened, flaring like an ember when air passes over it. Fay and Guire had a strong hold, but Jace, the Master of this magic, was closest. The cool green energy of his Soulkind glowed brighter, overwhelming the others. Straeten's eyes twitched more now, and his face grimaced. He wrenched his body forward, straining at the darkness pouring into him.

"Jace!" a voice yelled. Ranelle?

Jace ripped himself out of Straeten's mind only to see that three guards had run into the clearing, their swords out.

"We'll hold them off," Ranelle shouted, drawing her long hunting knife.

"We need to protect Allar while he works on Straet," Jace said. "But just stop them, don't kill them." He stared at Shey.

Shey ran directly at one of the guards and disarmed him with a quick flash of her knives. The sword clanged onto the ground and the man clutched at his bleeding arm with a groan. "He's not dead," Shey said and stood behind Jace as the remaining guards drew closer.

Jace scoffed. "Allar, you got this?"

Allar nodded. "That seemed to work, whatever you did." He drew his shield away from Straeten and the glowing light pulled back with it, making Guire's presence squirm like a maggot. Slowly, the shadow lifted out of Straeten's unconscious body, unmoving except for the occasional twitching.

Jace ran headlong at the guard closest to him. With a slight twist of his body, he slipped under the guard's swinging sword and slammed the handle of his knife upward into his chin. The guard dropped his sword and clutched at his throat, gasping for breath. Instantly Jace swung again at the back of his neck and the guard crumpled to the ground.

Shey pinned another guard face first into the dirt, favoring her left arm as she did so. "Hurry up!"

"I don't know if I can hold this thing," Allar said in a strained voice. A black mass spun in the air above Straeten. A slimy, shapeless arm reached back to Straeten's body.

"My turn!" Karanne stepped toward Allar and motioned for him to lower the mass. Her hand glowed with the summoning of her magic, the lines on her palm flared. The mass struggled within Allar's grasp and backed away from Karanne as she approached.

"Ready?" Allar asked.

Karanne nodded once and Allar released his hold. The second Guire's darkness dropped to the ground, a thin beam of intense light shot from Karanne's palm straight into the growth. It squealed and burned, breaking up into smaller bits as she continued to incinerate it. A larger portion scooted from the flame and sprouted three stalks.

"Over there!" Jace shouted and pointed. The clump, with its new jointed legs, scrambled awkwardly toward the trees where Shey sat on the ground.

"What the…?" Shey said, watching it come at her. She backed away on her hands and feet.

It seemed to notice her, or sense her, and quickened its awkward crawl.

"Get it away from me!" Shey yelled and backed into a thick tree trunk. The black mass reached her feet and she kicked out at it.

Allar appeared by her side without Jace even noticing his approach. Instantly the light from his shield grasped the growth, matching his hand's movement. He stared at the thing, scrutinizing it as it floated in the air in front of him.

"What are you waiting for?" Shey asked.

"I am trying to see how it works," Allar said.

"Can you hurry up and see how it dies?" Shey stood up and backed away, cradling her right arm.

Allar peered at it a moment longer. He shifted on his leg and then squeezed tighter with his hand. The light surrounding the black mass enveloped it, then both the darkness and the light blinked out of existence. Everyone turned to Straeten expectantly.

"Is he all right now?" Shey asked.

"That filth is finally out of him," Allar said. "But Fay is still in there."

Jace let out a deep breath and clapped Allar on the back. "That's one, at least. Thanks. Anybody know where Turic is?"

Ranelle shrugged her shoulders. "He should be here any minute."

"You okay?" Jace inspected Shey's right arm. Blood soaked through her sleeve as she stumbled to her feet. "Come on, let me take a look."

Shey reluctantly showed him her arm. "I wouldn't have gotten this if you let me do what I do best."

"He was a person, like you or me. Now you'll both be all right." He bound her arm up tightly to stop the bleeding. "I think this is pretty good, but we'll let Turic take a look at this to make sure it heals right. Wouldn't want you to be unable to use that arm."

Shey laughed dryly. "I can't imagine not being able to hit you."

Jace smiled back. "Thanks, by the way."

Shey punched him in the shoulder with her other hand. "You're welcome."

"And for what it's worth, I don't think that's what you do best." Jace sat down beside Ash.

Suddenly, both his and Ash's ears turned up. "Someone's coming."

Turic rounded the bend through the darkness, escorted by both Brannon and Burgis. "I can sense her. She is close."

"Turic!" Jace ran to him. "Straeten needs you."

"Can you do what you did for me?" Karanne pointed to her head. "Get her out of him."

Turic rushed to Straeten's side and knelt down. "I am not sure. You were not as far gone as he is, it never really had a chance to get hold of you." He placed his hand on Straeten's head and instantly a warm glow suffused his body.

"What is that?" Ranelle pointed into the forest. Jace glanced up from Straeten to see something large burst through the trees and barrel into Burgis' side. The boy flew into the brush and landed with a crash. He didn't get up.

It was a Darrak but it was far bigger and faster than any Jace had ever seen. Before he reached the trees, it swept its spear sideways into Ranelle, toppling her easily. Its next swing struck at Tare who was at least ready for the attack. He clung onto the spear as it hit his side and struggled to hold onto it. The creature followed up with a ferocious punch at Tare's head, sending him to the ground. He raised the spear over Tare's body as two other Darrak ran behind him.

"Stop!" Jace shouted. Jace reached to a pocket in his cloak. The metal rod he pulled out and held aloft glinted in the glow surrounding Straeten.

The first Darrak turned to face the other two, who both stared in awe at the relic. The larger Darrak spat some command and raised its spear.

"Turic, are you almost done?" Jace hissed.

Turic didn't respond.

The Darrak took a slow step toward Jace. A creaking sound emanated from behind Jace. Must've been Ranelle pulling back an arrow in her bow. He held up his hand to her without looking back. The Darrak took two more steps until Jace saw right into its red eyes. Then it moved so quickly that Jace couldn't even react.

It grabbed for the rod with one hand and kicked Jace back against a tree. Instantly Jace's eyes spun with stars.

So much for the rod.

Ranelle's arrow left her bow, yet it only plinked against the Darrak's chest, dropping harmlessly. The Darrak stared at the silver rod now lying abandoned on the ground. Karanne swept to Jace's side. Through the dizziness, he thought he heard her ask if he was all right.

The large Darrak raised the massive spear above its head and moved toward Jace.

Oh, you're dead.

It started to bring down the spear but it cracked in the air upon some sort of barrier. The Darrak's eyes narrowed. It reared back and lashed out with its fist. This time its bones crunched with an unsettling sound as it struck the invisible shield. For the first time, Jace saw the Darrak falter and step back, clutching its crippled hand. Off to his right, Allar stood holding his shield arm in the air.

"Allar," Jace said, gripping Karanne's shoulder to pull himself up. He shook his head to clear the stars. Allar saluted him.

"Stop this," a calm voice called out.

Jace froze. It was as if a wall of ice blocked him from moving, and apparently the others as well. Only the large Darrak moved, backing away toward the voice.

"Marathas," Fay said. "You're looking...older."

Turic kept his attention on Straeten. Through his blurred vision, Jace saw Fay's face contort as she noticed what Turic was attempting.

"Get away from him. He's mine." She took a step in his direction but Karanne finally was able to move. The Fireflash darted out in a quick burst of light in front of Fay's face but she only batted her hand at it. A sweeping wall of frost followed her movement. The

Fireflash spun away from the cold like a bug and Fay continued toward Turic.

Turic now squinted his eyes and bent deeply over Straeten's body. Jace pushed as hard as he could against his ice cage. Nothing. He watched the scene unfold, unable to move a muscle.

Fay walked to Turic's side and put her hands to his head. The old man fell sharply onto his back. She carelessly stepped over the old man's body.

"No!" Jace tried to shout, but only a muted sound came out of his mouth.

Fay affectionately caressed Straeten's cheek, beckoning him to awaken.

An urge to connect with Straeten rushed through Jace. He pushed into his friend's mind.

Turic had clearly done something. Straeten felt freer, more open. A little part of Straeten seemed to be listening for something. Jace crept closer inside.

"You've got to resist her," Jace thought with his last bit of energy. He fell back to his own body. Fay turned slightly in his direction and smiled briefly.

"So you survived that fall," she said. "Now that is a story I would like to hear." She turned back to Straeten. "Rise."

Straeten's eyes opened, blue and pale. He stumbled to his feet, reaching up to Fay for help. She held his hand and lifted him.

"Straet, no," Jace said weakly.

His friend looked at him, and for the briefest of moments, the blue faded back to brown. Straeten lifted his hand again, and this time, a thin blast of ice raced from his open palm into Fay's chest. She didn't flinch, but her eyes filled with a brilliant rage.

Using her own magic against her? That was stupid.

"Straeten?" Jace called out hesitantly.

Straeten glanced back at Jace. The blue in his eyes spun for a moment and then winked out until only his normal brown shown through. Yes! Using her magic against her must've worked somehow.

Fay... He had almost forgotten about the danger. Jace felt magic crackling in the air and turned to see Allar and Karanne with their arms outstretched. Fay's eyes darted about her, resting on Turic's prone body. Jace quickly stepped in front of him and brandished his dagger. The smile faltered on Fay's lips as she took them all in. Straeten joined Jace at Turic's side. Her smug expression disappeared altogether.

"Very well," Fay said and nodded to the large Darrak. "Next time." She shrank behind its form and stepped between the trees, the other two Darrak that had also come along slunk away after Fay without a word.

"I can't believe she just left," Karanne said after a minute.

"It was a fight she couldn't win," Jace said. "Especially without Straeten."

"Should we go after her?" Karanne asked.

"Probably," Jace said. "But there are more important things." Turic's unmoving body drew his eyes. Karanne rushed off to kneel beside him.

"Jace?"

Jace smiled. Straeten's voice. He tried to speak, but the words froze in his throat.

"I'm… sorry," Straeten said.

Before he could say anything else, Jace wrapped his arms around his friend in a huge hug. "I'm just glad it's you." Already Jace's head was beginning to clear, although he felt a warm dripping down his back. His own blood?

Stumbling to his feet he grabbed onto a tree trunk, only to falter and lose his grip. Straeten caught him before he could fall back down again. Strong arms, as solid as the tree trunk, supported him on his way to Turic. Straeten's brown eyes looked into his own, still begging for forgiveness. He gave him a reassuring grip on his arm.

"It's good to have you back."

Straeten smiled, but it slipped as Jace knelt beside Turic.

Jace looked over Karanne's shoulder. "Is he going to be okay?" Only when she gave him a brief nod did he breathe again.

"We've got to move him though." Karanne stood up and motioned to Tare. The large boy carefully picked Turic up and cradled him. "They'll be back."

Jace shook his head to clear out the lingering blur.

"You all right there Jace?" Shey asked. "That thing tossed you around pretty bad."

"Lucky we had Allar around." Jace patted Allar on his back.

"It took everything Newell had to slow it down. I don't really know what's happening when he takes over like that."

Straeten stopped Jace. "I've got to talk before it's all gone. It's slipping away." Straeten rubbed his forehead. "I know some things, I think. I don't know, it all seems like a dream now."

"Slow down," Jace said. "Try not to think too much and let it just come to you."

"It's about what Fay and Guire are doing. It's about Dorne."

Karanne turned around at this. "I saw him in the tower, they had him trapped up there."

Straeten nodded. "They're keeping him alive, but not letting him have his gloves back. I don't know why."

It all became clear to Jace then. "They want to be in charge, have all the power."

I could have told you that.

"What?" Jace said aloud.

Straeten looked at him funny. "What do you mean 'what?'"

Jace paused for a brief moment. "Nothing, nothing. I'm just exhausted. Anything else you remember?"

Straeten scrunched his eyebrows together. "Something about... no that can't be right."

"What can't be right?"

"That last thing they were talking about to the Darrak was the slaves. And something about..."

"About what?"

"No, it's not making any sense," Straeten said. He mumbled something unintelligible. "Something about... digging. That can't be right. I just can't remember."

Jace paused. "Those people back in the warehouse, what are they doing with them?"

"They've been shipping them out. Had them in a big hurry too."

"Shipping them out where?" Jace asked.

"Pretty sure the big boats have been heading north." Straeten thumped his head lightly. "But I can't remember where."

"Let's get Turic back to the caves," Jace said. "Maybe it will come back to you."

Chapter 6

The cold wind ripped past Cathlyn as she fell, threatening to pull her apart. How long had she been falling? Where was she, and how? It seemed like days had passed since she left the Library, watching Jace drop off the roof again. Or was it weeks?

Jace.

He said to trust him, but that didn't make her feel any less guilty about letting him go and saving herself. Could he be dead because of her? And what else had she done? Tried to lock magic away, for Mathes... Jace had made her see that Mathes had been coercing her, but was it all truly Mathes' fault?

Falling in silence had given her some time, but not clarity. All she knew was that she was far too dangerous to be used as a pawn.

Yes, she had awakened the ancient Masters and unleashed this evil upon the world. And yet, both Guire and Fay were still here because she could not separate them from their Soulkind. She had to figure out what she was capable of, and how to control it.

A call sounded almost in answer to these thoughts, faint and small, through the endless darkness around her. It felt familiar, somehow. Had it always been there, in the background?

She centered on it and it drew her toward a point of light in the distance faster and faster until the light blurred and a glowing haze surrounded her. She felt her body pulled in several directions now. Fear rippled through her and a terrible strain threatened to tear her in half.

Concentrate.

The thought had a voice now. It beckoned her. Yes, she had heard it before. Why had she ignored it? Cathlyn drew a breath or felt like she did. Was there even air in this place? It calmed her, nonetheless, and she fell toward the voice.

She stood alone on a mountainside, barren and exposed to the sky. No wind blew against her, no rain, just morning sun and coldness. But she was not alone. She felt the eyes of something older than the mountain itself gazing at her, boring through her with its stare.

Turning around, she drew her gaze upon what appeared to be a great gray pile of stones. No, not stones, something living, something greater than anything she had ever seen before. A dragon.

"I know you," Cathlyn said. "Jace spoke of you."

The dragon dropped his head slightly in greeting. "And he of you." The words reverberated in her head.

Her knees shook. She had only ever read about these creatures in the Library. Of all the beasts of old, through myth and legend, only the dragon ever called to her heart. And now…

"How did I get here?" She managed to walk to a small boulder and have a seat before her legs gave out.

"I called. And you finally listened." He raised a reptilian eyebrow.

Cathlyn glanced shrewdly at him. He couldn't be jesting with her, could he? She smiled weakly, not sure what to say next. Her hands knotted in her lap and she felt something solid in the pouch on her side.

"I think this is yours," she managed to say as she produced the artifact.

"The Lock." The dragon lumbered past her, down the side of the mountain. He glanced back over his shoulder when Cathlyn didn't follow him. She got up and, despite the wavering of her legs, strode alongside him.

"Its power is gone," he said.

Cathlyn nodded as she caressed the Lock. Jace had persuaded her not to use it on the Darrak, and by listening to him, she had ended its power. Something she had feared, but now Graebyrn had confirmed. The newly dawning sky warmed her mind even if it wasn't enough to thaw out her body.

"What is it you seek?" Graebyrn's voice entered her very mind. "Or, what is it you run from?"

Cathlyn was sure he already knew the answer to both of those questions. If only she did. "Can you tell me?" She halted.

He continued walking and began to blur and fade away. The whole mountain did, as did the blue sky, turning gray and cloudy. Where was she? Her magic felt more potent here.

"You had best keep up."

Cathlyn hurried several steps until she reached him and then reality solidified around her. Reality. This was real, wasn't it? Keeping up with him took some effort, the rocks slipped loose from the climb and she cut her hand catching herself on a sharp rock face. Her heart pounded in her chest and she fought to breathe in the frozen air, perhaps from sheer exhaustion or perhaps from actually being in the presence of Graebyrn now.

"Can you help me?" she asked.

"Doubt. You do not have the luxury of time for that. Even now the Soulkind Masters are seeking the power within the ruins of Aklareath. You and Jace will find them and save them." The vision began to fade again, even though Cathlyn fought to remain by his side.

"Save who?" Cathlyn asked.

The dragon disappeared, as did the mountainside, and once again Cathlyn fell into darkness.

Chapter 7

"It is I who should go before them," Brannon said. "My father is the head of the council, he will listen to me."

"Not if he's under their control, he won't," Jace responded.

Brannon paced between the dripping water from the cold rocks in the ceiling. The silence of the guild's caves surrounded Jace and his friends.

"Well, someone has to determine how much remains untouched by Fay and Guire's control." Turic placed his hand on Brannon's shoulder.

"Next you'll say that you want to go with him," Jace said and rolled his eyes. The old man smiled at him and slightly raised his eyebrows. "Are you serious? We just got you healed all up. And anyway, how would you get in there without being spotted? Fay would see you approaching the moment you set foot in the city."

"We would need an awfully good diversion then, now wouldn't we?" Turic said. "Can you manage that? I have to discuss some things with Brannon."

Jace half-smiled. "We've been making a lot of distractions lately."

"It would not have to be too big of a thing. And besides..." Turic leaned closer to Jace. "I know of a few ways into the Hall few have ever heard of. Not even your thieves."

Jace felt a pain in his chest at Turic's words. Had Turic not trusted him with that information? "I could go with you."

Turic rested his hand on Jace's shoulder. "The fewer that go with me the better."

"You think the council wouldn't listen to a thief?"

Turic's face turned red. "I did not mean that. You are a Master of a Soulkind, after all. I feel that you have greater things to accomplish now than talking to some boring people. And I am quite capable of taking care of myself."

"I suppose you're right," Jace said. "I'm sorry I suggested otherwise. But I've still got your back."

Turic smiled and then continued speaking to Brannon.

Jace joined a group of thieves standing around. "You want to help out?"

"What do you have in mind?" a young girl asked.

"Turic has to make it to the Hall unnoticed. Be creative."

The hooded boys and girls smiled and talked quickly in a closed circle among themselves.

Jace turned to Straeten. Regret still filled his eyes.

"You used Fay's ice against her," Jace said. "How did you know that would work?"

Straeten shrugged his shoulders and flashed his old smile. It was a relief to see that again. "Back in Varkran, one of those villagers who turned to Fay's side did the same thing to that dust creature right before he died. His eyes had gone back to normal. I just thought maybe that would work."

"You were right," Jace said. "But something's still bothering you."

"I keep losing this thought," Straeten said. "But something keeps telling me it's about Guire and Fay. Something they're doing with Dorne."

Karanne snapped her fingers and pointed at him. "They've got him as a prisoner, which means they're scared of him. We could use that fear."

The blood in Jace's heart ran cold.

"You mean, let him out?" Allar asked. "What do you think would happen if he got ahold of magic again? That's a bad idea. You do remember him before, right?"

"We don't have to actually let him have his magic back," Karanne said. "We just have to make Guire and Fay *think* he could get it back. Freeing him would be enough to get them out of Beldan.

"No." Jace clutched his Soulkind tightly. "There's no way we're even letting him get close to using his magic again. They're doing us a favor keeping him locked up."

"There's not much left to him," Karanne said. "He's just a shell."

Jace shook his head. "And that's how he tricked everyone a thousand years ago, too."

It isn't that bad of an idea.

Jace rubbed his forehead. There had to be a better way. "We're not getting anywhere." Jace sat down next to Straeten. "Any luck with your memories, Straet?"

48

Straeten ground his teeth. "Nothing."

"It is getting worse the longer we wait around here." Lady Danelia's voice emerged through the darkness.

"I know," Karanne said. "It's hard not to think about them. Mine started to die down recently, though. I had been going crazy. I'd started hearing their voices even in my sleep."

Something inside of Jace began to itch. Did they say *voices*? He crept closer to hear better.

"Did you... pass on...any of them?" Danelia asked.

Karanne paused. "Actually, I did. I think that's why they've faded."

Danelia stood. "Then I have to do the same. I cannot stand it any further."

"We'll stick together," Karanne said. "You, me, and the other Followers. We'll head out to see if we can give back these memories."

"How are we going to find them?"

Karanne scratched her chin. "I think we'll know. I felt a pull to Jace for his horse. And I know there are families that want to hear about any lost Followers."

Jace slipped on a loose rock and Karanne spun around to face him. "What are you two talking about?"

Danelia brushed herself off and lifted her chin a bit. Jace felt blood rush to his face as if he were a child who wandered into a grown-up conversation. Karanne didn't respond and only stood beside Danelia.

"Something we have to take care of."

All by themselves. Without you again. Looks like no one needs you anymore.

"It's those voices you keep hearing," Jace said. "Who are the people you're worried about finding?" His heart raced.

Karanne smiled at him and rested her hand on his shoulder. "The Followers who don't have anyone waiting for them. Or caring about them? What do I do with those?"

"Like who?"

"You know, like Jervis." Karanne suddenly squinted her eyes and looked at her hands, turning them over.

A sudden dread filled Jace then and a familiar laugh echoed in his head.

"Oh, no."

Looks like I'm stuck with you, eh Jace?

Chapter 8

Karanne held her hands over Jace's head, peeking through closed eyes every once in a while as she did so. "I don't think I can do it this way. I only collect these spirit memories right when they die."

"Well you're a Master, shouldn't you be able to figure something out?" Jace wrung his hands in his lap.

Karanne let out a long breath. "Maybe. Possibly. But it would take some time."

"Time we don't have, I know."

"Jervis is not… always talking to you, is he?"

Jace shook his head. "Only sometimes. But I don't want him *in* there. Is he going through my thoughts?"

Karanne shrugged. "When I gave Nilen her grandfather's spirit, she said he showed her some things before he left, warned her even about the attack that was about to happen."

"Will he be in here forever?" Jace pointed to his head.

Again Karanne shrugged.

"You're not making me feel any better about this. Everyone hated him." He paused and whispered, "Especially me."

"I don't know how this works," Karanne said. "He wasn't that bad, was he?"

Jace looked at her sideways. "You mean, before or after he decided to kill us all?"

Danelia rose, pressing her gloved hands to her forehead. "I cannot wait anymore, Master. I have to get rid of them!"

Karanne nodded. "I'm sorry, Jace, we have to transfer these spirits. It's getting worse for us."

Jace felt as if a tick was burrowing in his skull. His breath quickened and his eyes darted around the room.

"Just breathe," Karanne said. "It gets better when you don't think about it."

"It's like this for you?" Jace stood up, chasing her as she walked away.

She smiled weakly. "Only we've got a dozen or so of them in there." She gestured to her head with a finger and walked to the exit. Her few remaining Followers accompanied her. "You can come with us if you want. I can keep trying to figure out what to do with Jervis, but I've got to return these spirits to their families."

Jace saw the same anxious expression upon all those with her.

He wanted to go with her. She was like a mother. And he wanted Jervis out of his head more than anything. But something kept tugging at his mind. "I can't. There's something I've got to take care of."

Karanne studied him before responding. "I'll meet you back here after we're done." She hugged him tightly.

He hugged her back. "If not here, then I'll find you somehow."

Karanne nodded. "You be safe. Last time I thought you were dead. Don't do that to me again."

Jace shrugged.

"I'll make sure he doesn't do anything stupid," Straeten said, stroking Ash's neck.

"That'd be a change."

Jace shook his head. He watched the line of Followers wind out of the cave. First Turic decided to go alone and now she was leaving.

He returned to join the others and caught Shey and Allar discussing something. Loudly.

"We've got to do something about the prisoners they're keeping in those warehouses," Shey said. "I was in the shipping district this morning and I saw some of them north on the river. They can't be too far away yet. But if we wait any longer, they'll be gone and there won't be anything we can do about it."

"What do Guire and Fay want with them?" Allar asked.

"It doesn't matter, does it? They're prisoners and no one else is going to help them."

Since when does she care about this stuff?

The thought came so quietly that Jace barely noticed it wasn't his own. Was knowing better? He supposed he had Karanne to thank for this insanity.

"If we're going to try to save them on the water, we'll have to get past the Darrak. They're guarding every bridge." Allar paced as he spoke. "That's what your thieves have been reporting."

Jace smiled at the irony of this situation. Not too long ago Allar had scorned Jace for being a thief, and now he was working side by side with them. He'd come a long way.

"So how do we get through them?" Shey asked.

Jace pondered this. "First, we're going to need a boat of our own. A fast one."

Shey smiled at him. "I know where we can find one. Small though. Used for racing, and a bit of smuggling. Mostly smuggling."

"That still doesn't solve the Darrak problem." Allar scratched his chin.

Jace jammed his fists into his cloak pockets, gripping the metal artifact from Nilen's grandfather and running his fingers across the markings left by Sephintal's tribe. These creatures were herded here by the Call from Marlec's gloves, slaves to his will. But there had to be others within this army capable of ignoring the Call, like Sephintal. Jace turned the silver rod over in his hand. "I'll handle them. Just get that boat ready. How many can we get in there?"

Shey counted on her fingers. "No more than eight. With supplies. If we want any chance of catching them on the river."

Allar shook his head. "Not much of an army."

"But we have you, right?" Jace smiled.

Allar turned his shield over. "If I can get Newell to cooperate."

That cooperation was key. But Newell wasn't the only Soulkind Master along for this trip, and they also had a Deltir. Jace looked at Straeten, quietly sitting next to Ash and staring at the ground.

Yeah, some powerful friend you got there.

Jace scoffed but didn't dignify the thought with a response.

"When can you have our boat ready?" Jace asked Shey.

"By nightfall. I'll be ready in the Bay north of the shipping district. Out by Landers." Shey walked toward one of the exits.

"That should give me enough time to do what I have to do. Tell Karanne our plan, will you? She went that way." Jace pointed.

"Thanks, Jace." Shey saluted him and ran out through the tunnel.

Jace stood up and Ash raced to his side, tongue hanging out and tail wagging. "Straeten, learn as much magic as you can from Allar, and Turic before he leaves. We're going to need all the help we can get."

Straeten clenched his fists. "I… I don't know."

Jace pulled him to his feet and put his arm around his shoulder. "Look, I know you're worried about Fay's magic. But that's gone now. I trust you."

Straeten, still silent, walked toward Turic and Brannon.

Jace looked around and his eyes met with his own Followers. Ranelle and Tare both stood with him now. Evvy also seemed pretty adamant about coming along, despite the tired look in her young eyes. "Nah, Evvy, I need your help here."

"But…" Her freckled face fell.

"Burgis doesn't know where anything is that we need for the trip. We have to be ready, and quick. Can you help him out with that?"

Evvy took a breath like she was going to argue, but she just let it out in a sigh. "I suppose."

Jace ruffled her curly hair. "Thanks, kid. I couldn't do it without you." He also couldn't imagine dragging a child along for what he meant to do before leaving on the boat tonight.

Evvy perked up a bit with the task and hurried herself off into the various corners of the cave to gather food and supplies. Right off of people sleeping, but still. Jace smiled.

"We've got this." Excitement built up inside of him, making the hairs on his arms rise.

"We're with you," Ranelle said.

Jace knew Tare couldn't say anything, but he felt the boy's support through his Soulkind. The two Followers didn't even know what he was planning. They didn't know the danger that awaited them.

"You know, these streets are a little different than the hills and trees out in Tilbury. This will be dangerous," Jace said.

"We'll follow you wherever you lead," Ranelle said.

Jace clasped his Soulkind tightly in his right hand and the metal artifact Kedan had given him in his left. "Then let's go make some new friends."

Chapter 9

That boy. Would he be all right?

Karanne had never seen him so stretched. He always wanted to help others, everyone knew that about him. But would he understand that even he had limits?

The voices and images pounded in her head, even louder than when she first came into the city. She had felt better after releasing Blue, and unknowingly, Jervis, into Jace's mind, but…

"It's as if the floodgates have been opened and now I *need* to free the others."

"I know what you mean," Danelia said. "I think this is what we are supposed to do, it feels that way."

Karanne paused. "It is the right thing to do, to give them all peace. But I'm unsure at the same time. Ever since those spirits left, I've felt somehow weaker."

The darkness of the cave began to lighten as she approached one of the exits, this one a bit closer to the city. She waved the rest of the group to slow down and she signaled she would go and check out the opening. Couldn't have the guards or any of Fay's or Guire's spies spotting them.

"We're going to split up," Karanne said after returning. "We'll be harder to spot, and can get this done faster. You'll each have a thief with you, to guide you around the streets."

"We know them well enough" Barsal said.

Karanne shook her head at her chief Follower. "Not like a thief does. I've told each guide what section of the city you're to cover. Once you get there, your magic, I don't know, should show you where to go."

"Should?" Barsal asked.

Karanne raised her eyebrow at him. "Yes, should."

Five thieves paired up with the Followers, and Karanne joined with Danelia. She looked out upon her friends, eager to see their town and people after so long, even if only from the shadows. She also saw a bit of hesitancy.

"I'm worried, too," Karanne said. "But, you've been in the wilds all this time, what can't you handle back at home?"

Danelia spoke up. "It's not that, it's just that we've never been apart since the escape from the fortress. You've guided us safely wherever we went."

Karanne felt her cheeks warm. "I…" She cleared her throat. Their eyes all fell on her. Her mouth felt dry but she managed to get some words out. "I've seen you in impossible situations and you've always come out the other side. Today is just another challenge, no different from the last. Remember what you've learned so far." She held up her hand and the symbols glowed white. "And I'll be with you in here."

The Followers raised their hands, too, and the lines on their palms lit up enough to brighten the cave walls like daylight. Karanne walked around the room, patting them on their shoulders and clasping their hands. She smiled as the Followers left with their respective thieves. It was funny, seeing them all going out on their own. Pride swelled in her. She thought back to the beginning, to her own testing for the fire magic. She had never really thought of even trying to join the Soulkind Followers. Until Mathes had prompted that.

Mathes.

Her mind raced with thoughts of him. His school. All that he'd done to warp the minds of those young ones. Years of brainwashing, no doubt. How far had his handiwork reached? Many of those children lay dead within the Hall now, but he had many more students. His oldest had grown up years ago, with the same ideals burned into them. How strong was his grasp upon Beldan?

Karanne pulled the edges of her hood over her face as she walked through the woods. The frigid morning air chilled her deeply and a shiver ran through her body.

"Where should we go first?" Danelia asked.

Karanne slowed and stared at the marks on her palm. The spirits she had captured coursed through her mind.

"I'm getting something." Karanne held out her hand palm open to the sky. A faint glowing appeared, first on the left of her palm, but as she turned in that direction, the light shifted straight ahead almost like a compass. "This way."

"That's deeper into the woods," Danelia said as they shifted further west.

Karanne gestured to her hand with her head to show Danelia the glowing marks.

"Did these just appear?" Danelia asked.

Karanne nodded. "Just now, as we're getting closer."

She hadn't expected to go this way but at least they'd avoid the blue eyes of the guards and anyone else who might alert Fay or Guire.

They crept through the woods, stepping lightly over frozen branches. No one lived this far away from the city, did they? At least she didn't remember breaking into any homes out here.

The light pulsed brighter in her palm, driving her forward. Her steps quickened but she caught herself and slowed. "We're almost there, but they might not want any visitors."

The pulsing in Karanne's hand intensified and she held up the glowing signs to zero in on the location. Up ahead, a tiny creek wound its way along a thicker patch of trees. Karanne silently got Danelia's attention and pointed.

A small group of disheveled people sat beneath some overhanging branches. From this distance, Karanne spied three, maybe four of them. They didn't seem to notice her or Danelia yet. But when they finally did, they didn't even budge. The only sound they made came from a small boy whimpering in someone's arms.

Karanne approached and the woman backed away, clinging tighter to the child. "It's all right." Karanne held up her hands. The four people cowered and the child cried out.

Karanne quickly dropped her glowing hand to her side. "It's okay. I know magic, but not the kind that hurts others. Not the ice, or the sickness."

"It's the fire!" A small girl stepped from behind a large woman into the clearing.

"You're...you're one of the ones from Beldan," an older lady said, standing to meet Karanne.

"Like Saral," another said.

"Please." The old woman wrung her hands together in front of Karanne. "Do you know what happened to them? To my daughter?"

Saral. That name… Yes. She knew her. Not that she'd ever talked to her, or even met her. But ever since the fortress in Marlec's valley, she knew of her through the spirit racing around in her head.

"Mother!"

Karanne and Danelia jumped at the sudden scream but no one else appeared to hear it. "That must have been her," Karanne whispered to Danelia. "I can feel her pain." Burning tears fell on Karanne's cheeks as she embraced the old lady, patting her back. The woman shook as she sobbed.

"Here." Karanne clasped the woman's hand with her marked palm. A pulse of energy passed out of her, along with Saral's memories, of her whole life up until the moment she sacrificed herself against the Darrak in the dungeon of that foul castle.

Her mother wailed and sank onto the cold ground. The others, likely the rest of her family, formed a circle around her. The memory of Saral still floated in Karanne's head, but it was less tangible, less of a presence and more of a memory now.

Danelia gasped. "Something is gone," she whispered into Karanne's ear. "When you released her then, I felt as if the spirit left me. Could it be that they are connected to all of us?"

"Perhaps," Karanne said and turned to the others. "It is not safe for you here," she said. The weeping of the family echoed in the woods, despite the danger surrounding them. "Come." She reached for one of the people but they jerked back from her.

"Don't be afraid of her," the old woman said. "I can....*see* Saral now." She stared at Karanne and stood up. "And that you did all you could to save her, and the others. She is at peace now."

Karanne bowed slightly, avoiding the woman's eyes. The rest of the family continued crying but didn't appear afraid of Karanne anymore. "Really, you have to get going. Do you have any place to hide?"

"We do."

"Then go there, quickly," Karanne said.

"Bless you," the old woman said, placing her hand on Karanne's shoulder.

Karanne reached back and gripped her hand all the while staring at the city walls. *Just keep moving and then you can bless me all you want.*

After a few minutes after leaving, Karanne held up her hand and focused. "I think I can sense another one—" Karanne touched her temples in response to the intense dizziness there. Danelia did the same.

"This is what I felt when you passed on that spirit earlier," Danelia said.

"Do you think this is from the other Followers, then?" Karanne said when she could speak again.

"It has to be."

"Lucky we weren't climbing when it happened," Karanne said. She shook her arms to dispel the tingling in her fingertips.

After her head cleared, Karanne slipped through the thief opening in the city walls, avoiding any prying eyes from up above. The streets were dead silent in the market district. No booths set up, only empty stalls and shuttered windows that made Karanne's stomach drop. So many times before she would have slipped unseen behind some other city folk, now she was more exposed than ever.

"Stick to the alleys," Karanne said, glancing at the lights on her palm. "It doesn't seem like the next one's too far from here."

Karanne sensed the recipient of another spirit, drawing her along like the current of a river. Eventually, she came to a closed down building. She pulled back some planks blocking the entrance revealing a man, bent and skinny, scrambling into a corner like a roach. Behind his unkempt hair, crazed eyes flashed and he drew a long knife.

A wooden bowl flew toward Karanne's head and she dodged it instinctively. "Hey! We're here to help!"

"Don't need help. Don't want help. Don't need help." The man pushed a tall board toward Karanne and it clattered noisily onto the dusty floor. He backed away into another corner of the room, away from the window facing the street.

"Hey! Where are you going?" Karanne said. "Danelia, check to make sure no one is coming, will you?"

Danelia nodded and walked to the doorway. "Maybe this is not such a good idea."

"We have to do this." The throbbing spirit nearly bursting out of Karanne's head was motivation enough, despite the man's behavior.

"Be careful."

"Go away, go away, go away..." The man murmured and clutched his arms as Karanne approached.

"I have something to show you." Karanne took a few small steps in his direction. He whipped a clay pot past her head and it crashed into the wooden wall.

Karanne turned back to Danelia. The hair on the back of her neck stood up. "Someone's coming."

There was no other way out. How could she let them get pinned in? Karanne shook her head again and thought of the spirits. Karanne took another step in the man's direction.

"Can't help, can't help!" he shouted.

"Shut him up!" Karanne hissed.

Karanne glanced out the single window. In that second the man drew out a long knife and slashed at her. A hot searing pain shot through her arm and blood dripped heavily from the open cut on her palm. "Suffering!" she spat, biting back a stream of profanities.

The man stared wide-eyed around the room and started hurling anything he could at Karanne.

"You're not helping." She gritted her teeth.

"Look out!" Danelia screamed and ran into the small room, quickly followed by a black scaled Darrak.

Karanne drew out her Fireflash and sent a burst exploding in the Darrak's face. The scaled creature spun frantically onto the floor and crashed into Danelia's legs, knocking her down. "Let's get out of here."

Karanne jumped over the Darrak's twisting form and into the streets. Forget the spirit. That would have to wait. The moment she stepped back into the marketplace, a heavy spear swung at her. She ducked and it missed her by mere inches, driving into a wooden frame. The Darrak hissed at her and wrenched the weapon free. It rubbed at its eyes with the back of its hand.

"Can you do anything to stop it?" Danelia said.

Karanne thought back to the tower when she encountered Guire. She'd summoned a power she didn't know she had, unleashing a white blast of fire into his foul growths. She could do it again. She had to. She turned back to the Darrak as Danelia kept running.

But as Karanne reached for that power she sensed only emptiness. She stared blankly at her bloody palm. The whistle of a flying spear shot past her ears almost in slow motion.

Into Danelia's back.

"No!" Karanne screamed, watching her Follower crumple to the ground. She ran to her side, not caring about the Darrak. A crazed shout sounded behind her. She caught a glimpse of the man setting himself upon the lizard creature with a long knife.

Karanne knelt beside Danelia. "I'm sorry, I'm so sorry. I couldn't…"

But it was too late. Danelia's eyes stared lifelessly back into hers.

A clattering sound, the man's knife being knocked aside, rang against the walls. Karanne looked up to see the Darrak throw the man to the ground like a child's plaything. "Come on," she muttered as she knelt beside Danelia's body. She couldn't just abandon her friend here.

She could at least take her spirit. Her hand glowed as the Fireflash pulsed beneath the symbols on her palm.

A chunk of masonry struck her in the arm and she fell to the ground with pain piercing her mind. The Darrak stepped toward her and her anger-filled thoughts brought her to feet again. The Fireflash burst at the Darrak to blind it, but this time it only blinked away the light. Karanne glanced at Danelia and then back to the Darrak, weighing the time it would take to get her spirit. As she considered, two more Darrak dropped from the rooftops behind the first one and drew wicked-looking blades. Danelia's unmoving eyes seemed to stare into her, asking her why. Karanne raised her hand again but she shamefully turned her head and ran headlong into the alleyways. Tears stung her eyes as she fled.

Karanne ran into a section of town containing houses that backed up to a large hill and acted as a barrier around the town. The borders used to keep invaders out, but now trapped residents in. She felt the townsfolk watching as she passed, but kept her eyes on the ground with an occasional glance behind for the Darrak. What had happened? She was a Master of a Soulkind, wasn't she? How could she let one of her Followers die? That moment of indecision, that lack of power. What did it all mean?

And what now? She still had more spirits to return, and Danelia… Fresh tears sprung to her eyes. If she couldn't do anything for her, how was there any hope left against this army, with Guire and Fay at its head? With her own failing magic, and Turic and the others all separated, there wasn't any power to stand up against the darkness.

Or was there? Karanne set her eyes upon the Tower of Law and began running before she could think better of her idea.

Chapter 10

"And I thought it would be an easy walk back inside the Hall." Turic sat down upon the stone bench and stared out across the bridge. Surprisingly, many people walked about the city. Even Low Third rang casually and the townsfolk headed to the market like any other day.

Groups of guards patrolled the bridge each with three Darrak close behind. Other guards funneled people to a singular entrance and questioned them at a hastily constructed check station.

"We're lucky to have gotten this far," Brannon said. Both he and Turic had removed their robes back at the cave and now wore plain dark pants and simple tunics instead. "You haven't spoken of our way into the Hall yet. I'm not sure we can even cross this bridge."

Turic nodded, craning to see behind Brannon into the rest of the city. "Ah, there they are now."

A group of five or so people wandered amongst the crowd. They blended in so well, it was hard to count them.

"Time to go." Turic groaned as he stood, rubbing his legs. "These suffering pants are too tight."

"You sure whatever plan you've come up with is going to work?"

Turic shrugged. "Sounded like a good idea at the time."

Brannon squinted at the group coming toward the bridge. "Is that—?"

"Yes. Now stay with me." Turic grabbed Brannon's arm and pulled him to the side as the five figures approached in a cluster. Two familiar people stepped out from the middle. Well, at least what they were wearing was familiar.

"Hey, those are my clothes!" Brannon took a step in their direction.

"No, you don't." Turic turned him away from the thieves in Brannon's purple cloak and Turic's robes. Turic's double was even wearing a dusted gray wig and some spectacles to finish the job. "Admit it though, those robes you wear are a bit much."

Brannon opened his mouth as if to say something but closed it quickly and turned away.

"As I thought. Now, why aren't those guards making a move yet?" Turic tugged at his tight pants and watched the guards and Darrak turn around as they neared the middle of the bridge.

"They'll be killed!" Brannon said.

"I will have to help, I suppose." Turic lifted his hands and a reverberating booming shook the bridge and a white hot wind blew his white ponytail into his face. One of the statues along the bridge burst apart. Flames rained out and landed on the next statue, igniting it as well.

"Was that a bit much?" Turic asked.

The heat from the fire cracked the statue's head, sending it crashing into the roaring Crescent River below. The people on the bridge screamed as the fire leapt from the torches onto the bridge rails and into the crowd.

"Maybe."

"All right, now's our chance." Turic stepped to the side as the Darrak and guards sprinted after his impersonator into the city. "Now to get into the Hall."

Brannon stepped into the shadows and pointed to a group of people walking past them. "Those people don't look like they're under Fay's control." The group continued down to the bridge, still ablaze from Turic's handiwork.

Turic watched them. "True, I have not seen any blue in their eyes. Perhaps, even for her, it is too much to control everyone in the city." Another group of people in robes walked quickly toward the tower in the distance. Turic overheard Fay and Guire's names. "With magic, that is."

"I cannot imagine the people of our town giving in to them without fighting," Brannon said. Two Darrak shoved their way past three people walking along the path. "Although, I can see what might encourage that."

"We had best find out what is going on," Turic answered. "Now, come on, your father perhaps is still governing this town. Or at least he can tell us who is. We have to hope for that."

"He wasn't at home, and no one had seen him return in the past couple of days." Brannon picked at the stitches on his sleeve.

"Discouraging, indeed, but not hopeless. Now, I have an idea of how to get into the library."

"An *idea?*" Brannon asked.

"Now don't worry, at least one other person went into the Library this way." Turic unlatched a side door leading outside of the Hall. He pulled Brannon out with him and began to walk toward the Library.

"Who?"

"Well, it was a long time ago, when I first met him. You were there, it was a pivotal time in both our careers."

The two of them walked in silence alongside the high stone wall surrounding the Hall. Turic smiled as he watched Brannon struggle not to ask another question. At last, they reached the Soulwash, the icy clear pond fed by the cascading waterfall so high above the valley. A cool mist filled the air. Turic squinted toward the cave up above that started all this.

"Wait, you're not talking about Jace, are you?"

Turic placed his foot into the pool and grimaced as the iciness bit through his skin into his bones. He put both feet in and took two more steps toward the middle. The water quickly rose up to his thighs.

"But you told me he wasn't even aware of what he was doing. That you weren't even sure if he made it all the way inside."

"I did say those things, but I have a very good feeling about this. Now, come on." Turic gestured up to the roof where two Darrak perched and stood guard. "We've got to hurry if we don't want them to see us."

"How are we going to breathe under there?"

"You ask too many questions." Turic held both of his hands out and closed his eyes. "Now, do as I do. And trust me."

A bright glowing mark shown on Turic's hands. Around his legs, water began to bubble furiously and steam swelled into the air. A thin amount of space surrounded his legs where no water touched him.

Brannon smiled slightly. "You're using what you taught us in the mountains, against the cold."

"Precisely. I have just repurposed it. Remember what I taught, and do the same." Turic took two more dry steps along the bottom of the pool, pushing the water aside as he did so. Steam rose up between them and spread out as a cover of fog.

"Master, this is ingenious." Brannon called upon the same magic. "They can't even see us through this fog."

The heat bubble expanded, vaporizing the water instantly. Sudden panic gripped Turic as the water level reached his face, but the shield held. He stayed both warm and dry.

He couldn't see Brannon through the mass of bubbles but felt him following along. He exhaled sharply and continued farther below the Library.

"Are we going to run out of air?" Brannon said.

Turic drew in a deep breath. "No."

He hoped.

The sloping tunnel now leveled out. He could see only the pebbles inlaid into the path below. A thick stone wall entered the bubble and he rubbed his hand against the ancient masonry. Inside the Library now. Not much further.

Ten more strides. Twenty. Finally, the path sloped upward, slightly at first and then almost vertically. When he could go no further, Turic ran his hands along the curved surface of the pool that opened into the library.

Great. Now what?

Outside the shield, small bubbles rose quickly. How could they get to the surface without risking the ice cold water? Bigger bubbles?

He pushed the barrier farther from his body, widening the radius of his spell, and felt his feet lift. He kicked them back and forth. He was still underwater but was he floating in this bubble? He instinctively sought out his pen and paper but forgot about them as he rose through the water. Slowly at first, then as the bubble got wider, more quickly. Outside the bubble, there was only darkness. Hopefully, Brannon caught on to what he was doing.

Abruptly he burst into a dark room, lit only by the slight glow of his magic. A wave of claustrophobia hit him and he dropped the spell completely. Utter iciness surrounded him and his breath quickly exhaled as if being crushed out of him. He gripped the pool's edge and pulled himself out, despite the shaking in his arms. He crumpled onto the ground, hearing nothing but his chattering teeth.

A spasm of dizziness passed over him. Focusing all that energy on the spell had taken a lot. Still, he called that magic again and a wave of heat rippled over him drying him off. He wiggled his fingers to make sure he could.

He looked back over the edge of the pool into the depths of its inky blackness. Bubbling rose from below. Brannon was close. A massive hissing of steam and bubbles erupted from the surface and then suddenly stopped. Even the dim glowing in the water blinked out.

Turic shot his hand into the water and closed his eyes. He reached his mind further downward to seek Brannon out, finally sensing his weakly struggling form. With another push of his magic, he wrapped Brannon up in warmth.

More bubbles burst up out of the water. Turic pulled harder, willing Brannon to float up in the spell, his hand shook uncontrollably. Brannon shot up through the surface and flew past the pool's edge onto the floor.

Darkness and dizziness swept over Turic and he lost all thought.

How many minutes or hours later he woke up, Turic didn't know. But it was dark. And cold. Shivering, he called upon his magic and a bubble surrounded him and warmed him to his core. The dizziness that had clouded his vision was gone, replaced by a dull throbbing in his temples.

"Brannon?"

No answer. Where was he? Turic summoned a glowing ball from his outstretched hand and cast its light into the familiar room. There was the pool with its surrounding low wall in the room's center. The brick wall Straeten had knocked down opened into the darkness on one side. On the other was the staircase back into the Library.

But no sign of Brannon. What was he thinking? He would get himself killed wandering around here. With a great creaking in his knees, Turic began his ascent up the stairs to the Library. The sphere of light twinkled weakly and a wave of dizziness came across him again. His steps faltered and he clutched the railing along the wall.

"I haven't fully recovered, it seems. I guess I'll have to do this the old way."

He replaced the sphere with a small flame. The fire sought out a torch ensconced in the stone wall, surrounding the end until it blazed. Turic released the magic and lifted the torch out with two hands.

"Ugh, Straeten makes carrying these things look easy."

Turic made his way slowly to the lock on the door in the center of the Library. How he was going to get around it without the key?

He smelled something burning in the air.

The light from his torch revealed a door in mangled pieces on the ground, still smoldering. Could Brannon have done this? Had he fallen back into his madness? Turic quickly put the torch down and reached around his neck. With a heavy sigh, he felt his Soulkind with the red gem. He closed his eyes and allowed himself a couple more deep breaths. Now to find out what Brannon was up to. He picked up his torch, stepped over the melted metal of the door, and made his way into the Library.

Quiet.

Yes, it was a library, but it was even quieter than he had ever heard it before. No lights either. The shadows cast by the torch flickered in every corner, around every bookshelf, and each time Turic was certain a Darrak would be there waiting for him. But no, the entire building was empty. Lucky for him, since he wasn't built for stealth. Not at this age, anyway.

At least that dizziness had passed. The only thing he could conclude was that he had drawn upon the magic too heavily for too long. If he couldn't endure, how would he be able to confront Fay now that she was regaining her former power?

He passed hidden stacks and locked cabinets full of ancient texts and other artifacts. The main entrance of the Library opened in front of him. And still no one. Brannon must have gone this way, too, yet there were no signs.

Would Brannon turn himself over to Fay? No, that would be absurd. He wouldn't throw away his own life like that for nothing. It's not like she would give him power, would she? Turic sped up.

He turned a corner to see the Tower of Law pierce the sky, its top disappearing in the low clouds hanging over the city. Of course. There was someone else Brannon was in search of. Turic didn't slow down to check for guards, he had to stop Brannon before he did anything else foolish.

Despite the Darrak in the city, townsfolk and council members still filled the main tower entryway and the main audience chamber. Turic recognized a few of them, but they weren't conducting business as usual. They were, in fact, cowering around each other, silent with an eye on the main entrance. Prisoners.

No time to talk. Turic scanned the crowd as quickly as he could. But with no sign of Brannon or his father, he proceeded up the back staircase in silence, the cowls of his hood pulled over his face. Anyone with influence over this town would be further up the tower. Either in discussion in the main chamber. Or elsewhere in chains.

So many steps. Turic's knees creaked and groaned by the time he was halfway up them. Voices echoed their way down the winding staircase. Arguing voices. The Council had discussions daily about how to run the city, but these sounded different.

"They're basically letting us run things as normal!"

"So we just roll over then?"

The two voices sounded familiar to Turic, but it was difficult to tell through his heavy breathing. He had to get closer. Up ahead, the stairway branched off to the main chamber where the Council meetings were normally held.

"This is still our town. We still run the commerce."

That was Talhar, Brannon's father. Turic stood beside the doorway, staring in at the thirty or so people around the round room. Some glanced at him, too, but didn't waste more than a second doing so. His clothes, he mused. One look at them and they'd think he was no one special. Other citizens clustered at the door listening to the council, so he blended in well.

Turic was fairly certain the people here all had their own eye color. But why? Why didn't Fay control them, too?

"Yes, she has granted you that."

That was someone Turic didn't recognize. Although he squinted, he couldn't quite tell the state of his eyes, perhaps they were the bright blue that he dreaded.

"For a price," a familiar voice said. Turic adjusted his spectacles and focused on the man and his red robes. Mathes? What was he doing here? The traitor.

The heat of magic rose in Turic's chest. Before he could step into the room, a cloaked person held him back. He looked beneath the hood. Brannon. He had hidden in the crowd as Turic had. Brannon held up a finger to his lips and then pointed to the man Turic hadn't recognized earlier.

It was clear the man's eyes were bright blue now. He had to be an emissary of sorts. Turic nodded to Brannon in silent thanks for holding him back. Brannon pulled Turic away from the door.

"What is he doing here?" Turic stroked his beard and gave Brannon a questioning look.

"I'm not really sure." Brannon paused to listen next to the door. "I almost walked in, but saw that man with the blue eyes. I figured he would call Fay right to us."

A wave of heat ebbed away from Turic's fists but didn't fully dissipate. He eyed Brannon. "And why did you leave me down below the Library?"

"You weren't waking up." Brannon stared at his feet. "I thought I should get someone to help. But then I… I just had to find my father. I am sorry."

"It's all right." Turic patted him on his shoulder and the last of his magic faded. "Do we wait this out then? Until everyone but your father leaves?"

Fay's spy stood up and made his way to the exit where Turic and Brannon and a few others stood. Turic pulled his hood low over his face. The man slowed his steps as he neared the door. Turic bowed low and held his breath.

The man stopped in front of Turic and placed his hands on his hips. Turic's heart skipped and he took an involuntary step backward into Brannon.

The spy spun around to face the council. "Fay will be awaiting your response." And with that, he turned back and pushed past Turic.

After a moment's pause, arguments arose between the council members and Mathes. Turic hadn't heard the details of the spy's proposal, but whatever it was had obviously stirred the council members. He let out a deeply held breath.

"I believe we should stay and listen to her."

"Are you crazy? Let these creatures wander our streets?"

Mathes' voice rose up. "This is all very important of course, but how did we get here in the first place? Magic. We need to ban it from our city, as well as wielders of magic, including your son and the so-called Master, Turic. If it weren't for him, none of the other Soulkind would have awoken, and our town would not be in this predicament."

Cries of assent followed Mathes' words. Turic's blood boiled. So that was Mathes' plan. If he couldn't directly get rid of magic with Cathlyn, then he'd turn the council against it. He and Brannon exchanged a look of disgust.

Turic cocked his head slightly toward the staircase down below. The sound of swiftly approaching footsteps echoed through the hall, getting louder. Probably guards. Time to make themselves scarce.

A hooded patron outpaced them on the stairs past with quick strides. The doorway to the council twisted out of sight, and none too soon, as shouts began to ring out.

Turic and Brannon continued scrambling up the stairs. When the shouting died down and it was clear they weren't being followed, they finally slowed down and caught their breath. Eventually, they reached the next set of rooms, some with balconies overlooking the city, others closed up with bars in the windows. Holding cells. Burn marks from a recent fire covered the walls near the stairs. The hooded person who ran past them faced a locked cell door.

"Now what?" Brannon said, breathless.

Turic was too winded to respond.

"Brannon? Turic?" the person spun to face them. She removed her hood to reveal long red hair.

Chapter 11

"I see your talk with the Council went well," Karanne said.

"We never had the chance." Turic stopped to catch his breath. "How long were you there?"

"Long enough to hear Mathes' rant." Karanne continued peering through the barred window of a cell.

"I thought you were out freeing those spirits in your mind," Brannon said. "Did they lead you here?"

Karanne nodded. "More or less."

"This is your handiwork, isn't it?" Turic gestured toward the scorched walls in the upper room of the tower.

Karanne nodded. The Fireflash left her hand and spun into the locking mechanism, causing the metal to glow a deep orange.

"Who's trapped in there?" Turic asked, stepping forward to peer into the cell. His eyes adjusted to the darkness of the room and he grabbed Karanne by the shoulder. "Wait, what are you doing?"

"What I must." Karanne shook him off. She renewed her focus on the door until she heard a sharp click.

"This is not going to help." Turic pushed in between her and the door.

"What's going on?" Brannon asked. "Who's in there?"

"Step aside, Turic."

"Freeing *him* is the last thing we should be doing." Turic didn't budge. "I thought we already decided to drop this idea."

"You decided that. Things have changed." Karanne rubbed at the marks on her palm. "They're going to keep killing people that don't stand with them or ship them off to who knows where. All while we try to figure out how to use our magic. Dorne's the only chance we have."

Turic paused. "How would he help us?"

"They've got him in prison, right?" Karanne tapped her hand against the stone wall. "We can make him use his magic *for* us. Once we find his gloves."

Turic paused but did not move away. "He is too dangerous. He would turn on us before we knew it."

"But, he's just a shell, isn't he?" Karanne asked. "He barely said a word after we captured him. And besides, Jace got rid of Marlec, right?"

"This particular Soulkind has generations of darkness infused within. Marlec was only the last in a long line of Masters who left their mark upon the gloves. Surely, it has ensnared Dorne, I am afraid. Now, please. If ever you have thought of me as a friend, do not do this."

Karanne lost track of how many times Turic had helped Jace. Saving his life, giving him purpose when all his hope was gone. She turned her hand over to see the marks from her Fireflash and felt the spirits of those she collected, and the one she hadn't.

"You are more than a friend." She put her hand on his shoulder. "But this is bigger than just us. This whole land has lost too much. And we can't afford to lose anything else."

Something seemed to break in Turic. He slowly dropped his stare from Karanne and his shoulders sunk. A similar feeling hit Karanne's stomach when he stepped aside and let her pass. She wanted to say something to him, to make him understand, but no words came out. Instead, she opened the cell door.

There he was. The former dark master. The one who summoned armies to bind all the Soulkind to himself. Now, all she could see was a withered young man. His bloodied head rested against the stone wall and shackles bound him in place. Had he been… beaten? Two large crystals protruded from his temples, like the ones Jace had on the rooftop. The Fireflash flew from her hands.

"Wait!" Turic said.

But it was too late. The magical bolt melted Dorne's bonds in a spatter of molten metal. He dropped to his knees.

"So, you're back."

"Shut up and listen." Karanne pointed at him and the Fireflash hovered in front of his face.

Dorne responded with a smug stare but kept quiet. He seemed different now, no longer the husk of a person they had dragged through the ice.

"Your friends have outstayed their welcome," Karanne said. "You will help us get rid of them."

"And what do you expect me to do? I have these." Dorne pointed at the two crystals on his bloodied temples. Dried blood covered his fingers. Had he tried to gouge them out? "Surely there is no way they can be removed?" He glanced at the window overlooking the library's roof and raised an eyebrow at her.

Karanne followed his gaze to where Jace had been with Cathlyn. "You saw me do this before?"

"Don't," Turic whispered to her.

But she was already going down this path. Nothing would stop her. She reached for the power within her to blast them from his forehead. But nothing happened.

She had been enraged before when Jace was so powerless. Maybe that was what was missing. Conjuring up her anger, she gestured with her hand again at the crystals stuck in Dorne's head. Again, nothing.

"I did it before," Karanne said, staring at her palms.

"Perhaps you've lost something." Dorne sat back down on the ground. "Gave it all away, did you?"

Karanne closed her fists and opened them again. "I don't understand."

"Well, you'd better hurry up and do so. Those soldiers will probably be up here soon."

Turic stepped into the room and gently pushed past Karanne. "Whatever happens, you are coming with us."

"With you?" Dorne said, laughing. "Marathas? Are you sure you're up for it with nothing but petty fire and light shows?"

Turic said nothing. Only his tight fist betrayed his thoughts. He knelt and placed his hand over Dorne's chest. A bright glow emitted from his fingers, and when he released his grasp, the same glow showed under Dorne's shirt.

Dorne stood up and brushed away at his chest repeatedly. "What did you just do?"

Turic pointed at his chest. "Some petty fire and a light show. Try to use magic without my say-so and you will regret it."

Dorne's face twisted into a crooked smile. "You're lying." Perhaps he believed that, but his smile faded nonetheless.

Turic only shrugged. "Maybe. Maybe not. But I would not count on it. What I do know is that you're going to come with us. Now."

Dorne stood up slowly and silently.

"Are you going to take those things off his head?" Brannon asked.

Turic ignored the question. "When those intruders down there leave we'll need to get out of here. Karanne, why don't you go check?"

Karanne swallowed and nodded. Turic looked away. She had gotten what she wanted, but she hated herself for putting Turic in this position. Her thoughts drifted back to Dorne's words about her magic. Did she really lose what she had learned? He had insinuated that she had given something away. It couldn't be...

Could she have lost her power when she returned the spirits?

She no longer felt them calling to her. Was her power meant only to release them?

"Move!" Turic shouted.

"Master?" Brannon put his hand on Turic's shoulder.

Turic brushed it off and followed closely behind Dorne as he walked toward the stairs. "Any idea where they are keeping your gloves?"

Dorne shook his head. He closed his eyes then grimaced sharply.

"Jace said the crystals caused pain if he reached for magic." Karanne kept walking as Turic and the others halted at the top of the steps.

Turic raised his hands and placed them on either side of Dorne's head upon the crystals. He closed his eyes tightly.

"I'll be back shortly." Karanne crept down the wide staircase to the council chamber, listening for anything that may be around the corner. There was no getting out of the Hall if Fay found out they were up here. Karanne heard the sound of excited voices. When she reached the door, she recognized them.

Suffering.

Mathes' students. *Her* students. Much older, and better armed, than when she taught them years ago. And now they were clasping arms with Mathes and greeting the council members.

"They are here to help us escape this tower alive," Mathes told the council. "I had them wait until it was clear. Now is our chance. We can leave the Hall. With you all, we can assure the safety of Beldan."

One of Karanne's students, a young girl named Yorell, stood next to Mathes and looked up.

"She's here!" Yorell pointed at Karanne and the whole room quieted down and turned to face her.

How had she just wandered into the room? She stared dumbly at her feet.

74

The students drew their weapons, rapiers and thin daggers, with one question in their eyes: How could she betray them with magic.

Karanne raised her hands to ward off their accusing stares. The students jumped back from her. She looked at her hands. "No, no, I'm not going to do anything to you."

And still, they glared at her with disgust on their faces.

Mathes kept his calm and stepped toward her. "She is one of *them*." The council eyed her without speaking.

Talhar spoke to Mathes, his eyes still on Karanne. "What do you recommend we do?"

"I don't know what he's told you." Karanne glared at Mathes. "Between Guire and Fay invading our walls with Darrak and shipping our people to who knows where, we're trying to save the city. We need to band together."

When she finished, she noticed everyone wasn't staring at her anymore. They were looking behind her. She turned to see Turic, Brannon, and Dorne, the crystals no longer stuck into his skull. Slowly, she looked back at the room and muttered a stream of curses. One of her older students dropped her jaw at her words.

The crowd rose into a furor. The young fighters approached Dorne with their weapons held up. Karanne stepped back slowly until she was in line with Turic.

"I told you she wasn't with us," Mathes said. "She has freed the sorcerer."

"What are you doing?" Turic asked. When they did not slow, he too stepped back toward the stairs.

Dorne stayed put. In fact, he took a step into the room, staring at something on the table. A box. He would not take his eyes off of it.

Karanne exchanged glances with Turic, dreading what might be in there. Maybe this wasn't such a good idea.

"Fay kept them right below me?" Dorne walked and never broke his stare with the box. "Conceited, to a fault."

No one made a move as he approached. The box shook upon the table, vibrating until nails and bindings shattered off of it. Those closest to it flung their arms up to protect their faces from the oncoming splinters. When the shaking stopped, only a shiny black bundle remained on the table.

The gauntlets.

"I'll take those." The gloves slunk across the table, scraping against the wood and leaving thick gouges on its surface until they met

Dorne's waiting hands and shrank to enclose them tightly. The lights in the room dimmed, the sunlight outside faded away. Karanne felt a familiar darkness gripping her heart, just like in the Shadow Vale. But how could it? Marlec was gone. She found Turic's eyes and felt the guilt for not listening to him creep over her again.

A shadowy mist swept into the room, covering the floor and rising up along everyone's legs.

As if in response, a light surged around Dorne's chest and he doubled over. The darkness faded and the mist slowly left the room.

Turic stepped in. "I warned you about using magic again." The council and Mathes' students shifted their gazes between Turic and Dorne. Turic addressed them. "We still stand for Beldan. We have not forgotten you. Mathes may have turned you against us, but we will continue to fight anyway. When we return after the dark magic is defeated, please reconsider." Turic started to leave but stopped. "And Mathes? Stay out of our way."

Mathes held Turic's stare and straightened his back. Turic gestured with his hand and his students backed down. "It is as I have said. Magic clearly corrupts even the most righteous. You've allowed Dorne by your side."

"I will not explain myself to you." Turic turned to face the council. Nearly every person dropped their eyes to the floor. At the doorway, Turic paused again. "We will return."

Chapter 12

Jace ran with Ash at his side, staring up at the sun setting behind the mountains. Still a few hours left to do this. Valor swooped across the top of Beldan's walls while Ash kept constant watch along the river.

"I think they're right up ahead," Ranelle said.

"How can you tell?" Jace asked. He saw smoke from campfires in the distance, but it seemed farther than *right up ahead*.

"My dogs." Ranelle nodded to the hills in the distance. "They're watching them."

"And you can see what they see?" Jace said. "Like me and Valor?"

She nodded. "I think so. And there's a lot of them. Are you sure about this?"

Jace patted her on her shoulder. "I am. I have to believe there will be Darrak who are willing to listen. I met some in the mountains that didn't want to kill me when they first saw me. There's got to be more like them."

"You think any Darrak are going to have a chat?"

"I thought you said you were with me *wherever I led*?" Jace smiled.

Valor cried up above. Jace gripped his Soulkind, feeling the cool green stone and slick metal. His vision quickly jumped into the hawk's and he stared out across the wide valley floor. The dipping sun shone its light on thousands of camped Darrak. With Valor's vision, he could even see the food on their plates from nearly a mile away. He broke the connection and turned to Ranelle.

"You'll be able to understand the Darrak language with that magic I gave you," Jace said, "but not talk to them."

Tare and Ranelle stared at their new marks from the Soulkind.

"Can you teach us a few words?" Ranelle asked.

Ash tensed up and a low growl grew in his throat. Language lessons would have to wait. Jace waved down the other two and crept into the woods surrounding the plains up ahead. He touched the pouch at his side and pressed his hand onto the cold ground. A ghostlike vision of a small group of Darrak walked through him, right over this spot. The Darrak moved as if they were lost, stumbling about. No, not lost. Something pulled their minds in different directions, and Jace knew it well. When Cathlyn disrupted their attack on the city, they must have retreated here, but he sensed they could snap and attack Beldan again at any moment. It had to be the Call still commanding them somehow.

Could anything silence the Call permanently? He had calmed it down while with Sephintal, but could it be stopped?

"We may be too late." Jace ran to another clump of trees along the bank of the Crescent River. "Follow my lead."

Jace motioned to Ranelle and Tare to lower their weapons and led them to the edge of a small clearing where a group of five Darrak sat around a fire. A winged Darrak cried out as Jace emerged. The others leapt up from the fire. Five pairs of beady black eyes locked onto Jace, yet they did not attack.

"I'm not here to fight," Jace said in the Darrak tongue, approaching them slowly. The Darrak raised their swords higher and took steps away from him.

"You speak our language," a shorter, paler Darrak said. "But you shouldn't be here."

Jace reached into his pack, slowly. When he showed the metal rod to the Darrak, their eyes widened. The winged Darrak took two quick strides and gave the carved object a closer look. Ash tightened up near Jace's side but didn't make a sound.

"Is it real?" a rounder Darrak said.

"Yes."

"Are you sure?" another hissed.

The winged one glanced back at the others without a word and they didn't pursue it further. The Darrak turned back to Jace. "You haven't *stolen* this, have you?" It spat the word.

Jace took a step back with the sudden change in the Darrak's expression but then drew a deep breath. "A Darrak I met in the wild, Chran, inscribed this." He bowed slightly as he spoke, remembering the old Darrak who had trusted him in the mountains, right before the Call took over and Straeten froze them all. "He told me to show it to other Darrak—that it would help me gain passage through the land."

"We know what it's for." The Darrak turned to each other and spoke so low Jace couldn't understand their words.

78

Ranelle leaned forward to Jace and whispered. "Are you sure he meant you to use it with an army?"

Jace shrugged.

"You spoke of *Chran*?" the Darrak said. "We know of the old one. What is it you want, human?"

"I know about the Call."

A tall Darrak stepped toward Jace. "What do you think you know about it?"

"I know that it isn't as strong now, right?"

The Darrak all exchanged looks. "Strong enough that most Darrak will kill you on sight."

"But you haven't." Jace gulped as he stared at the circle of Darrak around him.

You better hope they don't.

Jace laughed grimly at Jervis' thoughts.

They all stood looking at Jace, waiting.

"I think I can get rid of the Call forever."

Chortles of laughter erupted amongst them. Two of their ranks even turned to leave.

"Impossible!" one of them said.

"The Call is as solid as magic itself," said the other.

You better be able to back this up.

"Yeah, I get that." Jace closed his eyes and called on his magic. It swept through him into one of the small symbols on his left hand. The mark glowed brightly and suddenly all his fears slipped from his mind. A blanket of peace settled over them all, or at least Jace hoped it did. He certainly felt it, and from his connection to Tare and Ranelle, he knew they felt it, too. The Darrak before him stood still and silent. The few that had turned away halted and turned back.

"What are you doing?" one of them asked.

Jace smiled. "The Call has lessened even more, right?"

"Some." The Darrak huddled closer to him, eyeing him like a curious specimen. "You are a Master? Can you make this spell stronger?"

Jace squinted his eyes tightly and drew again on the power that fed his Soulkind. The streams of magic rushed into the mark on his hand, now aglow with power. The mark stretched, widening across his skin.

When he opened his eyes, he felt all focus on him and took a hesitant step back. Their leader bowed and raised his claws to his forehead. "You *can* do it."

"And I can teach you to do it, as well." The truth hit him as he spoke the words. He could teach them the spells, and they could spread it throughout their ranks, crippling the Call from within. They seemed to realize it, too and walked toward Jace.

A cry from Valor suddenly screeched out through the golden glow of the setting sun.

Suffering! Ash barked in response and a low growl grew in his throat. A crashing in the trees drew Jace's eyes. Whatever it was snapped thick branches like twigs.

A few seconds later, one of the larger Darrak broke through into the clearing, swinging a large spear and leaving a swath of felled trees in its path. Its scaled muscles flexed as it gripped the spear. It eyed the Darrak and then glanced back and forth between them and Jace. Snarling, it leveled two of them in a single blow. Their bodies crumpled to the ground with the same crack as the smashed trees.

The Darrak raised the spear again. One of the remaining Darrak attempted to fly away, but the larger one grabbed him by the tail and dragged him to the ground. The Darrak screamed and struggled, but a blow from the spear ended it quickly.

"Help me!" Jace called to another Darrak. It should have been defending itself, but it wasn't. Instead, it turned to Jace and drew its sword. Its eyes clouded over with a rage that was too familiar.

Jace fought for his magic, but the enraged Darrak drove it from him. He gripped the metal rod tightly and scrambled to his feet as the large Darrak charged at him.

A gust of wind swept past as Valor swooped behind him, causing the large Darrak to falter enough for Jace to jump clear of his swinging spear. That thing was fast. Hot air exhaled sharply out of the creature's snout, filling Jace's nose with the smell of death.

"Look out, Jace!" Ranelle shouted from behind.

The creature raised the spear over his head this time preparing to shove it straight through Jace.

A dazzling white light appeared directly above the Darrak's skull and hovered there for a moment. The light then descended to the ground like a brush painting across a living palette, cutting straight through the Darrak's body. The creature's halves hit the ground with an unceremonious plop.

The one remaining Darrak, stunned, eyes still blinded by the Call, dropped his sword and stumbled away from Jace.

Jace raised his hand. "Wait!" he called, but the creature was gone.

The bright light that had severed the Darrak widened to form a doorway, but then closed shut an instant later. On the ground in front of the severed Darrak lay a mass of blue robes and bedraggled hair. The person staggered to her feet and turned to Jace, wobbling and reaching out for something to hold on to. It looked like her, but could it actually be?

"Cathlyn?" He ran to her side and held her up.

"I found you," she breathed and collapsed into his arms. "I found you."

Jace hugged her tightly and breathed her in. "It's really you. Are you all right? What happened?"

She clutched his wrist with one hand, her other gripping something else so tightly her knuckles turned white. The light reappeared above his head and arced down to his feet. When it reached the ground, the Darrak encampment faded away.

Chapter 13

Jace shook his head, trying to clear the dizziness. Cathlyn lay motionless in his arms. "Cathlyn?" She didn't respond. Where were they? The sound of running water surrounded him. He knew this place.

The cave at the top of the waterfall.

"Cathlyn!"

After a long moment, her eyes fluttered and she reached up to touch his face. "I found you."

"Yes." He hugged her again. How different she looked. Once carefully brushed hair now clumped in frizzy bunches. Dirt and blood stained her skin. And her eyes, usually calm and piercing, darted behind a glassy pall.

"Where did you go?" Jace smoothed her hair back from her face.

"I found you," she repeated. "I couldn't find you at first, I couldn't find anything. I was so far away. I didn't know where I was. Then you shone brightly."

"You did… you did great." A part of Jace's chest tightened as he rested his hand on her fevered forehead. "But what happened?"

I'll tell you what happened. She's gone nuts.

Jace shoved Jervis' voice down.

"I've got to show you something. He wants me to show you."

"Slow down, you're burning up." Jace rested Cathlyn on the floor, soaked a bit of cloth in the icy waters and dabbed it on her forehead.

"No, really." Cathlyn pushed his hand away and then raised herself up to a sitting position. She held her hand open exposing a dark gray chunk of rock, nothing special like any he would have collected. "I know what you can do with this. I can see it." Her eyes became unfocused and followed invisible pathways in front of Jace's face.

Wow, she's really lost it.

Maybe he was right.

He shook away the thought. She was just in shock, that was all. Something had done this to her, something she had seen. His heart

82

quickened as he thought of the companions he abandoned back at the Darrak encampment. Were they all right? Would Cathlyn be able to go and save them if they weren't? Definitely not.

He raised the cloth again to her forehead but she batted it away again and it dropped to the cave floor. She furrowed her eyebrows and thrust the stone at him.

"You have to look at this."

"But your head—"

"Forget my head." She shoved the stone into his hands and wrapped his fingers over it.

Jace nodded. He let the steady sound of the flowing water rush over him and through him as he embraced his magic. With his mark aglow and the flow of power thick in his head, he grasped the stone from her hands.

A thunder clap. An explosion of fire and then a shower of rocks falling to the earth. In the distance, gray hills with white stone towers on their shoulders stood amidst thick mists. Far below, torch lights flickered on cliff walls, exposing caves and staircases carved into the living rock.

Black shapes, scurrying like ants, bustled all about in droves carrying rocks and dumping them over the cliff. They tumbled down, down, and into something, some force, that shook him, and nearly swept him away. He had heard of it, read of it in many stories, but had never seen it.

The ocean.

The shapes were after something, unrelenting. This was a sacred place, he could feel that through Cathlyn's vision. Tears filled his eyes. Such desecration.

"Show him," a deep voice boomed, even over the crashing sound that came from below. "Tell him."

The vision teetered from side to side as Cathlyn swayed.

"Aklareath. Tell him the young need his help before it is too late..."

A bell began ringing, issuing forth from one of the great white towers on the cliff heights. Firelight shone out from its peak, a beacon to all who saw it. Cathlyn's vision spun to the sea showing several large ships tossed about on the white-capped waters. And further beyond that to the north, high on another cliff sat the many towers of the kingdom of Myraton.

"…before they are taken away."

"Cath?" Jace shook Cathlyn gently by her shoulders, but she had fallen in a deep sleep.

That voice in the vision. He had to make sure it was actually who he thought it was, or what in the suffering the *young* were. He gripped the stone. The vision ran through his mind again like a strong wind. The cliffs. The ocean. The deep voice.

Graebyrn. It was him. Graebyrn had shown this scene to Cathlyn, or brought her to see it.

Who is 'Graebyrn?'

"A dragon."

You found a dragon?

"Who was he talking about?" Jace ignored Jervis and spoke to Cathlyn. "Who was being taken away? And what is Aklareath?"

No response. He splashed water onto her face but she didn't even budge.

The water reminded him of the Beldan prisoners on the river. And Shey's plan to rescue them. He glanced out of the cave entrance. Already the sky was fading into the shadows of evening. She would be waiting for him at Landers by now, but for how long? Going with her was a sure way to get to Myraton. Maybe he could see what Graebyrn wanted. Cathlyn lay slumped on the stone floor without a hint of waking up anytime soon.

Leave her. She's crazier than I ever was, and besides she can just zip herself anywhere she wants when she gets up.

"I'm not going to leave her here." Was he telling Jervis, or himself?

Whatever. At least I won't be the one who has to carry her.

Jace lifted Cathlyn with a groan and shook as he tried to move her. This wouldn't do. "I know, I know, it'll never work."

Oh you can do it, you're big and strong and you can do anything.

Jace stumbled the whole way to the cave entrance and had to set Cathlyn down once he got there. "Cathlyn, wake up. I can't do this." He propped her up against the stony entrance. With a sigh he slid down the wall between her and the freezing water. He smoothed her tangled hair. The remaining sunlight glowed on her pale cheeks. He closed his eyes and listened to the water slide by, feeling its spray upon his face.

Graebyrn. Cathlyn had been with the old dragon somewhere near Myraton. Maybe he could talk to him from here. Jace focused on the water and called on his Soulkind. "Graebyrn," he called. The strands of magic rushed through him but the water remained clear. His heart dropped. Not an image of the silver dragon. Not a hint of his voice.

He tried again, this time with all his will pouring into his Soulkind, so much that his head throbbed. The faintest image appeared for a moment on the surface, but it just blinked and faded. Jace grimaced at the pain that gripped him as he tried to recall the image he had seen. Graebyrn had appeared, but he didn't even look at Jace.

Jace was simply too tired to use his magic. That was all. How much sleep had he gotten recently? Not nearly enough. Perhaps, if he rested a bit he could try again.

Maybe he's dead?

"He's not dead." Jace closed his eyes and squirmed a bit trying to find a comfortable spot against the wet rock entrance. "Only weakened, and focused on something else."

A warm gust of air puffed onto his cheeks. He smiled. "I was wondering when you'd get here." He gazed into the dark eyes staring down at him. Curved horns jutted from thick, gray shoulders. Jace patted Payt on the neck.

Are you crazy? What is that thing?

"A friend." Jace turned to Cathlyn's still body. "Think you can carry her, Payt?"

Payt lowered his two front legs slowly until his body lay completely prone beside Cathlyn.

"So you were just wandering these hills." Jace lifted her, gently moving her arms and legs away from the spikes on Payt's back. "Waiting for me." Jace sat behind Cathlyn and held her head against his chest. "Thanks, Payt."

Payt stood and began the slow but steady trek down the mountainside back to Beldan. Unsettled thoughts of Graebyrn surrounded Jace as he rolled the dragon's stone over in his palm again and again.

The sun was well behind the western hills and stars shone through the cloudy skies.

"Jace?"

A tight clump of dread loosened inside Jace's stomach as Cathlyn spoke. "I'm here. Are you all right?"

Cathlyn sat motionless in front of him. He placed his hand on her shoulder.

"I think so..." She reached up and touched his hand. "I'm just tired. What happened? The last thing I remember was finding you."

"You brought us to the cave, we're on our way back down."

"I saw the message in the stone you brought," Jace said. "I don't know exactly what it was all about, but I heard Graebyrn. Did you see him?"

Cathlyn nodded. "When I...left... the roof of the library, I showed up in the mountains somewhere. And he was there, waiting for me, I think."

Jace waited for her to elaborate but she didn't. "Then he took you to Myraton?"

She nodded then shrugged. "I think so. It's all a fog in my head, but I do remember the ocean."

"I saw something like a mine burrowing into the cliffs there. Someone was looking for something important. Graebyrn called them *the young*. Did he say anything to you about them, or maybe show you something?"

Cathlyn shook her head. "I don't remember it, only that I had to show you that rock."

Is she going to tell you, or what?

Jace tightened his grip on her arm and she turned back to look at him with a questioning silence. He quickly loosened his grasp. "Sorry, it's nothing. Just give it some time. It'll come back to you." He rubbed his temples.

"Where to now?" she asked.

"Myraton. That's what I got out of Graebyrn's message. Do you think you could use your magic again to bring us there?"

Cathlyn shook her head weakly. "I'm too exhausted, it took too much out of me."

"I have another way, don't worry. We're taking my friend's boat downriver to save the slaves Fay and Guire captured from Beldan. We can take the boat to Myraton afterwards."

"But the Darrak army. How will we get past them?"

"That's what I was trying to figure out when you showed up. Nice entrance, by the way."

She turned her head to smile at him. Her smile flooded Jace with relief, happiness, and... well, a feeling that reminded him of a being young again. It seemed so long ago.

"You were using your magic on the Darrak, I could sense it. What were you using?"

"I was trying to get their minds off the Call, but I don't think I got through to them. Not like I wanted to."

"I'm sorry," Cathlyn said. "I took you away… And your friends, I can't believe I left them there."

"No, don't worry. I'm connected to them, kind of like with Ash and Valor, and I can sense that they're all right. And I was there long enough to show them the rod I got from Varkran. It acted like a message, signed by other Darrak. I think they'll give me another chance, listen to me again."

Cathlyn leaned over and inspected Payt's spikes as if noticing them for the first time. "What are we riding? I remember seeing something like it before. In Varkran?"

Jace smiled. The Cathlyn he knew was back. "That's right. Payt has been with me for a long time. I don't think I would've gotten far without him."

"Payt, huh?" Cathlyn patted him on the neck.

"I'd watch out, he doesn't really like stuff like that."

The burra turned his head and eyed her warily. "I guess you know best." Cathlyn pulled her hand back. After a minute longer traveling down the hill, her head flopped to the side. Jace held her tighter and back upon his chest as she fell into a deep sleep.

Yeah, she's really going to be able to help you out.

"Shut up," Jace whispered to the voice in his head. Not for the first time he eyed a stick and considered jamming it into his ear.

Chapter 14

Karanne led the group through the woods to the secret guild entrance, keeping a careful watch on her surroundings. Dorne wore a cloth over his eyes and ears, but who knew what he could sense with his magic or otherwise.

"Do you think your spell will work?" Karanne whispered.

"It should be sufficient to stop him from using magic," Turic said. "Though I don't think it is perfect. I had to act quickly, so I simply changed other magic I had."

"I'm just glad you did something," Karanne said.

Turic suddenly bent forward as if under a great weight.

"Are you all right?" she asked.

Turic lifted his head. "I am always connected to him now. It's… exhausting."

"Do you have to keep an eye on him?" Karanne asked. "To make sure he isn't using magic?"

"No. The magic is watching and waiting of its own volition, like it did in the tower. But it is draining me."

Karanne put her hand on his shoulder. "You can't do this forever."

"Can you change it?" Brannon asked Turic.

Turic shrugged. "Perhaps, but not now. I would have to release him. And that would not be a good idea."

"We'll just have to finish this fight quickly," Karanne said. And even quieter, "Then we can end both him and his magic."

Turic walked silently for a moment. Dorne stumbled behind with Brannon leading him. "Do you not understand how this works? If he dies, then his Soulkind only needs to find another host to play Master."

"Maybe we could get him to give the gloves to someone we trust," Karanne suggested. "Like Brannon did with you. They could use their power for good."

"The darkness in the Soulkind cannot die," Turic said. "That is why Guire and Fay had Dorne in that cage in the first place. His Soulkind can only be used for dark purposes."

"But you escaped from Marathas' influence."

Turic grasped the glowing red gem around his neck. "This was never as far gone as those gloves."

"That doesn't mean his Soulkind couldn't be turned back," Karanne said. "I still think we can find a way to use him."

"Perhaps," Turic said, breathing heavily. "But I'm in no state for any of it." He stood silent for a moment, then tilted his head. "If I pass the magic along to my Followers they could take over this responsibility. And then I could work on lessening the spell's burden." He stumbled a step and reached out for a tree to steady himself. Brannon caught up and clasped his arm to help.

"I think I can do that," Brannon said.

Karanne caught Turic's eye. "You sure he can do it?"

"I believe he is ready." Turic patted Brannon's hand.

The sun dipped behind the mountains, casting long shadows on the ground. Karanne led them to what looked like a gray stone, knocked on its surface with a stick in a staccato pattern, and waited. It eventually cracked open, revealing a cloaked thief and a steep staircase.

Dorne's head sunk to his chest. Karanne knew that look well. Her old thief friends who had been captured eventually wore that same expression as they rotted away or went to the gallows. If he was as desperate and broken as he appeared, it would be useful in getting his help.

The light of day faded as Karanne stepped into the caves down the stone staircase. A small child, too dirty to tell the gender, stood at the bottom of the steps, waiting for her. "Go get Picks." Karanne pointed back at Dorne. "Tell him we need a room to lock him up." The kid nodded and raced off ahead.

Karanne released her Fireflash, lighting the way through the damp passageways. Dorne stumbled along behind her with Brannon and Turic.

"I see how this works," Brannon said, holding his hand up to Dorne's back. A slight glowing covered his chest and Turic's tensed shoulders relaxed.

"That's right," Turic said. "But it will begin to drain you." Turic trailed off and furrowed his brows in thought. "The Darrak are held in control by something Jace named the *Call*. Even though Jace helped rid the gloves of Marlec, the Call still lingers. We know Dorne isn't maintaining it since he can no longer use magic."

"His Followers?" Brannon asked.

Turic shrugged. "I feel that to use such a large spell would take an immense amount of control."

Brannon tapped Dorne on his shoulder with his finger. "I could ask him."

The inflection in his voice indicated how he would ask.

"No," Turic said, although Karanne didn't hear any conviction in his voice.

"They seem to be following Guire and Fay's orders," Karanne said. "Perhaps those two are controlling it?"

Turic shrugged. "I do not see how, but those creatures do heed them. Perhaps their submission could be a remnant from the Call that Dorne's Soulkind created."

Up ahead in the dimly lit cavern, a small group of people waited for them. One of the dirty-faced men pulled a heavy rusty gate open with a screech that echoed in the darkness. He made an overly extravagant and welcoming bow to Dorne.

Brannon pushed Dorne ahead into the cell. Dorne flinched as the door clanged shut behind him.

"We will keep the gloves safe from him," Turic said, touching a cloth sack he carried. "Until we can figure out what to do."

"How long before you regret trying to hold me, I wonder," Dorne said. He lowered himself to sit cross-legged in the center of the cell. Water dropped from the ceiling into a puddle next to him.

"I've cast the spell and I'll keep an eye on him," Brannon said. "He's not going to do anything for a while."

"Are you sure you can handle the toll it takes on you?" Turic asked.

Brannon smiled. "I can handle it."

"Yes, well," Turic said. "I will be back in a bit to check on you. Do not do anything rash."

"He'll be fine." Karanne added under her breath, "I hope." How long had it been since Brannon nearly turned his back on his own Followers? "Come on. We've got to get those gloves to a safe place before I go check on Jace."

Turic placed a wearied hand on her shoulder. "You are in charge around here. You lead the way."

Karanne squeezed his hand. "I'll do my best." Something moved up ahead in the tunnel.

In half a breath, she drew her knife and released the Fireflash from her palm. "What is *he* doing here?"

She continued to point her knife at Caspan Dral. The last time she saw him he had nearly captured her for Guire and Fay. She sent the Fireflash spinning in dangerous arcs, radiating her anger in pulses.

He held up both hands as she approached. "I know what you're thinking, Karanne," Dral started, "but I was only doing what was best for the Guild. I wasn't going to—"

"Keep your excuses," Karanne spat. "You're not talking your way out of this. I know you were doing what was best for only one person."

The circular meeting room seemed smaller than before and smaller still when several thieves and Dral approached her. "Already got some close friends?"

"You don't know everything I was doing," Dral said. "As I was explaining to everyone here, I just wanted us to be on the right side of this thing."

Karanne froze. "Does Fay know we're here? Don't lie to me."

Dral smiled his most persuasive smile, showing most of his teeth. "I wouldn't give up our best hiding spot to anyone, you know that."

Karanne scoffed. "I also knew you would never betray me." The Fireflash slowed its arcing.

"Well, I am sorry," Dral said. "I was doing what I thought was best for all of us. And thanks to Picks we've got the Guild working again. Thank you, Picks."

The old lock master nodded but remained silent.

"Where were you while we were evacuating?" Karanne asked. "Your people could have used your help."

Dral's smile slipped for a moment but returned almost instantly. "I was held up with Fay. And what I learned from her can help us. They'll be leaving soon to Myraton, and I think they may need to leave people here that they trust."

"They just told you this?"

"You know me," Dral said. "I can be a really good listener. Look, they need our help. *Your* help."

"You know that's crazy, right?" Karanne asked, glancing around the room. "They want me and Turic dead."

"I think they'd prefer you to be alive." Dral took a few steps toward Karanne and raised his hands. "Listen, they want to run this place, and I think that gives us a wonderful opportunity to come out on top."

"How can you possibly use this for personal gain? They are killing and enslaving our people. I don't have time for this," Karanne muttered.

"It's for all of us," Dral said and left with his advisors.

Karanne threw her hands up and walked away toward Turic. "Jace is leaving soon. I've got to go, I don't have time for Dral."

Turic nodded. "My remaining Followers are here. Both the gloves and Dorne are secure. We will be safe for a while. That is, unless your old boss here decides to do something stupid." Turic's head drooped and he raised a hand to his temple.

"What is it?" Karanne asked.

"Something is wrong. Back with Brannon." He looked up in panic. "You must hurry!" He collapsed onto a stone bench.

"Are you okay?" Karanne paused beside Turic.

"Don't worry about me! Go!"

Karanne sped from the room with the Fireflash bobbing just ahead of her to light the way. Everything seemed to be going wrong since they got here. What was Brannon doing now?

Shouting filled her ears up ahead through the passageway. Brannon's voice. Karanne rounded the last corner to see the two guards rushing toward her and Brannon with the cage key out.

"What's going on?" Karanne asked.

"He won't stop," Brannon said, gripping the cell bars. "Don't do it, Dorne!"

"Do what?" Karanne rushed to his side. Dorne lay on the floor with a pained expression on his face. What could possibly be hurting him?

Dorne raised his hand and drew with his finger in the air.

Karanne turned her head to Brannon. "He wouldn't try to cast a spell, would he? Won't the fire around his chest kill him?" After a second she blurted, "Brannon, release that spell on him!"

Brannon closed his eyes and his face strained. "I can't."

"Hurry!"

"I'm trying."

Inside the cell, Dorne's eyes locked onto Karanne's. A small smile crept onto his face through the pain. "That didn't take long, did it?"

"Brannon," Karanne urged.

Dorne's eyes took on a deep red and his chest started to glow brighter through his clothes. In a last effort to distract him, Karanne called her Fireflash into the cell and made it explode in a burst of light before Dorne's eyes. The burning fire faded from his body, but in seconds the blaze rekindled.

A mix of pain and pride showed on Dorne's twisted face. In the next moment, his eyes erupted in flames and a fireball burst out of his chest. He crumpled in a pile on the floor, flames enveloping his body. He disintegrated like a burning piece of paper.

"Why?" Brannon stared at his clenched fingers. "Why did he do that?"

Karanne peered at the ashes on the floor. Smoke rose from his remains forming a dark cloud that quickly dissipated. She ignited her Fireflash as she raced back through the tunnels to Turic, back to the gloves. She pushed away her fears about what might be happening, but still the thoughts crept in.

She ran faster.

And stumbled into the lit cave again to see Turic and Dral conversing quietly. She skidded to a halt.

"What happened?" Turic asked, looking up from the bag by his side.

"It's Dorne," she said. "He... he tried to use his magic."

"Didn't my fire stop him?"

Brannon entered the room, breathing heavily. "Yes, but he kept using his magic. I couldn't let go of the spell to save him."

Turic stared and pulled the bag containing the gloves closer to himself. "The Soulkind is free now."

"I couldn't control it," Brannon said, visibly shaking. "I couldn't let it go."

"If you had let it go, who knows how much worse things would be right now?" Turic said. "He would have his magic back. And you would probably be dead."

"But we can prevent another Master from being chosen, right?" Brannon asked.

"I suppose if no one touches this."

"Is contact necessary for a Soulkind to choose another?" Karanne said.

Turic rubbed his beard. "I am not certain."

"What's in there?" Dral asked, again his fingers twitching.

Turic held the bag more tightly. "What do we do now?"

"Nothing rash, that's for sure." Karanne looked sideways at Dral then back at Turic. "I think we'll be safe here tonight. We'll have to figure it out tomorrow." The sun had set and Jace would be leaving. If she was going to see him off at Landers, she'd have to run.

Whatever she was going to do about the thieves would have to wait.

"Watch him," Karanne said to Barsal and the few other Followers she had left. "See if you and Turic can scratch up a few more Followers here." She walked to Picks' side so only he could hear her. "Choose only thieves we can trust. And don't leave without me."

Chapter 15

Jace crept along a canal leading toward Landers Bay with Cathlyn and Payt. An uneasy feeling of being watched had grown in him after leaving the waterfall. He slowed Payt as they approached the small bay.

"I've never been here before," Cathlyn said.

"I can't imagine why you would," Jace said. "It's mainly used by thieves for smuggling things in and out of Beldan. They stay off the Crescent River anywhere near the town and guards."

Jace peered across the black water lapping gently against the canal's stonework. Lamps and torches bobbed in the distance across a network of docks as people loaded and unloaded crates and other supplies. "It's busy enough that we might not be noticed," Jace said. "But not you, Payt." The nimble burra stepped to his side and leaned his head closer. "It's time to go. There's no room for you on the boat. And besides, you might draw a little attention to us."

Payt stared at Jace for several seconds before bowing his head slightly. Jace patted his belt to reassure himself that he still carried a couple of Payt's shoulder spikes. "You sure you can't just bring us to Myraton with your magic?" Jace said to Cathlyn.

Cathlyn shook her head. "I can't." Jace sensed she had more to say but she hung her head forward in silence.

"Then this is goodbye for now." Jace tentatively reached up to pat the side of Payt's neck. Payt gave his hand a sidelong glance and Jace watched him disappear into the darkness. He'd be okay. "Did Graebyrn say anything about me?"

Cathlyn ran her fingers through her hair attempting to straighten the tangled knots. "I... I don't know. He gave me the stone, but that's really all I can remember."

"Did you mean he was *in* Myraton? Was he all right? Last time I saw him he had a lot of strength back, but he was still kind of slow."

A pained light came back into Cathlyn's eyes then—like the one she had when she first returned. She clenched her teeth and shivered.

I know that look. She's losing it.

"Shut it," Jace mumbled. Cathlyn's eyes shot at him and he held up his hands. "No, no! Not you. There's… um, it's complicated."

Nice one, genius.

"You still have that dark mark," Cathlyn said.

Jace rolled up his sleeve to reveal the marking. "You could see that?"

She nodded. "It's not as strong as before, though."

"Good." Jace clenched his fist and felt the magic like water behind a dam. The anger from Blue's loss. He reached out for Blue's memory and was suddenly aware that somehow the horse raced above in the darkened hills or maybe even the sky, watching down over him. "I'm dealing with it." He quickened his pace. "Come on. The sun is down and Shey will be waiting."

Darkness covered the stone pathways through the hills to Landers. Cathlyn reached for Jace's arm to steady herself. "Who is Shey?"

Jace tripped over a root but then quickly regained his stride. "She's a thief. I've known her forever." He turned to notice Cathlyn staring into the woods.

"You've never mentioned her before."

Jace felt heat rising to his face. "Nope."

Jervis' laughter echoed in his head.

"We're here!" Jace scanned the docks as the pathway widened and approached the bay. "They'll be back there." Jace pointed to a string of buildings. A familiar shadow passed in front of him toward an alley leading away from the water. "This way."

"You sure?" Cathlyn asked.

"Yeah. It's safe over here."

"How can you tell?"

Jace smiled as he held out his arm and a swooping form appeared from behind a building. A wave of air blew Cathlyn's hair back as Valor landed on Jace's shoulder.

"Valor!" Cathlyn smiled at the hawk.

Valor bobbed his head forward twice and with a quick flurry of feathers took to the dark again. "He's not alone. Ash is here, too." Both Valor's and Ash's vision filled his eyes at the same time, making the warehouses, back alleys, and the people within them clearer.

He saw the workers and guards patrolling the area, much sooner than if he relied on his own eyes. It took a moment to get over the jarring effect of three sets of visions, and he still couldn't move too quickly without a slight wave of nausea hitting him.

You know, if you had this skill back when you were a thief, you could've broken into any place you wanted. If this magic business doesn't work out for you...

"No thanks." He waved off Cathlyn's questioning look.

He signaled Cathlyn to move when he did, and pause in the shadows when they needed to let someone pass. "Let's not use magic here even if you're able to. Best not to be noticed at all."

Cathlyn nodded.

Alley by alley, they made their way until they finally reached a seemingly abandoned building atop the floating dock. A small whistle escaped from Jace's lips and was quickly answered by another from up above.

He felt a sharp tap on his shoulder and spun around, his dagger flashing in the moonlight. Shey's face appeared in the dim twilight.

"Easy there." She smiled.

"Yeah, you got me," Jace said.

"Don't just stand out here, get inside. Someone's going to see you. You and...?" Shey peered at Cathlyn's face.

"Cathlyn!" Allar rushed out onto the dock and clasped his sister in his arms. As the two embraced, Jace stepped into the rundown building with Shey.

"Nice girl," Shey said. "Interesting hair."

"She's had it worse than we have, trust me."

"She must've had it really bad then." Shey ushered Allar and Cathlyn in under the cover.

"Jace!" Straeten shouted and ran to greet him. "Ranelle told us what happened with the Darrak. Where did you go?"

"Cathlyn showed up and took me out of there. We went up to the waterfall again."

"You walked all the way up there?" Straeten asked.

Jace laughed. "No. She brought us there, with magic. I've got a lot to tell you, but where's Tare and Ranelle?"

Straeten gestured back toward the boat where Burgis and Tare were carrying supplies.

Jace ran over to Tare and clapped his shoulder. "I'm glad you guys are all right."

"We made it out of there without a problem," Ranelle said. "I'm glad you were taken by a friend and not a Darrak." She stood inside a sleek long boat with a folded up sail and tucked up oars. The words *Gray Ghost* were painted along the hull.

Ranelle saluted Jace quickly and got back to inspecting the vessel.

"Yeah," Jace said to Straeten. "Things could have gone better with the Darrak."

"Or worse," Straeten said, "if what Ranelle told us about those Darrak was true. Good thing Cath showed up."

Ash trotted through the door and jumped into the boat. He laid himself down at the bow as Valor landed on a rail beside him.

"Where's Karanne?" Jace asked.

"She wasn't there when I left with Shey," Straeten said. He looked almost like his old self, but something in his eyes looked worn.

"You okay? You look tired."

Straeten shrugged. "I'm fine. And don't worry about Karanne. She'll be busy with the thieves. You know someone has to get them all working together again."

Jace threw his light pack into the boat and some of its contents spilled out across the deck. "Suffering." He climbed in and knelt down to stuff his things back in as Shey walked past him. "Nice ride you got us, Shey."

"Someone owed me a favor."

Jace stood on one of the benches. "There's something I've got to ask you." Everyone turned to face him. "We're going to go save our townsfolk from those slavers. And I thank you, it's no easy thing. But after that's done I have a favor to ask. Cathlyn showed me a vision of something happening at the coast near Myraton, and I need to follow it."

Murmurs of consent and nods surrounded him. Burgis and Tare gave him looks that said, "Of course."

Shey lashed down the sail and lowered the short mast across the cabin. "How about you help us get moving so we can get on with this fool plan while it's still dark?"

The boat rocked as Straeten climbed aboard.

Jace grasped the rail.

"You going to make it, sailor?" Shey asked.

"I'm fine." Jace quickly let go. "We're not going to use the sail?"

Shey shook her head and gestured for Jace to tighten the canvas that came loose around the back of the boat. "Fay sent guards here to look for us, I don't know how we all made it here without them spotting us. The last thing we need is a big white sign telling them where we are."

Everyone gathered around the center of the boat with all eyes on Jace. He shook his head and pointed his thumb over to Shey. "She knows her way around this thing way better than I ever could. Isn't your father a sailor?"

Shey's smile slipped for a second but then she clapped her hands and looked about. "Dim those lights, and you, big guy—"

"Straeten," Straeten said.

"Big guy," she continued. "Grab the line at the bow…" She pointed when Straeten looked around. "Yeah, the *front*. Get that door open and pull us out. We'll make a break for the northern locks down to the river. Got it?"

Straeten grabbed Tare by the sleeve and together they climbed out and opened the large door leading into the main waters. Taking the line, the two led the boat effortlessly into the blackness with Shey at the till.

Cathlyn helped Jace tie down the tarp. "Shey didn't seem to like that comment about her father. Any idea why?"

Jace shrugged.

"Hey!" A guard shouted from the docks ahead and ran toward Straeten. "What are you doing here?"

Straeten turned and butted his forehead directly into the guard's face. The guard dropped to the dock and rolled into the water. Tare lunged for the man while Straeten rocked back on his heels, reeling from the blow. When he got his bearings back, he knelt beside Tare and helped haul the guard out.

"Just leave him." Shey hissed. "Hurry!"

"Hey," Jace said with his hand on Shey's forearm. "That guard is just being tricked by Fay and Guire. We couldn't just let him die like that."

"Sure, you'd just mash his face in, that's all," Shey said, but lost the harshness in her tone. "We just have to get out of here and after those boats."

Jace nodded. "I'll try to give us a better idea of what's ahead so that doesn't happen again." Valor flew off the boat and circled several times above them before disappearing into the dark. Jace felt the bird's sight wash over his own, yet it was too dark to see any details except the torches or lamps.

Straeten and Tare clambered onto the boat's decking and Jace took the oar and quietly swept it into the water. The *Gray Ghost* drew quietly along the dock toward the northern basin.

"I thought the canal was behind us," Jace asked. "How are we going to get back to the river this way?"

"See that open area up ahead?" Shey pointed. "There's a set of locks. We'll be lowered down to the river outside of Beldan. And hopefully far enough north of the Darrak. Trust me, it's faster this way."

The torchlight from across the bay flickered out dangerously onto the water and the *Gray Ghost*. Still, the guards hadn't appeared to notice.

Shey led the boat into the wooden chamber at the end of the waterway. A tall enclosed structure stood at this end of the bay. Probably the control tower for the lock.

Didn't spend much time out here, did you?

No, he really hadn't. Dral had kept him busy with all the break-ins and other work on land. He'd have to rely on Shey's expertise in this area.

"Won't there be guards watching?" Jace asked as Shey guided the boat in.

She touched her lips with her fingers and with a smile nodded up to the tower. A single guard sat near the balcony and stared at the ship. He stood quickly and ran to the railing and a dark figure appeared behind him. The guard dropped silently after a small cracking sound and the figure waved over the edge at the boat.

"Is that Tarolay up there?" Jace squinted into the darkness.

Shey jumped out of the boat and ran to a large crank off to the side of the lock. The mechanism spun easily, sealing the waterway off behind the boat with a huge gate. After several loud creaking and locking sounds, the gate shut and Shey nimbly hopped back into the boat. She signaled to Tarolay and the girl disappeared. The sound of gears grinding echoed again in the darkness.

The water level began to drop and the *Gray Ghost* drifted to the edge. A float attached to the side lowered with them and the boat eventually bumped up against it. With a creaking groan that lasted several seconds the water flow stopped, along with the boat, about ten feet down with no way out.

"That can't be good," Allar said.

"Tarolay?" Shey shouted up to the station. "What's going on?"

Silence.

"We're going to be an easy target for anyone up there." Burgis readied a bow for himself and tossed another to Tare.

Jace eyed the metal ladder attached to the side walls. "Allar, any idea what's going on?"

Allar pressed his hand up against the wet stone walls and his arm pulsed with magic. "It's not broken, if that's what you're wondering. And we're only about halfway down now."

A shadowy figure appeared alongside Allar's silhouette, wavering in the dim twilight. Jace started when he saw it, though he'd seen something like it before. Marlec, Guire and Fay's forms all appeared like this, but twisted. Why had this one appeared now?

"Hey," Shey said and slapped Jace on his shoulder. "Wake up."

"Sorry, I thought I—"

"Someone going up to check?" Shey asked. "Someone who's really good at climbing?" She shot Jace a pointed glance.

"Yeah, I'll go." Jace reached for the rungs on the wall. Guess he'd be target practice after all. Valor made a short chirp and Jace waved him down. "They might be waiting for this, Val, I don't want to risk us both. You stay down here."

"But what about you?" Cathlyn asked. "You're a bigger target than he is."

Jace climbed a couple of steps up the narrow ladder and glanced back down at those in the boat. "Well, I've got you all to cover me, don't I?"

Cathlyn nodded and rubbed her hands together.

Jace reached the top and its strange silence. Nothing. He crawled over the edge of the lock. Still not a sound. A dim light flickered in the tower structure where Tarolay had been operating the gears.

"Tarolay?" Jace whispered. He drew out one of his knives and held it loosely in his hand while he approached the building. A tall man with blue eyes walked out of the structure with Tarolay struggling in his arms. His silver blade pressed to her neck. "Put down your knife," the man said. "Or I'll slit her throat."

"Jace?" Straeten called from within the lock.

"Not now," Jace said loudly, lowering his knife to the ground.

You can use your magic on him. You know the kind I mean.

The thought had occurred to him even before Jervis suggested it, but he dismissed it quickly. He wouldn't go down that path again.

Five others men, each with arrows on their bows, stepped to either side of the lock and aimed down below. "Fay says we don't need the others. Just this one." The guards pulled back their bows with a creak.

"I hate to bother you Jace, but do you have this under control?" Straeten shouted up to him.

Jace locked eyes with Tarolay. Her gaze shifted from him to the man holding her and back to Jace again. Jace tilted his head almost imperceptibly to her and she nodded slowly.

Tarolay wrenched in the man's grasp and leaned to her left, pulling the man with her momentarily. When he righted himself, he stood with his back to the trees and away from Landers bay.

Nice.

"Well, I was a thief for a bit," Jace said. "Oh, and sorry about this."

The man furrowed his brows. "About what?" A sharp crack emanated from the tree line and a spike struck through his shoulder. His knife clattered to the stony ground and shock lit his face.

Jace saluted his friend still hidden in the trees.

Tarolay elbowed the man's gut and squirmed out of his hands as he gasped for breath. Indecision showed on her face, as she glanced from the tower to the woods.

"Go!" Jace shouted as he reached down for his own knife. Quick as a rabbit, Tarolay leapt into a tree off the side of the building and disappeared.

The men around the lock didn't waste any time and launched their arrows downward at the boat.

"No!"

Jace turned and glanced below, only to see the arrows bounce harmlessly off an invisible barrier and hit the water or rock wall. He sprinted to the control room and sent his vision spinning around into Payt's, locking the whole area in his mind. Another group of guards stamped across the docks with their weapons drawn, but Jace sensed something else approaching.

Darrak. Further down the dock, men and women flew into the water as the Darrak carved a path toward the boat. There was something different about how they moved, something stronger about the Call. It pounded so loudly in the air it throbbed into Jace's head through Payt. The men around the docks sent more arrows at the boat only for them to bounce into the water again.

"We're not going to be able to hold them off forever!" Straeten shouted.

"Working on it," Jace muttered, peering at the gears and levers in the tower control room. Someone grabbed him from behind, probably another guard. With a swipe of his forearm, Jace broke the hold on him and the man staggered in the doorway. Payt's vision showed that he had a clear shot at the man. The burra leaned over and the two shoulder spikes clicked into place.

Do it.

Jace hesitated, toying with the idea. No! Where did that thought come from? He berated himself for even considering it. He pulled the man out of Payt's way and struck the spike still jabbing out of his shoulder. The man screamed and Jace silenced him with a sharp strike to the base of his neck.

"Don't do that again," Jace said, but Jervis did not reply.

The approaching Darrak stormed into a group of guards, shoved them aside, and sprinted to Jace's building.

"If we don't get out of here quickly..." Jace ran back to the lock. "Just blast that door down, Straet!"

Valor screeched and left his perch on the boat, circling up into the night sky. With another cry, he dive-bombed the men around the lock as Jace attacked, taking advantage of the sight he got from Payt. He struck precisely with his knife and only disarmed them.

A great booming sounded from within the lock and the doors to the northern end splintered with a blast of flames. Straeten looked up at Jace with a smile. "That what you wanted?"

Jace nodded but then pointed at the door. "It's not open enough!" The boat listed to the side and wedged up against it as the water drained out quickly through the hole. "Hit it again!"

The guard at Jace's side suddenly flew into the wall over the boat. Jace stared up into the blazing eyes of a Darrak leader. Rage emanated from its every movement. It gnashed its teeth and spit slathered to the ground. The large spear in its grip swung so quickly Jace barely had time to avoid it.

A great creaking sound came from below. Allar sat at the bow with his hands held up. The great doors began to wedge open and the boat shimmied along as the water pushed it harder into the opening.

Jace sprinted toward the lock gate, ducking under another swinging spear that ended up smashing into the control tower. It reduced a window to splintered scrap. Jace leapt off the edge, flailing his arms as he fell. He landed right behind the boat with a splash, barely avoiding the tiller. Shey gaped down at him a second before she reached her arm over the edge.

Jace latched onto her forearm and she and Straeten yanked him onto the boat, only moments before the door cracked the rest of the way open. The force of the water shot the boat from the lock. It was almost as if the door had waited for him to get on board. Jace saw Cathlyn gripping the railing. He thought he saw a slight glow around her, but it quickly faded. He held on tightly as the boat skipped along the surface downstream.

In the moonlight, Jace caught a blurred image of a massive Darrak racing down the vast stones after them, leaping great distances to reach each boulder. Up ahead the canal would slow down and this chase would be over. "We're not clear yet," Jace said and scrambled to his feet.

Shey's voice shouted loud above the crashing of the water. "Pull together! Again!"

Straeten and Tare pulled hard on the oars, yet the boat didn't move as fast as Jace hoped.

"Cathlyn, do something about this guy!" Jace shouted.

Cathlyn stared out at the water. "I… I can't!"

Payt's large gray form pounded alongside the river. Again Jace felt the beast's shoulders drop to produce several resounding cracks. Multiple spikes launched across the river and over the boat, most implanting into trees or clattering off rocks. The Darrak wasn't slowing down, but the number of Payt's spikes were.

A brilliant flash appeared on the riverbank, knocking the Darrak back a stride. It dropped its spear and rubbed at its eyes but that was all that it took. Another crack and a spike whistled straight overhead and drove into the Darrak's chest. The beast tumbled forward onto its face beside the churning water and didn't get up again.

"That flash." Jace scanned the trees to his left as the boat sped downstream. "Was that one of you?" Nobody responded. Straeten and Tare kept rowing.

"It had to be Karanne." Jace tried to get a glimpse of red hair through the trees.

Cathlyn placed her hand on his. "She saved us, then."

Jace nodded. "I wish I could thank her."

"You'll get your chance," Cathlyn said. "Her Followers are here in Beldan. Together they'll be all right until we get back." Allar gripped her hand and brought her to a bench to sit.

"I don't know how we survived that drop," Shey said working the tiller. "Do you?" She stared at Cathlyn.

Cathlyn shrugged and took a drink from her flask.

"I see, I see," Shey said. "Keeping it close to the vest. I can respect that. Well, I'm glad you did whatever you did, we're on our way now. This channel will merge with the main river and we'll be away from Beldan."

Jace caught Cathlyn's eye and smiled his thanks to her. No wonder she couldn't help with the Darrak. She was already pretty exhausted before the escape. "I'm sorry I yelled at you back then."

Cathlyn just waved him off and looked away. "Let's just keep our eyes open for anything else that might be out there."

"Good idea," Jace said. Shuffling a bit from the unsteadiness of the boat, he tripped over a length of rope on the deck.

"Ow!" a small, muffled voice called from under the tarp.

"What the…?" Jace lifted the canvas. Definitely not rope. "Evvy?"

The young thief sheepishly looked out at him and got to her feet.

"Well great," Jace said. "Now we *have* to stop."

"But that lady just said it's good if we all stay together," Evvy said.

"No," Cathlyn said. "I said the Followers are going to be all right together."

Evvy wasn't listening, she was busy petting Ash who sat by her side. "Hey, birdie," she said. Valor flapped his wings and landed along the cabin roof.

Cathlyn gave Jace a raised eyebrow.

"Yeah, okay, she's one of mine," Jace said. He patted Evvy on her head and continued checking the supplies. "Some watch dog you are," he said to Ash. The gray dog closed his eyes and rolled on his back to get more rubs from Evvy. "Looks like our next stop is Myraton," Jace said, saluting Shey.

Shey locked in the tiller of the *Gray Ghost* to keep them in the middle of the stream, then helped Jace and Burgis pull the mast up and get the sail drawn. Soon Beldan's city lights slipped away to the south.

Chapter 16

Jace had escaped. He was safe for now. Karanne pushed back a strand of hair from her face and watched the boat finally slip away from sight. Part of her heart left with it and she fought back the urge to follow him. This was his path, she had her own Followers to worry about. He'd be all right. He was a Master, too, and he was with his friends.

It was never easy, seeing him off like this.

A gray creature swept past her and headed in Jace's direction, cracking branches as it stamped trees flat. It startled her at first, but something about it was familiar. Was that one of those creatures from Varkran helping him? And was that Cathlyn in the boat, too? Karanne breathed out a heavy sigh. Her son had all the support he needed.

The path back down to the river felt empty and quiet and the burden of what to do next lay heavy upon her heart. Guire and Fay must be stopped and she and Turic were the only Masters in Beldan. Well, on the good side, anyway. The Fireflash in her palm throbbed with its energy and she grasped her white stone necklace. Magic coursed through her and her palm glowed brightly with its power. The spirit memories she still held inside thudded against her skull, yelling at her to set them free.

She was a Master of a Soulkind. Time to start thinking like one. Guire and Fay's grasp covered much of Beldan and the way to weed out their evil was to go straight for the heart. But where were they hiding?

The thieves could find out. Their network had found Straeten and allowed Jace to set him free. Back when she was one of them, she even knew Council member schedules so she could break in without anyone home. Unfortunately, all Dral wanted for the thieves was to make money off this whole thing. No, she had to do this herself.

A yawn nearly split her face. How long had it been since she slept? Days? Too long for sure. First thing in the morning she would try to recruit more Followers. She held out her palm as she walked through the trees near Beldan. The mark on her hand glowed slightly brighter as she headed back to the guild and her remaining Followers.

She poured her thoughts into the Soulkind and her palm, thinking of finding others she could teach. The markings flared but then disappeared and a splitting headache blossomed over her temples. Karanne leaned against a tree and breathed deeply until the pain left. Okay, definitely time for a rest. She headed for the guild.

Karanne awoke the next morning with a start. Where was she? Like a dream, bits of how she got here popped into her head. The rocky shelf under her had been her bed, and someone had been kind enough to leave a blanket on her. Her neck still had a crick in it.

Her stomach gave a loud growl and she scanned for something to eat in the dim light. Someone had left her a chunk of bread and she ate it hungrily. She missed this life among the thieves, even though she lived on the outside with Jace for years and even taught with Mathes…

Mathes. He certainly wasn't helping with this takeover. Had he been waiting for this moment, waiting to spring his own "followers" to the town's rescue? Images of dead children sprawled on the ground came to her eyes, students she had taught and cared for. Their spirits rattled in her mind.

She walked to the meeting area to see Turic and Brannon already conferring with Picks and his remaining Followers. Her own Followers plus Turic's added to only ten. Not nearly enough.

"There's this." Turic held up a piece of parchment. Under rough sketches of Karanne and Turic were words proclaiming them traitors, with a substantial reward tacked on, as well.

"This had to be the work of Fay or Guire, the townsfolk wouldn't have done this," Karanne said. She turned to eye the thieves around her, but none met her gaze. "You can't be serious. All we've done is try to help them!"

Still, no one responded. And then, as if matters weren't bad enough, Dral walked into the room, strutting like he was a king.

"My people have just returned from the city," Dral said. "They spotted Guire and Fay near the Hall. They're giving the Council time to make a decision to join with them, but I believe they'll all be killed if they don't."

"We have to save them," Turic said.

"But we have so few Followers," Karanne said. "We need time to grow our numbers."

"It will all be over if we wait too long." Turic patted Brannon on his shoulder. "I have been holding back in what I can teach my Followers. I think that if I show them something stronger then we will have a better chance." Turic sighed heavily. "Will we have your help, Dral?"

"This is not the best move for us," Dral considered. "We should wait out the fighting and then—"

"Make a profit from it all?" Karanne asked. "I'm so glad we asked."

Dral smiled. "I never said we wouldn't help, I only said it wouldn't be the *best* move."

"So you will help," Karanne said. "Are the Darrak there?"

"Some. But most are out in the northern fields, away from the city. That doesn't mean we're clear, a lot of the city's own people support them, possibly willing to fight us."

"And that is worse," Karanne said. "The people aren't being controlled, they're deciding we're traitors. The longer we wait, the fewer allies we will have."

Turic stepped to the front of the room and the cluster of thieves and Followers turned to hear him speak. "Guire and Fay have remained hidden. I say we draw them out into the open and fight as best we can. Who knows when we may have another chance?"

"This is a crazy plan." Dral thumped Turic on his back. "I think I like it. We'll be at your side, old man."

Turic looked at Dral sideways. "We will need to get in to the city as quietly as possible."

"Tough with them watching for this," Dral said. "But we wouldn't be proper thieves if we couldn't do it, right, Karanne?"

Karanne frowned.

"I need to confront my twin Soulkind." Turic stroked the red gemstone around his neck. "How soon can we be ready?"

Dral smiled his most charming smile. "Anytime you need to go."

Karanne stepped to Dral's side and poked him in the shoulder so hard he winced. "You better not be turning us over for money."

"Money? Karanne, I'm disappointed. You know me." He gave her another smile. How could this one be more charming than the last one?

"You're right, I do know you." Karanne turned to her Followers. "Before we do anything, I've been working on something that might help us find other Followers."

Barsal joined her at her side.

"We leave within the hour," Turic said.

Dral nodded and started talking to Picks about organizing an attack party.

"Karanne," Turic said.

She turned to face him.

"The woman that Fay has possessed is still that young girl's mother, correct?"

"I tried to free her. Jace tried, too. There is little I think we can do for her."

Turic raised an eyebrow. "But she is still in there, yes? You focus on Guire then, perhaps there is something I can do."

Turic placed his hand on Brannon while his other Followers watched with wide eyes. "There will be fighting," he said. "And I need you to be careful with this."

Turic pulled his hand back. Would this power be too much for others to handle? He created this fire as a last resort. A power formed out of desperation. How could he trust anybody with this? Memories of incinerating the Darrak with a light brighter than the sun played over in his mind.

Be careful? It felt like handing a newborn the controls of a catapult. Perhaps he could take back what he gave them after this was all over, but he didn't really believe that was a possibility. "Soulkind were not meant to be weapons," he said. "They should be bringing this land to an age of enlightenment."

"You said we need this to win," Brannon said. "To even have a chance against her, let alone Guire."

He glanced at Karanne. They'd have to leave Guire to her. She stood at the corner of the cave with her own Followers showing them new magic, too. Bright lights glowed above their outstretched palms pointing out of the chamber.

Weapons or not, death seemed the likely outcome. Even if they survived, there would be no going back once Turic let the spells out.

He sighed. If creating a Follower army was the only way to rout this darkness, so be it. He uttered a curse but turned to face his own Followers.

"You make a shield of flame like this." Turic summoned an undulating wall of fire in front of him and it hovered in the air. "You can concentrate its power in any direction, even surrounding you." The fire closed in so he could barely see the others around him through the flickering flames.

"Use it wisely, as you will be blinded for a time following its use." The spell reduced itself to a shield again suspended in the air.

"Can we use it on others?" one of his Followers asked.

"They will be trapped in it, but it will draw on you as you hold it."

Turic grasped Brannon's hands and passed the spell to him.

A glowing mark appeared on Brannon's arm and he smiled. Focusing on that mark, he conjured a disk of fire like Turic's, although it was less stable and flickered out of sight soon after he cast it.

"Try again," Turic said. "Concentrate."

As Brannon practiced the magic, Turic turned to his other Followers and taught them as well. Before long, the room shone brightly with their fire. Shields and barriers. Suitable protection against any of Fay's spells, Turic thought.

"What about the other spell?" Brannon said.

Turic shook his head. "Let them focus on one in this short time. I can still use the other if it comes down to it."

When it came down to it, he meant. For it would.

Sighing, he turned to a group of people forming behind him. The thieves there were both young and old yet they all had the same look in their eyes. The young lady in front of them bowed her head in reverence.

"Master," she said.

Turic waved his hand. "Just Turic."

The woman smiled but didn't look up. "We were afraid to try to be Followers when the Soulkind first came here. We thought we would be thrown out, since we were thieves." The ten or so others behind her bowed their heads as well. "Will you teach us?"

"Everyone is allowed to try." Turic beckoned them forward and they formed a line. "Just know it is not I but the Soulkind that chooses the Followers. Chances are—"

Turic's eyes widened after he held her hands. The spell leapt from his body into hers and her eyes bulged. The mark burned bright on her forearm. She held her hands up in the air and laughed.

"Welcome, Miss…?"

110

"Chandril," she said and bowed her head.

"Well, Chandril. You are part of us now. You must know that we walk straight into danger."

"I am ready." Chandril gazed at the mark on her arm, now losing its glow and turning black.

"I hope I'm doing the right thing," Turic said under his breath. "Brannon, show her how to use it."

Chandril walked to Brannon and the other Followers. She held up her hand and the fires sputtered in front of her.

"All right," Turic said. "Let's see if any others will be joining us."

Out of that small group, nearly all who had lined up were able to learn. Turic's number of Followers doubled. Was this some result of the magic fully awakening? Or perhaps the need drew people able to learn? No matter the reason they learned so easily, he took a deep breath and stood up straighter. The magic of his Soulkind rumbled inside of him stronger than before.

"How many people will you send?" Turic asked.

Dral paused in his conferring with other thieves and faced Turic. "Not many. My thieves do not have your magic, which gives them less of a chance."

"I told you, we are more than happy to do this ourselves if needed." Turic gritted his teeth.

Dral smiled and held up his hands. "We will help, we promised. I only need to look out for the guild."

"You mean yourself." Karanne walked into the chamber and strode to Turic's side. "We were able to find more Followers, more than I expected. Barsal is taking the others to see if they can find more. They'll meet us on the way."

Turic smiled. "Good, good." He turned to Dral. "There is of course great risk, but this is our town. And our land. You understand that if Fay and Guire win here, they will be even stronger?"

Dral nodded. "Know I will be there with you at the front."

A hooded girl ran into the room, out of breath and sweating. "They are at the gates of the Hall right on the bridge. They're trying to get in. There is ice and… sickness everywhere. The doors are holding for now, but I don't know for how long. Those creatures, the Darrak, are not attacking yet."

"Thank you," Turic said. "They are overconfident. We don't have much time, but they will be trapped on NorBridge for a little longer. If they get into the Hall, our chances will weaken."

"As I said, I will be with you." Dral motioned behind him at twelve thieves all clad in dark clothing. "A group of my finest have volunteered."

"Thank you." Turic watched the hooded thieves. "Now, most of their people will be our own townsfolk. If we can avoid killing them…"

Dral snorted. "You fight your way to survive, let my people fight theirs."

There was no time to argue, but Turic's anger flared at his callousness. If only they could capture Guire and Fay's Soulkind, and free those people quickly… "We must be going now."

Turic handed Picks a wrapped up bundle of cloth. "Take good care of these," he whispered.

Picks nodded. "I promise I will keep them safe."

"Can you show us the best way to town?" Turic asked Dral.

Dral eyed the bundle in Picks' hands and then nodded.

"Then lead us."

Dral ducked into a side tunnel and Karanne and Turic followed him side by side up to the surface.

"He knows what he is doing," Karanne reassured him.

"Do you trust him?"

Karanne shrugged. "I have to, don't I?"

"Just be careful," Turic said. "Like you always are. As for our new Followers…"

Turic turned to address the small group of nearly twenty, both his and Karanne's. "You're scared. We are too. But together we do not have to be. Our town needs us. Your families need us. Stay close to Karanne and me. And remember your power. You have fire, strong fire."

The dark tunnels opened to the bright morning sunlight. Even from here amidst a field of boulders a mile from the city, Turic spied ice bursting near the main entrance of the hall and Guire's thick black growths clinging to the bridge and the walls.

"It begins," Turic said and followed Dral to Beldan.

Chapter 17

Karanne stared out at the burning buildings and armed guards marching through the streets of Beldan as the thieves escorted them and her Followers. So was this what she could expect from the magic of old? Wars? Karanne had never seen one, much less been a part of one. True, Myraton waged wars on other lands, but war had never struck home.

"Are we going to be enough?" Karanne asked Turic.

"To stop them?" Turic held onto her arm as he walked. "When I faced her last time, I did not fare so well, did I?"

"Straeten needed your help then. Now, you can focus entirely on her. You have her twin Soulkind and you said that would balance her power."

Karanne watched Turic only shrug and fiddle with the red gem hanging around his neck. It should be enough to stop Fay, but what about Guire? She had to be strong enough. Karanne's own magic had already tested him and he had run. She could do it again.

Her thoughts drifted to Jace. Maybe they should have waited for him to help out against these two Masters. And what about Cathlyn? Her magic was something entirely different, and had the potential to be more powerful.

"I wish Jace and the others were with us."

Turic patted her on the back. "We will be enough."

The thieves led them through the town by way of back alleys such that no one even noticed them. Once a guard turned toward them in the darkness and such a look of dumb shock crossed his face Karanne almost laughed. Before he could speak, a blade spun through the air and stuck in his chest. He tumbled to the ground.

"Hey!" Karanne grabbed Dral's arm. "I thought we said no killing unless we had no choice."

"I guess there was no choice." Dral strode up ahead, closely followed by his dark-clad thieves.

Karanne knelt by the guard and placed her hand on his forehead. His body burned brightly as he turned to ash and his spirit entered her thoughts. The spirit shuddered inside, longing to be free, but she also felt her strength surge with its presence. The Fireflash also throbbed in her palm. Her Followers, right beside her, awaited her lead before they reached the bridge.

"You ready Dral?" Karanne asked up ahead.

The leader nodded to her and waved to a young female thief that appeared from up ahead. "Report in."

"We've seen the bridge," the thief said. "Maybe thirty guards, and I saw some of those lizard things. Not sure how many. They move like snakes."

"And what about Guire and Fay?"

"They're trying to get into the hall," she said. "They're using ice and whatever filth comes out of that other one."

"And?" Dral asked after a moment of her silence.

"For now, the resistance inside the hall are holding them off.
The walls are still standing up
to that magic and they've got arrows inside. But it won't last too much longer."

"If they're preoccupied at the hall, they won't know we're coming," Dral said and clapped Karanne on her back. He signaled to his fellow thieves and they ran off, disappearing into the side streets.

"Where are they going?" Turic asked as the thieves disappeared into a tangle of side streets.

"Just a little surprise up ahead," Karanne said. "A lesser known path is all."

After a minute they finally reached the bridge with the first wave of town guards. When the Followers stepped on the bridge, the guards took a step back and glanced at each other.

"It appears they were not expecting us. Hopefully, there will not be many of them," Turic said and looked around. "We've lost our escort of thieves. Shields ready!"

His Followers in the front held up their hands. Some flaming shields sputtered in and out of existence, while others blazed furiously. Sparks flew and ignited nearby wooden stands. All of the Followers stood strong, however, as the guards advanced.

Bows twanged, arrows whistled. Those that shot true toward the Followers were incinerated when they collided with the shields. Karanne's Fireflash darted to the nearest guard and struck his arm. The little burning bolt sizzled through his sleeve and he dropped his sword with a cry of pain.

114

"Do the same!" Karanne shouted to her Followers.

Barsal easily cast his magic, disarming another guard. Her newer Followers had mixed results. Bolts careened off the stonework and others spun around in the air seeking out targets almost blindly. The guards scrambled back.

A thin whistling sound pierced the air and Karanne smiled. "Here they are."

Before the guards could find cover, Dral and his thieves clambered up from beneath the bridge. With precision, the thieves slipped behind the guards and in moments dropped them to the ground.

"That's the lesser known path?" Turic asked.

Karanne responded with a nod and blinded another guard. Turic pushed his group forward advancing to another line of enemy archers nearly halfway across the bridge. Karanne glanced at the motionless bodies of the fallen as she passed. The ones she saw weren't dead, merely bludgeoned or otherwise incapacitated.

"See?" Dral said. "I'm on your side here."

Karanne glanced at the sides of the bridge. Greasy black tendrils clung to the stonework pulsing with some unseen inner workings.

"Stay away from that!" she shouted.

At the same time, one of her newer Followers, a young man she knew from the guild, stepped on one of the living roots. The black mass erupted with a sticky fluid that covered the Follower's foot. Screaming, the man stumbled and fell on his knees, clutching at his foot. More black liquid covered his hands as he tried to free his leg and his screaming intensified. His tortured eyes met Karanne's as he tumbled into the darkness, the substance covering him.

Karanne reached for her power but found that it felt weaker than the last time she encountered Guire's magic. The white scouring fire wasn't there. Suffering! If only she had more time to collect spirits. Instead, she cast what she could at the bubbling mass trying to ease her Follower's pain.

The bolt seared through the black growth but his screams and struggling stopped. Karanne continued to cast her magic, knowing the poor soul might still be suffering. She consumed his body with fire and the bolt returned to her. Another bright mark formed on her palm and the young man's memory shot into her head.

"Burn them!" Karanne shouted to Turic. Fiery blasts shot from both his and Brannon's palms and sizzled over Guire's growths. The tendrils shrieked and curled in the fire, opening a path up ahead on the bridge.

Smoke rose from the ashes of Guire's magic and six Darrak leapt forward with their curved and notched swords. Karanne knew how to handle them. She raised her palm, but before she called her magic, the air chilled with a sudden frost. An icy sphere shot into a Follower's chest and frost quickly consumed his body. A Darrak smashed the frozen person with its sword, shattering it into tiny shards. Pieces of it skittered out on the bridge.

"Shields up!" Turic shouted.

The spinning disks of flame erupted in front of the Followers and the next volleys of ice hit the shields and instantly vaporized. The frozen blasts that hit the bridge made dangerously slick patches causing several Followers to stumble. The Darrak stood still for a moment, assessing the defenders.

"Blind them!" Karanne shouted to her own Followers.

Intense light flashed in the air leaving a green afterimage in Karanne's vision. The six Darrak clawed at their eyes and halted their attack.

"My turn." Dral and his thieves rushed past Karanne and downed the Darrak with thrown knives and stabbing blades.

A Darrak landed in a pile at Karanne's feet. Its empty reptilian eyes stared through Karanne and up at the sky. Decomposition started almost immediately—that rapid near melting of Darrak scales. Karanne knelt and placed her palm on the Darrak's exposed skull and for a second she wondered if her magic would work the same with a Darrak. She didn't have to wait long, as the rest of the Darrak's body quickly disintegrated and she consumed its spirit. The power welled inside of her and she had to push back the urge to release it.

The hall loomed up at the end of the bridge. They were almost there. Karanne watched the allied archers raining down arrows from the tall stone walls at the end of the bridge, pushing back the Darrak. Karanne smiled grimly. From here both Guire and Fay appeared to be held back, and even faltering a bit at the end of the bridge. The archers in the Hall and the Followers on the bridge pinned them in, and Fay alternated casting her magic up and behind her. Karanne almost relished the impending confrontation.

As Karanne passed more defeated Darrak, she knelt to claim their spirits and shared them with her Followers. Each one added to her strength. The Darrak in the distance kept casting the ice magic at them, but Turic and his people deflected them with ease.

"We've got them," Dral said and drummed Karanne on her back.

"It's not over yet." Karanne stunned another Darrak, giving the thieves a few seconds to finish it off.

"I say we hold here," Turic said as the last of the ice-wielding Darrak fell. His fiery shield still remained up.

"What?" Karanne forced herself to stop moving forward. "They're right there. We can finish them." She pointed to where Guire and Fay stood amongst the arrows still twanging down upon them. Their thick robes carried an air of nobility that covered whatever remained from their small-town origins, and perhaps who they once were could never be regained. Nilen, the young girl from Varkran, flashed before her eyes. Karanne had taken the girl's necklace to give to Lunara, her mother… this woman up ahead. "We have to finish this now. The townsfolk are doing their job inside the Hall. Fay's and Guire's Followers are almost dead." She gestured to the bodies lying at the base of the hall riddled with arrows.

"Guire and Fay could break inside the Hall at any time," Dral said. "We can't let them in, we'll never get the advantage then. We've got them."

Karanne nodded and looked to Turic. "What are you worried about?"

Turic shook his head. "I do not know, just a feeling."

"We have to try something," Dral said.

Karanne glanced back. Still no sign of anyone following them up on the bridge. "He's right. I don't think the townsfolk can hold them forever. Once they break through it'll all be over. We won't have another chance once Guire and Fay get inside."

Turic let out a big breath. "I guess you're right."

Dral smiled and patted him on the back. "We've got this. You lead with those shield things. And you, Karanne," he gestured to her hand. "Keep doing what you're doing."

"I'm right behind you," Karanne said.

Turic gathered his remaining Followers. "Hold strong and keep those shields going. I do not know everything she is capable of but I will watch over us all." He adjusted his spectacles and took a few tentative steps toward the hall. "Incoming!" he yelled.

A rain of ice shards flew up from the bridge and dove toward Turic. He lifted his arms and the fire around his body grew higher, blazing furiously. When the shards arced downward he steadied himself and his Followers did the same. The barrage of ice struck the barrier. Turic's footing faltered for a moment but the shield held, absorbing Fay's magic with a flash of sizzling steam as it did so. When the first attack passed, Turic lowered his shield briefly to give Karanne a nod.

Karanne motioned her own Followers onward. Memories of Danelia, and all the others who gave their lives since Marlec's fortress, flashed into her mind. A sudden chill passed through her as she thought of that dark fortress and gazed up at the vast tower in front of her. They were alarmingly similar.

"Get into position, but wait for me before you attack," Turic said. "I want her to see me first."

Karanne scurried to the side of the bridge and motioned her own group of Followers to follow.

Turic took three more strides. "Fay!" He released his shield and held up his hand toward her. Her blue eyes, a contrast to her dark hair, shone out in anger.

"Leave our town," Turic commanded. "And no one else has to die."

Fay laughed but she raised a hand and the fighting ceased for the moment. "Just like that? You think you have any chance of winning here? With your little army?"

"We may be small, but we will stop you." Turic met Karanne's eyes across the bridge. "And you know it."

Fay's eyes narrowed but then blinked as lights rapidly flashed in succession around her and the others beside her. She flailed her arms to ward off the bright lights.

Turic waited no longer. He formed a ring of fire around her chest, then clenched his fist to close it. The ring pulsed with life and closed in on her and she frantically turned her attention to it.

A storm of arrows pelted down from the Hall at her distracted form, but a black tentacle grew above Fay's head. The arrows stuck into the thick growth like a porcupine. Guire raised his arms and black groping fingers rose from the bridge to surround himself.

Time to act. Karanne felt the power of white fire surge inside her. That power, different from the Fireflash, burst from her outstretched palm and pierced the looming tentacle, slicing it in half. Like a fallen tree, the thick tentacle slammed onto the bridge, crushing several Darrak as it landed. Power beat within her as she directed the fire to other black growths creeping up the walls around Guire.

Below the black fluid spewing around the stairs, Fay tried to extinguish Turic's fire with a spray of ice, but for now it only slowed its closure.

Darrak jumped off the wall hacking at Followers on the bridge who failed to react quickly enough. Blasts of light shot out causing blinding flashes in Karanne's peripheral vision.

She focused now on her target, Guire, well-groomed even in the midst of battle. Perhaps fifty feet away now. "Nowhere to go," Karanne said. Guire looked about him and then an arrow from above drove itself through his left forearm. He howled in pain. Karanne moved in with her hands raised.

Darkness suddenly covered the mid-morning sun. Only the shields and Fireflashes lit the unnatural night. Karanne lost track of Guire in the dark fog. This was all too familiar. But from where? It was like a nightmare.

"Guire, Fay? You can come on out now."

Whose voice was that? Her voice trembled as she spoke. "Turic, what's going on?" She reached out for Turic but felt nothing in the dark. She stumbled into him and clutched his robes to get her footing.

"It cannot be," Turic said. "I gave them to Picks, I..."

"Gave what to Picks?"

Turic pulled her sleeve. "We have to leave."

"I...I can't move." Karanne compelled her feet to walk but they were mired as if in mud.

"It's okay, friends."

That voice. She knew it, but it sounded different. Some strange accent clung to the words.

Through the darkness, Guire and Fay both hung their heads as they walked through the shadows.

"No, no," the voice called. "Don't worry. I'm not mad."

Karanne tried to get Turic's attention. "What is going on? Who is that?"

A man stepped out of the dark fog and walked past Guire and Fay. Dral? But how did he get behind those two, unless... She gaped in horror. It was him, but it was also someone else. His voice didn't sound the same, and neither was the way he held himself. How much of him was still in there?

"Your friend, the fire Master, left these unguarded." The black gauntlets, now a smaller fit than on Dorne's hands, glimmered in the dark.

"But Picks…" Karanne started.

"Paid dearly for them, I'm afraid."

Anger and pain shot through Karanne. Light lashed out of her palm and cut through the darkness in the false night. Dral sidestepped the blast and raised an eyebrow at Karanne.

"That magic of yours, where did you get it?"

"I'll show you," Karanne growled.

"Not now, I'm afraid," Dral said, raising his hand. "Now please, let's end this and discuss what I really came here for."

Karanne took an unwilling step toward him.

"Karanne, no!" Turic urged, gripping her again.

"Yes, yes," Dral said. "You've known me for years. We're all friends here. Time to discuss this like adults."

A whistling arrow whined through the silence. A bloodied barb protruded through Dral's shoulder and he dropped to a knee. Above him on the walls stood a red-robed man holding a bow.

"Go!" a familiar voice shouted.

The arrows began raining, some plinking off the stones. In the chaos, Karanne grabbed Turic and pulled him back across the empty bridge.

"Run!" she shouted. But the word died on her lips. Darrak scrambled up from the underside of the bridge, their claws clicking, and blocked the way back across. The two large leaders she faced before stepped to the front and brandished their spears.

"Not that way," she muttered. She pointed to the edge of the bridge and cast her magic at it. When the beam of light faltered, Turic added to the blast with fire from his own hand. The stone shook and erupted in an ear-shattering explosion, flinging boulders and shards in every direction. A jagged path cut amongst its ruins to the riverbank. "Go!"

Turic waved to the Followers behind him and headed down the new path.

An icy canopy descended over Dral's head, deflecting the onslaught of arrows.

A loud, clear voice cut through the fighting. "I'll let them live."

Karanne stopped. "What?"

120

Dral took a few steps down toward her, holding out his hand. "Your friends. I'll let them live. I'm assuming that is your friend who shot me."

She looked up at Mathes standing on the wall, shrouded in a black cloud. *Friend* seemed too strong a word. He shouted out something unintelligible but was suddenly silenced.

"I'm losing my patience." Dral nodded slightly over Karanne's head. One of the large Darrak swung his spear into a Follower, flinging him screaming over the edge of the bridge into the river.

"No!" Karanne watched helplessly as his form sunk beneath the racing waters.

"I just want to talk with you." He reached out to her with a black-gloved hand. The arrow from his left shoulder dripped blood but he didn't seem to notice.

She shook her head as if fighting off sleep. Maybe she should talk with him, everything seemed to make sense when he talked. The words lulled her into a warm safe place and Karanne slumped her head forward and took her first steps up the stairs to Dral.

Chapter 18

"Look! What is that?"

Jace followed Evvy's pointed finger to a small creature basking in the midday sun along the river. Green scales sparkled like gemstones, that was all that Jace could see of it. Slightly bigger than a crow. It glanced up at them as the boat quickly slid through the water. As it dove in, Jace noticed a ridged back fin.

"Never seen one before," Jace said. It wasn't the first new thing they had encountered on this trip, either. "Graebyrn said more creatures are awakening with the magic."

Evvy gaped at him.

"Yes, I told you. He's a dragon. And yes, he talked to me. Right Straet?"

Straeten sat down on the bench alongside Evvy and Jace. "Sorry Ev. I think he's full of it."

Evvy dropped her eyes and frowned.

"Because all I ever heard from that old silver guy was a bunch of hissing and snapping of his teeth."

Evvy smiled again and got up to pace across the deck. She stopped and knelt down to pet Ash on his back. "Think I'll get an animal like you did?"

"I don't really *have* an animal," Jace said. Valor screeched from his perch atop the mast and Ash picked up his head for a moment before lying back down under Evvy's hand. "They just, I don't know, are friends, I guess."

"It's more than that." Ranelle sat on the other side of Ash. "It's more than the Soulkind. We have a voice that speaks to their spirit."

"You have them, too?" Evvy asked.

Ranelle nodded and closed her eyes. She pointed to the shore behind the boat and smiled. "Mine are following us. I was a little upset when Jace said we couldn't bring fifteen dogs along in the boat."

"That would've been fun." Evvy laughed.

"But don't worry, you'll find yours," Ranelle said. "Or, I guess they'll find you. Just keep your eyes open." Ranelle left to speak quietly to Allar.

The sail filled with a steady breeze and pushed the boat downstream. Jace thought about what Ranelle said. He had bonded with his companions after helping each of them in some way. Valor with the crows. Ash with the town of Tilbury. Payt after releasing him from captivity. Though with Payt, *bond* might've been too strong a word since he always felt the burra would bite his hand rather than accept a pat to his shoulder. And yet, he could point to where the burra was racing along the riverbank.

He let the comfort of his connections fill him. Somehow, he sensed even Blue watching over him.

"Sorry to crash your little magic tea party," Shey said. "But do you mind helping out at the tiller here?"

Jace stumbled past the others and sat down next to Shey. "Nice job getting us out of there."

"Are you sure Tarolay made it out all right?" Shey asked.

"I saw her leave, and I'm sure she knows how to stay unseen."

"She does." Shey fidgeted with a strap on her waist and arched her neck to stare downstream.

"We'll catch them. This is a fast boat, you said so yourself." Jace paused. "Why do you want to get there so badly?"

Shey stared for a few more seconds. "I need to sleep. I'm about to fall over." She laid down near a tarp and pulled it over her head. "Let me know when you need to rest."

Straeten walked over to Jace. "Seems like she's hiding something, doesn't it?"

"You think?" Jace asked. "Probably someone she cares about onboard the boat."

"Oooh. Someone she cares about." Straeten nudged Jace in the arm.

"Hey, why don't you go check in on the brothers. Looks like they're struggling a bit."

Straeten turned toward Burgis and Tare leaning over the boat's side. "You boys never been on a boat before?" Burgis answered with a moan.

Cathlyn walked past Straeten and lightly cuffed him on the side of his head. "Good observation. Now find me a few cups. I'm going to fix them some tea." Cathlyn rummaged through the bags and found what she needed.

"You're feeling better, it seems." Jace smiled at Cathlyn.

"A good night's rest was all I needed."

"And a good comb through her hair," Shey muttered. Jace was pretty sure no one else heard her but he shot her a pointed look.

"Are you able to remember anything else, you know, from Graebyrn or the sea?" Jace swerved the boat to avoid a large rock jutting out of the water. Burgis looked back at him with a sour expression and Jace mouthed a, "sorry."

Cathlyn shook her head.

"What about your magic?" Jace whispered to her. "Can you use it now?"

"Ever since I left the library, it seems so out of control. It took a lot out of me. I felt nearly torn in half from it all."

"And then you saved us at the lock," Jace said, fishing for a definitive response on that.

Cathlyn shrugged and gave a half smile.

"It does seem you go all or nothing," Jace said. "Have you tried anything smaller than, you know, trying to wipe out all magic?"

"Not yet." Cathlyn shook her head. "But the day is still young."

Jace laughed. "It's good to have you back." He turned to the water. "Now that you have some time, maybe you really should slow down and try something."

Cathlyn nodded. She filled a kettle she found in the gear and sat it on the deck. Raising her hands, she focused on it.

"Right there," Jace said. "Right on the deck. Right on the thing keeping us afloat?"

Cathlyn raised her eyebrow at him. "No faith? After I saved you on the tower?" The kettle began to shake, its metal handle clanking, and rose two feet into the air.

Evvy looked up from Ash. Her jaw dropped.

The kettle tilted awkwardly and Cathlyn adjusted her hand slightly to keep the pot aright. Water spilled from the top but vaporized before it hit the deck. Straeten backed away from it slowly. The pot spun too far and Cathlyn compensated in the other direction quickly. The rest of the water splashed out hitting Straeten's arm.

"Tea's ready," Straeten said through gritted teeth. He nursed his arm and bit back other words.

124

The kettle clanked to the decking and Cathlyn dropped her head. Jace, with his free hand, touched her arm. "Hey, it was a nice try. And the boat is still in one piece."

Nice one. You wanted to make her madder, right?

Cathlyn stayed silent for a few more seconds. "I just wanted to do something simple. Lift the pot, heat the water." She eyed the resting kettle.

"Well, you certainly did that." Straeten rubbed his arm.

Cathlyn narrowed her eyes. The kettle crumpled like paper and shot like an arrow right at him. Straeten raised his hands but before it hit him, the kettle struck an invisible wall and clattered back to the deck.

No one moved.

Cathlyn's eyes widened and she raised her hands to her mouth. "Straet, I'm sorry, I…"

Allar limped over and put his arm around her. He led her off to the front of the boat as she erupted into tears.

"I didn't mean to do that. I'm so sorry," she cried over her shoulder.

Straeten smiled weakly at her. "I know you didn't." After she walked past him, he locked eyes with Jace. "What was that?"

"I don't know," Jace said. "But you're lucky."

"What stopped it?" Straeten reached over and picked up the collapsed kettle. One side of it was completely flat. "Looks like it hit something hard."

The memory of it all played over in Jace's mind. Cathlyn looking at Straeten. The kettle folding in on itself. It shooting straight at him. What next? Jace slowed down the images and caught a shadow standing behind Straeten. The shadow covered someone. Jace replayed the image again and tried to slow down his thoughts.

"It was Allar." Jace nodded. "Or Newell, actually. You ought to thank him for that."

"You bet." Straeten huffed out a deep breath.

"We'll soon be going up against some pretty serious trouble," Jace said. "We're going to need you to learn everything you can."

"I'll ask him." Straeten threw the flattened metal ball up in the air a few times. "Think she'll teach me that?"

"You might want to wait for her to cool down a bit."

"Yeah. Good idea."

Jace sighed.

"Can you all keep it down?" Shey said, lifting her head up from the tarp. "Trying to sleep."

For the next few hours, they floated along in silence. Even Evvy stopped her constant questioning, and with some help from Tare, tried to use her newfound magic to connect with Ash and Valor.

Soon, Evvy laughed as she saw through Valor's eyes. Tare's face beamed with pride. Valor swooped across the water and into the trees to catch some food for him and Ash. Whenever he returned to the side of the boat, Evvy greeted him with a cheer.

Cathlyn still sat covered with a thick blanket beside Allar. She avoided everyone's eyes and ignored their comforting words.

"What are we going to do when we catch the boat?" Straeten asked.

Jace gave a mirthless laugh. "Hadn't thought of that."

"Maybe you could point your friend, the cannon, at it?" Shey asked.

"Sure, if you wanted the boat to sink with everyone on it," Jace said. "And be nice, she doesn't know what she's doing."

"Do any of you?" Shey asked. "Looks like you're all making it up as you go along."

She's right.

"Yeah." Jace hefted the stone Graebyrn had sent him again. Images of the caves and the threat of attack hung over him as he watched the memory in it. He'd have to figure out how to deal with the boat first.

"I keep trying to focus on the memories in the rocks around us," Jace said staring into the water. "I get images of the boat going past them. From the angle of the sun, I'm guessing we're not too far behind them now. An hour, maybe?"

"Doesn't leave us much time, then," Shey said. "But we should probably wait until it gets dark. Stop them from seeing us coming."

"How big's the boat?" Jace asked her.

"She's slower, fatter. Meant for hauling big freight. The people'll be down below deck."

"Do you know how big their crew is?"

Shey shrugged. "Regular crew to manage that boat is probably four or five people. As for guards, not sure. They could have those creatures."

126

"Darrak." Might not be a bad thing. Could be another chance to try to contact them, like he did at the camp before things went wrong. "Listen, let's do our best not kill the crew. I'm guessing they're being forced against their will. Everyone needs to get back home."

"Home?" Shey asked. "You didn't see the crew loading the prisoners. I did. They're not being forced. They're doing this for themselves, all right? We're getting the people off that boat however we have to." She gripped the tiller, her knuckles turning white.

Jace walked to the bow and held out his arm to Valor. The hawk leapt to him, gently kneading with his talons. "I need you to look ahead for us." Valor gave a few soft chirps and nodded his head. Jace lifted him up, and with a great flapping, Valor swept out across the water.

The hawk circled into the waning afternoon light. Jace entered his sight when he leveled out a couple hundred feet up. Even at this great height, things below were clear and detailed. Their own boat appeared amidst the wide river. Further and further he soared to the east.

In the distance he spotted their quarry. A mile downriver, perhaps? A heavy set ship with its hull riding low in the water. How many people did they get in there? With their plan and magic, they'd find a way to stop the boat and save the townsfolk. Hopefully, Cathlyn would be able to help out somehow. Jace just about let go of the sight when something caught his eye. He focused in a little closer. With a start, he released his magic and ran back to Straeten and Shey.

"What's wrong?" Straeten asked.

"There's more than one boat."

Chapter 19

"Everybody linked to Valor?" Jace asked.

"Whoa," Evvy said, clutching the sides of her head. "This is weird."

Jace smiled. "It'll help us keep track of everything going on. Now, it's going to be hard to hold on to it while you're doing other things but now's your chance to practice.

Jace paired off the others with his Followers. Burgis and Tare, Allar and Ranelle, Evvy and Cathlyn, Straeten and Shey. His Followers' thoughts filled his mind through Valor's.

Evvy, think you can stay on the boat and keep an eye on everything for us?

Evvy's connection broke off suddenly. "Did you just *say* that?"

"What do you mean?"

"I heard you say that, but not in my ears. It was in my head."

"Yeah, I didn't hear anything," Shey said.

"I guess I didn't say it," Jace said. "I only thought it."

You better watch what you think through Valor's connection.

Jace nodded. "Ok, everybody try thinking something into the link."

At first, Jace only heard the sound of wind and water. Then a few small indiscernible voices rose in the distance. In moments they grew louder.

I'm here, Ranelle's thoughts appeared.

When was the last time Jace took a bath? Straeten asked.

Nice, Jace said.

Laughter echoed in the strange link.

Hello? a deep voice sounded.

Is that you, Evvy? Jace asked with a laugh. Evvy shook her head and a meek, *No,* came through. *Who was that then?*

All eyes landed on Tare, whose face had turned completely red. A huge smile crossed his face. *I can talk in my mind. And you can hear me.*

The link suddenly became filled with everyone talking to Tare at once.

Okay, okay. Tare laughed.

"What's so funny?" Burgis asked through their laughter. He glanced at his brother who shrugged.

"Nothing," Straeten said. "Except that Tare here says you need to learn how to cook."

Tare smiled widely and put his large arm around his brother's shoulders. This time it was Burgis who was at a loss for words.

"This is great," Shey said loudly, silencing them. "Now, if we can avoid any more family reunions perhaps we can focus for a minute."

Jace opened his mouth to say something but Burgis waved him off.

"Good," Shey said. "I think we need to drop the sail and go in rowing while it's dark. Anything we can do to stop them from seeing us."

"Cathlyn, can you do anything?" Straeten asked. "You know, with the weather or something?"

Great. A lightning storm would be a big help.

"I don't know," Jace said before Cathlyn could speak.

Hey! You agree with me? That's new.

Cathlyn locked eyes with Jace.

"I mean, what do you think, Cath?" Jace asked.

"No, you're right." Cathlyn crossed her arms over her chest. "We don't want our boat sinking, do we?"

"I didn't mean anything, I'm sorry," Jace said. "I—"

"Really?" Shey said. "We're making a plan to free those slaves and you and Miss Magic are having a spat?" She said something unintelligible and then grabbed Straeten to lower the sail.

Jace rose to follow Cathlyn but Allar caught his eye. He knew that look and backed off. Allar smiled and put his arm around his sister. Jace walked to the bow and gazed down the darkening river.

"There's things in the water," Evvy said, appearing by his side.

"Really? Like what?"

Evvy shrugged. "I don't know, I just know."

Jace ruffled her hair. "You stick close to Cathlyn, and don't leave the boat, all right? I mean it."

"But what if—"

"We've got this. You help her see things she can't."

"I want to help *you* though."

Jace sighed. "If you got hurt, kid…"

Evvy shrugged. "I helped you before. Remember?"

Yes, he did remember. Somehow, Evvy had broken into the barracks and gotten him out. "I just—"

Jace froze for a second, listening to the silence and instinctively ducked below the boat's rail, pulling Evvy down with him. "We're there," he said. Peering over the rail, he spied two large boats around a bend in the river. "This is it. Let's tell the others."

Night closed in. Up ahead Jace could still spy the two boats and their lamps painting light across the water. Straeten and Tare pulled back on the oars heavily as quietly as they could. Shey manned the tiller and kept her eyes straight ahead.

Evvy sat at the bow and peered at the water keeping an eye out for rocks like Shey had told her. They were going to be drifting as close to the banks as possible to stay under the cover of the overhanging trees.

As they approached the two boats, Jace sat close to Cathlyn. "I'm sorry about earlier," he whispered.

"I know you don't trust me. And I don't blame you. I don't trust myself."

"Cathlyn," Jace said. "I trust you with my life. I always have."

Cathlyn paused and Jace thought he saw her smile in the darkness. "It would've been a good storm."

Jace squeezed her shoulder then walked over to the grappling hooks. Burgis already stood there hefting the tool. "Okay," Jace said in a low voice. "I'm sending Valor."

The hawk leapt from the rail and with silent flapping circled up above the river. Jace's vision filled with Straeten's, Tare's and Ranelle's thoughts, and then briefly, Evvy, who quickly faded out.

Suffering, Jace thought. *Try again, kid. Come on.*

After a few seconds, her presence reappeared, but still only weakly.

It's tough to hold it, she thought.

You need some practice, that's all. Do your best.

All three boats appeared then in Jace's eyes. In this darkness, it was difficult to spot how many guards stood on deck, or even if they were all human.

I'm losing our boat, Straeten's voice echoed through the link.

Me, too, Jace said. It wasn't dark, but a thin yet growing fog enveloped the little craft. *That can't be normal, right?*

Jace glanced back at Cathlyn who stood holding out her hands. No. Not normal. She had her eyes tightly closed. He didn't dare talk to her and risk startling a storm out of her.

The fog grew so much that it covered their eyes. Before anyone could worry too much, Jace spoke. "Some of us can still see through Valor." Evvy stepped quickly to the back of the boat to Shey's side.

Closer now, their boat drifted to the slave boat on the right. *All right. I'm going to get on this boat first*, Jace said through the link. *I go in and scuttle it so it runs aground. Remember, the other boat hopefully won't see us and will come to help them.*

Jace, do you see that? Evvy asked.

Valor dove closer until Jace saw what Evvy noticed. Several Darrak on the other side of the boat were hauling up something from the river. Something large and wriggling.

Perfect, Straeten said. *That'll keep them busy over there while you go onboard.*

Are they going to kill it? Evvy's thoughts rang shrilly in Jace's ears.

Straeten and Tare pulled the oars back in as the boat drifted closer now through the fog right alongside the slave boat. "We're going faster than it," Straeten whispered. "Get it, now."

"Here goes." Jace spun the grappling hook in the air and released it, aiming at the rail of the other boat. With a clank, the hook latched on and the rope pulled itself taut. Without waiting to see if anyone heard the sound, Jace reeled in the rope through the rail. Their boat crept toward the bigger one while Shey kept the tiller angled so they wouldn't slam into it.

Jace removed his cloak and pack and grabbed onto the rope. He motioned to Straeten to come with him and he nodded in agreement. He pointed to the others and signaled for them to head to the other boat.

Cathlyn smiled at Jace, but the strain of holding the fog was visible on her face.

Jace clasped her hand and then quickly scaled the side of the boat and crouched on the deck behind a crate. Luckily, as Straeten had guessed, the crew gathered around their catch still flopping about in its suspended net.

"That thing is huge," Straeten whispered as he followed Jace, "and it has a lot of legs."

A few of the sailors hoisted the thing up over the side of the rail using a pulley. The Darrak cheered and drew their weapons. Memories of the trophy creature the Darrak had claimed back upon the mountain pass came to Jace's mind, but he couldn't save this one. Not now.

Straeten struggled with the grappling hook for a moment until he freed it from the boat. He leaned over to drop it to the others below in the fog. "Okay, now what?"

Jace surveyed the boat. Shey had described it to him before, but now he had to take it all in. *The people are being held in the center hold there. Shey said to get below deck, get this boat pointed to shore and take out the steering.*

Oh, that's it? Straeten asked. *Do you have any idea how to do that?*

I'm kind of winging it with you here. Just like old times.

I don't remember old times being like this.

Jace beckoned him to follow to the back of the boat. One set of steps led up to the guard steering the craft and another below. Down they went passing by the ropes of the steering mechanism.

You guys doing okay out there? Jace thought to the group.

So far, Ranelle answered.

Valor circled above the river slowly allowing Jace to see the two large boats and the bank of fog covering the other. *We're inside now.*

A flurry of thoughts crossed through the link then. *What's going on?* Jace asked.

Evvy's not on the boat, Tare said.

What? Where is she?

Don't know, Ranelle said. *We're almost at the other boat and we just noticed.*

Great. Jace ran his hands over the steering mechanism. *She must be up on deck with that creature. Suffering!*

"Hey, it's all right," Straeten said aloud. "Allar showed me some of his magic. That guy is good at figuring out how things work, and I'm starting to see what to do. Sort of." He held out his palm and the Fireflash he learned from Karanne shot out. "You head back up there. Go help out the kid."

Jace ran up the stairs two at a time until he reached the deck. The crew gathered around the netted creature, still suspended a couple feet in the air and wriggling like a bunch of eels. Unwillingly, Jace felt the creature's pain. Darrak began to prod the thing causing it to hiss and flail about. The Darrak laughed.

Jace brought his senses back to himself and caught a slight bit of movement up above in the rigging. Evvy. She clung to the ropes and mast leaning out over the netted creature.

Four Darrak. Three sailors. And how many below the boat? No time for it. Karanne would have plenty to say about not spending more time to observe.

Jace opened himself to his Soulkind and felt the flows enter. He stretched out with his calming magic, but it was too late. With a giant thud, the river creature landed on the deck, its ropes cut. Jace spied Evvy up above with a blade in her hands. The boat lurched toward the bank knocking two of the Darrak into each other. The sailors sidestepped and yelped as the netted creature lashed out with its paddle-like appendages.

"What's going on?" one sailor asked.

"Steering's gone!"

Jace glanced to the back of the boat to see the steersman frantically spinning the wheel.

"Signal the other boat!" a man hollered.

Another sailor raced across the deck to the main mast and set foot on the ladder there. A thundering boom and a brilliant flash of light appeared across the river, barely visible through the thickening fog.

Before the man could take a step, the boat lurched again and came to a crashing halt. The deck tilted backward, wedged upon something, possibly a rock or maybe even the shore.

"Come on." Straeten ran up the stairs and slapped Jace on the back. "If we can get those people out, they can make it to the shore now."

Jace nodded dumbly. Evvy waved to him with a sheepish smile and began to climb back around the rigging. Jace ran down the stairs and entered a long passage leading to the hold. He followed shouts and cries echoing through the dark boat. A Darrak stood in front of the caged prisoners.

A brilliant flash appeared in front of its face. It bent over clawing at its eyes. Time slowed down. Jace scanned the Darrak's body and *knew* things about it. The strength of its bite, how high it could leap, and something about its chest... Grabbing a wooden pole from the floor, Jace charged and drove a solid blow beneath its arm. The Darrak crumpled to the deck unable to shout out in its pain. Following up Jace's strike, Straeten knocked the Darrak out soundly with a blow to its skull.

"Nice hit," Straeten said appraising Jace's handiwork. "We ought to remember that for next time."

The cries of the prisoners escalated when they saw Jace. He held up his hand and called his calming magic. Instantly the others quieted beyond the metal door as a cool breeze drifted across the room. "We're getting out of here. Hold tight."

Jace glanced around for and spied a ring of keys hanging from a post. He grabbed them and with a click, the door unlocked and opened.

"Now what?" Straeten asked.

Jace closed his eyes and focused on Valor. His sight shifted and he took in the boat which had, indeed, run aground. Those on deck were either avoiding the whip-like strikes from the freed creature or heading to the back of the boat.

"There must be a way up front," Jace said. "We can still get them off quietly. Get them up above and I'll make sure whoever is left out there is distracted."

Another of Cathlyn's loud thunder claps sounded so close that some of the prisoners covered their ears and cried out.

"Come on!" Straeten yelled with a laugh, he pointed to a barrel with swords and bludgeons in it. "Take one." Those strong enough to heft a weapon took one and followed him.

"You're going to need supplies, too," Straeten said to the others. "It's a long way back home." Young men and women grabbed anything not bolted down in the hold.

"Anyone know a girl named Shey?" Jace asked as they passed by. Some shook their heads, but most didn't respond. Maybe on the other boat?

Jace stretched out his mind like he did back in Graebyrn's caves, first sensing Valor and then Ash. Then that strange creature on the deck still lashing about. What had Evvy said before? Something in the water? He pushed down into the water's depths with his Soulkind.

Cold surrounded him. Loss and anger filled him. Another one of those creatures—a sibling, a mate? Jace felt crashing against the hull and the boat rocking free of the sandbar. Jace cast images to its mind, images of Evvy freeing the netted one on board. A mix of relief and anger rose through the link.

Through the water, Jace saw a Darrak leaning over, stabbing the water with a spear hook The water creature lashed out with its tentacle, grabbing the Darrak's arm and dragging it under the water.

Jace let go of the creature's thoughts and switched back to Valor. *Almost clear?* No reply. Jace peered down from above and watched the prisoners scrambling off the edge of the boat onto the bank.

Yeah, Straeten's thoughts finally called. *The last of them is getting off now.*

Evvy?

Don't see her.

She didn't respond, either. Jace scanned the boat and spotted her on the deck now edging closer to the dark-skinned creature. It had slowed down its thrashing and its mouth gaped open continually.

Evvy, get out of there! Jace thought to her. Instead, she moved ever closer to the creature beckoning it to her.

One of the Darrak approached the trapped creature, its sword raised. Evvy jumped onto the Darrak's arm and broke the swing. The Darrak butted her with his head and flung her overboard.

The creature swung its tentacles around the Darrak's head and swung it over the rail. Still attached, the weight of the Darrak dragged the thing over the edge and into the water.

Jace ran to the front of the boat, climbed onto the deck, and peered into the river. "Evvy!" He stared into the dark water seeking out any movement. The back end of the boat erupted with fire further plunging the Darrak and sailors into chaos.

Jace returned his gaze to the cold water. Not a movement. Time to go in. He prepared to jump when something popped up, adrift on a log. Evvy? Jace let his mind follow that image and focused on the young girl. *Are you okay?* Evvy didn't answer, but before he could push further, Ranelle's voice filled his head.

Jace, Ranelle called. *We have a problem.*

He glanced once more in Evvy's direction and noticed she was not on a log, but something slimy and moving. But she was okay. He'd just have to trust his gut. A quick scan with Valor's sight showed the fog lifting from the river, exposing the *Gray Ghost* and the larger vessel on the other side. Cathlyn leaned over with her head in her hands. Allar stood at the tiller.

Where's Shey?

On that boat, Ranelle said. *And I'm pretty sure they know we're out here now.*

Arrows flew through the night air, some plunking in the water, others embedding into the wood of the smaller boat. "Get up there!" Ranelle jerked Allar away from the tiller and took his place while he ran to the front of the boat. He held up his shield arm, knocking arrows into the water.

The *Gray Ghost* lost some distance to the other ship as Ranelle settled in to steering. "Row!" Ranelle yelled. Burgis and Tare quickly pulled the oars back and forth. *Jace?*

The Darrak onboard the prisoner ship finally noticed Jace through the confusion and ran toward him.

Straet, they're coming for you, now, Jace thought through the link. With a deep breath, Jace jumped off the deck and in a flash of light his body instantly merged into Valor's flapping form. Vertigo gripped him as he adjusted to the bird's height and movement gliding across the water. With a keen cry, Valor dove toward the other boat. Jace felt his spirit lurch with the speed.

Jace bent Valor's wings ever so slightly and aimed for the front of the boat. When he got close enough, Valor began to pull out of the dive and Jace let go of the magic. He shot through the air flailing his arms in an attempt to slow his fall. With a crash, he hit the deck and slid to the other side, coming to a halt when he collided with a pile of netting. He patted himself down. Nothing broken. And all his clothes on.

But he had to work on that landing.

The crew of this other vessel stood at the back, raising their bows and spears against the smaller boat behind them. Twenty or so comprised the crew, some Darrak, others human. Too many to face alone. Were there, though? He had broken through the Call at the Darrak camp with worse odds.

After a deep breath, Jace grasped his Soulkind. The black metal claws around the green stone now felt smooth and a part of the whole, no longer like an intrusion. He let the magic flow into him and through him.

A calming breeze blew past him to the back of the ship. The yells and twangs of bows ceased and all eyes turned to Jace walking with his hand held up toward them. It was working. Both man and creature would listen.

"I don't know what you were promised," Jace began. "I don't know how you were threatened. But this ends tonight." No one moved.

The driving force of the Call reached for the Darrak and tugged at Jace like a whirlpool. It felt stronger now, like a current trying to drown him. Carefully he pushed that away with his mind and held up the silver metal rod with the Darrak markings on it.

"Crajit," Jace said and crossed his fingers.

The Darrak exchanged baffled glances.

They seemed to understand his use of 'peace' so he continued in the Darrak tongue. "You are free."

Jace sensed no anger or confusion in the Darrak, only relief. A metal sound creaked followed by a splash of water. Moments later the boat came to a halt. It had to be the anchor.

"You don't need to do this," Jace said to the Darrak.

"Who are you?" one of the Darrak asked.

"I'm here to help." Jace took a step toward them with his hand held up.

"Back off," a human voice called out. A tall man with a scar across his nose stood in between them and struck the Darrak with a whip. "I'm captain here." The Darrak cringed, but only glared at the man.

He looked familiar. Jace must have had dealings with him back in Beldan when he worked as a thief. His eyes didn't have the blue tint of Fay's touch, and that made him extra dangerous. Shey was right. He chose to do this to his own people. Four other crewmen took a few steps toward Jace. None of them with blue eyes.

"Why did you do this?" Jace asked. "Just for money?"

Another large splash drew everyone's attention to the front of the boat. Then another. The captain shoved past Jace to the rail and peered over.

"The shore boats!" he yelled. "The prisoners are leaving!"

Jace smiled as he saw the people rowing back up the river. They might struggle against the current but at least they were away for now. Nicely done, Shey.

The captain drew a long blade from his belt and faced Jace. "You're going to pay for this."

"No, he won't."

The man turned and faced Shey. She held a dagger in her hand.

"What are you doing here?" he asked.

"You took these people. I'm taking them back."

"I warned you at Landers, girl. You're not going to cost me everything again." The captain swung his blade at her. She tried to deflect it, but it struck her arm with a glancing blow. Shey cried out and jumped back clutching her bleeding arm. The man lunged. Shey lost her balance on some coiled ropes and fell on her back. He raised his sword again and she held up a hand.

Jace jumped on the man's back and knocked him over. The long knife clattered out of his reach upon the wooden deck. He stood up eyeing both it and Jace. Jace reached out with his magic to calm the animal rage in the man's eyes, but it did nothing.

"I'll kill you both," the man said through clenched teeth and leapt at Jace with a smaller metal blade glinting in his hand.

The captain's face contorted in pain and he unceremoniously dropped onto the deck. A dagger stuck out of his back and Shey stood over him, her hands shaking. The remaining human crew backed away and then disappeared below deck.

"See?" Shey said with a shaky voice. "It's what I do best."

Jace nodded his thanks to Shey, who silently removed her knife and knelt down to turn the captain over.

Jace reached for her blood-soaked arm. "You're hurt."

She pushed him away. "I'm fine." She ripped a piece of cloth from the dead man's tunic and tied it around her arm, warning Jace off with her eyes.

Jace turned to the Darrak, suddenly aware of them staring at him. "The Call will be back, but you must try to fight it."

The Darrak gathered around him. "I am Tark. And we await *your* call." The Darrak bowed slightly at the rod now back in Jace's hands. And with that, they leaped off the boat and swam across the river.

"I can't believe that's over," Jace said. "Thanks for that. You saved me." She didn't respond.

She killed a man, give her a minute.

Jace put his arm around her to help her up but she pushed him away again. "Hey, we have to go," Jace said. After a few long seconds she stood up.

Shey stumbled along in silence toward their small river boat now riding up alongside the one they were on.

"Did you find who you were looking for in there?" Jace asked.

"I… did. My father."

Jace put his hand on her arm and gestured to the two shore boats with the townsfolk on them. "Did you want to go with him?"

Shey pulled away from him and climbed down a ladder to the others. "He's dead."

Chapter 20

Karanne lifted her head only to see darkness. The sun had set some time ago but the night surrounding her seemed more complete than any she could think of. Her head ached. Her throat grated with dryness when she tried to swallow. How long had it been since she'd seen anybody? And where was she?

Her mind reeled with the madness filling her. She knew this darkness, she had experienced it before. But where? The Fireflash called to her and she held up her hand. The light spun out of her palm and floated, pulsing, in front of her face. Its dim light barely cut into the dark.

"You know, this reminds me of Marlec's fortress." The voice… was it Dral's voice? It was hard to tell as several other voices seemed to echo around the room.

Karanne called the Fireflash back into her palm and the symbols glowed when it returned. She opened her mouth to speak, but no words came out, only a cracking sound. It felt as if dust filled her mouth and throat.

"And now it is mine. Come, look."

Karanne realized she could see a path to a window now and walked to it. The Tower of Law. The view below reminded her again of the Shadow Vale for the courtyards teemed with the bodies of the Darrak.

"Guire and Fay had no real vision. Take over these people. Destroy that building. Wait for Myraton to attack us here. They would have failed if I had not intervened. They did do one thing right, it seems." Dral glanced to the north where the Darrak army lay encamped.

Karanne tried again to speak but only sputtered.

"Oh, I am sorry. Forgive me," Dral said.

A wisp of black smoke flew from her mouth and she drew a few deep relieved breaths. "Where are my friends? You said they'd be safe." The words ran out of her.

"Yes, they are. For now."

"Where?"

"Trust. You must learn to trust me. As I was saying, Guire and Fay had no vision without me."

Karanne clenched her fists. "How can I trust you?".

"Just give it some time." With each word spoken, several voices echoed ever so faintly. They itched at Karanne's mind and she shook her head to clear it.

"Who *are* you?" Karanne asked.

"That is a long story. You are probably wondering this since Marlec is no longer with us. Truly, we were sad to see him leave the Soulkind. But he was only one part, and we will not be so easily cast out."

"We?"

"Yes," the voices began. "When one of the first Masters of these gloves died, he refused to leave. And then the next, and so on. Wouldn't you like to learn of this immortality?" Dral reached his hand out to her.

This was madness, wasn't it? Karanne bit her tongue. She had to play along with these spirits, not anger them. They held her here alive for a reason.

"Your son," the voices began again slowly. "Where is he now?"

"Why do you want Jace?"

Dral smiled a crooked smile. "I like to keep all the loose ends near at hand. Now, where is he?"

Karanne's mouth started to open and she clamped it shut. Dral raised an eyebrow and her mouth opened again, the word forced out.

"Gone."

"Yes, but where? To Myraton? I know you sent some of your own there with the Soulkind."

Black wispy smoke solidified around her arms and embraced her in darkness. She felt the malice they contained, and the power to crush her. Her mind drifted, words formed without her control. "The river. He was heading to the river to save the people. And then..."

Karanne caught herself. Shey had told her of Jace's plan to go free the prisoners on the ships, but was there more? That boy was always going off on adventures, maybe there was something more to it.

"Aklareath," Dral said in a singular voice, all echoes ceased.

The gripping force around Karanne turned back into smoke. "What?"

"Not for you to concern yourself with."

140

Dral's presence in the darkness quickly faded. She had to get him back, to delay him.

"What do you want with me?"

The presence hesitated. "Fay spoke highly of you, and Guire ran from you. We've never seen a Soulkind like yours. I saw you on the bridge with the fallen bodies and I enjoyed what you did with them. You could say I'm interested."

Karanne paused. "Keep talking."

Dral smiled. "Somehow, yours is a new Soulkind. I do not know how this happened, but it did. Each Soulkind follows a path. Which have you chosen?"

"I haven't decided. What do you have to offer?"

The smoke lessened around her further. "An opportunity to join me. A very *rare* opportunity."

"And do what?" Karanne asked. "What do you want?"

"You have not been a Master long enough to know, I suppose. But even now you must feel the draw to the magic, no? The *need* for it?"

The spirits within her, the memories of those fallen warriors she absorbed. They pounded in her head now wanting freedom, but also her chest blazed with their power. Dral already knew the answer to his question.

"Together, we can grow in power. And don't you want to be on the winning side? This land is ripe with magic now, and for growing our Followers. If you join me, we can choose how magic will be used."

An image entered her head, like a dream but more real. Myraton. The castle by the sea standing tall above the white cliffs. The tall spires shooting hundreds of feet into the air. She and Dral sitting in high chairs in the throne room ruling over the bowing courtiers. Thousands of Followers parading in the streets below cheering for their leaders.

"So tell me, how do you feel about this?"

The dream faded and a feeling of powerlessness replaced it. She reached out for the dream with her eyes closed tightly, desperate to have it back. Dral smiled.

Karanne dug her fingernails into her palm. "I haven't decided yet. Show me more."

The room grew colder. "I believe you have," he said.

Black smoke crept around her shoulders and over her mouth. As it filled her lungs, she smiled bitterly. She had given Jace at least a few more moments.

Chapter 21

"You sure you're okay?" Jace asked Evvy, checking her over for injuries again.

"I told you last night, I'm fine." Evvy leaned over the edge of the boat and peered into the water.

"That was a pretty brave thing you did," Jace said. "I just can't believe that creature saved you." He ruffled her hair affectionately.

Evvy smiled but Jace thought she might not really be listening to him. Instead she just kept staring intensely at the water.

"Is Shey all right?" Straeten whispered. "She hasn't said a word to anybody. And I don't think she slept much last night."

Shey was sitting at the front of the boat next to Cathlyn. The two weren't speaking.

"She didn't want to go back with the others to Beldan, or wherever they're going," Jace said.

"Maybe she wants to see where the people were being sent," Straeten said. "I do."

Jace shrugged. "I guess so. Shey's dad, did you…collect him?" Jace asked.

Straeten nodded and showed Jace his still glowing palm. "Right after I got back to the big boat. I'm not even going to ask if she wants it."

Allar tossed Jace and Straeten some bread.

"Allar, you look terrible. Didn't you sleep?"

Allar shook his head. "I don't sleep much anymore." He pointed to the shield latched onto his arm.

"You're going to have to," Jace said. "We're going to need your help when we get to the coast."

"I know he needs sleep!" Allar slammed his fist into the side of the boat. Ash and Evvy both lifted their heads from their spots on the deck then rested them again. Burgis glanced up with a wary expression on his face.

Straeten gave a questioning look to Jace, and mouthed the word, "He?"

"Allar," Jace emphasized the name. "When you saved everyone on the boat with Newell's magic, was that you or him?"

"Who do you think?" Allar said. "Do you think I could do it all by myself?"

Jace frowned. "I just think you might work better together if you had control."

Allar's face turned red and he took a step toward Jace, the limp prominent in his gait. Straeten rose from his seat, but Jace held him off with a wave. A small breeze drifted past the boat and everyone visibly relaxed. Allar's expression softened and he turned to limp to the front of the boat behind Cathlyn. He hesitantly reached for her shoulder then pulled his hand back.

"He is a complete mess, isn't he?" Straeten asked.

Jace nodded. A shadowy form reverberated just outside of Allar's body. "Do you see that?" Jace pointed to Allar.

"What do you mean?" Straeten said.

"I can see something. Someone. It has to be Newell." The black form vibrated violently but Jace could make out a person's head and body.

"What, you see ghosts?" Straeten whispered.

Jace nodded. "I think so. I've seen Marathas, Marlec, even Guire and Fay. Something to do with my Soulkind."

"What does it look like?"

"It's a shadow, but there's something wrong with it. It's shaking, struggling. I think Newell is getting worse the longer he stays around. Remember what Karanne said happened to him when we split up in Varkran?"

Straeten made a 'crazy' gesture to Jace.

"Yeah, that's one way to put it," Burgis said. "I was there. Nearly killed me."

Jace nodded. "And if he's getting worse, he might not be able to stop next time. I'm going to go talk to him."

"And do what? Ask him to leave?" Burgis asked.

"Not a terrible idea," Jace said.

"You sure?" Straeten took the tiller from Jace. "I mean, we're on a boat here in the middle of a river."

"I'll be careful," Jace patted Straeten on the shoulder. "Here goes." He walked slowly to the front with a smile on his face and sat next to Allar.

"What now?" Allar asked through gritted teeth.

144

Jace pulled out his Soulkind and placed it on his knee. A calming breeze drifted across the river and lifted Cathlyn's brown hair gently. She turned her head and smiled at him. Allar's shoulders relaxed slightly and the shadow coming from his body slowed its shaking.

"You've been with us for a long time." Jace tensed briefly but Allar didn't move, so he continued. "You've helped us, and taught Allar, too."

"It is difficult to, hold on, sometimes." Allar clenched his fist.

"I can't imagine. But," and Jace paused. "Your companions, the other Masters, they all let go of their Soulkinds and passed on."

The spirit shadow drifted a few feet away from Allar and then froze. The features of a young but proud man with his eyes shut. Newell.

"Why do you still hang on? We can do this without you. If you just trust us."

His ghostly eyes flashed opened and a wave of anger spread across his face. The shadow slammed back into Allar and those same dark eyes opened on Allar's face. "Stay away from me." Allar walked off to the back of the boat. Cathlyn gave Jace a sympathetic smile and then followed her brother.

The sun rose over the river in distance to the east, blinding Jace. Sighing, he placed his Soulkind into his memory stone pouch. In the relative peace of the morning, he took some time to brush past some of his old memories, particularly of Turic and Karanne. Something disturbed him when he thought of them. Karanne's memory on NorBridge with him was the same as it always had been, yet there was something looming over it all. Same with Turic's. What was it?

He sighed again and put the stones away.

Shey shifted in front of him.

"You doing all right?" Jace asked.

"Look at you, trying to help everybody?" She didn't turn around.

"I'm sorry. I don't know what to say."

Shey looked back at him with red eyes. "How about, *Sorry you killed your father.* Or even, *He must have been pure evil for you to do such a thing.*' She turned back to the river in front of them.

Jace fidgeted with one of his knives. "I'm sorry, I guess."

Shey sat quietly for a minute. "Karanne said you had some magic around memories, right? Can you, get rid of them? Take them from someone?"

"No." He laughed. "That's not how it works."

"That's not how *what* works?"

Jace shrugged. "You know, this magic thing."

She stiffened. "Well, thanks for trying."

"Hey. I would if I could."

"Aren't you a *Master*?" Shey poked him right in his chest.

"Ow," Jace said. "What was that for?"

"That was for me thinking you were something more." Shey turned away. "It was a stupid idea anyway."

"No, it's a good idea, it's just, well, not something I can do." Was it?

He placed his hand on her shoulder. "I'm sorry."

She shrugged away. "Don't bother. Sorries never help anyone."

Jace followed her gaze out to the river. It was true. He was a Master. Wasn't it at least possible he could create this? He'd made much worse. But how to even start?

The green stone Soulkind appeared in his palm. He rubbed his thumb over the smooth lines and the lingering black marks still attached to it.

He stood up and glanced around the deck.

"What are you looking for?" Shey asked.

"I don't know, I've never done this before."

Jace suddenly noticed Cathlyn staring at him. She mouthed a word.

"*Rock?*" Jace asked. Cathlyn nodded.

Jace's heart raced as he reached for his memory stones. "You're right. Something to put the memory in."

"What, like this?" Shey reached down and picked up an ordinary gray rock from beneath one of the boat benches.

"Sure." Jace took it from her. He stared into his green stone. Back in Graebyrn's cave, he could see the magic flowing into his Soulkind. He could bend the streams. But not out here. How was he supposed to make something new with his magic if he couldn't see anything?

"You don't have any idea what you're doing, do you?" Shey asked.

"I'm also not sure erasing a memory is a good idea."

"Got it. Whatever doesn't kill me, right?"

"All right, all right. I'll try." Jace sat down and focused on his Soulkind. His thoughts passed by the many marks on his body thinking of the flows of magic they contained.

The sound of water flowing trickled in the back of his thoughts. Not from the river, but here, all around him. He pressed the gray stone, sharp and jagged, into his palm.

"Try to think those thoughts now. The ones you want to forget."

"Okay." Shey let out a deep breath.

Jace called on his magic and felt the familiar power push on his mind. He thought about taking Shey's memory, the one from last night. *Take the memory, and place it into the stone.* He repeated these thoughts over and over again.

Nothing. Jace sat for several minutes then moved next to Shey. He placed the stone on her head. He touched her forehead with his other hand, then placed the stone in her hand.

"That's weird." Evvy tapped Jace on his shoulder and looked at him funny. "You okay?"

"Not now, kid. I need some quiet for this. Sorry."

Evvy backed away to the others in the boat, all watching Jace now. He smiled weakly and waved.

Jace stretched out to the magic again and listened for Shey's thoughts to capture into the stone. Every wave that lifted the boat slightly jarred him. Every word someone spoke behind him. He just couldn't hold his concentration.

He couldn't—

Wait, what was that? An image of the big ship last night appeared in his mind. Then it flashed to Shey's father. Then back to the present. The small boat dipped suddenly and caused all of the images to run from Jace's head. He cursed.

"It's still there." Shey stood.

"I know," Jace said. "I think I'm getting it, though. Want to try again?"

"Maybe later." Shey walked to the back of the boat and took the tiller from Burgis.

Jace flipped the gray stone in the air and placed it into a pocket. He scanned his arms for any sign of a new mark, but only noticed a faint outline. Probably only dirt. He'd try later, maybe when there were fewer distractions.

Cathlyn sat down beside him and placed her hand on his forearm. The warmth from her touch filled him up and he smiled up at her. She had brushed through her tangled hair finally and it shone in the morning sun. Her smile put him at a loss for words and his heart beat faster.

Speaking of distractions…

"Oh go away," Jace muttered.

Cathlyn lifted her hand from him. "What?"

Jace's face burned bright red. "No, I meant, I mean…."

Smooth.

Jace grabbed her hand as she stood up and gently pulled her back down beside him. "I'm sorry, it's, *him*." He pointed to his head. "Are you feeling better? How is Allar?"

"I saw what happened."

"What do you mean?"

"I can see magic as it is being formed," Cathlyn traced a pattern in the air with her finger. "Whatever you are doing with Shey's memory, I don't think it's a good idea."

"I was only doing what she wanted."

"Memories are what make us who we are. Even if terrible things happen, who we are and what we'll become are because of them."

"Don't you have some things you just wish you could forget?" Jace asked.

Cathlyn sat quietly for a moment. "I guess."

"Well, I know I do, and even though they didn't involve me killing my father, I'd just as soon get rid of them." Jace rubbed the dark mark on his arm.

"You're saying you want to forget about Blue?" Cathlyn asked, pointing to his movement.

Jace stood up. "Don't make this about me."

"I'm not, I just want you to—"

"Look, we don't have a lot of time to figure out what to do about Graebyrn's message. Can we just focus on that?" Jace fished the stone Cathlyn had brought to him out of his pouch and spun it in his hand. "We're getting closer to where he wanted us to go, and any information would be helpful."

Cathlyn placed her hand on Jace's arm. "I'm sorry. Blue was special to us all. I didn't mean to make you feel guilty." Jace sat down.

Cathlyn said, "When you looked into the stone before, you said the name, *Aklareath*. What does that mean?"

Jace shrugged. "I think it's a place. In my vision I saw ruined towers on the sea cliffs."

"What do they want with it? And why send all those townspeople there?"

"Whatever it is it must be important," Jace said. "Maybe there's a relic or some sort of weapon down there."

He unrolled a map of the countryside and studied the river. A few days traveling and they'd be at the ocean, but before that lay several small villages and branches in the river leading north and south.

"Where was the ship going?" Jace asked. "Myraton wouldn't let a prisoner ship from Beldan pass on through, would it? Any ships that came before must have to veer off well before that. Or drop off passengers to march the rest of the way. But how far away?"

Jace rolled up the map and shoved it into its case. Out of all of them on this boat, only one might know something. "Do you think Newell might be familiar with this place?"

Cathlyn stood up and waved him off. "I don't think he's in any mood to talk to you right now."

Can't win everything, can you?

Not today, apparently.

"But maybe I can ask him." Cathlyn leaned over and kissed Jace's head.

And with that, all else left his mind.

"No!"

Jace woke to someone screaming. Was it Shey? Straeten sat at the tiller, waving and pointing to the front of the boat. Jace shuffled in the darkness to where she lay whimpering in her sleep. Should he wake her?

She turned back and forth muttering indecipherably. He rested his hand on her forehead. Her breathing evened. He looked down at the stone that suddenly appeared in his hand *Memories make us what we are.* Who was he to take away a part of her? *Blue…* He closed his eyes and felt the familiar pain in his chest. And Shey's pain was even more haunting. How could he let her live with it if there was anything he could do to help?

He drew in a deep breath and let it out slowly. The faint marking he'd thought was dirt glowed with a weak light as he turned the stone over in his hand. Much like he'd done with Sephintal back in the mountains, he attempted to peer into Shey's head.

Images like passing dreams flashed across his eyes, too light to grasp, too fleeting to remember. He plucked streams of magic from both the calming and sight spells and directed them toward the new mark on his arm. Its glowing pulsed slightly.

Shey's breathing slowed and steadied as from a deep slumber. The images went by more slowly now, and were easier for him to follow, like a child's play toy spinning round and round.

Focus.

Jace's heart beat evenly as he drew in a deep breath. Since he was in her memories, he sought out visions of himself drifting through her consciousness. The first one he came upon was Tarolay at the locks being freed and running away. The memory felt malleable in his mind, somehow.

When he grasped it, it bounced about like one of the thin paper balloons he had seen drifting in the market. The memory felt attached by a few strings, but as if he could pluck it out. Another memory illuminated inside Shey's thoughts, this time of leading Karanne through Beldan to help Jace find Straeten. Again, this one felt held down by only a few strands.

And then, like a wave crashing, the memory of striking down her father with a knife appeared. Not a floating leaf like the others, but a tethered bull.

Jace centered his thoughts, but couldn't see around the scope of it. The memory was tied to her mind in many spots, and not all from this location. How was he going to get all of that out?

Memories are what help make us who we are. Cathlyn's words echoed again in his mind.

It's Shey's choice, though, isn't it?

Not if I'm the one making the magic, Jace shot back at Jervis.

Cathlyn was right. Taking people's memories was far from the "right thing" to do. But he couldn't leave her with this. He would hold on to the memory and give it back if she wanted it.

But how would she know when that was if she didn't know *what* it was?

He gripped the stone tightly. Deliberating the morality of this decision in the middle of someone's brain was hardly a good idea. Time to make a choice. He tightened his grip, feeling every point and jagged edge.

He tried to cover the entire image in a bubble and began tugging it out into the stone. The little rock bit painfully into his hand.

Instead of drifting along like a feather in the wind, the image raged about like a wild animal. Luckily, he knew how to deal with wild animals.

Calm. That's it. He kept loosening the grip the image had over Shey, like plucking out every bit of root from a weed. When he was down to only a few more connections, the memory jumped free and Shey convulsed.

For a second, he wondered what would happen if he let it go. He knew he could do it, knew it would be gone forever. But he kept it in his grasp.

From there his thoughts moved it to the stone. He felt a warm glow. It was done.

For a second longer, he kept his hand on Shey's forehead and listened as she slept peacefully. As he lifted away, Shey's warm hand touched his forearm and stayed there holding him gently.

"What are you doing?"

Jace pulled back but she held on. "You were having a nightmare, and I—"

Shey's hand slid behind his neck and drew him down toward her. Before he knew what was happening, the warmth of her kiss pressed into his lips.

Whoa. And to think I wanted out of your head. Forget it now.

Jace stood up.

"What's the matter?" Shey asked.

Jace stepped back, tripped over a coil of rope, and landed on his backside on the deck. "Just, I didn't mean—" He scrambled to his feet.

"I won't tell, see? They're all asleep."

"But…but…"

"I didn't see anything," Straeten said loudly.

Luckily it was dark, for Jace's felt his face grow completely red. He gripped the rail of the boat not knowing which way to turn.

"Never seen you trip over yourself like that." Shey yawned widely. "Oh well, if that's all for tonight." She turned over and away from Jace, waving lightly.

Jace stared at her lying motionlessly.

"That seemed to go well," Straeten said.

Jace started. "Yeah, I'm pretty sure I got the memory out of her." He pushed Straeten aside and took over the tiller.

"Not what I meant, but okay. Good for that."

Jace punched Straeten in the arm. "Come on. I have her memory, you know, the one of her killing her father? That's pretty serious."

"Yeah, good luck keeping it from her," Straeten said. "You're sure it's all gone, right? I can't imagine you got everything out of her head."

Jace sat in silence for a minute running his fingers over the new mark on his arm. "Maybe it wasn't the right thing to do."

"You do have a way of skating that line." Straeten yawned.

Jace glanced over the sleeping forms of his other friends and a pit grew in his stomach. "I have an idea, or actually Jervis had one."

"That guy is still in there?" Straeten said. "What did he say this time?"

"Something about helping me get him out of my head."

Straeten yawned again. "Sounds like a good idea. Then you could use it on Guire and Fay."

"Wait a minute, what did you say?" Jace sat up straight.

"Yeah, you know? They're spirits stuck here like Jervis. You learn that type of magic and it'd be over for them."

Jace turned the thought over in his head. "That's actually a good idea, I really think that could work. We should have more talks like this when you're half asleep. Jervis?" Jace paused. "Jervis?"

"You know, I never liked him around when he was alive," Straeten said. "I'm going to bed now. Do you mind erasing the memory of this conversation, so I can pretend I got more sleep?"

Jace shook his head and smiled. "Who was going to relieve you?"

"Cathlyn, I think? Doesn't seem like she's back to normal yet. Not sure she should be steering this thing."

"I'll take over. Let her get some sleep."

Jace took the tiller and watched Straeten find a spot in the boat to lie down. He waited several more minutes until he heard only the river sounds in the background.

"Jervis. You there?"

And now the incessant frogs and Ash snoring.

"I don't get it. When you were alive, you wanted nothing to do with me, and now you want to stay?"

I had my chance to leave. When Karanne passed me on to you, I felt it. I could have just… gone.

"Why didn't you?"

Hah! You know I like messing with you too much to leave.

"Aren't you worried you might end up going crazy? Like Newell, or Guire and Fay? You don't want to end up like that."

I'm not that different from them. I took their magic and liked it. Made me feel good. You know what's going to happen to me when I leave? I'm going to a dark place, that's what. I've done nothing right my whole life.

So that was it.

"Straeten said something earlier..."

I heard.

"Whoa. Sometimes I forget you're there. That's messed up. Anyway, let me finish. Help me. Help all of us."

Save my soul? Oh, good idea. I'm already dead. Nothing worth saving here.

"But you're not gone yet. Come on. Don't be an idiot."

The sound of the river filled Jace's ears for a minute.

You promise to kiss Shey again if I help?

Jace laughed. "If you felt this way about her, how come you never said anything when you…"

Were alive? Look I know I'm dead. You don't have to tiptoe around that anymore. Anyway, who says I didn't tell her?

"Because we both know Shey and that wouldn't have gone well for anybody."

This time Jervis laughed. *All right. You try to get me out of your head if you think it will help.*

"It will." Jace scratched his head. "And thanks."

Chapter 22

"Thanks, sailor," Shey said as the sun rose. "I'll take it from here."

Jace smiled awkwardly. "Sure. Kept it warm for you." He winced.

"Okay," Shey said slowly.

How much do you think she remembers? Maybe it was all a dream to her?

"Let's hope so," Jace said under his breath. He walked away with a farewell wave.

"Morning." Straeten lowered his voice as he handed Jace a mug of water and some bread and dried meat. "I told everyone about what you did. They won't say a thing." He winked at Jace.

"Wait, what did you tell them?"

Straeten's eyes widened and he laughed. "No, no. Not about that. About the memory. I didn't tell *everyone* about that other thing."

Tare raised his chin to Jace and smiled.

"I figured he can't say anything," Straeten said. "Not out loud anyway."

Cathlyn abruptly sat down on a water barrel next to Straeten. Jace jumped.

"Hey, what's the plan for today?" Cathlyn asked. "You had a busy night, huh?"

Jace's face heated up.

"I came to relieve you, remember?"

Jace nodded slowly and wiped sweat from his forehead. Had she seen something after all?

"You told me to just go back to sleep," she said. "Thanks. I needed that."

Jace let out a breath. "Well, you've been through a lot."

Jervis chuckled in his head. *Looks like you're safe this time around.*

"I also saw what you were working on," Cathlyn said. "With your magic. It looks good."

"I'm going to try to use it on, with, uh…" Jace pointed to his head.

"The virus?" Cathlyn said. "I'm sorry you're stuck with him in there."

"It's not that bad," Jace said. Hard to believe the words came out of his mouth.

Straeten snorted. "Really? We're talking about the backstabbing maniac, right?"

Jace forced a smile. "Anyway, I think we're getting really close to where the people were being shipped. We might even be there today."

"Don't change the subject. What are you going to do about him?" Cathlyn pointed to Jace's head. "I might be able to help."

"You can follow what I did?"

Cathlyn nodded, looking at the black angular marks on his arm. "Most of it. I think if you can just keep him still, you can pull him out of there. Want to try?"

Jace gaped at her for a moment. "Yeah," he said. "Of course I do." *Jervis?* No response. Jace concentrated on searching for him, but his mind was surprisingly empty. He still sensed something like a tick embedded way down in. "Hey, Jervis? You in there?"

Again, no response.

"Did you already get him to leave?" Straeten asked.

Jace shook his head. "I would have known. I don't think he's ready to go yet."

Straeten laughed. "Don't think he's ever going to be ready. He's having too much fun messing with you. Just get him out of there."

"Not yet," Jace said. "I want to practice more, you know. Get it right." The mark on his arm was more solid than yesterday, but not completely filled in. The magic didn't feel totally connected to him yet.

"Don't get too attached," Straeten said. "Remember, he pretty much sold us all to death, just so he could learn a few magic tricks."

"Hey take it easy on him," Jace said. "What happened to him could happen to anybody, right?"

Straeten grimaced. "You made your point. But this is *Jervis*. I don't want him getting his hooks in you." Straeten stood and walked to the tiller next to Shey.

Jace watched the countryside as they passed. Straet was right, this was the same Jervis he grew up with in the Guild, it was hard to forget all of that. And yet he'd come a long way since then.

The mountains and the tall trees gave way to flatter plains and rounder vegetation as they approached the coastline. Evvy came to sit by him and stared into the dark and muddy river.

"Is your friend still following us?" Jace asked.

She smiled widely at Jace and nodded. "Toola."

"Toola, huh?"

"She's a river queen."

Jace patted Evvy on her back. "I bet she is."

"Yeah, remind me to never go for a swim again." Straeten looked at the river over Jace's shoulder.

"No, dummy," Evvy said. "She wouldn't eat you."

"Yeah, dummy." Jace shook his head at Straeten.

He could feel Valor and Ash's presence and even Payt's way in the distance. As the wind blew Evvy's hair, the mark on the back of her neck shone like a badge of honor. A small black diamond, with... What was it? Looked like a loose coil like a tentacle. That was something different.

"Straeten, let me see something." Jace turned Straeten around and lifted up his shoulder-length hair at his neck. There was the same initial mark Evvy had, with the black diamond at the center. Straeten didn't have the squiggle like hers but instead showed other black markings. An animal's paw and a curved set of talons. Those had to be Ash and Valor.

"What do you see?" Straeten asked.

"Remember when Graebyrn first looked at my mark? He said it had dragon wings on it. Yours is made of Ash's and Valor's marks. Take a look at mine, will you?"

Jace lifted up his hair and both Straeten and Evvy looked.

"Whoa," both Straeten and Evvy exclaimed.

"What?"

"It's grown." Straeten rubbed his own mark and walked to the back of the boat.

Evvy's eyes bulged. "It's branched out across your neck and onto your back. All black lines making wings, claws, and this spikey thing. Looks like a horse's head on there, too. Some are bigger than others and have more lines on them." A wide grin spread over her face and she twisted her neck to try to look at her back.

Above her head in the distance, a thin drift of black smoke grew from the tree line. "Come on Evvy." Jace pointed ahead to the smoke. "Practice with me and Valor."

156

Evvy quickly nodded. Jace set his sight into Valor's and the hawk leapt from the mast to circle up into the heights. *Let's check that out,* Jace thought to the bird.

"Wait for me," a distant voice called. Slowly Evvy's presence appeared next to Jace there inside of Valor's eyes.

"Nicely done." Somehow, Jace felt Evvy smile with pride. Then something new appeared.

"What is that?" Evvy asked.

A wide expanse of dark blue spread across the horizon through a bank of clouds. "That's got to be the ocean."

Both he and Evvy watched silently for a minute until the clouds covered the distant water again. He heard her laughing through the link. "That is amazing."

He agreed with her in silence.

"How do you actually turn into Valor?" Evvy asked after Valor wheeled about the sky.

"That one takes a while, and you have to be pretty close to the animal, I think. Close like I am with Valor. Payt won't let me do that yet. He barely lets me see through his eyes."

"And Ash?"

Jace laughed. "Never tried. I'll show you how to do it when we have more time. Maybe you could turn into Toola."

"Really?" Evvy giggled.

Valor spun around and faced the river ahead. Plumes of what looked like smoke arose from a small village built right on the river. Several docks stretched into the water. All the boats were still moored there.

"What happened there?" Evvy said.

Jace didn't respond. He followed Valor's eyes to scour the banks. No one. He urged the hawk to fly closer to see through the trees. "Do you see anything?"

"Just smoke and… what are those?"

Black shapes blurred between the trees. Branches shook and leaves scattered. "Darrak."

Evvy dropped out of the connection quickly but after a few seconds returned.

"You all right?" Jace asked.

"Yeah. But they scare me."

"I know. They scare me too. Some of them. I think we'll be safe out here in the boat—"

Valor wheeled about and scanned the western horizon. Several more plumes of smoke rose in the distance along the river behind them, all at the same time. "Okay, maybe not. Come on. Come back now, Evvy."

Jace steadied himself on the boat after leaving Valor's sight so quickly. Evvy wrapped her arms around Jace's waist and he patted her back. Soon everyone looked up at the skies noticing the smoke all around them.

"Why is it happening?" Evvy asked.

"The Darrak are setting fire to the woods," Jace said. "They're all doing it at once."

"They were waiting for us?" Straeten asked. "How would they know we're here? Maybe it's just a rogue group of Darrak, planning to invade Myraton."

Jace shrugged. "I can't tell." An itching feeling made him think the target of their attack was much closer. "I think the Call is involved, but I don't know why it's suddenly so strong." Could Straeten be right about the Darrak knowing they were here? How could they? The Darrak at the ship didn't know where they were going, and even if they had told others to come, they wouldn't have arrived so quickly.

"We have to leave the river." Allar stood and started stuffing supplies into his pack. "They'll be able to spot us, if they haven't already."

"How can the Call be so strong?" Cathlyn said. "Dorne is locked up in Beldan."

"Is he?" A pit grew in Jace's stomach. "They know we're coming, somehow." If it was Dorne, this could have been avoided if Jace hadn't been so selfish about keeping his Soulkind intact.

What do you mean?

"Never mind," Jace muttered to Jervis. "We're close to the ocean. Evvy and I saw it."

"And Toola is slowing down, too. I don't think she likes the water here."

"Well, we're getting off the river now." Shey steered the *Gray Ghost* to the sandy river bank. It slid several feet onto it. "Pull this thing out of here and try to hide it. We might need it later."

Straeten and Tare were the first to jump out and grab a line. In a few short tugs, the boat easily rode up onto shore tilting only slightly in the process. They busied themselves for several minutes pulling the boat under the trees. Evvy and Shey smoothed out the boat's tracks in the sand using branches.

"Look." Straeten pointed north. In the distance, the high castle towers of Myraton shone upon the cliffs next to the sea.

"No time for that now," Jace said, gawking a bit at the towers himself. "They'll be on the banks of the river looking for us."

"Think Stroud made it there?" Straeten asked.

Allar paused in his packing.

"We should know soon enough," Jace said. "He was bringing the rest of the Soulkind with him. He'll tell the king to prepare his army."

"Enough to match the Darrak?" Allar asked.

"We better hope so," Straeten said.

Allar bent over to pack again. "Back when Stroud asked me to go with him, I told him I needed to help my sister. Now that she's with you, it's my duty to join up with the Guardians again."

"But we still need your help," Jace said. "At least until we find out what's going on in Aklareath, and what happened to the rest of the people who were shipped here."

"But if these Darrak are going to attack the castle, I'll be needed there with the rest of the Guardians."

Cathlyn walked by and placed her hand on Allar's shoulder. "After we find our people, I think I can get you there all in one piece with my magic, okay?"

Allar nodded.

Those 'Guardians'? Some good they did.

"Maybe Allar can help them now that he has magic," Jace said quietly.

If he ever loses that crazy guy, right?

"Right. Sounds familiar." Jace shoved the final bit of food into his pack and threw it over his shoulder. "Let's go."

"Bye, Toola." Evvy waved to the river. Jace caught a glimpse of dark ripples along the water's surface.

Ash darted all about leading the group into the woods, sniffing the ground and bushes vigorously. Must've been a relief to be off the boat. Connecting to the dog's senses, Jace became aware of a salty tang in the air.

Valor kept to the skies. Jace held his sight in the back of his own almost continuously. Jace's other Followers stretched out with their own magic, now, as he had taught them. He sensed other creatures among the trees and their awareness, like tickling thoughts in the back of his mind.

"Animals surround us," Jace said. "Use their eyes if they let you."

Ranelle saluted Jace and the others followed. Jace smiled. He hadn't seen that in a while.

High winds gusted against Valor and he adjusted to stay facing east. Jace's mind reeled at the sight that opened up before him. The clouds parted and the vast blue horizon spanned out in both directions curving slightly at each end.

"Straeten, are you seeing this?"

"Uh huh."

Massive cliffs lined the coast with the great walled kingdom of Myraton sitting atop the highest. Ships with triple masts sailed into the great bay next to the city.

The city. His home.

Not that he knew it. Only what he got from Karanne's memories. Was his father still alive? Had he survived the fire? Had he sought Jace out after everything, or had he given up when the house burnt down?

That's where you're from? Evvy thought through the link.

Jace shook his head. "Didn't know I was sending that. We better focus on what's in front of us. We've got that big hill to climb."

Valor flew back above Jace and showed a fresh trail carving through the woods further east, heading up into the massive hills near the coast.

"I think the Darrak were taking the prisoners there." Jace pointed to the path.

"See anyone on it?" Allar asked.

Jace shook his head. "Too many trees. We're going to have to break trail beside the path to keep us far enough away, just in case. Burgis, Tare, you help make sure I'm not going to drop us off a cliff or something."

Jace opened his senses to the new woodland area. Valor's sight and Ash's sense of smell were the strongest, but he felt the other creatures around him, as well, some lending their own senses to further fill his mind. The earth never felt so alive.

Colossal white stones littered the climb, some jutting from the ground, others forming piles at the bottom of the hill from some fall.

Jace placed his hand on their precisely cut surfaces seeking some vision they might offer. Following his lead, Evvy also touched the boulders. The stones revealed nothing, at least nothing recent. Faint whispers of the distant past brushed near his thoughts.

Burgis, Tare and Ranelle strung their bows, arrows ready. "So we go in, free the people, and get out, right?" Burgis asked.

"I'm not going to lie. There's probably going to be some big resistance waiting for us. I can feel the Call everywhere." Jace slashed some undergrowth with a long knife.

"Nothing will stop us." Allar rubbed his hand along the shield on his arm.

Burgis glanced at Tare. *This sounds familiar,* Tare thought through the connection with Valor.

From before? When he attacked Burgis? Jace asked.

Jace felt Tare's agreement.

Jace paused in his hike up the steepening hill. Allar approached and the dark shade of Newell's form flickered around his body. The flickering calmed when he reached Jace.

"I'm going to try to reach out to the Darrak when we get there. See if we can bargain with them," Jace said.

"That's crazy, and you know it," Allar said. "They're going to try to kill us. You said you could feel it, right? And what about the last time you tried this? That didn't go so well."

"Yes, but I have to keep trying."

"You don't know how many there are. If there are people with them who came on the boats. People like Shey's father. You don't know anything!" The shadow wavered outside of Allar's body.

Jace took a deep breath and focused. "That's why we need your help. To get a layout of this place. Find out what we're up against."

Gradually, the shadow completely disappeared inside Allar. "I'll see what I can do. Newell is pretty good at figuring out how things are made. Maybe there is some weakness, some entrance that no one noticed yet."

"Good. You do that." Jace looked up to see Tare point his nocked arrow away from Allar, but he didn't stop staring at him.

"We're getting close," Cathlyn said. "I can feel it."

"Me, too." The magic felt stronger here, much like it had in Graebyrn's cave. Even more so. More potent. Jace touched the stone Cathlyn had given him to see the vision again.

The dragon hadn't sent him here to save the people of Beldan. Of course, he'd free them, but something else was going on. Something Jace was sent to find.

"We're getting near the top," Jace said. "We'll be able to see everything once we get there."

"These are definitely ruins." Allar pointed to the carved stones jutting from the ground. "Some sort of temple."

"But a temple to what?" Straeten said.

They reached a clearing and swung around the south side of the ruins. Several flat stretches broke out along the length of the hill like massive steps all the way to the ocean.

Jace looked beyond the stretches and caught his breath. Blue sky greeted them and the sun sparkled off the surface of the water a thousand feet below them. Waves crashed upon the rocks and sprayed into the air. The great spired kingdom of Myraton lay many miles to the north.

Jace turned to see everyone staring out at the sea for the first time.

"All right. We're not here to admire the sights," Shey said after a minute, still gaping a bit herself. "Can your bird see anything down there?"

Valor wheeled above the peak of the ruins, crying out in the salty air. Ocean birds, gulls he thought they were called, covered one of the stony flats. Their strange calls echoed up the hilltop. A dark fissure in the ruins opened up a hundred or so feet below.

Fly closer, Jace urged Valor.

The hawk dove toward the path that led up from the river and to the opening. The constant breeze twisted him about in his flight and Jace had to briefly close off from the sight to avoid nausea.

"I see crates, wagons," Jace said aloud once he connected again.

"Any Darrak?" Allar asked.

"I don't see anyone, yet." Valor dove further now threading through the branches.

Without warning, a net shot through the air, wrapping Valor and pinning his wings to his side. He crashed through the trees with a terrified shriek.

"No!" Evvy cried out. Ash whined.

In the brief moments of flailing, Jace saw a Darrak and felt Valor being shoved into a crate. Then darkness covered his vision.

"Is he okay?" Ranelle said.

Jace nodded numbly. "I'm having a hard time connecting with him, now. He's... he's in a cage with other animals."

"Do they know we're here?" Allar asked.

"I can't tell, but I don't think so."

"Then we go on as planned," Allar said.

"Should we go get him?" Evvy asked with a soft voice.

"No," Allar said. "There's no time for that."

Jace put his shaking hand on Evvy's back. "We'll get him." Ash started to run down the hill. "No, Ash! Not now." Ash whined softly but listened. "Hold on, Valor." Jace tried to push that thought to wherever his companion was trapped.

Allar scanned the hillside and the plants that overgrew the surface. "You were right, Jace. He has been here before. A long time ago. At least, he knows how it was built."

"What is this place?" Jace squinted his eyes but failed to see anything down the hill. No movement toward them. He tried to connect with Valor again, but sensed only more darkness.

"I'm not sure," Allar said. "But he remembers a few of the entrances. Come on."

Allar ran along the length of the ruins to a jutting stone structure. He waved for everyone to follow him. "We've got to open this. It's blocking a way in."

Straeten and Tare leaned into the white stone, embedded with shells. Allar lifted a bleached tree branch and wedged it under the stone. "Give me a hand."

Straeten added his grip to the lever and leaned into it. The massive rock shifted slightly, allowing the lever to slide under even further. With a few more shoves, they lifted the entire rock away exposing a narrow opening.

Jace went in first. "I'll go check this out. Figure out what's going on."

"And the rest of us stay out here?" Straeten said. "I don't think so."

Jace sighed as Straeten pushed him into the ruins. "Just don't make a sound."

"What?" Straeten said loudly with a smile, then held up a finger to his lips. "You're going to need a light in there." He cast the Fireflash, filling the darkened tunnel with spinning light.

Jace proceeded with Ash right at his heels. He had to turn sideways to walk through the passage. Straeten and Tare had a much

163

tougher time, needing the others to gently push them through narrow sections.

"Maybe, we should have stayed outside," Straeten said sucking in his gut.

Jace smiled but didn't say anything. The passageway went on into the darkness for several hundred feet without any change. The sound of striking metal reverberated and grew louder as they approached the end of the passage.

Jace turned a corner into a wider passage to see a man and a woman hitting rock with hammers. Their hunched backs were to Jace and they didn't notice him coming. Ash walked over and sniffed at the man's leg. The man cried out and fell back, wielding his hammer like a weapon. He and the woman turned to the nine of them, the Fireflash flickering between them.

"We're here to help," Jace whispered.

A look of relief spread over their faces and they lowered their hammers.

Jace shared some water with them and noticed they were alone in this section of the ruins.

"Where are the others?" Jace asked.

"I'm not sure," the woman said, leaning back against the wall. "They just sent us this way to dig."

"Do you know how many Darrak are down there?" Jace asked. "And prisoners?"

"Fifteen, maybe twenty of those… Darrak," the man said.

"A hundred prisoners, maybe?" the woman said. "A lot of people from Beldan. But also from other places."

"There's a way out back there." Jace pointed down the path they just came up. The two dropped their hammers, pushed past the group and disappeared. "Keep going through the dark, you'll see it."

"Okay, bye," Straeten said. "We're just the people who freed you."

Allar stopped Jace with his hand on his shoulder. "This way opens into a main chamber. We'll be exposed there if we're not careful."

"Got it." Jace took the lead with Ash and scrambled over and around piles of rocks left by the mining prisoners. "You remembering things now?"

Allar nodded. "And what I can't remember, I can figure out by reading this place."

"So now what do we do?" Shey said from the back of the line.

"We stick with the plan," Jace said. "I'm going to talk the Darrak into letting us out of here with the prisoners."

"I think it's time to change the plan. We're past talking," Allar said. "After all we've seen? Better to pick them off one at a time. We can scour them from this building."

Cathlyn placed her hand on Allar's shoulder and said a few quiet words to him. Allar pushed it off and glared at her. He turned the glare toward Jace but only nodded.

"Let's keep it quiet," Jace said. "Straeten and I'll take the lead."

Jace slipped behind Ash's eyes. Thoughts of Valor thudded in his head and filled him with anger. If anything happened to that hawk...

The passage grew clearer. He noticed scents from everyone, smelled their anxiety and fear. Vague sounds became sharp. Focusing on the path ahead, he heard faint scratches of movement and moans of prisoners. Jace signaled straight ahead when they reached an intersecting tunnel.

"We've got to let them know that we're coming to talk," Jace said to Straeten and his Followers. "Let's try something all together."

Jace called upon the calming magic of his Soulkind and found the magic came more quickly to him here. He even saw faint streams of light flashing in the air as he drew on the power. Similar strands drew toward Straeten and then to Tare, Ranelle and Evvy. This place was almost like where he trained with Graebyrn, the magic was stronger here.

"That's right," Jace said. "All of us." A gentle breeze filled the passageway and Jace took an easy breath.

"What is this place?" Cathlyn stared around at them, at the air between them.

"Graebyrn said there are places where magic enters our world." Jace smiled at her. "This has to be one of them. Strongest I've ever felt."

Cathlyn slowly nodded.

They reached a staircase heading down and Jace stepped onto it. "These symbols on the walls, I've seen them before." Jace ran his hand over the carvings as he walked down the stairs. "From Graebyrn's lair."

The staircase ended and their path passed under an elaborately carved arch and into a much larger room. Dozens of prisoners hammered on rocks, some lifting and dragging them. Darrak overseers also heaved rocks from the walls, examining the openings behind them.

"This is it." Jace breathed deeply and scanned for the nearest Darrak. It screeched at a pair of prisoners next to it and waved its clawed arm. With a hand on the silver rod, Jace approached the black-skinned creature. He felt the power of his magic multiply, perhaps from the magic surrounding him or even from his own strength. The calming magic settled upon the room and peace entered Jace's mind.

The Darrak stopped its yelling, and gazed at Jace with wonder reflected in its round black eyes. Its hand moved reflexively to the sword at its side, but it didn't grasp the hilt. Jace made sure not to make any sudden moves and held out the rod toward the Darrak.

"Kru-ra." Jace spoke the greeting learned from Sephintal. He bowed as she had taught him and presented the rod to the Darrak.

The Darrak glanced back at the other black and gray creatures that now walked to Jace. They seemed to stand taller as they approached, much like Sephintal had, as if a weight had been lifted from their backs. Two others behind them poised ready to spring, but whether to attack, raise an alarm, or something else, Jace did not know.

"These people, what are they doing here?" Jace asked, again in their tongue.

The Darrak did not answer and spoke to each other too quietly for him to understand. They took the rod and inspected the markings upon it, all the while keeping a suspicious eye on Jace.

Why does everyone think you stole that thing?

Jace ignored Jervis to maintain his concentration.

"They are digging for something. What is it?" Jace asked.

One of the Darrak from the back brought the rod forward to Jace. She—Jace could tell from the way her snout curved to her neck—handed it back to him with two hands.

The magic streams surrounding Jace grew stronger, or at least more perceptible. What was this place? Something about it made the connection to magic clearer. Whatever it was, Jace had to find it before Guire and Fay did.

"Hey, where's Allar?" Shey asked.

Jace lost track of the trails around him. "What?"

"I don't remember the last time I saw him." Straeten uttered a curse under his breath. "He must've left at one of those other tunnels, known a faster way and didn't tell us."

Jace took a deep breath. His heart raced and his breathing quickened. The strands of magic drifting in the air faded. He focused again and they regained their glow.

The sound of metal scraping rang out in the dark as the Darrak drew their swords. Ash growled and stepped in front of Jace.

"What's happening?" Evvy called shrilly.

Shouts from the prisoners echoed from within the chamber. Ten or so of them ran from the room as a group guided by some unseen force. The Darrak looked at the prisoners and then at Jace. Their eyes narrowed.

"I'm not doing this!" Jace protested.

A massive cracking shook the cavern. Dust and bits of rock fell from the ceiling. A section the size of a small house broke free and landed on top of the Darrak. All of them. The connection Jace felt from them severed. In the stunned silence that followed, the rest of the prisoners stumbled toward where the others had exited.

"Allar." Jace spun around and scanned the room. No sign of him. "Cathlyn?"

Cathlyn pointed to another archway. "I only see traces of his magic. That way."

He's going to destroy everything here.

"Even us." Jace checked on the buried Darrak, but the rocks were too big to lift. "We'd better hurry or he's going to level this whole place."

"He did get those prisoners out of here," Shey said.

"At what cost?" Cathlyn responded. "Jace was making headway with the Darrak."

Jace rushed to the archway and ran down the steps with Ash at his side and Cathlyn close behind. Torches lit the way, sputtering their weak light across the worn stone. "We're going to have a tough time negotiating with the Darrak if they think they're under attack."

Jace ran his hands over the carved walls, catching faint glimpses of the memory of Allar running past. "You were right, Cath. Over here."

A bright light shone from up ahead through the staircase. A stiff breeze accompanied it. Ash's nose perked up and he slowed a step. "You find something?" Jace glanced back at the dog for a second while running. In two more strides he found out what.

He skidded to a stop at a ledge overlooking the ocean hundreds of feet below. Ropes and winches ran along the cliff walls to his left and right, suspended over dozens of people digging into the rocks of the ruins. Waves crashed upon the rocks and a heavy mist filled the air.

"What is this place?" Straeten peered over the edge down at the pounding ocean.

"I don't know, but we have to get going." Something beyond the collapsing cave called for Jace to hurry. A whole new set of steps cut back into the building and spiraled up and down. He motioned down and everyone followed him.

"Save them. They have almost taken the last one."

Jace glanced around to see who spoke. The "last one" what? No time to think, he had to keep going. Down, down the stairs went, opening at different levels. Upon reaching the end of the stairs, they entered a wide room with a familiar pool in the center of it.

With a gentle blue light.

The dim glow shone off Newell's shield in the center of the room.

A few Darrak and some humans walked around the edge of the room carrying mining tools and pushing carts. The Darrak watched Jace enter the room and turned to face him, weapons drawn. Jace pushed his magic through the room and everyone stilled.

"Newell," Jace said. "Let me handle this." He approached with the silver rod in front of him.

"That's right," Allar whispered. "Lure them in, and I'll finish them."

"No! What's wrong with you?" Jace said. "We don't have to kill them. Let me do this."

Behind Newell, one of the townsfolk removed some debris from what looked like a small altar within an ornately carved section of the wall. When the woman turned around, she held something in her arms carefully, much like holding a baby. A Darrak shouted something almost triumphantly and rushed over to her. A terrified expression flashed over her face as she looked at the Darrak coming to claim the prize. She turned and tried to keep it from him.

"It is too late now," Allar said.

Allar made a fist and swung it through the air. The ceiling from the right side of the room collapsed onto two of the Darrak, covering them and one of the prisoners with debris. A huge rumbling shook the ruins and dust filled the room. The remaining Darrak reached the woman and ripped the round object from her arms as she wailed. The

168

creature darted around the pool toward the back of the room where another staircase opened.

Allar raised his hands again and a massive crack extended through the ceiling. The Darrak stumbled and fell as the room shook but it still clutched onto the artifact. A sickening pit formed in Jace's stomach. The object looked too smooth to be carved. It was almost as if...

"Cathlyn!" Jace shouted. "Stop him!"

Cathlyn extended her arms toward Allar and a brilliant flash of light surrounded him for a moment and an invisible force thrust him to the ground with a sickening thud. Allar traced his hands through the air and the crack up above the Darrak widened.

For a second, Jace's mind wavered between the Darrak and Allar. Who to stop? If he went after the Darrak, he might get whatever he was carrying, but Allar might end up leveling this whole place while he did it. The lines of magic streamed off him and led straight to Allar, now pinned to the ground.

It's time.

Jace knew what to do. The magic flowed through the air and wound itself around and through him, in and out of the now gleaming mark on his forearm.

"Hold him." Jace raised his hands over Allar. Newell's pupils widened and his shadowy form lurched away from Jace. Cathlyn strained and shut her eyes tight.

"Hurry," Cathlyn said through clenched teeth.

Like Shey's dark memory, Jace felt Newell's connection to Allar and the shield like the many roots from a weed. His magic grip encircled the mad soul, containing the darkness radiating from it. Cathlyn's magic slowly narrowed down his movements as he squirmed like a roach avoiding the light of a candle.

You can do it. Show him.

Jace directed his thoughts to the blue glowing water and the peace it held. "That can be yours," Jace said. "Go rest. You earned it." Slowly the fingers holding the soul to its host loosened their grip.

Jace held his breath as the spirit teetered on the edge. The darkness in Newell's eyes flared at Jace and reeled momentarily. Jace could push him. He had the power to do it. He felt it, but he also knew he couldn't. Newell had to leave by his own will.

"I'll watch over Cathlyn," Jace said.

And with the gentle push of a cool breeze, Newell turned to the light and let go his grip on the Soulkind and Allar. The anger faded from his eyes and Jace saw the proud Master he once was. Newell drifted to the streams of magic spinning within the room and disappeared into them.

Allar opened his eyes after a minute of Cathlyn shaking his shoulders gently. "He's gone."

Cathlyn smiled weakly. "It's good to have you back."

"Yeah," Straeten lifted Allar to his shaky feet. "You were being a real ass."

Jace laughed but then his smile faltered as he heard the voice again.

"That is the last one. They have them all."

"Did you hear that?" Jace asked but everyone shook their head or shrugged. He knew that voice. He ran to the pool and glanced at the image floating upon its surface. Graebyrn. "We've got to stop him. Whatever he took, it's important."

"These people are hurt." Ranelle helped one of the prisoners to her feet, dazed and bleeding from her forehead.

Jace glanced back and forth from the stairs to the people.

"Go," Straeten said. "We got this."

Jace and Ash sprinted to the steps but stopped just as the last remnants of Newell's destruction collapsed in front of them partially blocking the way up. Jace wedged himself between the rock pile and the wall but couldn't make it through. Ash jumped up on the debris, easily slipped through and began to bark. Jace tore a loose piece of stone off and smashed it onto the floor with a grunt.

"Not that way," Evvy said. Jace furrowed his eyebrows at her. She pointed straight through the fallen stones. At Ash.

Jace smiled and reached out with his mind. The streams of magic enveloped him and pulled him through their light until he saw the stones blocking the stairs again, but this time from the other side. He caught the fear and pain of the prisoners with a whiff of the air. Looking down, he saw the gray fur on his paws in the dim light and felt the call to run.

He looked up at Evvy through Ash's eyes and laughed, though it sounded more like a bark.

Ash sprang away in surprisingly swift strides and the stairs blurred past. Trails of the Darrak's scent spun in the air much like the magic and Ash followed them like an arrow.

This staircase led to a more central part of the ruins where twenty or thirty prisoners hauled dirt and stones away. The smell of their sweat told Jace they were tired, hungry, and scared. The emotions nearly overwhelmed him. A group of Darrak parted as Ash ran into the area, barking. The ones behind him closed in after seeing him run into the room. They were fast, but he was faster.

A tall but narrow opening let in the light from outside. A stunned Darrak fell back reaching for his weapon and Ash bounded over him. A vicious growl escaped Ash's throat. The Darrak stumbled as the sight of Ash's bared and gnashing teeth.

The outside light momentarily blinded Ash, but he kept going. If Jace had run this much, he would have passed out by now. The Darrak's scent led down a well-worn trail to a horse-drawn cart. The cart churned up dust as the horses dragged it along under the Darrak's whips. The back of it was enclosed and covered, like a prisoner's wagon.

Ash suddenly veered toward the boarded up cart. Jace soon knew why. A shrill cry rang out from within. Valor! He was alive. Ash barked in answer to Valor's call and he wagged his tail. Now that was a strange feeling.

Before Jace could quiet Ash, the three Darrak on the cart spun around to face him. "There's his dog!" one shouted in the Darrak tongue.

Why would they care about a random dog running alongside them? Did they say, "his" dog? Maybe he just misheard them. Ash cut into the undergrowth to the side of the path and bounded through the trees and stones. A loud clang sounded behind him and he twisted his head to look back.

Darrak spilled out from the ruins and onto the path, all of them abandoning the building. They had gotten what they came for. And now they were leaving.

In a big hurry.

Ash sprinted through the brush until he broke onto the road right behind the cart. He sprang up to the wooden planks behind the enclosed section. Jace reached for the lock but faltered when his gray paws scratched at the door.

With a jolt, Jace dropped out of Ash's body right next to him on the back of the cart. He peered around the side to see what was happening up front. Nothing. The Darrak driving the cart hadn't heard him. And behind he could only see the dust kicked up by the wheels.

Perfect cover. The door was a simple one, with merely a latch holding it shut. The metal creaked as he lifted the latch. He winced. With his teeth clenched, he slowly tried again.

Jace slid the latch the rest of the way and opened the small door with his heart pounding. Would his friend be all right? Light spilled through the prison opening onto Valor flapping his wings. Jace bit his tongue to stop from shouting out his relief. Valor locked eyes with Jace and quieted. Instinctively, Jace slid briefly behind Valor's eyes. He smiled as Valor's gratitude flooded his mind. Jace reached out for Valor to climb upon his arm, but the hawk darted past him to the corner of the enclosure.

Jace's eyes followed him and landed on a round object, about the size of a large melon. The object from the ruins. Had to be important. "Don't worry, I'll get that too."

At those words, Valor headed for the end of the cart. Jace stooped over to pick up the stony artifact. A large crack ran halfway across it, exposing a dark fissure. Jace hefted the artifact and stepped to the door. The dust still filled the air behind and around the cart and made Jace smile. "They even provided our cover."

His smile dropped as a large shape emerged from the dust. Instantly, Jace recognized it as one of the larger Darrak. Damn. The Darrak noticed Jace and fumbled for the spear strapped to its back. In that moment of hesitation, Ash and Valor dove from the cart and crashed into the Darrak and knocked it over into the brush. Jace jumped after them but was blinded by the dust. The cart continued rolling through the woods down the steepening path, its riders unaware of the fight behind them.

Jace reached for either Valor or Ash's sight but even their eyes were no good in this. Valor flapped his wings and took to the sky to get a better view while Ash stayed at Jace's side. A snap of a branch to the right. Then another to the left. This thing was fast, and big. Jace held his breath and scanned the forest around him, using Ash's sense of smell to help. The dog sneezed in the dust and Jace motioned for him to be quiet.

Before he could let out his breath, Jace heard a weapon slamming into a tree, followed by it being ripped from the ground. A trunk came swinging at him and though he ducked away, the tree crashed into his right shoulder. With the artifact cradled under his left arm, Jace ran behind a thick tree keeping it between him and the beast.

Muscles rippled under the scales on its arms as it clenched the spear. Two sets of horns from its thick skull pointed at Jace as it leaned over, possibly preparing to skewer him like a bull. Nothing left to do but fight. He reached for a weapon around his belt. He slipped past his throwing knives and blades and settled on Payt's spike. Something tickled the back of his mind as he touched it.

A clicking sound sprang from the woods behind him followed by a soft whoosh. A thick spike drove itself into the Darrak's neck and disappeared out the back. The Darrak stumbled, a garbled cry rising in its throat. Jace flipped the spike from his belt and threw it at the Darrak. This one struck it in the back of his opened mouth and it dropped to the forest floor.

Jace turned around and saw the dust settling to reveal the burra standing there, his great gray flanks heaving and sweating from a long run. He bowed down and Jace reached up to pet his neck.

"How many do I owe you now?"

Chapter 23

The sun dipped further below the trees, casting wide shadows upon the crumbling stones. The blue-green sea sparkled as the four friends made their way back to the ruins. Jace looked back down the hill for any sign of the Darrak and saw a dust cloud rising through the branches in the distance. What else had they taken? He turned around back to the ruins.

Little sound emerged from within the structure now that the Darrak were gone. Still, Jace felt uneasy.

"You guys stay out here, all right?" He slapped Payt's thick gray hide. "Keep an eye out?" The burra's sides had only just stopped their great heaving. "You need a rest from that running." Ash and Payt promptly turned and faced outward while Valor took to the skies.

Jace walked back inside the temple. A cool blast of wind greeted him. A small twitch emanated from the large stone he carried and he almost dropped it.

"What the—?"

Looking at the crack running along it more closely, he noticed a faint discoloration staining the material. "What are you?" He held the stone up to shake it, but something told him not to.

The prisoners wandered about the open room, staring as Jace made his way to the staircase he'd come up earlier. Were they expecting him to tell them what to do? He waved awkwardly and sped down the steps.

You sent Newell away.

"Hey, you're back. Yeah, he's gone, thanks to you. If you hadn't helped me figure out what to do, I don't think we would've made it out of this place alive. Or at least with this thing."

I didn't do anything. You all worked together, you and your friends.

Jace laughed. "Don't get all soft on me. Anyway, at the end I think Newell went on his own. I just showed him the way."

Jace focused on going down the steps two at a time. Soon the stairs ended and he met up with Straeten and Tare clearing stones away from the entrance. They backed up allowing Jace to walk past them into the chamber.

174

"Did you get it?" Straeten asked.

Jace held the object up. "And Valor, too. He's all right. This thing has got a crack right down the—"

Jace stopped and looked around the room, for the first time taking in all the smashed stones and platforms located around the central pool. One platform remained intact, with an impression big enough to hold… Hmm. He wondered. Jace placed the object on the nearest platform and it held it perfectly. It felt safe there. The stone twitched again and he blinked as realization started to creep in.

"It's an...an egg!"

"Yes," Graebyrn's voice rose from the glowing pool.

"A dragon's egg." Somehow, Jace already knew the answer. He held his breath and reached his shaking hand out tentatively to the egg resting in the blue light. The others crowded behind him to gaze at it in silence.

"Yes," the dragon replied again in his ancient voice.

Jace's stared in awe but then fear gripped him as he looked at the crack with new understanding.

"Is it okay?"

The rippling image of the great gray dragon faded slightly and then reappeared on the water, sadness in his emerald eyes. "I hope so. I am not certain how many survived."

"You mean there are others?" Jace asked. His heart quickened. Just a moment ago, he'd thought Graebyrn was the only one.

Graebyrn nodded. "The Darrak took them."

Jace stood. "We'll get them back. They can't be too far ahead of us." He took a step toward the door, then stopped and turned. "What do Guire and Fay want with them?"

"To control them. And to harness their magic to strengthen their own." Graebyrn paused. "Can you find out how many were taken? I cannot sense them all."

Jace glanced around and saw a few of the injured prisoners gaping at the dragon's image in the water. "He asked how many were taken."

"We have been here for a month and have seen four or five brought up," the woman who found the egg said through tears. "I did not know what we were digging for." She bowed before Graebyrn. "I am so sorry."

The dragon nodded at her and turned back to Jace.

A sharp cry from Evvy broke Jace's heart. She pointed towards some broken, rounded fragments among the wreckage. "I see little wings over here." Tare put his arm around the young girl.

"Some didn't make it," Jace said into the pool.

Graebyrn roared so loudly Jace had to cover his ears. The cracked egg rattled at the sound of Graebyrn's mourning. Everyone stood silently.

"What do we do?" Shey whispered. "What about all these people?"

"They can't go back home now," Allar said. "Not with what's going on there."

"We bring them to Myraton," Straeten said. "They'll have to take them in."

"But what about the eggs?" Jace asked. "We have to get them back." Energy pulsed in Jace's head, calling him to stay at these ruins. He could learn much here.

"This one is dying," Graebyrn said so softly Jace almost thought he imagined it.

A chip of the egg fell, exposing a tiny silver arm moving weakly within. A reddish fluid covered the scales. Jace peeled off the top of the stony shell and saw a tiny version of Graebyrn grasping at the air with feeble claws. A bloody gash cut across her face, through both of her now sightless eyes. She fought for each breath with a shudder through her entire body. Evvy cried softly behind Jace. Cathlyn quietly consoled her and patted her head.

Instinctively, Jace gently picked off the broken shells and cradled the dragon. She arched her neck to press against Jace's hands with the side of her face. The dragon's wings didn't move, sitting limp against Jace's grasp as he lifted. Her long tail wrapped tightly around his left arm as he carried her to the pool, spreading warmth pulsing throughout it.

Jace knelt down at the water's edge and lowered the dragon in it to wash off her wounds. At first, she struggled against the cold but then her body calmed, her tail still tightly clutched his arm. The water darkened.

Graebyrn said something and the little dragon twisted her neck to find him, but gave up with a pained sigh. "Goodbye, little one."

"No," Jace's voice caught in his throat. "Cathlyn, do something!"

176

Cathlyn stretched out her hand and touched the little wings. After a few moments in deep concentration, she pulled back shakily. "It's too late, Jace."

Jace desperately reached for his magic, anything he could use to help her, but he was no healer. A spasm ran through her body. Her tail gripped Jace so hard the scales cut into his skin, and yet, caused no pain. Even without Ash's senses, he could feel her fear.

He took a deep breath. At least he could try to create some peace for her as she passed. He reached for his magic and felt the flows enter and warm him while a calming breeze blew through the chamber. Everyone quieted and the dragon's tail relaxed.

Jace approached her mind with his thoughts. Immediately he felt a fear and pain he could not calm. His magic wasn't enough. If only he could take on her pain himself, like he had taken on Shey's memories. He breathed deeply and drew in the power that seemed to fill the air around him. He touched the pathways he used for Shey's magic and redirected them, tied them to the dying dragon. The warm glow from his Soulkind turned to burning pain as the dragon's suffering passed through his body. He gritted his teeth as it filled him. He could do it. He could sacrifice himself to ease her passing. He owed that to Graebyrn. And to her. The burning increased. His shoulder blades ached as he felt her crushed wings. When he forced himself to open his eyes, he saw that she had calmed even more. How had she been able to bear so much pain? He drew more in so she wouldn't have to face any before she left.

For a moment, he felt her understand what he was doing for her. Her presence lingered in his thoughts.

"It's okay. You can go now," Jace said.

Her tail constricted for a brief second and then completely relaxed. The weight of her body in his hands felt like a feather. A blinding blue light emanated from all around Jace and he shut his eyes tightly. All the pain he held drained out of him like water from an urn. The light faded and when he opened his eyes again, the dragon's body had disappeared. Only a warmth and tingling in his arm remained. The pool's water dripping from his fingers was the only sound.

"Graebyrn," Jace whispered.

The pool darkened. The old dragon watched it for a few more seconds in silence before turning to Jace. He fixed him with a look that Jace couldn't discern. Was it gratitude? Perhaps it was only sorrow.

"I'm sorry."

Evvy's sobs echoed quietly through the cave.

After several minutes of staring into the water, Jace turned around. Ash, Payt, and Valor stood behind his human friends, each head bowed low. "When did they come in here?" Jace massaged his left arm where her tight grip left an imprint of tiny scales.

"In time to see the little one go," Straeten said.

Jace's animals and the others turned to walk silently up the stairs. Valor rode on Payt's wide shoulders. Straeten was the last to leave and patted Jace on his back before going.

"You tried." Straeten put his arm around one of the injured prisoners and helped him up the stairs.

"Yeah, some help I was." Jace picked up a stone, a small piece of the shell that lay crumbled on its platform. He rubbed it between his fingers for a minute and then placed it in his pouch. He'd never forget her.

Jace.

"Not now."

No, right now. You did try to save her, and that is important.

"Not to me it isn't. Not to Graebyrn."

To me.

Jace scoffed.

I'm serious. You took on so much of her pain. And now she's safe.

Safe? She's dead! Jace stared into the water.

No. Safe. He paused. *I'm going to leave.*

"What do you mean? Why now?" Jace couldn't believe he was even questioning this. A week ago he'd have taken a sharpened stick to his ear if he thought it would help get rid of him.

If I stay too long, I'll turn into Newell.

"You don't know that."

No, but you do. And... your mind is needed for other purposes.

Jace sighed. "I never thought I'd say this, but you did good. You'll be all right."

For what it's worth, I'm sorry, about everything.

"What, no comebacks or jokes?"

Well, does it help to know that before I died I always hated you?

Jace laughed. He took a deep breath and held onto his Soulkind. Magic quickly poured into him and he sought out the spirit lodged somewhere deep in his thoughts.

Before I died.

Jace trudged up the stairs still rubbing his arm. He was gone. Jervis… was gone. He always thought he'd feel relieved to get him out of his head, but there was something about him he would miss. He entered the main chamber to see his friends gathering up the refugees from Beldan. Cathlyn awaited him at the top of the steps and hugged him. That was better than anything she could say, and she knew it. He held on and pulled her close for a while.

"Are you all right?" Cathlyn asked.

Jace nodded. "I'm fine."

"You look different." Cathlyn cocked her head to give him a look over.

"I'm just tired."

"No, it's not that."

The last thing on his mind was his appearance. "Does Allar have control of the shield yet?"

Cathlyn raised her eyebrow at him. "I don't think he's tried, and now he's set on taking these people to Myraton and reuniting with Stroud and the other Guardians." Cathlyn waved her hand to the forty or so people huddled together with Allar. "Says he can help with the defense against Guire and Fay."

Jace grunted. "Based on what happened today, I don't know if this was caused by them. I mean, they started it, but something changed. The Call is out of control. I had no chance of talking with that Darrak outside. It's dead because of me."

"You had no choice," Cathlyn said.

"I guess," Jace said. "But I can't go to Myraton. I need to find the other dragons. You have to understand."

"I do." Cathlyn walked to the exit. "And I'm going with you. I've been a part of this since Graebyrn sent me here. We'll find them."

Jace smiled, the hollow feeling in his chest subsiding ever so slightly. "Think Straeten'll come along with us?"

"I'm pretty sure he'd follow you anywhere."

"Who'd follow Jace anywhere?" Straeten said over his shoulder.

Jace smiled and gathered his friends together for one last time. "I'm going after the Darrak, wherever they go. I think I can find a way to track them." He patted Ash.

"I'm with you, and I'm sure my pack can help Ash," Ranelle said.

Evvy stood close to Jace and he placed his arm around her shoulder. "Me, too," she said.

Tare pointed over to his brother who now stood beside Allar. Tare's eyes dropped a bit when he caught his brother's glance.

"Burgis is going to help Allar," Cathlyn said. "He wants to join the Guardians."

"He's your brother," Jace said to Tare. "You should go with him."

Tare held up his arm and pointed to the Soulkind's marks and then pointed at Jace. Jace nodded his understanding.

"Looks like I'm the last to decide." Shey leaned against a stone pillar. "Do I tag along with you magic people? Not sure I'll quite fit in."

"You should come with us," Jace said.

Straeten nudged him playfully and winked. Jace hit him in the arm. Better to keep her close in case she needed his help.

"I didn't know you cared," Shey said.

Jace felt the heat rush to his face. "I think it's best for us to stick together. Plus, if we're going to get on that boat again, there's no one else who can manage it like you."

"If you insist."

"It's settled then." Jace gathered some wood scraps lying around and handed them to Straeten. "Want to start us up a fire? I don't think we're in any condition to march out there tonight. We'll head out as early as we can." Jace walked toward the stairs again. "And there's someone I need to talk to before we go."

Chapter 24

"I am sorry."

There was no response. No motion except the slight rippling of blue light onto the cavern walls.

"I need your help."

A great sigh emanated from the pool. "I am not angry with you and your friends, only at these thieves. For years, I have raised the young here. They were still in their eggs, but I have spoken to all of them. They have my knowledge. But now…"

"When will they hatch?"

"Soon, if not already."

"I will get them back."

"I have no doubt. You have the heart of a dragon."

Jace turned his green stone over. The black metal still clung to it, but it had definitely gotten smaller. Or blended in with it.

"Why is the Call stronger now?"

"I am uncertain. But we cannot allow the dragons to be taken. If the dark Soulkind Masters possess them, they could use their magic to amplify their own. The balance of the Soulkind depend on you." Graebyrn's image faded.

"What was her name?" Jace rubbed his sore arm. The scaled-shaped marks were still fresh.

Graebyrn's face reappeared with a smile upon the surface of the pool. "Rismantalia. A strong name for one strong with spirit and fire. I sense that she is at peace. You did that."

Graebyrn paused and looked closely at Jace. Jace looked away, guilt still burning inside him.

Graebyrn's voice faded. "Find them."

Jace sat staring at his Soulkind until he fell asleep next to the pool.

Jace woke early the next morning in a panic. In his dreams, he had been lost, stumbling about the ruins blindly. Falling down deep shafts of cold air only to float to the bottom. He rubbed his eyes and breathed a sigh in relief when he saw the pale blue light surrounding him. Ash scrambled to his feet and pushed his nose into Jace's hand. Jace obliged him with a rub on his side. Jace glanced into the pool again, hoping that Graebyrn would appear this morning. He didn't.

"We're on our own now." Jace shouldered his pack and made for the stairs. A longing to remain in the comfort of the chamber pulled at him but he climbed up, nonetheless.

The markings on his wrist where the little dragon had gripped him were less visible, smoother. A shudder ran through him as he thought of her dying in his hands. She was a part of the magic again and he'd helped her along her journey. Graebyrn said he wasn't mad at Jace, but a guilty feeling burned deep in Jace's stomach. If only he had been quicker, she might have survived.

Up in the main chamber, his friends were all awake, too, and the former prisoners scrambled about, eager to get the trip to Myraton underway. Allar guided them from the ruins toward the main road while Burgis stood by with Tare.

"You take care of Jace," Burgis said while clasping his brother's arm. Tare replied with a big hug that enveloped him.

"Good luck with the Guardians," Jace said. "We'll miss you for sure."

Burgis smiled at Jace. "I don't know if I ever thanked you for letting Tare and me follow you out of Tilbury. It has been an adventure."

"Until the next time, then," Jace said.

"Until the next time." Burgis gave Jace the two-finger salute from what seemed like so long ago. Jace returned it and led his friends out of the ruins into the forest.

"Which way do we head first?" Straeten asked.

Jace closed his eyes and held the gray stone from the dragon's egg. A light called to him, some distant power that throbbed in his head. He held his hand up until it centered to the west. "That way. The dragons are there. Heading home."

"Then let's get going," Straeten said, hoisting up his pack.

"The boat ride will take longer this time," Shey said. "We'll have to use the sail to help us upriver."

"It might be a big signal to the Darrak that we're coming," Jace said.

"Let's hope not," Cathlyn said.

Allar led the people north along the trail and waved to them, keeping his eyes on Cathlyn. "Be safe," he yelled.

Cathlyn nodded and called back, "You too."

The path veered away from their course, but going through the trees wasn't too difficult. Payt and Ash stayed by Jace's side in the front. Valor screeched in the morning air. Movement in the trees drew Jace's attention and he raised his hand to Straeten.

"Don't worry," Ranelle said. "They came in the middle of the night."

Jace caught a glimpse of a few scruffy, wolf-like dogs walking beside them under the trees. Her pack must've tracked them down, just like Payt. He opened his mind to them and they willingly allowed him to connect to their sight and other senses. Being linked to so many creatures made him aware of every sound, smell and movement in the woods.

"Do you sense the dogs?" Jace asked Evvy.

She nodded and laughed.

"Ask them nicely before you jump in their heads."

Evvy stumbled a bit as she tried to walk and stretch out to the dogs at the same time. She clung onto Jace's arm for support.

"I'm sorry that you didn't get to see a dragon," Jace said to her after they had walked a quarter mile into the forest.

Evvy frowned. "But I did, though. She was beautiful, all silver."

"Her name was Rismantalia. Graebyrn told me."

Evvy nodded. "I like it. I'm sorry we didn't get to know her."

Jace thought about that. "I suppose we did, a little bit. And look, she left me something to remember her." Jace turned his arm over for Evvy to see the little scale-like markings.

"We'll get the other ones," Evvy said, stumbling along, still latched onto Jace's arm.

"Yes, we will."

The *Gray Ghost* remained untouched from yesterday and nothing appeared on the river nor on the main road far on the other side. Jace still sensed the other dragons somewhere to the north and west. Valor flapped while on Payt's shoulder.

"Soon, buddy. I want you to find them, too."

"How far do you think he can go and still keep contact?" Straeten asked.

"I can't send him far. I don't want him to get spotted again." Just imagining Valor trapped in that cage, or worse, was too much.

"You're not making him," Straeten said. "These animals would do anything for you."

"I know. That's what worries me."

Valor jumped onto Jace's shoulder and squeezed until Jace flinched.

"Well, if you're going to claw my shoulder all day, might as well try. Be safe." Jace jutted his chin up at the hawk and Valor flapped away. Ash and Payt both bucked to follow him.

"All right, all right." Jace pointed into the woods. Payt and Ash bobbed their heads at Jace before darting through the trees after Valor. Ranelle signaled her own pack of dogs and they dashed after them, too.

Jace lined up with the others beside the boat while Evvy jumped onboard. They all dragged the boat together and it easily slid through the grass and sand into the water. Evvy waved her hands and cheered as the boat slipped into the river and then she peered expectantly into the dark water.

Once the boat floated freely, Shey vaulted over the side first and ran to the tiller to straighten it out. Everybody else splashed in the river and clambered up the sides. Jace shivered in his water-soaked clothes as he pulled himself in.

"Ahhh," Straeten exclaimed.

Jace faced a completely dry Straeten. "Hey, what did I miss?"

"Something I picked up from Turic before we left." Straeten pulled up his sleeves pointing to the black marks lining his arms. There were many symbols Jace hadn't seen. The one he pointed to was curved with jagged edges, like a flame. Those he got from Turic all had a similar shape. The rounded marks had to be from Newell. Jace's had a different feel altogether, like an ancient script mixed with animal tracks.

"Think you can share that with us?" Jace gestured to the group dripping with water.

"Gladly," Straeten said. "And if you're doing breakfast could you make something for me?"

"Deal," Jace said.

In moments, everyone was as dry as Straeten.

Tare opened the sail, but the early morning breeze barely filled it. The boat tacked slowly upriver.

"Going to be heavy on the rowing," Shey said. "Better get your backs into it, crew."

Jace groaned and grabbed an oar. "Looks like we only have time for four-day-old bread." Then it was Straeten who groaned.

The boat jarred suddenly. Jace glanced back at Shey.

She shrugged. "A shoal, I think."

Evvy stood beside Shey grinning widely at the water below. The boat pitched back slightly and pointed directly upstream. It then began to move steadily without anyone paddling. Jace peered over the edge and jumped a bit at the cluster of gray tentacles clasping the sides of the boat.

He looked back to Evvy and smiled. "The river queen?"

"That's right!" Evvy jumped up and down on the deck and clapped.

"Maybe now we'll have time for you to make us breakfast, huh?" Straeten pounded the sides of the boat.

Jace smiled. "This might be a good day after all."

Chapter 25

"Master?"

Turic rubbed his jaw and tried to clear his ears. They still rang from the explosion on the bridge several days ago. "Yes, I can hear you."

Brannon pushed back his hair, not as perfect as it once was, and handed Turic a cup of broth. "You've barely eaten since we escaped."

"Hmmph. Escaped." Turic stood up and looked out over the trees and river. "We should have saved Karanne. Now she is locked up. Or dead." He rubbed the red stone necklace in his hand. "I should have saved her."

"We still can," Brannon said. He pointed back into the house from the balcony. "Most of your Followers survived, and now we are at least thirty strong. Half of them are out there now following your plan. It will work."

"Yes, but we are only saving one person at a time." Turic stood up and returned inside, Brannon beside him. "All the while their army grows with Darrak. There is little we can do while they are all inside the Hall."

The Followers bowed to Turic as he entered but he waved them off. "And it won't be long before one of them sniffs us out here in your family's estate." He looked over his initiates and took in the determination in their eyes. Would it be enough to face the enemy?

"Then we'd better move faster." Brannon ushered in a cloaked young man. "This one reached us from the city this morning. Go ahead, tell him what you saw."

The man lowered his head as he spoke to Turic. "Just this morning, I saw Fay."

"Where?" Turic asked.

"She rushed out of the Hall." The young man's head remained bowed. "She seemed to be leaving the city. Got close enough to hear her—" He cut off and began to twitch.

One of Turic's Followers jumped up and grabbed the man from behind, pinning his arms to his sides.

186

"Don't let him see anything," Brannon said and the Follower yanked him away from the balcony trying to cover his face with a robe.

"I know you're out there," a hissing voice spoke through the young man. "You can't hide from me."

Brannon scrambled in front of the man and touched his forehead. A mark on his hand glowed bright red. The young man slammed back into the Follower and they both crashed into the wall. His arm lock broke and the younger man looked around with bright blue glowing eyes. They met Turic's and a wide grin spread across his face. He twitched again, this time with a spasm that wracked his entire body. Frost filled the air and quivered with energy. All the ice swirled around like a whirlpool until it sucked inside him, and for a moment his body compacted.

With a wave of Turic's hand, a fiery sphere formed around the young man the second before shards of ice exploded from his body. The shards struck it and instantly vaporized. When the frost disappeared and the man dropped to the floor, Turic removed the shield.

Brannon rushed in to grab the fallen body. He placed his hand on the man's head and cast the spell again. This time the young man's eyes glowed red behind his closed eyelids and tears flowed out.

"Check on Nin." Turic pointed to the fallen Follower and Brannon scrambled over to him. He placed his hand on Nin's forehead and after a time helped him to his feet.

"He's fine. We all are, thanks to you."

Turic nodded. "That is a new one, huh? I think she meant to lie dormant in him and then turn us all in one shot. It's a good bet she knows we are here now, though."

"Do you think he spoke the truth?" Brannon asked. "About her leaving Beldan?"

"He seemed to think he was telling the truth."

"Then this is the chance we need, to get her out in the open."

Turic knelt over the young man. "Or for her to get *us* out in the open. It seems we have no choice but to oblige fate."

Brannon smiled wryly. "I'll make the preparations."

"She's making her way east to get a weapon," a weak voice whispered.

Turic leaned over the young man. "What weapon?"

The man shook his head and buried it in his hands. "I'm sorry, I don't know."

"But east, you are certain?"

The man nodded his response and then passed out.

"Perhaps we should go north," Brannon said. "We could hopefully cut her off there."

Turic nodded. "I will attempt to call back our Followers. We must leave immediately." He closed his eyes and reached out for them across the city and then faltered.

Karanne.

How could he leave her?

This was perhaps the best opportunity to get Fay alone, but what if Karanne was alive and needed his help?

Turic grimaced and reluctantly resumed calling out for his Followers. It was what she would want.

Chapter 26

Two voices. Two men.

Then darkness.

No day, no night, just darkness.

"Time to go out," Dral called to her. "Earn your keep."

That's right. She was breaking into the lord's house south of Beldan tonight. She'd been casing the place for weeks now and tonight was the…

No. That wasn't right. How could that be? She hadn't been a thief in—

Darkness again.

Dreaming. That was it.

Daylight broke through her window and she rolled out of bed, trying to remember that dream she just was having.

"What are you doing up?" Jace asked groggily from the next room.

"Mathes wants me at the school this morning."

"This early?"

Karanne smiled. She hurried about quietly. Mathes finally had asked her to join him, and she had been going crazy this first week after leaving the Guild. A lot was changing. She rubbed the white stone necklace on her way to the school.

"This is your new teacher. Karanne," Mathes said to a group of young children, some as old as Jace, many much younger.

"You teach them to use swords?" Karanne asked.

Mathes looked at her with kind eyes and nodded. "And so much more. I'm glad you're a part of it now."

Wait, hadn't Mathes tried to kill Cathlyn? Images shattered in her mind and she clutched her head.

Darkness overtook her again.

She woke up in a prison cell. The screams of the other Followers echoed in the dark hall outside her room. She could hear Darrak walking toward her room. And the fire Brannon showed her spun in the air in front of her, despite her trying to snuff it out. The fire shrunk down to the size of a coin but the Darrak would still surely see

189

it if they peered in her room. Her heart raced and she reached around for anything to cover the magic, yet all she found was her hand.

The fire seared her palm as she covered it but only for a second. She backed into the corner of the room and stared at the door waiting for the creatures to come in.

"So that's how it began." Two sets of eyes watched her through the small window in her door.

This wasn't right. Who was that?

Clouds swirled in her mind and the room disappeared. She tried to speak, to question those eyes, but her throat refused. Her palm, the fire, did it make the pattern of the... what was it called again?

She held her hand up but didn't see anything. The Fireflash. That was what she called it. Faint lines glowed in circular patterns on her palm and the tiny pulse of light leapt out of it.

Her mind swirled again and when she could see, she was looking at Mitaya's lifeless body. "I'm sorry. We can't leave you here like this." The Fireflash spun in smaller and smaller arcs around the fallen until the bodies glowed like embers. In seconds, they disappeared and the brightly glowing fire returned to Karanne's waiting hand. More complex lines and patterns grew upon her palm.

"And this is the beauty of it all."

Karanne paused and everything in the room stopped cold. That voice again. Who could it be? She fell to her knees and clutched her head.

"Can't we kill her and take the Soulkind?"

"We can't do that now. She might take it with her. It is so new and fragile we don't know what might happen. Let us watch."

"Aren't you worried she might escape?"

"No. In a few days she won't know what or who to believe. Isn't that right?"

A face appeared in front of Karanne and she jumped back. "Who are you?" Karanne said. She cowered into a corner.

"We're here to help." The face smiled, but she felt no help in it.

"Go away!" The Fireflash burst out of her palm and spun in wide circles, lighting up the small and meager cell. She was alone. Memories flitted on the edge of her thoughts and faded as she tried to remember them. Two voices. Two men. Two voices. Two men. Those were real, she knew that, so she repeated it over and over to make herself remember.

Two voices. Two men.

And no darkness. That was different, something was different. This was real.

She ran to the door and pulled at it. Locked. With a thought, the Fireflash entered the keyhole and spun a bright white until liquid metal spattered from inside. The door opened quietly into a corridor and she stepped out into it. A man stood guard twenty paces ahead of her, but his back was to her now. Magic pulsed inside of her. She could kill this man, claim his spirit and have more power to escape from this dungeon. She crept toward him. The Fireflash could end him from here but a nagging feeling stopped her.

Closer she walked, pausing to observe him. The funny thing was he didn't move. He just stood there. Easy then, one quick motion and he'd be dead. Karanne pulled a knife from her boot and took another step.

Right in his back. Do it. End it.

But something held her shaking hand back.

Two voices. Two men.

A sharp pain rang in her head and she doubled over. The hall flashed with light briefly but then both the light and her pain disappeared. The guard still didn't move.

Instead of attacking, she reached up and put her hand on his shoulder. She spun him around and his face screwed up in fear. Fear? The knife fell from her grip and clattered to the floor.

His uniform faded away, revealing rags and a thin man beneath them. He kept shaking his head and tears stained his filthy face. A gag covered his mouth but his muffled sobs and screams still came through. He was chained to the wall.

Karanne staggered back from what she had almost done. She turned and ran down the hall, but the hall shrank to a small chamber.

And then darkness surrounded her.

Two voices. Two men. She repeated this but the words lost all meaning.

Chapter 27

The wind had picked up. Toola and the other creatures with her were still carrying the *Gray Ghost* forward. Water sprayed onto the passengers as the boat bobbed up and down on the surface.

"We've got to go faster." Jace leaned into his oars and his muscles burned.

"Yes sir," Straeten said through heavy breaths. "I don't suppose you can do anything back there, Cath?"

Cathlyn stood on the deck above the cabin, her long brown hair blowing about her shoulders. The rising sun shone behind her and cast shadows on Jace as he glanced at her. "I'm pretty sure I'm helping."

"Well, you look really amazing doing whatever you're doing," Straeten said. "With the hair and sun and everything. Keep it up."

Cathlyn only smiled, but it was the half-smile Jace always remembered her doing before this all started. She looked like her old self, and pretty amazing like Straeten said. Jace started a bit when Tare tapped him on his shoulder. His face turned red. Tare gestured for him to switch places. "Thanks." Jace stood and stretched his arms and neck, and headed for the tiller at the rear of the boat.

Shey stared upriver.

"You all right?" Jace asked her.

"About time you said something to me. If I didn't know better, I'd say you were keeping secrets."

Jace's smile dropped for a moment. "No, it's been a mess since the ruins. Sorry. But really, how are you feeling?"

"Asking about my feelings? Now you're really scaring me. I'm doing fine. Just, forgetful lately, I guess. Ever since our attack on the boats."

Jace had prepared a story to tell her about how the prisoners were freed on the river, but since she'd never asked, he never told it. He found the stone he used to trap her memory sitting in his hand. Cathlyn caught his attention and shot him a disapproving head shake. She never cared for the idea, after all.

"What's that?" Shey asked.

Jace fumbled to put it away into his memory pouch. "Nothing." He was even worse at lying than Straeten.

"Hey, what's your friend all upset about?" Shey pointed to Tare.

Tare had stopped rowing and was staring at Jace with wide eyes. "I don't know, but it doesn't look good." Jace reconnected with Valor. He had forgotten he had even let go. Tare's voice filled his head, although it was more distressed sounds than words. It didn't take long for Jace to see what was going on.

Black smoke rose from the trees on the northern side of the river and slivers of flames roiled within the trees. The forest was alight with fire, but that wasn't the worst of it.

Valor dove toward the destruction. Flickering tongues of flames grew sharper in the vision. "This isn't natural," Jace said. "Where are the animals? They should be flying from it."

A field opened up. Livestock from a farm lay motionless and burnt. Valor flew closer revealing wild animals among them. Wolves, birds… how did they not get away from the flames? It must've spread too quickly.

You think the Darrak did this? Tare asked. *Why?*

Jace paused. "This has to be more than a random Darrak attack. Somehow Guire and Fay know we're here. I don't know how, but they do. The Darrak are killing everything to get to us."

"I hate them," Evvy said softly.

Jace scanned as far as he could but the smoke now rose to block Valor's sight. "They're not doing it on purpose."

"Are you sure?" Evvy asked. "You saw them with Toola."

"It's the Call." Jace wanted to burst out of the boat and face the Darrak then and there. To stop this senseless mayhem.

"Doesn't the Call come from the gloves?" Cathlyn asked.

Jace nodded slowly. The Call felt stronger now, but how could that be with the gloves safe in Beldan with the thieves? "We've really got to hurry. Valor, fly higher." The hawk spun around and found an updraft sending him wheeling in the sky. Through Valor's eyes, Jace saw Cathlyn standing next to him on the boat. A veil of shimmering light shone over her body.

"You've gotten stronger," Jace said to Cathlyn.

"I don't feel it." Cathlyn sat down and slumped against Jace's arm.

"We've got trouble up ahead," Jace said to Shey. "Looks like they're waiting for us."

"I'll try to get us closer to the bank, under those trees." Shey turned the tiller and drifted to the southern bank.

"There's a farm on the other side. I want to see if anyone needs help."

"You sure?" Shey asked. "I thought we were in a hurry?"

Jace nodded. "Someone could be hurt."

"Everyone okay with this?" Shey glanced around at everyone nodding. "Whatever. I'll stay in the boat with Evvy. Hey kid, is that sweet river thing of yours still there?"

Evvy glanced at Jace. "But I want to go with them."

"Who's going to protect me, then?" Shey patted Evvy on her shoulder and winked at Jace. "I don't have any magic."

"Okay." Evvy sat down and pouted. "And her name is Toola."

"Hey," Cathlyn said to Shey. "Here's something to help." With a wave of her hand, Shey's hand began to glow and a metal sword grew from her grasp. She almost dropped it but gripped the hilt tighter when the sword fully formed.

Shey's eyes widened and she turned the blade over to inspect its lines. When she felt Cathlyn watching, she cleared her throat. "I'm used to something smaller."

Cathlyn waved her hand and the blade shrunk to a glinting edged dagger. "Better?"

Shey swung the blade back and forth in the air several times. "Yeah, all right. Thanks."

Cathlyn smiled and sat next to Jace.

"Umm. I think I'd call that stronger."

Cathlyn shrugged and turned to face the river.

Jace removed the metal rod from his pack. "We're coming up on a dock."

Straeten grabbed a long club from the cabin. "In case they get too close, you know, past my magic."

"I'm just going to talk to them," Jace said as the boat ran against the dock.

"And nothing ever goes wrong talking to Darrak," Straeten said.

Tare jumped over and hooked a line to one of the moorings there.

Jace peered through the thick smoky haze to the other side of the river where he faintly caught a glimpse of Ash and Payt waiting expectantly. "We'll be right back." He jumped off the boat onto the rickety dock followed by the others.

"What's that burnt smell?" Straeten scrunched his nose and pointed to the scorch marks on the tree trunks. "They used their fire on them, looks like."

Jace stepped over dozens of dead birds littering the ground. Some were burnt, some were frozen. "Let's head to that farm we saw from above."

An emptiness spread over Jace. He couldn't detect anything out there. It was like his senses were cut off and he was blind, perhaps more than blind. He took a deep breath and tried to seek out any sign of life.

Ranelle and Tare held their bows at the ready at the rear while Straeten and Cathlyn walked beside Jace. "Jace, everything is dead here." Cathlyn placed her hand on Jace's shoulder. "We can't do anything now."

"Wait." Jace ran ahead and called back over his shoulder. "There's some people by that shed."

Jace raced to the shed through the trees and came upon some cloaked figures bent over some of the dead animals. "Hey," he shouted. "Need some help?"

The group stood there as if Jace hadn't spoken.

Jace approached them. "Are you all right?" He took several more steps and halted. The group pulled back their cloaks to reveal the black scaled long snouts of the Darrak. The four of them started in Jace's direction.

"Darrak!" Straeten yelled. Tare and Ranelle's arrows whistled through the smoke over Jace's head.

"No, wait!" Jace turned and held up his hand. The arrows bounced off an invisible barrier and fell to the ground. A mark on Straeten's raised arm glowed.

"You better be sure about this," Straeten said.

"There's more!" Ranelle pointed far to the left where a larger leader led a small band of Darrak.

"Can they fire now, please?" Straeten asked.

Jace paused. If this larger Darrak was like the others he encountered, there was little chance he'd get two words out before being attacked. Still, he had to try. He held up the metal rod and drew as much power into his Soulkind as he could.

The Darrak slowed and lowered their weapons, however slightly. Even the leader.

"Do you need help?" Jace shouted, not certain why he said it.

The Darrak exchanged looks of confusion. An offer of help must've been the last thing they expected.

"No," the leader uttered. "But you will." The brief calm ended as the large Darrak roared and goaded the others into charging.

Arrows whistled through the air at the approaching Darrak, some bouncing off the ground, some finding their mark, but none slowing the Darrak. The massive leader bounded at them in a blur, knocking three smaller Darrak to the ground as it did so. It roared a challenge and brandished its weapon.

Jace reached out for his animals, but they were too far away to offer him their senses. They couldn't help him now. Nor could he sense any other animals. Had this fire been caused just for this reason? By the Darrak? The thought made him feel suddenly very exposed.

Straeten shoved Jace aside and ran to meet the leader head-on, raising his left arm and returning a shout of his own. The Darrak swung its club through the air but it hit upon an invisible barrier so hard the wood cracked and shattered. Straeten staggered back a step under the blow but still faced his opponent. With his other hand, he released a ball of fire into the Darrak, knocking it onto its back. It roared and jumped to its feet, sizing Straeten up before attacking. Black scales on its chest smoked from the blast, sizzling and crackling.

Five Darrak caught up to the leader and sprang with their weapons drawn. Arrows pelted them but did little to slow them. A fiery ring appeared around Jace and the others. The Darrak stopped short, their eyes glinting with the fire blocking them.

The leader shoved one of the other Darrak through the ring. It screamed as its scales burned, yet didn't stop attacking. Jace ducked under its sword strike and plunged his knife into its chest. The Darrak dropped to the ground.

The large Darrak leaped over the flames and swung its arm at Straeten like a hammer. It struck the shield barrier again, but this time Straeten fell backward hitting his head on the ground with a thud. The fiery ring vanished and Straeten groaned.

"Cathlyn?" Jace held up his knife and retreated to where Straeten fell.

Three of the Darrak suddenly disappeared, including the leader. One Darrak remained and lowered its weapons, looking around for its companions. It settled its stare onto Jace and pulled its lips back in a snarl.

The three Darrak reappeared, falling from the sky at a great speed and directly onto the snarling Darrak, flattening it with a bone-crunching sound.

Another group of Darrak ran from the south and surrounded them.

Tare swung his bow into the face of the one closest to him and then jumped onto it. The Darrak swung its arms lightning quick and struck Tare hard, dropping him to the ground with a gash across his forehead. The Darrak's tail whipped around and lashed Tare across his front side, spinning him over and away from the group.

"Stop!" Jace shouted and held up the metal artifact in his left hand. He had to try again. This caught the Darrak so off guard that they actually did stop. "You don't have to do this!"

The large leader made a sound, perhaps a chuckle, but that sound died as it looked past Jace. Jace whipped his head around to see what drew its attention.

A hunched-over Darrak, an elder by the look of it, yelled some words Jace didn't know including "Gora" as it approached them. The large Darrak bowed its head and, for the time being, didn't try to kill Jace. What was the significance of "Gora"? He'd heard a large Darrak addressed by it before. Must be what they were called. Three other cloaked direct joined him and they all pointed to the artifact in Jace's hand.

Valor flew from the sky and fluttered onto Jace's shoulder. The Darrak muttered something and glanced at each other. In the confusion, Jace ran to Tare's side and turned him over. "He's still breathing. Come on, we've got to get out of here." Jace wrapped his arms around Tare but he was too big for him to lift alone. The Gora snorted like a bull about to charge but waited as the elder Darrak approached.

Cathlyn knelt by Tare and placed her hand on his forehead. Warmth radiated from her touch and Tare's eyes fluttered open.

"Can you get up?" Jace asked. Tare's arm wavered as he reached for Jace and strained to pull himself up. Valor jumped off of Jace and circled the area.

A loud roar escaped from the Gora and it lashed out at the Darrak, sending a cloaked one to the ground. They were fighting each other? The remaining Darrak drew their curved swords from beneath their cloaks and advanced on the Gora.

Jace watched the cloaked Darrak and blinked. He knew them.

"Watch out, Tark!" Jace said. They were the ones from the riverboat!

Two other Darrak moved around to flank Tark and the Darrak with him. Tark shouted out words Jace didn't follow and the attackers held off for a moment. All except for the Gora, who grew even angrier and swung at its own Darrak, clipping one across the side of its head. The other Darrak growled and turned on the Gora, circling like wolves around a weakened prey, making small but deadly jabs at it. Despite its strength and the fierce swinging of its claws, the Gora soon fell to their persistent blows. The Darrak swarmed it.

Time to get Tare to safety. Jace and Straeten supported him between them and made for the *Gray Ghost* as quickly as they could.

Valor swooped down to Evvy near the river. Jace felt her mind link with the hawk's.

Get the boat ready!

Evvy shook Shey's shoulder. Shey scrambled to release the mooring and hold tight to the dock post while Jace dragged Tare onto the boat. "Things not go like you thought they would?" Shey asked.

"Yeah, not quite," Jace said, laying Tare down safely. Cathlyn tended to his wound. "Your friend is still here, right Ev?"

The boat jerked forward seemingly under its own will. Evvy gave him a thumbs up. Jace turned back as the shore receded and saw a large group of Darrak clustering together. He held Kedan's metal rod aloft and it glinted in the muted daylight. One of the Darrak, raised his fist to Jace.

If only he knew what that meant.

Chapter 28

The blood-red sun barely broke through the layer of smoky haze hanging over the river. The unnatural quiet put everyone on edge and no one spoke a word over a meager breakfast. Valor winged above Ash and Payt on the southern shore. Ranelle's small pack of dogs followed close behind, darting in and out of the trees.

Jace connected with Ash and sudden exhaustion hit his legs and body. "You've been running for days, boy. I don't know how you're doing it." Jace drew a deep breath and coughed. "This smoke isn't helping, either."

Evvy waved at Jace and showed how she had draped a rag over her mouth. Jace waved back at her and tore a piece of cloth off one of the supply bags for himself.

"I think Ash is hungry," Evvy said, pointing out into the woods.

"Valor and Payt will go hunting soon," Jace said. "They'll bring back food like they always do. He'll be all right."

"He's slowing down though," Evvy said. "Everyone is. Even Toola."

"How many of those things are down there?" Shey pointed to the water.

Evvy finished the last bite of her bread. "Two at a time on the boat, and there's three others following along to take their place when they get tired."

Jace tried to sense them, but couldn't quite place all five of them as well as Evvy could. Still, the water creatures offered him their sight. This sight was less seeing and more sensing of sound, similar to when he used the bats in Graebyrn's cave. Underwater vibrations showed him the shallows in the river and the fish swimming past. Toola snapped up one of them and swallowed it whole.

"How's Tare?" Jace asked.

"Better," Cathlyn said. "Weak though. But he won't admit it."

Tare waved her off as he struggled with one of the oars opposite Ranelle, his face turning red.

"Come on, Straet, wake up and take over rowing for him."

199

Straeten yawned and stumbled over to Tare. "My turn." He tapped him on the shoulder until he stood up. "No sleep for me around here."

"I can't see anything this morning, not through this." Jace gestured at the smoke to the west above the water.

"They really don't want us following," Cathlyn said. "I mean, burning everything? It's insane."

Was it all just to slow them down? Or had they planned for it to sever his connection to animals? Jace shuddered. If so, their plan was effective.

"What do they want with those dragons?" Cathlyn continued. "Did you find out?"

"I think that if Fay can control them, she'll get stronger," Jace said. "Graebyrn said something about dragons strengthening magic. We can't let that happen." Jace turned his left hand over and inspected it.

"Is your arm any better?" Cathlyn asked.

Jace rubbed the scaled lines on it. "The marks aren't going away. Here, look." He showed her his arm.

"It should have healed more by now." Cathlyn turned his arm over lightly. Her warm hands felt nice in the cool air. "They shouldn't be black like this. Here." Cathlyn closed her eyes and concentrated.

"Just take it easy on me." Jace smiled, relaxing for the first time in a long while.

"That's right, keep smiling." Straeten pulled hard on the oars. "I'll do all the work. Is that okay?"

"This is strange." Cathlyn's smile faded as she traced the pattern on his arm.

"What is?"

Before she could answer a loud thud came from the front of the river boat. "We hit something," Shey shouted. "Check up there, kid."

Evvy ran to the front and peered over the edge, pointing. "It's a big chunk of… ice?"

"Ice?" Jace asked. "What's it doing here?" It wasn't the right season to have ice in the river. Fear rippled through his mind.

Another crash sounded, this time shaking the entire boat. Evvy dropped over the edge with a short scream and a splash.

Jace jerked his arm from Cathlyn's hands and ran along the edge of the boat. Several large blocks of ice knocked against the hull but there was no sign of Evvy. "Evvy!"

Valor shot into the air and Jace felt sudden vertigo as he slipped into his sight. The smoke still blocked anything he could see through the hawk. He cursed.

"I see her over there." Ranelle pointed behind the boat to Evvy's struggling body. Ranelle grabbed a rope to toss back to her but hesitated and gasped. Dark tentacles surrounded Evvy's body gently, almost with a mother's touch. Evvy waved and laughed as the river creature swept her toward the boat.

"That kid is lucky to have a river friend like that," Cathlyn said.

Jace started to agree but fell silent. A cracking sound grew from near the northern shoreline. The sound intensified and Jace's heart beat faster in his ears. "There's something out there."

Still looking through Valor's eyes, Jace's fears sank his heart. The hawk, now swooping directly over the surface of the river, saw winter cover the water in a matter of seconds. It froze instantly and the ice stretched toward the boat like a grasping claw. "It's her. Fay's here."

He looked back to Evvy in horror. The creature sped her to the boat with a white bubbling wake behind it, but the expanding ice was catching them.

"Evvy! Tell her to move faster!"

Evvy looked back and forth from the ice to the boat and gripped the black tentacles around her tightly. The icy fingers nearly reached her just as Toola lifted her from the water and launched her through the air.

Straeten reached over the edge and clasped her wriggling wet form in his arms. He pulled her inside as a wave of ice crashed into the *Gray Ghost's* hull and knocked it at an angle. The boat froze in its place and the ear-splitting cracking continued past them to the other shore.

Jace slid to the side of the boat that now leaned awkwardly toward the river. He caught Cathlyn as she slid into him. He held her close to avoid the gear sliding past them.

"Toola!" Evvy's screams rang out. She broke from Straeten's grip and dropped onto the solid river. She slipped and scrambled around the boat and fell to her knees beside a frozen mass of what had to be tentacles. "No!"

Jace reached her and pulled her away. "I'm sorry, kid, we've got to go."

A pillar of ice exploded through the frozen layer of the river. Straeten dragged Tare out of the upended craft and the others followed. Another explosion cracked and skewered the boat with its frozen spears, blasting it into a shower of splinters at Jace. He lifted his hands, but the pieces deflected harmlessly off an invisible barrier. He turned to Straeten.

"Thank Allar for that one." Straeten lowered his arm and the glow on it faded.

"Go!" Jace yelled and pointed to the northern shore. "We need to get some cover."

Jace took a few steps and slipped on the icy river. Straeten slid into him as he tried to move forward. "We're sitting targets here," Jace said. In a sudden flash, the shore appeared to shift toward them by about fifty feet. "What the—?"

"Keep going," Cathlyn shouted. "I can't carry us all the way all at once."

Jace glanced back to see a shower of ice explode from below the river's surface where they had just been standing. Another burst of light and again he was closer to the other side, almost there this time. "She's that way." He pointed to the western shore.

"Then we're heading right toward her." Shey slipped this time but Tare grabbed her arm and held her upright.

"No turning around now," Jace said. "We need to get off this river and under those trees."

"Is Guire here, too?" Cathlyn asked, her voice sounding weak after the magic she just cast.

Jace shook his head. "I'm pretty sure it's just her."

One more time they advanced to the shore, finally reaching the bank. Cathlyn hung her head forward and stumbled along the shore but luckily Jace grabbed her arm. He helped her clamber up under the tree line before another pillar of ice erupted spikes into the riverbank.

"I'm starting to think they don't want us in Beldan." Straeten leaned up against a tree, panting.

"I can't see anything up above with the smoke and I'm blind in the woods with the animals gone," Jace said. "You got anything? Anybody?"

"Those Darrak aren't close by, are they?" Straeten asked.

Jace shook his head. "I can't sense them. But that doesn't mean they're not near. I can't tell with this fire."

"Stay behind me." Straeten held up his arms and a fiery shield appeared in front of him. The flames flickered around the edge as if being pushed by an invisible barrier. "Both shields should help."

Two cloaked humans ran through the trees and stopped when they spotted Jace and the others. One called back through the woods but his call got cut short by an arrow piercing his chest. The other threw a handful of ash onto the ground, held her hand over it, and mumbled strange words. A blue glow covered the ground where the ashes fell and a thin mist arose.

Tare pulled back on his bow and shot again but the projectile froze mid-flight before reaching the blue-eyed woman. A withered hand materialized through the fog and clutched the arrow. The rest of the being pulled itself out of the ground, a faceless human-shaped creature with skin stretched across its thin bones.

"Not one of these again," Straeten said.

"Cathlyn?" Jace said.

Cathlyn faltered. Her skin paled and her eyes glazed over. "My magic. I… I can't. I need more time to recover."

"We've got to get out of here," Jace said.

"No," Straeten said with a sudden calm. "Get us to Fay."

"Are you crazy?" Shey asked. "You want to find this witch?"

Straeten nodded.

"I don't know if I can remove her from her Soulkind," Jace said. "When I got Newell out it was different. It was—"

"Trust me," Straeten said.

That was enough for Jace. He ran in the direction he sensed Fay waiting.

He glanced back to see the demon contorting and bending over onto its arms so that it resembled a bug scrambling toward them. A long slit opened on its head revealing a single black eye focused onto Straeten. "Deltir," a creaky voice uttered through a thin crack in its stomach. "Come back to us."

Fire burst from Straeten's hand and hit the creature's chest. A scream gurgled from it as it flailed about, but as soon as the fire ceased its burning, the charred creature stepped toward them again.

"She can see us through that thing," Straeten yelled to Jace. "Hurry up and get to Fay. I'll cover us from behind."

Another Follower appeared on the slope ahead and knelt down with his hand on the ground. A mass of ice burst from the soil beside Jace, spitting rocks all around. He dodged the ice's groping fingers and kept running toward Fay.

"They'll grab us with those if she sees us," Cathlyn said, struggling to keep up with Jace. "Careful."

Before the Follower could cast the spell again, Straeten bounded up the slope and drove his fist into his nose. The Follower dropped back onto the ground without a struggle. Another of the demons arose from the ground to their left. Thin gray flesh raced to cover its body, but its bones jutted out at awkward angles. Two bulbous black eyes split open atop its skull and fixed on Jace. It raised its leathery arm to him and hoarse laughter spat from an opening in its neck.

"Wait!" Straeten shouted.

Jace turned to see a thick icy finger wrap itself around Straeten's leg. Quickly, Jace mashed it with his fist. Part of it shattered only to be replaced by another that gripped his other leg. The fiery shield reappeared in front of Straeten's hand. He drove it at the ice cutting through it with ease, then jumped away as the ice grabbed for him again.

Straeten fell behind Jace and the others.

"Hurry!" Jace said.

"Keep going over that hill." Straeten's fiery shield doubled in size and he held it up behind them as he ran.

Jace cleared the top of the hill and looked out over a sunken area before the frozen river. He ran to the bottom while holding Evvy's hand. "Come on."

"Are we going to be okay?" Evvy asked.

Jace didn't tell her how distanced he felt from his magic without the power from the surrounding animals. Instead, he squeezed Evvy's hand.

"We'll be all right."

He scanned the hillside for Fay or her Followers. As soon as they reached the bottom of the hill a wall of ice thrust up from the ground, preventing them from going any further. "We're stuck here." Jace looked Straeten right in his eyes.

"No, I'm not leading you into a trap." Straeten turned around and spun a ring of fire around their small group. "Up there."

A group of people reached the top of the hill and stopped to look down at them. Twenty of them, at least. The two demons from the woods floated over the edge in jerking movements. Streams of ice flowed along the ground, seeking out Jace and the others. Each time the ice got too close, Straeten struck out with his fire and pushed it back.

"You're going to have to come down here and get us," Straeten yelled. He turned back to Jace and winked. "Right?"

Fay, dressed in fine clothes exposing her dark-skinned arms, appeared at the top of the ridge. The snaking ice stopped as she lifted her hands. "I think we are done with the pleasantries. Now, will you please lay aside your magic so we can… talk?"

Straeten hurled a bolt of fire at her but she casually absorbed it with a cloud of fog in her outstretched palm. She clicked her tongue. "How can you expect to win? Look at your Deltir." She flicked a spinning ice dart at Straeten who raised his shield but her magic penetrated the fire and pierced his side.

Straeten shouted out in pain and fell to his knees.

"And your sorceress?" Fay smiled at Cathlyn. "Useless."

Cathlyn scowled at her words as she bent to examine Straeten's wound.

"How kind of you to bring me fresh meat, though."

Jace followed her gaze to his friends behind him and landed on Shey. At first she fell back a step, but then drew Cathlyn's magical blade and faced Fay.

"You have lost the dragons. Can you not feel it?" Fay waved her hand and her Followers walked down the hill.

Emptiness filled Jace's heart and a chill crept into his mind. He *could* feel it. The dragons were gone. What was he doing here then? How could he defeat such an experienced and ruthless Master?

Fire appeared in the air to Jace's left and he wondered if Straeten or Cathlyn somehow caused it. More flames came from the right side of the hill, crashing into Fay's Followers. They screamed and flailed about as the fire raged.

"What's going on?" Jace asked.

Straeten pointed up the hill then doubled over again. Jace followed his finger and at first thought his eyes were tricking him. Red and blue light glowed upon the trees with the clash of fire and ice. Only one could wield fire magic like that against Fay. And there he was, approaching Fay with light like the sun shining from his hand.

"I've got to get up there." Jace caught Cathlyn's eye.

Cathlyn followed his gaze to Turic and nodded quickly. "I'll stay with him." She focused back on Straeten's prone form and opened his shirt, exposing a black bruise on the right side of his body. She laid her hands upon the injury and Straeten winced.

Valor swooped from above. Jace almost joined with him when another presence entered his thoughts. A powerful one. Trees snapped like twigs as a gray blur bounded down the hill and skidded in the dirt beside him. "Payt!" Jace grabbed hold of the burra's horned shoulder and clambered onto his back. "How did you get here?"

Like a dart, Payt sprang up the hill with Jace barely holding on to his shoulder spikes. Jace turned back to see the river stretching out behind him. "The ice. You came over on the river."

Payt rammed into and tossed one of Fay's Followers who got in the way, flipping the body into a burning tree. His hooves thundered up the rocky slope and he thrust three other Followers aside along the way. Upon the ridge molten sprays of fire cascaded to the ground like a fountain. Turic's horse's legs froze to the ground and Turic splayed out forward onto his face.

Fay's dark skin glowed in blue light, and she smiled at Turic now lying at her feet. Her lips curled back down as she noticed the ring of flames circle her and begin to close in around her chest. She grabbed onto the encircling fire and screamed in pain, but soon the fire faded into an icy ring.

"Now!" Jace shouted. Two spikes shot out of Payt's shoulders into Fay's arms flinging her back and skewering her to the trunk of a large burning tree. She glanced side to side like a trapped animal and tugged at her arms, yelling when they didn't move. A shadowy image grew from her body, shaking like Newell's shadow had.

Payt knelt over again, pointing toward her chest. "No, hold!" Jace slid off his back and ran to Turic and helped him to his feet. "You okay?" When Turic nodded, Jace pointed to Fay. "Can you keep her there?"

Turic nodded again and raised his hands. A ring of fire encircled the tree and her body. Jace stepped forward cautiously. Magic flowed into him, rushed into him like a river, channeling into the angular mark on his forearm which was now a solid black.

"Stay away from me!" Fay shouted as Jace approached.

"It's time to leave." Jace focused his magic on the spiked ring on Fay's hand, her Soulkind, where her shadow bound to it like a spider web to an insect. The webbing twitched and squirmed as Jace pulled on it. Fay's soul shadow lurched toward him, but he didn't flinch. A cool breeze blew across the hillside and Fay's shadow drew back into her body. She stared at Jace with a blend of fear and rage.

"Just go," Jace said.

"Never." The shadow lashed out at Jace with an ice blade gripped in its wispy hands. Jace jumped back just as Turic's fire formed a barrier that vaporized the blade in a flash of steam. The fire pulsed like a living thing. The strings attaching Fay to the Soulkind spread and grew apart as if seeking a new host, but Nilen's mother's life force held her tight. She bucked at the spikes in her arms and blood flowed from the widening gashes.

"I won't let you kill her." Jace pulled all the strings together until the shadow held fast with one thick band. His left hand appeared to turn into a silver edged sword and he swung it down upon her soul. The line tying Fay to the Soulkind frayed and then snapped as it split apart. Jace looked at his hand but whatever he thought he had seen was no longer there.

Fay's soul opened her mouth to scream but nothing came out. The black shadow vainly reached for Jace then back to Nilen's mother's body, clasping at her arms, but then faded like smoke in the wind. Lunara slumped her head forward and Jace rushed to her, pulling on the spikes. She moaned softly when he finally removed the last and slumped into his arms.

"Nilen," she said in barely a whisper.

Jace gently laid her onto the forest floor. "She's back in Varkran, waiting for you."

A weak smile spread across her face and then she passed out of consciousness. Jace then checked on Turic. "Are you all right?"

Turic adjusted his spectacles. One of the glasses had shattered and the final pieces fell out of the frame. "I am fine, but she needs help. They all will need help." He gestured down the hill where the fighting dwindled. "Her influence on her Followers is over. Without her, they should go back to their former selves."

"Unless they chose to be her Followers." Jace reached for the jagged crystal ring on Lunara's hand and slid it off her finger. "You'd better hold onto this."

Jace dropped it into Turic's hand and in seconds the Soulkind began to transform. The spikes melted and reformed into a smooth metallic ring, plain without any adornments except the blue gem.

"I can't stay here to clean this up," Jace said. "I need to get back to Beldan."

"I understand," Turic said. "But I need to tell you something before you go."

Jace locked his eyes onto Turic's.

"Karanne was taken. She is being held in the hall now."

"Who took her? Guire?" Jace's heart started pounding in his chest.

Turic shook his head. "No."

"Then who?"

"The gloves," Turic said. "They have claimed someone else."

Jace staggered from Turic's words. "But we had them safe! How could this happen?"

"Your old boss, Dral, killed Picks and took them. I am sorry."

"Picks is dead?"

"I'm afraid so." The old healer placed his glowing hands upon Lunara's wounds.

Jace stumbled away from Turic. The gloves? It had to be true. He had felt the change in the power of the Call, so much more intense and powerful. Now he knew why.

"I have to go." Jace ran faster toward Straeten and stopped when he reached Tare and Shey. Brannon stood over Straeten's body and Cathlyn patted him on the shoulder with a relieved smile on her lips.

"Turic taught you well," Cathlyn said. Brannon beamed.

"You did it." Straeten sat himself up and waved to Jace when he caught his eye.

"We all did." Jace clasped Brannon's hand and thanked him. "You good, Straet? Time to go." He offered his arm to Straeten who grasped it and pulled himself up.

"You must take our horses then." Brannon gestured to a group of horses making their way over the edge of the hill. "Some have riders that have fallen. Take those."

"Thank you. Tell Turic to hurry and return to Beldan." Cathlyn deftly pulled herself up on one of the horses. "We're going to need him there."

Brannon bowed his head and hurried to other Followers who needed healing.

Tare pulled Evvy onto the back of his horse and the others mounted theirs, too. Jace spied Turic on the hill. The old Master raised his hand and waved. Jace returned it and then Payt kicked off at a sprint to the frozen river. There were more than just dragons to worry about now. Would they be ready for this? Jace clenched his jaw. They would have to be.

Chapter 29

"Why was Fay alone?" Cathlyn rode closer to Jace.

"Dral thought she could stop us, I suppose." Saying Dral's name as the new master of the gloves didn't sit well with Jace. How could he have killed Picks? Picks wouldn't have hurt anybody.

"It doesn't make sense," Cathlyn said. "If they wanted to stop us, why not send them both at the same time?"

"Good question." Was Dral toying with them? "Maybe he is heading for the dragons? And Fay was just to delay us?"

"Possibly. Should we cut through these hills and head straight to Beldan?" Cathlyn asked. "If that's where the eggs are going anyway, maybe we can avoid anyone. Let them slip right past us."

Jace shook his head. "We can't risk Guire getting to the dragons first. We're so close to them. If Fay hadn't shown up, we'd have them by now."

"But what about Karanne?" Cathlyn asked.

Jace reached for his memory stones but held his hand back. "I've got to believe she is all right. I feel like Dral may be using her as bait."

"A trap?" Cathlyn said.

Jace nodded. "And then he'd get the dragons and have even more power, and then it would be too late. No, we have to get the dragons first."

"Seems like you're trying to convince yourself of that," Cathlyn said.

Jace sighed. "I guess I am. You know I want to get her out of there, more than anything. But we've got to think ahead, or it will all be for nothing."

Jace turned back to his companions. Evvy sat slumped forward in front of Tare, fast asleep. She'd barely stopped crying since hearing about Picks. Ranelle rode through her pack of dogs next to Straeten but neither of them spoke.

"Straet," Jace said as he walked over to his friend. "How did you know Turic was coming?"

"I felt him in my head, in the magic. You know?"

Jace nodded. He had felt something similar with his own Followers when they were close.

"Hey, what's wrong with her?" Straeten pointed back behind Jace.

Jace turned to see Shey, her eyes watering over. When she steered her horse through the trees closer to the bank, Jace fell back to join her. A large, familiar ship leaned over on the shore. New patches of black charring scored the hull and the sails hung in burnt tatters.

"Magic?" Straeten asked.

Jace shrugged. "Probably."

"This is my father's ship." Shey dismounted and walked to it, stumbling a bit through the undergrowth. "What's he doing here?"

Jace swallowed and reached for his memory stones while trying to avoid Cathlyn's eyes.

Straeten leaned over to him and whispered. "She won't be able to remember, will she?"

"I have her memory right here." Jace showed Straeten the stone.

"Dad?" Shey climbed aboard the tilted ship and over the toppled mast. She hesitantly reached for her knife.

Jace caught up, stepping over the bloodstain on the decking. "Shey?"

She waved him off and proceeded into the cabin. "There's no one here." Her voice floated back to them. "I'm sure he got off…" She reappeared through the doorway carrying a large book under one arm. Her other hand was on her forehead.

The log. Jace walked to her and tried to take it but she held on and flipped to the last pages of writing. "He left several days ago from Beldan, destination near Myraton, cargo… people?"

Jace reached for the book again but she slapped him away. "What happened? Where is he?"

Jace shrugged tentatively. "I don't know? How would I know?" He looked around for Cathlyn or Straeten but no one was offering any help. Cathlyn shot him her best "I told you so" look.

"I feel like I'm going crazy here." Shey pulled on the pages of the log until they started to rip. Tears crept down her cheeks. "I know something happened. With my Dad. I dream of it. I sit awake thinking it. Little thoughts just pop into my mind. I see the river, the darkness, the… It's all so confusing." Shey looked pleadingly up at Jace.

"I'm… I'm so sorry. I…" Jace let out a deep breath.

Shey stopped and stared at Jace. "'Sorry? What does this have to do with you?" She took a step back. "What did you do?"

Jace stepped closer and took her hands in his. "Something happened. Something bad. You asked me to help you forget it. You saved us. You saved me." Jace placed the small, ordinary gray stone in her palm. He looked at Cathlyn and she nodded.

"I'm sorry I couldn't help after all." He closed Shey's hand over the stone.

Shey looked down at her hand while Jace called the magic to him. Her hand began to glow and thousands of tiny strands of lights wriggled from it then floated in a pulsating bubble toward Shey's face. The veins of lights grew and reached for her, passing through her forehead. When it all vanished Shey's eyes widened and she gasped.

She pounded her fists on Jace's chest, tears and sobs shaking her body. Jace held her tight in his arms and pulled her close. "You saved my life," Jace said.

Shey yanked up her sleeves and shirt to expose faded scars across her arm and stomach. "He did all this to me. I shouldn't feel bad. Right?" She wiped her eyes on her sleeve and suddenly pushed Jace away. Fresh tears ran down her face. "Go. Get away from me. Back to Beldan."

"But Shey—"

"I can't. Not now. And I'm no good to you all anyway."

"That's not true," Cathlyn said.

Shey scoffed. "I can't do anything you can."

"I could say the same thing." Cathlyn smiled at her.

Shey turned away and kicked at the rail. "Well, I was hoping to rebuild this thing, but I've got a better idea." She glanced at Straeten's hands.

"You sure?" he asked. She nodded emphatically.

"Here, let me help," Cathlyn said.

As the group sat on the bank to eat, Shey waved to the flaming ship floating down the river.

"Good riddance."

"You seem better," Jace said.

"I thought it would be easier to forget it all." Shey threw a stone into the water. "But it wasn't worth going crazy."

Jace stared at the water. "I'm sorry. I guess I couldn't get everything out of there. There were too many memories tied to that one. And they didn't want to let go." He turned over his Soulkind to look at the dark side of the stone.

"It was my mistake for asking it of you." Shey hurled one last rock at the burning ship.

"Evvy," Cathlyn said gently rubbed the young girl on her back. "You've been quiet. Do you want to talk about... anything?"

Evvy threw a stone and it skipped several times across the still water. "Nah."

"I'm really sorry about Toola. She was very brave to save you like that."

"Oh, she's not dead. She's just really mad."

"Mad?" Jace said.

Evvy nodded. "Mad she can't come with us."

"What do you mean?" Cathlyn asked.

"She can't swim until her legs grow back."

Jace smiled at Cathlyn's confused expression. "Hey, Cath, you want to ride up here?" He held out his hand to her.

Before she could answer, Evvy grabbed Jace's hand and scrambled up onto Payt. "Love to." She smiled and touched the spikes and bones sticking out of Payt's back. "This is great."

Jace shrugged at Cathlyn. "Now nudge him with your feet." Evvy booted Payt's flanks and he sprang to a gallop while Jace fought to hold on.

Chapter 30

Hills rose in the distance through the trees surrounding Beldan. The smoke thinned enough to see the blue skies, but the haze still kept drifting from the north where the fires burned. Jace felt his senses sharpen slightly as they travelled, but not nearly as much as they had been before the fires began. He felt… less blind.

"We're almost in the valley," Jace said. "We can make it to the northern bridge before the Darrak."

"And you're not worried about Guire?" Straeten asked.

"Of course I'm worried," Jace said. Valor circled far overhead and Jace watched the Citadel tower appear through the fog over the Crescent River. "We're real close. We get there, set up an ambush, and we get the dragons before Guire even shows up."

The dragons were out there, to the north. He sensed it. But something else pulsed through him, something extremely faint, emanating from further west. Was it a challenge? A warning? He swallowed hard. It was hard to tell, but if it was Guire, he was closer than Jace wanted him to be. "They have to cross the bridge here. We wait until then and we can trap them."

"Just like that?" Shey asked. "They don't seem to go down easy in a fight."

"I can talk to them," Jace said. "The Darrak."

"And the people?" Cathlyn asked. "The ones who are still following Fay's Soulkind? Or even Guire's? We got lucky with Turic showing up to slow Fay down, but I don't think Allar is coming to face his Soulkind's twin."

Straeten shrugged. "Maybe I can help stop Guire. I've got a few of Allar's spells."

"Look, I don't have this all planned out," Jace said to everyone. "But we've got a good chance with Cathlyn, Straeten, and my Followers."

Shey scoffed. "Your followers? What can they do? Make them forget why they showed up to kill you? No offense, but your magic isn't exactly what we need to fight these things."

Jace held his hand out toward Shey and closed his eyes.

"Hey!" Shey said, backing up and tripping over her own feet.

Jace cracked open one eye and gave her a smirk. "It works on you."

"Not funny," Shey said doing her best to cover her own smile.

Jace laughed then turned his attention back to Valor on the other side of the river. He saw only the smashed branches and deeply rutted cart trails the Darrak left before he lost connection with him.

He rolled up his sleeve on his left arm to inspect the marks. Cathlyn had been about to share something strange before the battle and his mind kept drifting to it. More and more tiny black marks had grown there. He caught Cathlyn looking over at him and quickly pulled his sleeve back down. No sense worrying her about this, best to keep her focused on the task at hand.

"You want us to go up this hill?" Straeten called from the front. "Maybe we should go around through the north of the valley? It might be quicker that way."

"I considered that, but if Guire is coming to stop us, I'd rather trek through the trees here and maybe get a drop on him. This doesn't look like too bad of a climb."

"You're the boss." Straeten urged his horse up the ever increasing slope with a kick of his boots. And then he added under his breath, "But I'm not liking the look of this hill."

For while, the horses had no problem with the climb, but after an hour, the undergrowth became so tangled, everyone was off their rides and leading them through by their reins. Maybe this wasn't the greatest idea after all. He tried to avoid Straeten's eyes.

As usual, everyone followed his lead without a word. Payt plowed through the branches with ease, snapping off ones that would have blocked the other horses. Everyone formed a line behind him and slowly made their way up.

Finally, after hours of stumbling to find any sort of path, they reached the top. At the far northern end of the valley, the Citadel tower rose like a spike. That's when something in Jace's chest dropped. The path down to the valley floor sloped steeper until it became a nearly fifty-foot sheer cliff. Valor flew out and Jace linked up his sight.

"There's no easy way down here." Jace scanned the wall. "But it appears to be a more gradual slope further south. About a mile or so from here."

"What about Cath?" Straeten asked. "Can you do that thing again? Use magic to bring us down?"

All eyes turned to Cathlyn and she shied away from his question. "I don't know how far away that is. I could drop us somewhere up in the sky."

Jace felt the dragons calling out.

"Try."

Cathlyn stared back at him for a moment, then picked up a rock and concentrated. It disappeared only to reappear as a flash over the valley, where it fell to the earth perhaps a hundred feet. "I…I can't do it here. I'm sorry."

"Well, unless we can all fly…" Straeten said.

Jace sighed. "Head south until you can get down to the valley, then hurry to the Citadel as fast as you can."

"You sound like you're not coming with us," Straeten said.

Jace shook his head and turned to the cliff. "Just go, and take Payt with you." With a wild sprint, he careened down the hill avoiding trees and boulders. Branches slapped his arms and legs but he couldn't stop. He reached the edge of the cliff and dove off.

"Jace!" Cathlyn screamed from behind.

The valley floor raced closer. A bright light surrounded him. When it faded, he flapped his wings and Valor's cry rang off the valley walls.

Evvy first, then Ranelle, Tare and Straeten linked with Valor, their voices dropping in one at a time.

That was crazy, Straeten said.

But really amazing, too, Evvy said.

Straeten grunted but Jace could sense his agreement, and perhaps some envy, too. *You'll fly someday, Straet.*

Valor spun around and headed toward the Citadel, bringing the river and the road clearly into Jace's sight. *They're coming.* A hundred or so Darrak and three carts rolled down the road perhaps two miles out. Valor's head twitched to the side. *And there's more on the way from Beldan.* If Jace and his party had gone around the hill, they would have run into the group on the road.

Okay, Straeten said. *I see them. You were right about the hill.*

Just hurry up and get down here, Jace said as Valor dove.

The Citadel grew closer quickly and Valor glided toward the high bridge. Jace jumped out of his body and came to a skidding halt, kicking up dust. He spun to the valley walls behind him, wondering how far back the others might be, but couldn't spot them among the rocks and trees. A mile away? Maybe more?

The Darrak were fast approaching and would be at the gates in minutes. The dragons, he sensed them more vividly. They felt... afraid? A swelling rage churned inside him and he clenched his fist.

Are you down the cliff yet? Jace thought.

We're almost there, Straeten answered. *When we get down, Cath says she can move us closer.*

Jace climbed down the bridge toward the arch. Now what? Stop them from coming through the gate? Maybe Straeten or Cathlyn could destroy it, but there was little he could do about it himself.

Jace tried to sense them, to get a better count, but when he got near their thoughts, he felt the torrent of the Call pulling him in and quickly let go. He scanned the Citadel. There was nothing he could do but use the magic he'd created. He stood in the middle of the path leading into the valley and waited, focusing on his breathing and the power inside his Soulkind.

A cool breeze flowed from behind him. The first of the Darrak neared enough for him to see their eyes. The Darrak slowed a step when they saw him. He rose to greet them, holding the carved metal rod out in front of him.

Dust settled around the hundreds of Darrak as they clustered around him. Jace held up a hand and called out a few words in their language and they slowed even more. Two Gora continued forward and huffed out great breaths of air.

"Return the dragons you bring," Jace said.

The Gora snorted what could only be a laugh. "Back to the temple?"

"To me." Jace's sense of the dragons grew even stronger. He felt a connection with them like with Valor and Ash.

Through Valor's sight, he focused on a single cart in the middle of the group. One had to be within. Had it hatched yet? Where were the others?

Some of the Darrak at the front lowered their weapons as they stepped closer to Jace. He held his thoughts on peace and calm and showed them the engravings on the rod.

Jace felt the Call fall away in a ripple across the horde. Many of their eyes met his, but without the anger and hate he'd come to recognize. He had reached almost all of them. Almost. One of the Gora yelled and struck the two nearest Darrak. They fell back and crumpled to the ground.

The Gora darted toward Jace with its arms pulled back in a hammer strike. Time seemed to slow as the Gora swung its weapon. Darkness covered Jace's eyes but when the light came back to him, he had moved ten feet forward closer to the group of Darrak. A long groove in the dirt road ran back from him to the crumpled over Gora. Dark red liquid covered the ground. It had to be blood.

What just happened? Something had killed it, but what? His thoughts flew to Cathlyn. She'd ripped open that one Darrak with her portal, but she was too far away to do that now. With a start, Jace gaped at the blood covering his hand. He didn't do it, did he?

The group of Darrak at the front turned on the other Gora and drew their weapons. The Gora opened its mouth wide in a screeching yell and swung its massive spear in a wide arc. Two fell under its blow and the others hesitated then struck back. A wave of power crashed over Jace and knocked him to the ground, the metal artifact clattered out of his reach. His mind reeled from the blast. Through the haze, he saw the Darrak slow their fighting and turn to him.

"It's the Call," Jace yelled through the splitting pain. "Don't listen to it!"

Jace pushed his magic at the approaching Darrak, anything to slow them down or stop them from listening to the Call. They circled him and herded him onto the Citadel's bridge. In the storm of enemies closing in, his magic faltered.

The Darrak stepped hesitantly toward him, their curved blades brandished. He overheard them whisper the words, "Soulkind Master." Were they afraid of him?

Jace turned the green stone over in his hand and thought of how Lu'Calen had this Soulkind so long ago. What would he have done? Jace scoffed. He wouldn't have put himself in this situation in the first place, that's what he wouldn't have done.

"Come on, Cath," Jace murmured as he backed away from the Darrak. "I can't do this alone."

The Darrak lunged at him with their blades. Again his vision blurred. When his sight returned, blood dripped from his fingers. He flinched when he looked more closely at his hand, or what should have been his hand. A silver ripple slipped over his fingers and then disappeared. What was that? He was met by shocked expressions on the faces of the three Darrak in front of him. No one moved.

"You saw that, right?"

The Darrak backed away from him. Jace held up his arm to look at it but something thrust his body backward to the edge of the bridge. A burning pain shot through his left arm and through his cloudy eyes, he saw a thick arrow protruding from his shoulder. He fought to stand up but the dizziness knocked him back down.

The Darrak who fired on him held another arrow to his bow and pointed it at Jace. Behind the Darrak, two carts rolled by and inside the closest cart, he spied a tiny creature with swept-back horns like Graebyrn's on his head.

"Hey!" Jace cringed with the pain the yell caused but tried to stay focused on the newly-born creature trapped before him. The dragon didn't look at him even though Jace stretched out with every bit of magic he could to reach his mind. Something else drew the dragon's eyes toward the west, toward Beldan. There was only one thing strong enough to do that. The Call.

A Gora prodded Jace with his clawed toes. He laughed and spit on Jace and then kicked him so hard in the side that he skidded over the edge of the bridge into the river.

The cold water swallowed him.

Jace had the sensation of spinning and falling in a blind dream. He fought with the current then gave up and drifted. Time slipped away and still his eyes remained dark. Gentle arms gripped and held him up and even with the mild awareness of the pain in his shoulder, a sense of peace covered him.

"Get up."

The words came from a distance, nudging him back. Graebyrn? No. He couldn't be here.

"Get up, idiot."

Ah. Straeten. Jace groaned as light slowly filled his sight showing him the rocky bank of a river. He reached for the arrow in his shoulder but found nothing. Not even a wound where the arrow would have been. Had he dreamt it? He could never dream up pain like that. His sight drew into focus and he saw Straet wasn't alone. Cathlyn knelt over him with a relieved but tired smile on her lips.

"You healed me."

Cathlyn nodded. "I'm getting better."

Jace grunted as he pulled himself to a sitting position. He pushed off Cathlyn's hand to hold him back. "We have to get to the dragons. If they reach the city, Dral, or whoever has the gloves, will be unstoppable."

"We'll go." Straeten hoisted him up to his feet. "Here, you dropped this."

Straeten handed Jace the metal artifact he'd dropped on the bridge. "Thanks, I thought it fell into the water and wasn't looking forward to going after it."

Straeten smiled. "Glad we found you."

"Yeah, I thought you were dead." Shey walked beside him and gently nudged him in his shoulder.

"Not me," Evvy said. "I knew they would bring you out of the water."

"Who would?" Cathlyn asked.

"Toola's friends." Jace reached for Evvy's head and ruffled her hair.

"That's not all who came." Straeten lifted Jace up and thumbed over his shoulder

Jace nearly jumped when he saw the four Darrak atop burras. Squinting, he noticed the smooth curved back and slightly tapered snout of one of the Darrak. "Sephintal?"

"I guess you can tell us apart after all." Sephintal stepped off her mount and strode to Jace's side, bowing her head and holding her hand up in his salute. "Master."

Jace wondered if it would be against Darrak protocol to hug. He returned her salute instead. "How did you find us?"

Sephintal smiled and showed Jace the mark on her neck. "You gave me this, remember? More of these creatures appeared after you left us, and they helped lead us here." Sephintal stroked the burra's thick neck.

"I can't believe you're here." Or could he? Before the attack, he had sensed *something* approaching from the west. He had thought it might have been Guire but maybe he'd felt Sephintal. Jace looked behind her to see Straeten clasping arms with another slightly bigger Darrak. Harkra.

"Do all of you have magic now?" Jace asked.

"After you taught me, I passed it on to my people. And yet, these creatures still were not easy to connect with. We suffered some of their anger before riding them."

"Yeah, they can be a little...stubborn," Jace said. "Where are the other Darrak we saw in the mountains?"

Harkra laughed roughly and hefted one of the burra's spikes in the air. "Not all of us could ride after…" The rest of his words returned to the harsh Darrak language and he gestured to his backside with the spike.

Sephintal laughed. "Yes, that's true for some. But others stayed behind, like Chran, to find more like us among the other Darrak. More who are willing to listen."

"We could really use your help." Jace wobbled a bit but then steadied himself.

"That is why we are here," Sephintal said with a smile.

Jace's eyes went wide. "What about the Call? You must be going crazy with it right now."

Sephintal shook her head with a smile that showed her sharp teeth. "I sense it." She waved her hand in the air. "But somehow it does not touch me."

"And the others?" Jace gestured to the other Darrak with her.

"They are the same. They know the Call is still there, but it does not take them."

Jace smiled. It had to be his magic doing this.

"Give me your hands. I've learned other things from the Soulkind." He held out his hands to her and she grasped them with her claws. He concentrated on his Soulkind and willed all his magic to her.

Curved marks appeared on her arms and hand, glowing at first and then settling to black on her dark scales. When the passing was complete, Sephintal smiled. "Thank you for trusting me."

"Of course." Jace looked about the road near the citadel bridge. "How long have I been out?"

"An hour or so." Straeten frowned. "We got here too late to save the dragons."

"I saw them." Jace flexed his left hand. "Something happened when I was fighting the Darrak."

"Tell me about it," Straeten said. "I was watching through Valor when that big guy attacked, and you.... you should have died right there."

"You saw that?" Jace asked. "Did you see anything… strange?"

"Like what?" Straeten asked.

Jace turned his hand over. "Something's going on with me. It's happened a couple times now. I black out, and when I can see again, whatever was attacking me is… dead. And I mean, brutally dead."

"Was it your magic?" Straeten asked.

"I don't think so," Jace said. "That's not how mine works. Maybe it was the dragons? I saw one that had hatched, in a cart as they passed by."

"Cath, did you do it?" Straeten said.

Cathlyn shrugged. "It wasn't me. I was barely strong enough to shift us after getting down the hill."

"You sure you didn't do something to my arm when you looked at it before?" Jace pointed to the faded marks. "Maybe you put some magic in here?"

Cathlyn took his hand. "Nothing."

"Well," Jace said, flexing his arm. "We don't have time to worry about it. We have to hurry to Beldan."

"And do what?" Shey asked. "We didn't really make a dent over here, did we? What do you think we'll be able to do in town against their whole army?"

"We have friends." Jace gestured to Sephintal. "And maybe even more on the way."

"Friends, huh?" Shey said. "It could be worse, I suppose."

"Yeah, someone could go off by himself again and get killed," Straeten said.

"I had to hurry," Jace said.

"You always think you can do everything by yourself. We'll save the dragons. Then we'll deal with Dral. Together."

"Sounds easy enough." Jace mounted Payt and kicked him with his heels. Time to head home.

Chapter 31

After riding hard for several hours, the walled city of Beldan appeared miles in the distance. Jace kept Payt in check continually to prevent him from running ahead on his own. Sephintal and the other Darrak would have sprinted with him, but he wouldn't leave his friends.

"The army of Darrak heading toward Myraton will destroy it." Sephintal pointed away to the east. "The fires they set for you are nothing compared to what they will do to the city. Even if your friends warn the king, there will be little they can do to stop them."

Jace held himself back from nudging Payt to speed up. "That is why we have to stop Dral. If we can end the Call, we'll have a chance." If not, who knew what Dral could do with the dragons and their power? Graebyrn feared it would make the gloves stronger. What if Sephintal could no longer resist the Call?

"This sounds like the last time we met," Sephintal said. "I'm sure you have a plan?"

The others rode closer to listen. "Not really." Jace shrugged. "I'm kind of making this up as we go. But, as Straeten says, we'll do it together."

"Think Karanne's in the Hall somewhere?" Straeten asked.

Jace's heart raced. "He might have her locked up in the tower where they held me. That's where I'm going to need your help."

Straeten nodded. "I think I know what you're talking about. I could sense Turic coming because I am his Follower, so maybe I could sense her too."

"Right. You'll need to find her quickly since this is all going to happen pretty fast," Jace said. "We have to assume they're going to kill her if we don't do what they want."

"I'll work on it." Straeten rode off to the side focusing on the glowing lines on his palm.

"Shey," Jace called.

"What do you want me to do?"

"If Dral took over, he'll have the thieves somewhere. I need you to get in there and find them. And once you do—"

"I'll make a big noise somewhere. Got it." Shey smiled.

222

"They'll be waiting for us at the north entrance," Jace said. "Let's head around to the southern gates. And Evvy?"

Evvy looked up at him expectantly.

"You stick with Shey. Keep her out of trouble and watch her back. And Ash's." Jace nodded to the gray dog. He bounded over to Evvy's and Shey's horse. Evvy's face brightened.

"I'll keep Valor above the city the whole time for us all." Jace gestured to his Followers, including Sephintal. "You four come with us. I have an idea."

"What should I do?" Cathlyn asked.

"I'll need you with me," Jace said. "I don't think I can get Dral out of that Soulkind all by myself."

"He's your Soulkind twin," Cathlyn said. "Will it work the same way?"

"It better."

Jace lifted his arm and sent Valor into the air where he settled upon the city wall. Below, Shey, Evvy, and Ash disappeared into a culvert.

"Are they going to be all right?" Straeten asked.

"Shey will be able to find the thieves without us," Jace said. "All of us going in at once might draw attention. Plus, don't you think the pipe is a bit narrow?"

Straeten nodded.

They crept along in silence along the outskirts of Beldan, constantly looking for but never spying any guards. Shortly, they arrived at the south entrance with its seemingly abandoned gate. "Empty. Like last time."

"I don't like this." Cathlyn glanced at the sky. "It's late in the day, but not this late."

She was right. Darkness rolled over the walls but outside of the city it was only late afternoon. "Some of the glove's magic, maybe. I can barely see through Valor's eyes." Jace focused through the connection but it was only getting worse.

"Seems like they're expecting us," Straeten said. "Maybe Cathlyn and I could light this place up." He cast a small Fireflash bolt into the air and it zipped around his head.

"I don't want to announce that we're here yet." Jace sighed. "We'll have to deal with the darkness for now." He sought out Evvy through Valor's connection. *Are you three in?*

No response. Valor swooped over the city, trying to get low enough to pierce through the dark.

We're in, Evvy's thoughts called. *It's quiet. And dark. I can't keep this going with Valor, the sight I mean.*

Just be careful, Jace said.

As Valor soared around the town, Evvy's connection dropped in and out. This shadow magic was interfering with his own, but the more passes Valor took, the better he could perceive Evvy's location based on her thoughts. After two more sweeps back and forth, Jace figured she was near the market district by the river.

"The street lights aren't even cutting through this," Jace said. "Maybe we can use this darkness to our advantage. If we can't see them, maybe they can't see us."

"Let's not count on it." Straeten patted Jace on the back and together they ran closer to the city gates.

"You down there," a guard shouted from atop the closed gate at the southern entrance. "What is going on?" The two men behind the guard drew back their bows and aimed at Jace and the others.

"So much for this entrance being empty," Jace muttered. From this distance, he couldn't tell if the guards still had the blue eyes from Fay's Soulkind. She was gone, but he didn't know if her spells remained.

Jace looked sideways at Sephintal from under the hood of his cloak and nodded. She took a few steps forward from the others and held her weapon up over her head while speaking. Jace understood what she said, but the guards just stood there and stared blankly. Jace saw the other Darrak positioning themselves around his friends.

Soon a Darrak appeared on the wall next to the humans. "What do you have there?"

"Human scum," Sephintal growled. "We found them causing trouble in the south."

"Why bring them? You have orders to kill them."

Sephintal hesitated. "They have strange marks on them. Thought we should bring them in for questioning."

"I'm glad she's on our side," Straeten whispered to Jace.

Harkra shoved Straeten so hard he stumbled forward.

"Okay, I get it, take it easy." Straeten fell back in line next to Jace and grasped his cloak. "Are you sure about this?"

The Darrak on the wall stared down at them for a moment before disappearing from sight. They all waited for a long minute.

"Those burras haven't gotten far, have they?" Straeten asked.

"Hold on." Jace clutched at the knives hidden under his cloak.

Finally, the massive wooden gate creaked opened wide to the dark city beyond and the Darrak staring at them. Harkra shoved Jace this time to get him moving forward and he stumbled under the arch. He kept his eyes down but used Valor above him to see the guards and Darrak as he entered.

When they walked all the way inside, the doors shut tightly behind them with a resounding clang. Another group of three Darrak walked up to Sephintal. She held up a clawed hand. Jace looked around and didn't notice anyone else watching them.

"What kind of marks do they have?" one Darrak asked her. "They didn't abandon Fay or Guire, did they?"

"No, not theirs," Sephintal started.

"Wait." The Darrak grabbed Sephintal's wrist and turned it over. "What are these?" Its lips pulled back over its sharp teeth in a snarl, pointing at the marks on her arm.

Before it could release a sound, Sephintal whipped around and struck the other Darrak's head with her tail. The Darrak dropped to the ground, a surprised look in its eyes. Harkra slashed with his claws, silencing the others in a blur. In a matter of seconds, they pulled their motionless bodies into an alleyway and quietly returned.

"Did I say I was glad she's on our side?" Straeten stared at the alleyway but no one came out of it. "Sheesh."

Jace shifted around to see above them but the street was clear. As they stepped out into view of the upper wall, Sephintal and the other Darrak surrounded Jace again and walked quickly to the center of Beldan. The guards on top barely gave them a glance as they passed by. Jace held his breath as another group of Darrak and people walked toward them. He kept his head down and soon they passed by.

We're getting lucky, Straeten thought through Valor's connection.

Jace silently wished that's all it was.

These people, Sephintal said in a choppy fashion through Valor. *If they are not under Fay's power, why are they involved?*

Fear. Jace saw it in their eyes. They kept glancing up at the darkness now over the town, probably wondering if the storm was going to pass if they rode it out long enough. *It's Dral and the Darrak threatening them. If he gets more power, he can use the Call on them.*

"Let's get moving then," Straeten said.

They arrived at the open space before NorBridge. The far end of the bridge was in charred pieces, probably from when Turic blasted his way off of it. Over the Hall, the darkness grew the thickest and seeped its way across the river over Beldan.

A single figure stood, awaiting them perhaps, on the near end of NorBridge. Jace tried to see through Valor's eyes but the shadows blocked him. Valor started to dive, but Jace commanded him not to, and he spun away back to the skies. *I'm not going to lose you again.*

It wasn't Dral, but Jace sensed a darkness like he had with Fay and Newell. Jace stepped into the clearing surrounded by his Followers and friends. It had to be Guire.

Guire lifted his hands and the shadow of his spirit grew from behind his body into giant arms reaching into the air. The shadowy tendrils merged with the darkness in the sky, fading the light even more. Truly night had fallen. The clouds thickened and drops began to fall from the sky. One of them landed on Jace's arm and he winced from the sizzle it made on his skin.

More drops fell. Jace scanned the area for cover. The way they'd just come was blocked by a group of Darrak and humans The other alleys and streets soon filled up as well. All those surrounding them bore the same pallid skin and sunken features. Guire's Followers. They stood waiting.

"Why aren't they attacking?" Straeten said. A drop of rain hit his head and he flinched. "Oh."

"What do we do?" Ranelle pulled her cloak over her exposed hands. "They've got us trapped out here, and that rain is going eat through our clothes."

"Our clothes if we're lucky." Straeten crouched in front of the group and held his arm out in front of him. The air shimmered and quaked with a pulse of energy surrounding them. "Good thing you got me."

The next drops of corrosive rain fell harmlessly off of Straeten's shield. Behind them, no one stepped forward into the rain. Stinging pangs ran across Jace's back and he cried out in pain and realization. *Valor, go away!*

Valor screeched high above the bridge, but not high enough. The pain seared his arms and even his eyes. *Go!* But his friend wouldn't leave. The acid storm splashed large drops onto the street. The link with Valor dropped out. With an anguished cry, Jace pushed Straeten forward. Guire stood before them on the bridge with a wide smile on his lips.

Jace's blood boiled and his mind flashed to the faded dark mark on his arm. In the distance, a quiet whinny echoed. His mind calmed. *Blue.*

Cathlyn put her hand on his shoulder "Valor's all right, I took care of him." She squeezed his shoulder. "Now stay focused."

She'd moved the hawk. That was it.

"Send me, Cath. Out there on the bridge, right behind him."

"But there's no cover from that stuff. And I don't know if I can—"

"It's all right, I trust you. Now trust me and do it!"

With a flash, Jace blinked out of existence and then reappeared in a blurred daze ten feet above the bridge. He flailed his arms to balance himself as he dropped soundlessly to the stones below. Spinning around, he faced Guire's back. Cathlyn had shifted him halfway across the bridge, but that was better than over the water or even higher in the air.

A bolt of lightning struck from the middle of the dark storm. The shock of the thunder knocked Jace off balance. One of the statues at the end of the bridge toppled over and crashed a few feet away from Straeten's shield. A sudden impulse took Jace, a tingling instinct that told him something wasn't quite right. He jumped to the side and tumbled to the stone bridge, narrowly avoiding a bolt of energy exploding right where he had been standing.

He crouched next to a tall statue and peered back at the origin of the magic, rubbing his eyes to see past the blind spots from the bright light. Wind swept over the bridge past a single figure twenty paces from him. Thick red hair cascaded over her shoulder.

Jace's chest went cold. "Karanne?"

A spinning light wrapped around her in tight arcs. She lifted her hand at him. The Fireflash seemed to hesitate but Karanne forced her hand forward and the bolt raced to Jace again. He tumbled to the middle of the bridge. The post behind him erupted in white fire.

"What are you doing? It's me!"

Karanne stepped toward him with her glowing and pulsing hand raised. The power inside of her throbbed outward. Jace felt it in his chest.

Rain began to fall on his side of the bridge, burning his hands. A look back showed Guire's features in a curled sneer, finally noticing

Jace behind him. Without wasting another second, Jace scrambled up onto the ledge of the bridge and dropped straight down toward the churning water.

He landed on a small wooden ledge that extended from beneath the bridge and he looked up to see Karanne peer over the edge. He swung from suspended ropes to the bridge where Brannon showed his fire magic only a few months ago.

Seconds later, Karanne vaulted over the bridge's edge. She scrambled down to the ropes with a glowing fist pointed where Jace should've been. But he wasn't there. She twisted her head around and sent her Fireflash dashing about. The high waters of the river splashed up at her as she sped along the rope bridge.

"Where are you?" she shouted.

Jace watched her go past him as he clutched the wooden perch with his talons.

Quietly, he transformed out of Valor's body back into his own and dropped to the rope behind Karanne without her even noticing. "Knew I'd get the drop on you someday," he whispered. He motioned to her with his hand.

A cluster of black tentacles arose from the frothing river and gripped Karanne's legs and arms, twisting them behind her. The roiling shapes of Toola's river family appeared above the water for a moment, revealing their wide dark eyes.

Jace reached Karanne as she tried to twist out of the creatures' grasp. She spun her bedraggled hair around so her darkened eyes met Jace's. He pushed with his magic to calm her, and soon her thrashing slowed.

He reached into his stone pouch, although he already had the memory he wanted at the forefront of his thoughts. When he touched the stone, the memory of Karanne bringing him across the bridge to the Library for the first time ran through his mind as clear as the day it happened. He placed his hand on Karanne's head and she twitched violently under his touch. He felt through the clouds in her mind, saw what she now thought were real. Her mind was a maelstrom of images. Everyone was trying to kill her. And it was not Jace, but a Darrak touching her.

He replayed the memory from the stone into her head. "It's me, Jace. Your son." The tension in her limbs lessened. Jace motioned to the river creatures below him. They released their grip on her and returned to the depths. He took in her tired expression, but most importantly, he saw her own eyes. Relief washed over her when she touched his face, a smile touched her lips. She wrapped him in a hug.

"I didn't know what was real anymore."

"You're all right now." Jace hugged her back. "Well, sort of."

"Jace, I think I did terrible things." Karanne held up her hands and Jace could sense again the pulse of energy from within her.

"Well, let's go and make them right, okay?"

Karanne nodded and followed him up onto the bridge. Guire's attention was back on the others so the acid rain no longer pelted Jace's side of the bridge. Red sores covered Jace's hand and arms from earlier. Luckily Valor had chosen to remain under the bridge for the time being.

Karanne stood beside Jace and raised her hand. Her raw power built up, strong enough for him to feel, and strong enough to level a building.

He touched her forearm. "If you kill him, his spirit will still remain in the Soulkind. When I get close enough I'm going to try to rip him out. So don't kill him. Yet."

Karanne lowered her quaking arm and pulled Jace with her toward Guire. "That's Straeten out there?"

"Yeah, and he's not going to last much longer with the rain and Darrak." Jace ducked low and ran along the edge of the bridge with Karanne next to him.

They stopped about twenty feet away. The air around them suddenly turned even darker, as if something didn't want them to proceed. Karanne stood tall. "I've been waiting for this."

A thin intense beam of white light sprung from her open palm and cut through the darkness, slamming into Guire's leg. He dropped to his knees and grimaced. "Go!" Karanne shouted.

Jace sprinted the last distance to Guire and focused on his Soulkind, opening his mind to the flow of magic pouring in.

About five feet away, a sickly green wall rose up from his feet, blocking him. Orbs of pulsating blobs raised up and towered over him. He reached for Guire's spirit but couldn't even sense it through the wall of sickness.

Karanne's white bolt shot over Jace's head and sliced neatly through the green growth, carving a wide path through it. Guire's eyes shifted to Karanne, a hint of fear wavering there, but the wall regrew and solidified around the hole. Karanne blasted the wall again, but this time the magic did barely any damage. Guire's laughter rose behind the barrier.

"I am ready for you this time," Guire said.

A second later, a searing drop of water landed directly on Jace's left arm. He winced as he wiped it off. Karanne yelled and cast another bolt at the wall but it did little but cascade off in a splash of fire. Jace's heart raced as he considered escape. They might never get another chance at Guire being alone like this.

A battle cry sounded from the middle of the city, fierce horns blaring through the unnatural night. Warriors on horses rode through the streets attacking Guire's Followers and the Darrak blocking the way. Chaos erupted as the Darrak spun to face the new attackers. Arrows and spears flew through the air.

Jace's heart lifted as he recognized the insignias on their armor. The Guardians and soldiers of Myraton! And of course, Allar and Stroud in the lead. Stroud's sword swept through stunned Darrak, and he was backed by Allar holding his arm aloft. His magic covered them with a dome of energy. The Darrak and Guire's Followers fell over each other trying to form ranks but the fighters pushed through.

Sudden hope coursed through Jace's body, then darkness fell over his eyes. Moments later, he stood before the green wall, but a new massive hole had appeared, exposing Guire standing there dumbfounded. Shards of the barrier lay in piles around Jace's feet and his left arm felt numb. He glanced at it as a glowing silver sheen faded from his skin. This was crazy. What was happening to him?

Through the pain of the poison rainfall, Jace pushed his magic. He caught the shadowy soul around his neck and began to yank it from the corroded Soulkind Guire wore. The spirit clung tightly as Jace pulled. Like a trapped animal, Guire glanced all around as he realized he couldn't run from this.

Karanne sent another blast of white fire and it zeroed in on Guire's spirit. Jace's flows of magic wrapped around it in an embrace and, with one severing motion, wrested the black soul from the shield like plucking a weed from the ground. The spirit floundered and screeched as it reached for its Soulkind, but Jace's magic barred the way.

In seconds, a gusting breeze blew Guire's soul away. The storm clouds faded. Guire's body dropped to the bridge.

Chapter 32

The sun gleamed off the armor of the battling armies as they clashed. The Myraton army initially had surprise as an advantage, but the strength of the Darrak and the Gora leading them began to turn the tide. Some of Guire's Followers darted away from the fray but most stood there, stunned, lost.

Karanne and Jace beckoned for their friends on the other side of the bridge to cross.

"How did you do that?" Karanne asked while they waited.

"What, remove his soul?" Jace asked.

She shook her head. "You... you smashed right through that wall. Your arm, it was all... different, metal-like."

Jace shrugged. "I don't even know what happened." There was nothing on his arm now except for the small markings. "But this isn't the first time it's happened."

"Nice work," Jace said as his friends and Followers joined them. "I'm glad you're all okay."

"So are we," Straeten said.

"I've got to get to the Hall." Jace stepped off the bridge onto land. "Before Dral can use the dragons."

The other side of the bridge held no opposition. Several figures curled in a pile near a tipped and broken cage. Jace's heart raced as he scanned the figures. Among the lifeless Darrak, a gold creature gleamed brightly in the sunlight. It lay motionless. Jace rushed to the young dragon and knelt by its side. A young male. Jace cupped his hand gently around the dragon's unmoving head.

Another dragon lost? His other fist clenched in anger.

But the young dragon's golden eyes flickered open and locked onto Jace's.

"You're alive!"

Jace stared into the golden eyes and felt acutely aware of the other dragons nearby, as if he were already connected to them. He closed his eyes and sought the closest one and effortlessly linked to its sight. He watched as a chaotic group of Darrak carried a cage down a circling flight of steps. The dragon's sight vanished, swallowed by darkness. It had to be the gloves.

"You were brave, little one," Jace said. The dragon's head went limp in his hands. "No, wait!"

"I've got him." Cathlyn raced to Jace's side. "Go finish this." She lifted her arms above the injured dragonling and a warm glow surrounded them both.

Jace couldn't make himself stand.

"He's going to be all right!" Cathlyn said. "Go!"

Jace stumbled to his feet and ran a couple of steps to the hall entrance. "Ranelle, stay here. Talk to him, keep him calm."

Ranelle followed his orders without hesitation. Jace felt her magic reach out for the dragon's mind. One of Sephintal's Darrak shot Jace a questioning look.

Jace nodded. "You too."

The Darrak stood guard over Cathlyn and Ranelle and faced the bridge while stealing glances at the dragon on the ground.

Straeten, Tare, Karanne and the remaining three Darrak followed Jace past the smashed bridge through the unguarded hall doors and into an empty courtyard. Jace paused and tilted his head up at the sky. Instantly, he linked to Valor soaring high above and the hawk's sight filled his own eyes.

"Valor is up there. Link up and try to find Evvy."

The courtyard appeared empty, even from above.

No one's here to stop us, Straeten said. *I don't like this.*

Me either, but I've got to get inside. Jace turned to face Sephintal who had come to a stop behind the group. "How are you holding up?"

Sephintal looked up, dazed. "The Call is getting stronger. But I can do this." She made a fist, closed her eyes and Jace felt her draw upon the magic of his Soulkind. "What will happen when they get the dragons?"

"I don't think we'll know for sure until it happens. But it's probably going to be bad." Jace ran up ahead to the Tower of Law and stood on its steps. *Evvy is close, somehow.*

I am. Evvy's tiny voice cut into the connection with Valor.

Where are you? Are you all right? Is Shey with you? Jace asked.

We're both okay. We're up in the tower. They've trapped lots of people here. Thieves, and a lot of kids from a school, I think. Darrak are holding them. I think they're going to kill them.

"He's got Mathes' students?" Jace muttered. *Stay put, we're coming up now.*

"Jace." Karanne gripped Jace's shoulder. "If those kids are trapped, I need to get them out of there, and you need to find Dral."

Jace hesitated. His group was slowly dwindling. What if that was part of Dral's plan? "Take Tare with you. You'll need some help."

Sephintal made a few motions with her hand and Harkra and the other Darrak went to Karanne's side.

Karanne nodded her thanks. "Be careful," she said to Jace. "And thanks for helping me out on the bridge."

"I'll see you when it's over." Jace returned Tare's salute and ran around the other side of the tower with Straeten and Sephintal behind him.

"You're pretty confident the three of us can stop Dral, huh?" Straeten ran harder to keep up with Jace.

"I don't see anyone else coming. Now keep up, all right?" Jace smirked back at his friend.

Jace? Evvy's voice crept into Valor's link again. *I don't know if what I'm seeing is right.*

What's the matter?

I see some thieves up here, and in the middle of them is…Picks.

Picks? Jace asked. *Didn't Turic say Dral killed him when he took the gloves? Why would he say that?*

Well someone who looks like Picks is alive up here.

Jace didn't respond but kept running. The dragons appeared in his thoughts again and he sought out their sight. He caught glimpses of hallways and passageways and a long staircase. It all felt familiar. "I know where they are. Dral's bringing them down below the library."

"You sure?" Sephintal asked.

"I don't think Dral's coming out to greet us like the others. He prefers to stay hidden. We've got to get to the lower levels where the pool was. Remember, Straet?"

"I remember it took us a long time to get there, and we had to go right through the building itself. There's going to be a lot of Darrak between here and there. Too bad there's not another way."

Jace ran quietly, then paused. He looked up at the roof.

"No, no," Straeten said. "You're not thinking…"

"It's the only way."

"But last time was different. When you got in the water, Lu'Calen brought you through."

233

The light in the sky darkened abruptly like a candle being snuffed out. A dark cloud billowed from the rooftop, threading its way out of the tall windows. Strong arms pinned Jace's hands by his side and he bit back his anger.

"Uh, Sephintal," Straeten said slowly. "What are you doing?"

Jace twisted his head to the side to see Sephintal gripping him. "It's the Call," Jace said. "They've got the dragons, and they're trying to get us all, too." Jace's head spun with the pull of the Call's magic.

A wide snarl crept over the Darrak's normally calm face and her claws bit into Jace's shoulder. A warm trickle of liquid dripped down his arm.

He took a deep breath. "Sephintal, look at me."

The snarl lessened and her eyes cleared up, but in a moment they darkened again.

"What do I do?" Straeten pulled back his long club.

"Not that," Jace said.

A shadow flitted over Straeten's face. That wasn't a good sign. How many dragons did Dral already have under his power? Jace thrashed in Sephintal's grip.

"Okay, maybe a little of that."

A sharp crack sounded behind Jace and Sephintal's claws loosened enough for him to break free. He turned to see her dazedly reach for the back of her skull. She pulled her hand away with dark blood on it. Her black eyes narrowed and she faced Straeten.

"I'll hold her off. You get going." Straeten stepped between Jace and Sephintal and held up his arm. The marks Allar passed on to him glowed now as he summoned his shield again. "Hurry! I'll get there as soon as I can."

Sephintal hammered on the invisible barrier with both hands and Straeten staggered back a step. She shoved him aside and approached Jace.

Jace glanced upward and saw Valor drop from the top of the Library. Sephintal growled and sprang at him again, this time with her claws fully extended and her mouth wide open.

Jace gripped his magic and jumped up toward Valor, fully in his dive. For a second Jace's sight vanished as he swept into Valor's body. The hawk pulled out of the steep dive barely in time to wheel away from Sephintal's flailing attack. Valor stole a glance at Straeten backing away from Sephintal. A bright flash of light erupted in front of the Darrak's face and she shrunk back. With a swipe of her tail, Straeten fell to the ground but was able to block her next attack with the shield again. They'd be okay. If he worked quickly.

Jace and Valor flew to the Library roof. The black smoke emanated thickly and Jace dared not release himself from Valor yet. He flew out over the ledge and peered down at the Soulwash behind the Library. He gulped hard. If he hit the surface of that water, could be sure he'd make it all the way inside the Library to the hidden pool?

He squinted at the silvery surface as he glided above. Even with Valor's more powerful sight, he doubted the image he saw. It was a face of a gray-scaled creature he knew well, and his eyes beckoned Jace to him.

Graebyrn.

Without another thought, Valor swept his wings back and entered a steep dive for the Soulwash. The world blurred past and the wind rocked against his body. Halfway to the pool, Jace signaled for Valor to level out of the dive.

Valor screeched loudly as Jace shot out of Valor's body and toward the glistening surface of the water. A fraction of a second before he struck, Jace thought that his arm... changed. Darkness covered his eyes and he was yanked through the water with undulating movement like a fish. In seconds, his sight returned and the shock of the freezing mountain water snapped him back. He gripped the ledge of the pool and slowly lifted his left arm out of the water. As his eyes cleared, he swore he saw scales covering his skin. He shook it and water droplets cascaded off. No, there weren't any scales. Was he going crazy? He scanned the torch lit room and took in the shadows surrounding him.

It was different than the last time he was here. Ornate tables and chairs filled the room. One chair stood above the others, a makeshift throne with elaborate gildings around its edges. It was empty, but he could guess who it was for.

The sound of footsteps clicked on the stone and echoed through the hall, but Jace couldn't tell if they were approaching or retreating. Quickly, yet quietly, he pulled himself out of the pool. Water dripped in a steady stream onto the floor on his way to one of the five shadow-covered shapes. These were cages, much like those that trapped him and his friends in Marlec's lair.

But he had gotten rid of Marlec, or at least Lu'Calen had, and dragged his spirit away from the gloves, hadn't he? Yet somehow the darkness remained.

A throbbing pain threatened to split Jace's head apart. These cages weren't empty, they contained dragons. He rushed to a cage to penetrate it with his magic, to connect with the dragon, but a jolt forced him onto his backside.

He tried to calm himself, calling on the power of his Soulkind to bring a peaceful breeze into the room. The wind picked up and swirled away wisps of the dark cages. The oppressive power within them waned.

"Come on," Jace said. He channeled his magic into the mark he used to remove souls, trying in vain to open the cages, but the cloudy wisps returned. The dragons remained trapped. Cold fell over Jace's body. Someone had entered the room.

Dral walked in with a cautious step that fell silently on the floor. His fingers still twitched like they did when he thought about gold This time, the twitching arose when he reached the cages. He waved his hands over the shadows then stepped back toward the pool to face them all.

He hadn't yet seen Jace.

Jace snuck down to the pool's edge. Should he throw a knife? Try to knock him out somehow? His heart thudded rapidly in his chest and the blood pounded in his head as he inched a few steps closer. Dral's eyes were closed. A mark on the back of his gloved hands glowed brightly.

Jace's own magic coursed through him, preparing to yank the dark spirit he sensed floating inside Dral's body and attached to the gloves he wore. It was now or never. With all his concentration, he cast the spell, clenched onto the dark spirit and held on. Dral gasped and attempted to turn to Jace but was held in place.

The magical arms enveloped the spirit in a bright light and Jace slowly, inexorably, began to pull it from the gloves. "It's over."

The shadow soul quaked as Jace forced a wedge between it and the gloves. Jace smiled. He could do this. He felt it. Then his smile faded. The steel grip he first felt on the darkness faltered. Shifting smoke slipped between his fingertips. He doubled his focus on the spell and the grip solidified again. But only for a moment.

"I cannot believe you got in here without me knowing. Must've been trained by the best." Dral turned to Jace, a smile on his lips. "Was it through the water? You came through the water like you did when you were a child, didn't you?"

Jace froze in place as smoky tendrils latched around his wrists and attached to the floor. "That was when Marlec still inhabited the gloves. You know, the battle between these two Soulkind has been around long before those two brothers squabbled over a kingdom, and it will last longer than you."

Jace felt his feet moving beneath him without his control. When he focused, they slowed down, but he couldn't stop them. Dral continued dragging him until a cage of shadows enveloped him beside the dragons.

"You've become much stronger since the last time we met. But not strong enough, I'm afraid. Even with *that*." Dral pointed to Jace's arm.

An intense pain burst in Jace's back and spread through his whole body, bringing him to his knees. The markings that before only faintly covered his arm now shone like dragon scales. His arm clenched into a fist and his claws scratched into the stone floor. What was going on? It looked just like a dragon's arm.

Jace stretched out to Valor, to anyone out there who could listen. "Straeten! Cathlyn!" His thoughts floundered about and found nothing. He couldn't sense anything beyond the room.

Dral gestured to the pool and Jace craned his neck to see it. Inside, the vision showed Straeten and Sephintal no longer fighting each other, but kneeling down. It shifted again to Cathlyn and then Karanne and his other friends, even Stroud and Allar across the bridge. The fighting had stopped. Had they all given up?

"If you had pulled me from this body, I would only have returned again," Dral said. "No matter what you do, you will never get us fully out."

Jace reached for his Soulkind with his silver hand. It wasn't there. Frantically, he reached through his other pockets and pouches, turning out his memory stones onto the floor. It was gone.

"Looking for this?" Dral's fingers twitched. Up near the ornate chair above the dragons a shadowy hand lifted Jace's green stone into the air and placed it in a tiny dark cage, slowly rotating in place. "As you can see, my new skills haven't detracted from my old. Now, listen. I'm not trying to pick a fight with you. I think if you sit back and relax, we will get along just fine. We were once family, after all."

Dral walked to Jace's cage and held his hand over his head like he was about to pet an animal. His words triggered a distant thought inside of Jace and he reached for his memory stones strewn about on the floor. He found the right one instantly and conjured up the memory, not only in his head but into Dral's mind.

"Why didn't you kill him?" Jace asked.

Drawl furrowed his brow and his hand faltered. "What?"

Jace pushed the memory harder. Dral's face softened and his eyes lightened. His old boss appeared through the dark mask.

"Picks?" Dral whispered.

"You let him live. I know you're in there, Dral." The darkness shifted behind Dral's body. Jace took advantage by slamming a wedge between the two of them. The cage holding Jace flickered and faded, as did those around the small dragons. Their silver and gold colors shone in the torchlight now that the darkness fell away. The dragons' eyes followed the spirit, which slowly pushed away from the gloves. They were helping him, now.

The many fingered wisps of smoke crept around the magical wedge, always connected to the gloves by at least one tendril no matter how hard Jace and the dragons pushed.

"See? You'll never find a way to keep me away!" the spirit yelled.

Well, there was one way.

Graebyrn's voice from long ago echoed in Jace's head. Words he'd pushed far from his mind and thought he'd never heed in a thousand years. A lump formed in his throat, but he lifted his chin. Words he would heed now. He pulled the gloves from Dral's hands and threw them in the center of the floor. The dragons looked down at them and bowed their heads to Jace.

"What are you doing?" The spirit pushed its entire force against the magic holding it back from Dral's body. The room shook and dust fell from the ceiling.

Jace nodded to the five dragons. This was a sacrifice he had to make. For his friends. For the dragons. For Blue's memory. Fire flew from the dragon's mouths and converged upon the heavy black gloves before them, heating them until they glowed red. The bandings of the Soulkind peeled apart under the blast of the intense fire.

"You can't do this!" The darkness heaved like a wave surging and finally spilled over the wedge. Like wind snuffing out candle flames, the shadowy cages enveloped the dragons one by one ceasing their fiery breath. Dral shook from the effort of quelling their power. The gloves were gone, and a single charred stone remained in the middle of the floor.

A deep voice echoed around the room. "Are you sure? It will be lost forever."

"It's not about what I want anymore, Graebyrn." Jace gave the pool in the center of the room a sad smile.

"Truly you have the heart of a dragon."

Jace closed his eyes and nodded. Suddenly, images of Rismantalia flashed through his head. Her tiny form, him taking on her pain, her going limp in his arms. His eyes shot open. Now he knew. He stared at his silver scaled arm. Rismantalia's arm. He not only kept her spirit alive, she had become a part of him. And now her strength coursed through him.

The dark spirit slammed itself back into Dral's body and he lifted his hands toward Jace's throat. Before his twitching fingers could clasp around his neck, however, a soft blue glow shone from the pool's surface and covered Dral in its light. He could not move.

"You can't do this. You won't. You'll be nothing." Froth collected around Dral's lips as he spat these words. Quickly his expression changed to one of pleading. "We can join together, make peace. Anything."

This final Call, with all its pull, gave Jace only a second's pause. "I should have done this a long time ago."

Jace raised his scaled arm high above his head and its power grew with a blinding aura of light. With one final strike, he drove his fist into the cursed Soulkind stone on the floor. Sparks flew, the floor smashed into fragments of heated rock and the Soulkind split in half. At the same time, another crack sounded from near the ornate chair and tiny shards of rock clattered to the floor. Green stone fragments.

Screams rang out, howls of rage. Swirls of darkness fled from Dral's body and reached for the shattered Soulkind, only to find nothing to hold on to. For a moment, the spirit's eyes caught Jace's with anguish and loss in its gaze. "You'll be nothing!" the voice hissed until a strong breeze blew through the room taking the black smoke away.

In the silence that followed, Jace looked down at his hands and arms to watch the Soulkind marks on his body glow one last time and then drain entirely away. He dropped to his knees with an emptiness he didn't think possible. He slumped against the pool's ledge, buried his face in his hands, and wept.

Chapter 33

Jace lay sprawled against the pool. His world was empty, cut off from the power that he'd for so long taken for granted. The connection to his Followers, to Valor, Ash, Payt. Blue... It was all gone.

Cathlyn walked into the room still lit by the pool's faint blue light. Her footsteps echoed as she approached Jace. The young dragons, now freed from their cages, bowed their necks to her. She looked only at Jace.

Light returned to his eyes.

"Jace." Cathlyn knelt by his side and placed her warm hands on his. She withdrew suddenly. "What did you do?" Her look of horror slowly changed to pity.

His voice came out a hoarse whisper. "There wasn't any other way." He had to believe that.

Cathlyn pulled her hands away and held them over the small pile of green stone on the floor. Nothing but shattered pieces. "There's got to be some way to fix it." A glow emanated from her hands.

Jace sat up and rubbed his forehead. "Just stop." The magic faded and the room dimmed.

"You doubt me?" Tears brimmed in her eyes.

"Never." Jace glanced at the pool.

Cathlyn smiled and turned his face to hers. "Let me help you." She slowly drew closer. He felt her breath upon his mouth. His heart pounded in his chest.

The soft touch of her lips sent warmth through his body. He nearly forgot what had happened.

Nearly.

He pulled away.

"I can't do this." He could hardly believe the words he heard himself say.

Cathlyn pulled his face back to hers more abruptly than before and fixed him with a stare. "You gave up your magic. If you have the strength to do that, you can do anything." She looked down and said under her breath. "I know I couldn't have done it."

This time he lifted her face to his. "I don't believe that for a second."

He kissed her gently.

Cathlyn sighed and rested her head on his chest.

Jace smiled. For a moment, his pain lifted ever so slightly. How he wanted to cling to that small glimpse of happiness.

But it was an illusion. What point was there in torturing himself? He lifted her to her feet. "I have to go. I need to take these dragons back to Graebyrn."

"I'll come with you."

"You're needed here. With the other... Masters." Saying the word brought a new wave of pain. He held up his hand when she started to speak again.

She stepped closer and put her hands on his chest. "They need you, too." She looked searchingly into his eyes but he avoided her gaze. "I need you."

"I…" He wanted to tell her he would stay with her. Isn't that what he'd wanted his whole life? But the pain was too deep. "I have to go."

He kissed her forehead. A smooth stone from the pool's edge caught his eye. He rubbed it a few times and then placed it in his pouch.

The memory faded as Jace put the stone away. A cold wind blew through the valley. He stared at the mountains and reveled in the silence. Rugged peaks covered in snow, distant hilltops bursting with the new green of spring, and wide blue lakes surrounded him.

He breathed the cold air and absently reached for his neck before catching himself and dropping his hand to his side.

Two months. Two months since he had destroyed the gloves and the darkness trapped inside them. Since he had destroyed his own Soulkind. Nothing remained but the green fragments bound together by wire. And the memory of what he once was.

A Soulkind Master. And now he was up here in the mountains back where he first trained with Graebyrn, far away from any prying, pitying eyes. Ash nudged Jace's arm and he scratched him behind his ears.

He wanted to be with them. Needed to be. He owed it to his friends and family. And yet...

"My work is not done," Jace said aloud.

Look around you.

Jace gazed at the valley before him. The woods were alive with those who'd come to help the dragon younglings. Nilen and her mother sat laughing with each other under a tree. Picks waved from beside the lake. And Evvy ran out of the water, splashing with the rest of her young thief friends.

A cluster of black writhing tentacles burst out of the lake. Evvy screamed as they latched onto her and dragged her back into the water. A second later, she shot out with a cheer toward the deeper part of the lake. Toola hadn't left her side since she'd arrived.

Thanks to the thieves, this was now a safe place for the dragons to grow.

And others are already taking up the cause.

True. Ranelle, Sephintal, and Tare had already located other convergences Graebyrn told them to seek out. The dragons would thrive in such places where magic was at its strongest.

He was running out of excuses.

"Why would they need me? They've got an entire Soulkind Council now, with all new Masters, and even a Deltir."

Graebyrn always says for you to follow your heart, it is your strongest quality. And you'd hardly be returning empty-handed.

"But..."

But nothing. He also says you're stubborn. And a bit of a whiner.

Jace laughed. "I guess you have a point." He closed his eyes and breathed deeply. "All right, I'll go. Can you ask Graebyrn to send a message to them?"

I'll tell them to expect us.

Straeten peered over the edge of the cliff at the city of Beldan, trying to catch his breath. The waterfall cascaded into the Soulwash hundreds of feet below.

"Couldn't... we have just... used our magic to get up here?" he said, still trying to catch his breath.

"We've been stuck inside with the Council for so long," Cathlyn said. "I thought we could use the exercise. Now come on, don't you want to see what's in there?"

"I am afraid I am going to have to side with Straeten on this one," Turic said. "I will opt for using magic on the way down." Cathlyn shot him a raised eyebrow. "Just this once."

"I've never been up here, you know." Karanne gripped Turic's hand to help keep his footing upon the slippery rocks at the entrance.

As daylight faded, the cave grew nearly pitch black. Almost as one, all four summoned fire to light the path. A brilliant light filled the chamber exposing the elaborate mural on the wall.

The scene told Jace's story. From the finding of his Soulkind as a child, the rescue in Marlec's fortress, Guire and Fay's return, and the dragons, to Jace sacrificing his own Soulkind. Laughter and tears filled the room alongside the bubbling of flowing water.

"There's more." Cathlyn stared at the end where a new image was forming through the rocks. Stone cracked as the wall shifted until an image of a cloaked person stood alone at the top of a waterfall. Everyone spun to face the cave entrance.

Straeten slopped through the freezing water to reach his friend. He wrapped him in a huge hug, lifting him off his feet. "You're here!"

"Yeah," Jace wheezed. "Barely."

Karanne practically had to pry him free. Her squeeze was nearly as tight.

Jace turned to face the others just as Cathlyn came running into his arms. He stumbled backwards. Turic cleared his throat.

Jace pulled one of his arms away from Cathlyn and embraced his old friend and teacher.

"You all look great," Jace said.

Soulkind marks covered their necks and arms. Straeten pulled his sleeves down, covering blank spots where once there had been the outlines of animals.

"It's okay." Jace touched the shards of the Soulkind around his neck with gloved fingers and traced over the wire binding them together. "I know you're wondering where I've been. And why I didn't come back sooner. I've been practicing what to say to you for the past months." He took a deep breath. "I've been helping Graebyrn, and the dragons. And the Darrak. I've—"

"Are you all right?" Karanne asked.

Jace reached over and squeezed her hand. "I am now." He nodded to himself and let out a deep sigh. He walked back to the ledge overlooking the valley. His friends followed.

Jace held his hands out to the sky.

"And…you got a new ring?" Straeten asked.

Jace laughed. "Just hold on."

Straeten squinted. Several specks appeared in the sky, growing larger as they approached.

Cathlyn gasped.

Sunlight glinted off the silver and gold scales of four young dragons.

"Okay, this is much better." Straeten clapped him on his back.

The gusts of wind from their wings forced back Jace's friends. Jace stood his ground with his arms outstretched as the dragons' landing shook the rock ledge. They folded their wings while Jace patted each of their heads in greeting. Turic bowed, and the dragons bowed in return.

Straeten laughed. "Aww, would you look at them? They grow up so fast, don't they?"

Karanne elbowed him in the side.

"Wait, how did *you* get here?" Straeten asked.

"Oh, they're the slower ones." Jace smiled at the dragons. "No offense." They exchanged glances.

"What do you mean?" Karanne asked.

"Seeker," one of the gold dragons said. "I think you've kept them waiting long enough."

"*Seeker?*" Cathlyn said.

Jace removed the thick glove that rode up his left arm and scales glistened upon his skin. He knelt and placed his silver hand on the ground. Dragon skin cascaded all across his own like hundreds of coins flipping into place. A long tail stretched behind him and his neck stretched high over Straeten's body.

"That's new." Straeten took a step closer. "Your coloring… You look like that dragon from the ruins. Rismantalia."

"Ris," the dragon said in a voice clear like a morning bell. The dragon dropped her head in a bow.

"But you… We saw you…"

"Jace took on more than just my pain that day."

"He sure did." Straeten looked up at the scars covering gray, sightless eyes. The dragon smiled in his direction.

"But I don't understand. Jace's magic is gone. How can he do this?"

"The Seeker's Soulkind is broken, but his magic will always remain in this world. He gives me sight, and I help him with… other things." The dragon's pale eyes met his and a familiar feeling stirred in his chest.

Straeten almost cried when he recognized it.

Connection. To the dragon. To Valor.

To Jace.

It's me.

Straeten's eyes widened. "Jace? You have it back? Magic?"

Not exactly. It's… different.

Valor's familiar screech called out as he swept past the mountain ledge. Everyone stood watching as Rismantalia beat her wings and followed the bird's call into the air.

"You coming?" Ris called down.

The four of them climbed onto the dragons and held on tightly.

"I'm just glad I don't have to share a ride with one of you guys." Straeten nudged his golden dragon. "Come on, I think he called you slow earlier. Did you catch that?"

"Yes," the dragon said and clawed at the stone ledge. "I did."

"What's your name?" Straeten asked.

"Skywatch. Now, are you ready?"

Straeten peeked out over the edge of the waterfall.

"Oh yeah." Straeten grinned. "Let's fly."

The End

Steve Davala is a young adult sci-fi and fantasy novelist who resides in Oregon. Now that the Soulkind Series is complete, he has more time to write that sci-fi story that's been kicking around in his head.

The Soulkind Series is available as an audiobook on Audible and iTunes. Stay in touch with the story on Steve's web site: **www.sciteachah.blogspot.com** or follow him on Twitter and Instagram @sciteachah and The Soulkind Series on Facebook.

Made in United States
Troutdale, OR
10/16/2023